Tessa Dare is a part-time librarian, full-time mother, and swing-shift writer. She makes her home in Southern California, where she shares a cozy, cluttered bungalow with her husband, their two children, and a dog.

She is the award-winning author of *Goddess of the Hunt, Surrender of a Siren, A Lady of Persuasion, One Dance with a Duke, Twice Tempted by a Rogue* and *Three Nights with a Scoundrel,* all available from *Rouge*.

www.tessadare.com

Also by Tessa Dare:

Goddess of the Hunt
Surrender of a Siren
A Lady of Persuasion

One Dance with a Duke
Twice Tempted by a Rogue
Three Nights with a Scoundrel

TESSA DARE

TWICE TEMPTED
BY A
ROGUE

RΦUGE
REGENCY

1 3 5 7 9 10 8 6 4 2

This edition published 2012
First published by *Rouge* in 2011, an imprint of Ebury Publishing
A Random House Group company
Originally published in the US by Ballantine Books in 2010,
an imprint of The Random House Publishing Group

The Random House Group Limited Reg. No. 954009

Addresses for companies within the Random House Group can be
found at www.randomhouse.co.uk

A CIP catalogue record for this book is available from the British Library

The Random House Group Limited supports The Forest Stewardship
Council (FSC®), the leading international forest certification organisation.
Our books carrying the FSC label are printed on FSC® certified paper.
FSC is the only forest certification scheme endorsed by the
leading environmental organisations, including Greenpeace.
Our paper procurement policy can be found at:
www.randomhouse.co.uk/environment

Printed and bound in Great Britain by Clays Ltd, St Ives PLC

ISBN 9780091948832

To buy books by your favourite authors and register for offers visit:
www.randomhouse.co.uk

For Amy, Courtney, and Leigh
Thanks for a great weekend in the mountains,
and for all your help with this book.

Many thanks to Jennifer Haymore, Janga Brannon, Sarah Kirbo, Elyssa Papa, Lindsey Faber, Santa Byrnes, Diana Chung, and Kim Castillo for their insight and encouragement. As always, I'm grateful to my agent, Helen Breitwieser, my editor, Kate Collins, her assistant, Kelli Fillingim, my copy editor, Martha Trachtenberg, and everyone at Random House. Last but never least, much love to my wonderful husband and children.

Chapter One

❧

Rhys St. Maur, newly Lord Ashworth, was a broken man.

Literally.

By the age of twenty, he'd fractured his left arm twice—once in a schoolboy brawl at Eton, and then again during an army training drill. Cracked ribs . . . he'd lost count of those. Fists driving through bar-room haze to connect with his face had snapped the cartilage in his nose a few times, leaving him with a craggy profile—one that was not improved by his myriad scars. Since sometime around his thirtieth birth-day, the little finger on his right hand just plain refused to bend. And in damp weather like this, his left knee throbbed with memories of marching through the Pyre-nees and surviving the Battle of Nivelle unscathed, only to catch a Basque farmer's hoe to the knee the next morning, when he left camp for a predawn piss.

That left knee was on fire tonight, sizzling with pain as Rhys trudged through the granite heart of Devon-shire, leading his horse down the darkened road. The moisture in the air kept dithering between fog and rain, and the night was thick with its indecision. He couldn't see but a few feet in front of him, which was why he'd decided to dismount and lead his horse on foot. Between the poor visibility and the surrounding terrain littered with chunks of stone and boot-sucking bogs, the risk of fatal injury was too great.

For the horse, that was. Rhys wasn't in the least concerned for himself. In fact, if he thought this godforsaken moor had any chance of claiming his own life, he'd cheerfully saddle his gelding and charge off into the gloom.

But it wouldn't work. It never had. He'd just end up with a lamed or dead horse, another broken rib perhaps, and the same curse that had haunted him since boyhood: unwanted, undeserved, and wholly wasted good luck.

No matter what misfortune befell him, this or any night, Rhys St. Maur was doomed to survive it.

The wind's low moan played his spine like a fiddle string. Behind him, the gelding balked. With a reassuring shush for the beast's benefit, Rhys marched on, turning up the collar of his coat to keep out the mist.

Yea, though I walk through the valley of the shadow of death, I will fear no evil . . .

He'd been walking through this valley for a long, long time. Trod so far into death's shadow he'd felt his feet turning to dust in his boots, the breath in his lungs burning acrid as sulfur. A living ghost, that's what he was. He'd returned from war to a newly inherited barony, and his sole duty now was to haunt the English aristocracy. Hulk awkwardly in the corners of their parties, terrify their delicate young ladies, and cause the gentlemen to rub their temples self-consciously as they tried not to stare at the gnarled scar marring his own.

As Rhys rounded a sharp curve in the road, a vaguely familiar sight emerged from the gloom. If he'd read his landmarks right, this had to be it. The tiny village of Buckleigh-in-the-Moor. At this distance, just a meager constellation of amber pinpricks against the black night.

The horse, scenting straw and safety, picked up his pace. Soon the cluster of stone and cob buildings came into focus. It must not be as late as it felt. A fair number of the cottages still showed light through their windows— yellow eyes peering out from beneath thatched-roof hats.

He halted in the center of the road. Wiping the moisture from his eyes, he squinted in the direction of the old inn. Fourteen years he'd been gone, but the same sign still creaked on its chains above the door. It read, in retouched gilt letters, The Three Hounds. Below the words, the pictured trio of dogs remained at perpetual attention. A burst of coarse laughter rattled one of the inn's unshuttered windows. Old Maddox was still doing a brisk trade, then.

Though his mount stamped with impatience, Rhys stood motionless facing the inn. Finally, he tilted his face to the sky above it. Fog covered the village like cotton wool, obscuring the craggy tors that loomed high on the steep slope beyond. Without their ominous shadow, the village of Buckleigh-in-the-Moor—this hated place he'd been running from since before he could remember— almost appeared . . . quaint. Charming. Welcoming.

And at that fool notion, Rhys almost laughed aloud.

This place would not welcome him.

No sooner had he formed the thought, than the inn's front door swung out on its hinges, tossing a shaft of light and warmth into the courtyard. The dull wave of laughter he'd heard earlier now swelled to a roar of excitement—one punctuated with a crash of breaking glass.

"You bastard son of a bitch!"

Ah, now that was the sort of reception he'd been expecting. But unless the old superstitions were true and some witch had foretold his arrival, Rhys knew the words couldn't have been meant for him. No one was likely to recognize him at all—he'd been just seventeen years old when he'd been here last.

Pulled forward by curiosity and the smells of ale and peat smoke, he approached the open door, stopping just outside.

The tavern was cramped, and much as Rhys remembered it. Just big enough to hold a small bar, a half-dozen tables, a mismatched assortment of chairs and stools, and—on this particular occasion—complete pandemonium.

"That's it! Pound 'im good!"

Two neckless apes faced off in the center of the room, spitting and circling one another as the onlookers pushed aside tables and chairs. The taller of the two brutes took a clumsy swing that caught nothing but air. The momentum carried him into a startled onlooker's arms. That man took exception and shoved back. Within seconds, the room was a blur of fists.

Standing unnoticed in the shadowed doorway, Rhys shifted his weight. An echo of bloodlust whispered in his ear. As a younger man, he would have hurled himself into the thickest knot of violence, eager to claw and punch his way back out. Just to feel the surge of his racing pulse, the slice of broken glass scoring his flesh, the tang of blood in his mouth. The strange, fleeting sensation of being alive.

But he wasn't that young man anymore. Thanks to the war, he'd had his fill of both fighting and pain. And he'd long given up on feeling alive.

After a minute or two, the peripheral scrabbling defused. Once again the two louts faced off, huffing for breath and clearly hungry for more. They chuckled as they circled one another, as though this were their typical Saturday night fun. It probably was. Wasn't as though life on the moor offered a wealth of amusements other than drinking and brawling.

Now that he studied their faces, Rhys wondered if the two might be brothers. Or cousins, perhaps. The taller one had mashed features, while the shorter sported a beaky nose. But their eyes reflected the same empty shade of blue, and they wore identical expressions of willful stupidity.

The shorter one picked up a low stool and taunted his opponent with it, as if baiting a bull. The "bull" charged. He threw a wild punch over the stool, but his reach fell short by inches. To close the gap, Bull grabbed a brass candlestick from the mantel and whipped it through the air, sucking all sound from the room.

Whoosh.

Beak threw aside his stool, and it smashed to splinters against the hearth. With Bull's attention momentarily diverted, Beak dove for a table still set for a meal. Half-empty dishes and bread crusts were strewn over white linen.

Rhys frowned. When had old Maddox started bothering with tablecloths?

He stopped wondering about it when Beak came up wielding a knife.

"I'll teach you to raise a club to me, you whoreson," he snarled.

Everyone in the room froze. Rhys ceased leaning against the doorjamb and stood erect, reconsidering his decision not to intervene. With a brass club and a knife involved, someone was likely to get seriously injured, or worse. As tired as he might be of fighting, he was even more weary of watching men die.

But before he could act, a series of sounds arrested him where he stood.

Crash. A bottle breaking.

Plink, plink, plink. Glass bits trickling to the floor.

Thud. Beak collapsing to the table unconscious, rivulets of wine streaming down around his ears.

"Harold Symmonds, you'll pay for that wine." A slender, dark-haired woman stood over Beak's senseless form, clutching what remained of a green-glass bottle. "And the tablecloth too, you great lout." She shook her head and tsked. "Blood and claret will never come out of white linen.

"And as for you, Laurence—" She wheeled on the second man, threatening him with the broken bottle's sharp glass teeth. Though he was twice as big as the barmaid and a man besides, Laurence held up his hands in surrender.

In fact, every man in the room had gone still. As though they all feared the harsh discipline this tiny barmaid might dole out. Interesting. To a man like Rhys, who'd spent several years commanding soldiers, that snap to attention spoke volumes.

Jabbing the bottle at Laurence, the barmaid backed him up against the wall. " 'Twas your own master who brought that, you know."

"This?" He stared at the candlestick in his fist. "It's Gideon's?"

"No, it's the inn's." She wrenched the brass club away from the stunned brute and curled her arm, lifting it to eye level. "But Gideon delivered it. Hauled it and its mate all the way up from Plymouth just last week. The set came very dear, and I'll thank you to keep your grimy mitts off the bric-a-brac."

The thing must have weighed a stone, but it cost her no effort to heft the candlestick up on the mantel with one hand and nudge it back into place.

"There," she said to herself, apparently satisfied with the symmetry. Standing back, she threw the jagged remnants of the bottle into the fire, and a wine-fueled blaze surged in the hearth.

The reddish flare illuminated the woman's face, and Rhys got his first good look at her.

Holy God. She was beautiful.

And young.

And . . . and beautiful.

Rhys had never been especially good with words. He couldn't have described exactly what it was about this woman that made her appearance so striking. He just knew he'd been struck.

She had pale skin and dark hair coming loose from a thick plait. Her figure was slight, yet feminine. Her eyes were large and wide, but to discern their color he would've had to stand much closer to her.

He wanted to stand much closer to her.

Especially now that she was no longer armed.

Fury radiated from her slender form as she propped her hands on her hips and scolded the assembly. "It's the same damned scene, again and again." Her tone was sharp, but the voice beneath it was husky, warm. "In case you haven't noticed, this inn is all we've got in Buckleigh-in-the-Moor. I'm trying to build a name for this place, make it a respectable establishment for travelers. Now tell me, how am I to make this inn fit for the Quality, what with you overgrown clods destroying my dining room once a fortnight?"

She swept an angry glare around the room, silently confronting each offender in turn. When her gaze collided with Rhys's, he noted the first crack in her veneer of poise. Her eyelashes fluttered. That was the extent of her visible surprise. The rest of her remained granite-still as she said, "And all this in front of a guest."

Rhys sensed every head in the room swiveling to face him. But he couldn't have torn his gaze from the barmaid's if he'd tried. Jesus, what a woman.

Between the travel and the damp, his body had been grousing at him all night. He wouldn't have believed one more part of him could stiffen . . . but evidently it could. His riding breeches pulled snug across his groin. He'd gone hard enough to rival that brass candlestick. He hadn't reacted so intensely to a woman since he'd been a randy youth. Perhaps not even then. His heart pounded. Blood surged through his veins, carrying orders to his every limb. He felt his whole body tightening, mustering strength, readying for a purpose. A very specific, very pleasurable purpose.

Damn. He felt *alive*.

Still holding his gaze, she said steadily, "Now put this place to rights."

Rhys blinked. He didn't recall this woman—he couldn't possibly have forgotten her—but had she somehow recognized him? Was she calling him out for his gross negligence as lord? It would be a fair enough accusation. If there was anything that needed putting to rights in Buckleigh-in-the-Moor, the responsibility should be his.

But as the men before him lurched into motion, scraping chairs and tables against the slate floor as they dragged the furniture back into place, Rhys realized her words hadn't been meant for him. He was almost disappointed. He would have liked to put things to rights for her. Starting with that mussed dark hair.

With an impatient sweep of her fingers, she tucked a lock behind her ear. "Welcome to the Three Hounds," she said. "Are you coming in, or aren't you?"

Oh, he was coming in. He was most definitely coming in.

Rhys stepped forward and closed the door behind him.

Before he could acknowledge her welcome, the barmaid's attention jerked away. "Not there, Skinner. Left side of the hearth."

Skinner hurried to obey. All six burly feet of him.

"I've a horse outside," Rhys said, once he had her attention again.

She nodded and summoned a twiggy youth from the bar. "Darryl, see to the gentleman's horse." To Rhys she said, "Will you drink whiskey, sir?"

"Just ale."

"I've rabbit stew and mutton pie."

His stomach rumbled. "I'd welcome both."

"Have a seat, then."

Rhys crossed to a table, lowered his weight onto the most sturdy-looking of the chairs, and accepted a tankard of ale from her hand.

He sipped at the cool ale, watching the barmaid and her band of reformed pugilists clear the room of debris. No wonder this place still did a brisk business. To Rhys's recollection, old Maddox had never kept barmaids this fair, nor this fierce.

She kept stealing looks at him, even as she swept broken glass from the floor and rolled up the soiled linen tablecloth. There was an intriguing softness to her gaze.

That couldn't be right. Perhaps she was looking at someone else. Under the guise of stretching, Rhys rotated his neck and turned an unhurried glance about the room.

No. There was no one else.

Strange.

Everything about the woman—her bearing, her voice, the reactions she inspired—declared her strength. But her eyes were telling him something else. They spoke of hopes and fears and vulnerability, and Rhys had no idea why she'd be revealing all that to a complete stranger, least of all him—but he knew one thing. Those looks she kept giving him contained more direct human contact than he'd known in years.

She was touching him. From across the room, with

her hands otherwise occupied, she was touching him. He felt it deep inside.

Rhys sipped his ale and pondered the queer nature of fate. He was a steadfast believer in destiny. There was no other way to explain the fact that his heart still beat. In his eleven years in the light infantry, he'd spent battle after battle charging headlong into the bloody fray, eager to meet his death. Only to be cruelly disappointed, when fate spared him once again. He simply could not die. But for once, maybe for once his wretched good luck was about to throw him a true boon.

As she bent to sweep splintered wood from the corner, he observed the gentle curve of her neck, the loose strands of hair at her nape. He could spend a very pleasant minute winding that lock of hair about his finger, counting how many times it would wrap around. Five, he guessed, or maybe six.

When she straightened and their eyes met again, he raised his ale in a silent salute. She smiled shyly before looking away. Odd, because she didn't seem the shy type.

As if to prove the point, she called across the room, "Laurence, get Harry back in the nook where he belongs. He's bleeding on my flagstones, and I just scrubbed them yesterday."

"Aye, Meredith."

Meredith. The name pulled a thread in his mind, but the memory unraveled before Rhys could grasp it.

Laurence slid an arm under the moaning heap that was Harry Symmonds and shouldered the unconscious man to his feet.

"Don't 'Meredith' me." She shooed them toward a secluded alcove with her broom. "So long as you're going to behave like boys, it'll be Mrs. Maddox to you."

The ale soured on Rhys's tongue. *Mrs. Maddox?*

Ah, hell. This young, strong, beautiful woman was

married to old Maddox? Not a barmaid after all, but the inn's landlady. So much for fate throwing him a boon. He should have known better. There'd be nothing so beautiful for him on this earth.

A trencher of stew and a wedge of mutton pie appeared on the table before him. Rhys dug in, keeping his gaze stubbornly trained on the food rather than his lovely server. He didn't pursue married women, no matter what sort of looks they threw him. Not to mention, if she was married to Maddox and making eyes at Rhys, the woman must be not only fickle, but daft and half-blind in the bargain.

He was hungrier than he'd realized, and he cleaned both plates in a matter of minutes. He'd always been a fast, efficient eater, even more so since the army. More than once in the year since he'd inherited the Ashworth title, he'd looked up from a finely laid London dinner table to discover his table manners the object of intense, horrified scrutiny. Just another of his acquired traits that sent English ladies groping for their vinaigrettes.

He bolted the rest of his ale and carried the empty tankard to the bar for refilling. Mrs. Maddox had disappeared for the moment, and a gap-toothed young man stood behind the counter. Rhys recognized him as the youth she'd charged with stabling his horse. What was his name again? Dylan? Dermott?

"Darryl Tewkes, at your service, sir. Will it be another ale?"

The young man took the tankard from Rhys, and his left eye creased at the edge as he did it. Rhys couldn't tell if it was a wink or some sort of nervous twitch. The latter, he hoped, when the eye flashed shut a second time. He had an amusing look to him, this Darryl Tewkes. Sharp nose, pointy ears. Like one of the piskies old moorfolk still believed in.

"Yours is a fine horse, sir," Darryl went on, handing

him a mug of fresh ale. "I've seen him settled in well. He's unsaddled, watered. I'll go back out to brush him down and give him hay in a minute or two."

Rhys nodded his approval and raised his drink.

"Does he have a name, sir? The horse?"

He wiped his mouth with his cuff. "No." He never named them, not anymore.

"Will the gentleman be staying long in the neighborhood?" Darryl asked.

"Just one night."

At the outset, Rhys hadn't been sure how long he'd stay. But now he knew—one night of this place was all he could take. In the morning, he'd ride up the slope and take a long, slow look at what he'd come to see. And then he'd leave. Surely he could hire a steward or land agent to come tend to any matters here that needed attention. That was what titled gentlemen of means did, wasn't it? Where he'd go after that, Rhys had no idea. Wherever fate took him, he supposed.

"One night?" Darryl's eye gave an eager twitch. "Sir, you must stay more than one night. One night isn't anywhere long enough to see the local attractions."

Rhys frowned. Attractions? There were local attractions?

The younger man's eyebrows rose. "I give tours to travelers," he said, his face brightening. "Two hours, or half a day. Best value for your coin is my full-day Mystic Moor excursion, complete with guided commentary and a picnic lunch."

Rhys chuckled at the image of genteel travelers picnicking in the shadow of Bell Tor. He hoped they took precautions against the ravens. He cleared his throat and asked, "What sort of attractions?"

"Why, it's a mystical trip through time, you see." He made a grand, expansive gesture. "I'll start by taking you round to the ancient burial cairns, and the abandoned tinners' works from centuries past."

Rhys was well familiar with those sights. They looked remarkably like random piles of stone.

"Then there's the old monks' crosses. And Bell Tor, of course. On a clear day, you can see—"

"Even more rocks?" Rhys grunted, still unimpressed.

"Oh, but that's nothing. I haven't yet told you the best part of the tour. The haunted ruins of Nethermoor Hall."

Now he had Rhys's attention. "Haunted ruins, you say?"

Darryl settled both elbows on the counter and leaned forward, as though he didn't dare speak too loud. "Yes. Nethermoor Hall. The cursed House of Ashworth. Generations of evil flourished in that house. Till one summer night fourteen years ago, when it burnt to the ground in an unholy conflagration. My tour ends there, just as the hour turns toward dusk. Sometimes, if you listen sharp, you can hear the crackle of flames, or catch a whiff of brimstone on the wind. That blaze was the judgment of God, folk say. After that night, the family was never heard from again."

"What happened to them?" Rhys asked, surprised to hear the question come from his lips. He had to credit the younger man. Darryl did have a knack for spinning tales. "I mean, you spoke of haunting."

"Ah yes. Well, the old Lord Ashworth's ghost hasn't been seen. He never returned to Devonshire. Died just last year, somewhere in Ireland, I think. Lady Ashworth, she died several years before the blaze. There are some folk here—the ones with the touch—who've seen her ghostly form hovering high above the ruined house. As though she's still pacing the upstairs corridors. But it's the son people see most often."

Rhys choked on a mouthful of ale. "The son?"

"Aye. He was a wild youth, always making trouble. Churned up the moor with his reckless rides. Folk say he had bit of devil in him."

"And he died in this fire?"

"Not precisely. He nearly perished—should have died, by accounts. But even though he survived, it's like he left a ghostly imprint on Nethermoor Hall. People spy his phantom wandering the place, especially on warm summer nights. They've even seen him gallop across the moor on a spectral horse, flames licking at his heels."

Rhys blinked at the youth, unsure whether to be amused, bemused, offended, or . . . mildly concerned. Outlandish as Darryl's tale might be, parts of it held the faint ring of truth. All these years he'd spent feeling half alive, could it be because he'd left some ghost of his adolescent self behind? He shook his head to dispel the fool notion. This Dartmoor fog must be creeping in through his ears, muddling his brain.

"So." Darryl leaned forward and waggled his eyebrows. "The tour. Are you man enough? Do you dare risk an encounter with Rhys St. Maur, the living phantom of Bell Tor?"

A smile tugged at Rhys's lips. Now this could prove amusing. Before he could decide just how to respond, a figure joined Darryl's on the business side of the bar.

Meredith.

Mrs. Maddox, he corrected himself.

"Darryl," she said, clouting the youth on the back of the head, "you idiot. This *is* Rhys St. Maur. Lord Ashworth now. You're talking to your 'living phantom,' live and in the flesh."

Darryl's pale face went whiter still as he stared at Rhys, jaw working to no audible effect. At least his eye had finally ceased twitching.

The youth swallowed hard as Rhys braced his arm on

the bar and leaned forward. Until their faces were just inches apart. And then, when he was certain Darryl was paying very close attention, he lowered his voice and whispered . . .

"Boo."

Chapter Two

"I . . . You're . . ." Darryl stammered. "I mean to say, it isn't . . ."

"I'll see to him, Darryl." With a tone that would brook no argument, Meredith shooed the addlewit groom from the bar. "Back to the stables you go."

Rhys was staring at her. To avoid staring back, Meredith quickly looked away, making a show of straightening bottles. So far, she'd made do with furtive glances, but she'd gaze at him all night long if she could, exploring his every contour and shadow. Cataloging all the ways he'd changed and all the ways he hadn't.

His hair was the first thing she'd noticed. Or rather, the lack of it. He kept it shorn close to his scalp now, and that had thrown her for a moment when she'd seen him in the door. All her memories of Rhys featured long waves of dark hair pulled back with a bit of leather cord. Or falling loose in roguish locks over his brow. He'd tried to hide his face sometimes back then—the new bruise purpling beneath his eye, or a fresh split in his lip.

He seemed to have given up on hiding his injuries now. His face was a map of scars she didn't recognize, but she blessed those healed wounds. They told her she wasn't dreaming this time. This was truly Rhys St. Maur sitting there on the stool, one elbow propped on the counter. Huge and defiant and rugged and—holy God—right there in front of her. In the flesh. After fourteen years.

"I know you," he said slowly. His tone made it a question.

"Do you?" Desperate to disguise her shock, Meredith reached for his empty tankard.

His fingers tightened over the handle. Large, roughened. Strong.

Her gaze snapped up to his, and again he snared her with those gorgeous eyes. In all the years she'd spent living on the Nethermoor estate, Rhys St. Maur had never looked at her like this. He'd scarcely looked at her at all. Now she could see that his eyes were wild and beautiful, just like the rest of him. Deep, rich brown streaked with amber. Like the finest cognac, or . . .

"Brandy," she breathed.

His brow lifted. A thick scar split it in two.

"Care for a brandy?" She cleared her throat. "Cool night out there. A man needs something more than ale to warm him."

"Does he?" His lips quirked in a sensuous way.

She cursed silently, realizing the flirtatious implication of her words. That hadn't been her intent. Not that she found it repulsive, the idea of . . . warming Rhys St. Maur. To the contrary, fantasies of doing just that had steamed her bathwater for years. "I . . . I only meant . . ."

"I know. Thank you, Mrs. Maddox. But I don't drink spirits."

Well. He might not need a drink, but Meredith did. She reached for a bottle under the counter—her private reserve—and poured herself a generous amount.

"I know you," he said. Not a question this time. His

voice was deeper than she recalled, and it reached different places inside her. "I don't remember you, but I know you."

She tilted the glass of gin slowly, taking a fortifying swallow before answering. "Meredith Lane," she finally said, giving him her maiden name. "You likely don't recall, but my father—"

"Managed our stables. Of course I recall." He cocked his head and narrowed his eyes. "You're George Lane's girl? Impossible. When I saw that girl last, she was nothing but freckles and bone."

Her cheeks heated. He did remember her. Not precisely the way she'd have wished to be remembered, but it was something.

"Merry Lane," he said, his voice gone soft. A low chuckle caught in his throat. "Can't believe it. You're little Merry Lane."

The warmth in her cheeks was a full blush now. That was the only notice he'd taken of her as a girl—her silly, sentimental name. If they crossed paths in the stables, he'd say it with a mocking lilt in his voice as he impatiently brushed her aside.

Run along home, Merry Lane.

"I'm not Merry Lane anymore." Wiping down the counter with a rag, she kept her tone light. "That's the magic of being gone from the neighborhood fourteen years, my lord. Things change in your absence."

"So they do, Mrs. Maddox. So they do." Suddenly serious, he cleared his throat. "Your father . . . He's still living?"

"Upstairs as we speak. He oversees the inn's stables now, with Darryl's help. Though we seldom shelter anything finer than pack ponies and the occasional traveler's mount."

"I'd like to see him."

"Then you'll have to wait. He'll be sleeping now, but

tomorrow you can . . ." She paused. "I'm assuming you mean to stay the night here. It is the only inn for miles."

Please stay, a fool voice inside her pleaded. *Please don't walk away again just yet.*

"Yes, for the night."

"Just the one night?" Not that it mattered. Whether he stayed one night or ten, he was sure to leave again eventually. There was nothing for him here. His inherited lands were largely worthless moorland. Nethermoor Hall itself was a burnt-out ruin, and it ought to stay that way.

"Just the one night." He gave her a slight, self-effacing smile. "If you've a room for a living phantom, that is."

"Don't mind Darryl Tewkes," she said quickly. "He's been embroidering that tale for years. He plies it on all the travelers passing through, trying to entice them to stay in the neighborhood an extra night. More money for the inn, you know, as well as for his pocket. He even has some of the cottagers along the touring route making souvenirs to sell. Miniature stone crosses and the like."

"How enterprising of him. An industrious employee, a capable young wife . . . Old Maddox seems to have done quite well for himself."

"The man's six years in the grave. Depends on your point of view, whether that's doing well or not."

His jaw tensed. "You're widowed."

She nodded in reply.

"I'm sorry for it."

"Don't be." She fumbled with the glass she'd been wiping clean. Devil take it, she was a widow, an innkeeper, and turning thirty in two summers. How did he make her feel like an awkward girl again? "I mean, it's been years. I've been widowed longer than I was married, by now. And he left me the inn, so we get by well enough."

"We? Have you children?"

The familiar pang came and ebbed in a heartbeat. She shook her head. "No. Just me and Father. And Darryl, since his aunt died. And all the villagers, for that matter. We had to find a way to get by, didn't we? The primary local employer deserted us fourteen years ago."

Rhys stared at his ale a moment. Then he lifted it and drank in silence.

He looked chastened, and she rued the bitterness in her tone. But he should know the truth—it hadn't been easy. The late Lord Ashworth had been a right bastard, but at least he'd paid wages on occasion and given the local merchants some custom. After Nethermoor burned down and the family deserted the region, the village was left at loose ends. There was very little agriculture in the area, this being the rocky heart of the moor. Buckleigh-in-the-Moor lost an entire generation as the young men left town, one by one. The new war prison at Princetown gave some work for a time. Others went further, to Exeter or Plymouth. Those few who remained in the village relied on what wages the Three Hounds could provide—as Darryl did—or else made a living through shady dealings.

Speaking of shady dealings . . . As if she'd called him in from the cold with the thought, Gideon Myles strolled through the door.

The assembled men greeted him with a rousing cheer, to which Gideon responded with a gallant tip of his low-brimmed cap. As always, he took a moment to savor his notoriety, vigorously shaking the outstretched hands of several men. All too soon, however, his keen eyes sought her out. Meredith knew better than to wait for him to approach.

"Back in a trice," she told Rhys, hurrying out from behind the bar. Rhys was only passing through, just staying the night. He and Gideon Myles had no business with one another, but only trouble could result if they met.

Gideon greeted her with a roguish grin. He was a young man—at least three years her junior—but he'd never lacked for arrogance. He was also far too handsome for his own good. "Well, well," he said. "Don't you look eager to see me? And for good reason, too. I've a cask of Madeira for you this week."

"Fine, fine," she said distractedly, darting a glance at Rhys. "Can we go outside and discuss it in the courtyard?"

"The courtyard? I just came in. It's cold as a witch's cunny out there, and near as damp." His eyebrow arched, and he lowered his voice to a suggestive murmur. "Unless you wanted a bit of privacy, in which case I'd suggest a different location . . ."

She blew out a frustrated breath. Now was not the time for flirtation. Pulling him aside, she said, "You can't unload the wagon tonight."

"What do you mean? I know the mist's a bit thick, but by the time the men load up the ponies the weather's sure to—"

"No, no. You mustn't load the ponies, either. I mean it, Gideon. Tonight won't do. You can pull the wagon into the barn, and we'll cover it with blankets and such. Darryl will sleep atop it, for safekeeping."

He made a scornful sound in his throat. "I wouldn't trust Darryl Tewkes to guard my drink while I went out to piss." His eyes went serious. "It's a valuable take tonight, Meredith. I've two men out there already, armed with pistols and shot. It's too risky not to transport the goods immediately."

Even worse. Two men with guns? She hesitated, casting a glance toward the bar.

"As usual," he said, "there's more than Madeira in it

for you. You know I pay handsomely for the use of your father's ponies."

"I know, I know. But you don't understand."

"I understand your eyes keep straying to that gent by the bar. Great ugly fellow, isn't he? Where'd he come from?" His voice darkened. "Has he frightened you?"

"No, no. He's just a traveler." Inspiration struck, and she added, "So he says. If you ask me, he's on errand from the Lydford magistrate. Best not to give him any reason to suspect, you know? Wait until morning, after he leaves."

"You know I can't transport these goods in daylight. And the Lydford magistrate's been in my pocket for well over a year." Gideon shrugged out of his coat and tossed it to a waiting man. "Perhaps I'll introduce myself. Add his drinks to my account, will you?"

Meredith tried to protest, but Gideon was already halfway across the room.

"I'm Gideon Myles," he announced, tossing his cap on the counter beside Rhys's elbow.

Rhys looked up from his ale. "Should I know that name?"

"I daresay you should. But then, modesty's never been one of my virtues."

With a reluctant sigh, Rhys braced his hands on the edge of the bar and stood. Meredith saw a flicker of hesitance cross Gideon's features. Gideon was a big man by most measures, but Rhys dwarfed him with his shadow alone.

"Don't tell me," Rhys said, stacking his arms across his massive chest. "You want to show me your enchanted cave and sell me a bottle of piskie dust."

And now Gideon's face went blank with confusion. "I don't know what the hell you're implying," he said slowly, "but I know I feel like hitting you for it."

This was hopeless. Meredith had no choice but to step in.

"Pardon the interruption," she said to Rhys. "Mr. Myles is our local . . . dry goods carrier." She ignored Gideon's expression of offended pride. He'd understand the reason for her falsehood soon enough. "Gideon, this is Rhys St. Maur. The new Lord Ashworth."

The entire room went still. Conversations died mid-syllable. The name Ashworth had the same effect as the sound of that brass candlestick whipped through the air. It was a dangerous sound. A threat.

"Ashworth," Gideon repeated, staring down Rhys with vengeful eyes.

Rhys stood impassive and said evenly, "Yes. I believe we've established our names, Mr. Myles."

A grumble spread through the room. Chair legs scraped slate.

"What are you doing here?" Gideon asked.

"Whatever I please. I don't answer to you."

Meredith knew she had to draw a close to this scene, and fast. She'd only just tidied up from the first brawl. And now Gideon had two men outside armed with pistols, and a wagonload of smuggled goods he'd no doubt kill to protect.

"He's only here for the night," she announced to the room. "And I was just going to show him to his accommodations. Mr. Myles, our trade will wait for tomorrow morning."

There, she told Gideon with her eyes. *Now do you see why you can't go unloading that wagon tonight?*

He did. But he wasn't happy about it. He struck a petulant pose. "Darryl can show him upstairs."

"It's my inn. He's my guest." She turned to Rhys. "If you'd follow me, my lord?"

She didn't wait for his reply, just turned and headed for the back stairs and hoped he'd follow. He did. The ancient bowed planks groaned beneath his weight, and the stairway suddenly felt too narrow.

"I'm sorry to make trouble for you," he said.

"It's no trouble," she replied, slowing her pace. "But if you don't mind my asking, why *are* you here?"

She heard him sigh. "Honestly, Mrs. Maddox?" *Creak.* "I'm asking myself the same thing."

Fair enough.

"Your room's just here," she said, leading him down the corridor. She waited to the side, holding the door open for him to enter.

He strode a few paces to the center of the bedchamber and turned a slow circle, surveying his accommodations. Meredith held her breath, wondering what he'd make of them. She'd only finished redecorating the room this week. It was the opening salvo in her campaign to remake the Three Hounds into a quality establishment. A real inn, the type where well-heeled travelers would *plan* to break their journeys, not just reluctantly stop over if they'd broken a carriage wheel.

Meredith sighed as she went to start a fire. She really hadn't the slightest notion what she was doing. Just this afternoon, she'd stood in the center of this room, feeling terribly proud of the new ruffled drapes and quilted counterpane. The blue china vase above the mantel added a touch of elegance, she'd fancied.

Now that she saw the small bedchamber from Rhys's perspective, she noted the exposed rafters overhead, the dingy walls, the choking tang of peat smoke from the hearth . . . . It all looked hopelessly meager and drab. She could only imagine how it appeared in a titled gentleman's eyes. Who was she fooling, anyway?

"Darryl will bring up your bags. Shall I tell him to act as valet?"

"No," Rhys said quickly. She thought she saw him shudder. "Not necessary."

"There's the washstand in the corner." *Please don't chip the new porcelain.*

He nodded.

"We serve breakfast downstairs in the morning. And if there's anything you need in the meantime, you've only to ask."

"Thank you." He tipped his gaze to the ceiling. "This room is rather . . ."

"Drafty," she finished. "I know. I'm sorry. I'll send in Darryl overnight to add peat to the fire, and there's an extra blanket in the chest. But then you might become overheated, in which case there's always the window." She felt, with distinct horror, that she was blathering on like a bedlamite, but she couldn't seem to stop. "I know the room must be poor indeed, compared with what you're accustomed to, but I do hope you'll find it adequate to your . . ."

He turned to her and smiled.

And suddenly she had no more words.

"Adequate?" He shook his head. "In the army, I grew more accustomed to sleeping on hard ground than anything. My rooms in London were barren and cold." He looked around the bedchamber. "I can assure you, this is the finest bedchamber I've known in years. True luxury. I'll sleep well tonight."

His words made her heart float in her chest. Blast it. She couldn't start yearning for him. Well, she'd *started* yearning for him as a girl, but she couldn't afford to take the practice up again now. He was leaving in the morning.

"In fact," he said lightly, crossing to the window and peering out, "I'm so pleased with this room, I think I could kiss you for it."

Oh, Lord. Now that wouldn't help with her yearning problem.

His head jerked up, as though he'd surprised himself

with the words. Of course he had. They were a ridiculous notion. The last time he'd looked at her, he'd seen naught but freckles and bone.

Confirming the foolishness, he said, "That's strange."

She tried to laugh, but couldn't. He was drawing too near. Her pulse thundered in her chest as those giant boots carried him across the old, creaking oak floorboards. Floorboards she'd scoured with sand on hand and knee just a few days ago. Her shoulders still ached.

His deep brown eyes searched hers as he drew to a halt. "I think I'd very much like to kiss you." He reached out and plucked a stray lock of her hair from where it lay on her shoulder, twisting it slowly between his finger and thumb. "What do you say, Merry Lane? Show me a proper welcome home?"

She could make a joke, or step away. She knew well how to deflect a man's advances. Down in the tavern, she did it all the time. For each of the few men she'd taken to her bed since her husband's death, she'd refused dozens more. But she'd spent her girlhood dreaming of *this* particular man, staring down at her with exactly that glimmer of desire in his eyes, speaking precisely those words to her.

I think I'd very much like to kiss you.

It was simply all too much. In a flutter of nerves, she blurted out, "Is there anything else you require, my lord?"

At her brisk tone, he recoiled instantly. "No." He turned away, but not before she caught a wounded flash in his eyes. He rubbed one palm over his short dark hair. "No, I apologize. That was . . . wrong of me. It won't happen again."

Meredith stood there for a moment, watching him return to the window.

He didn't turn back around as he said, "You'd best leave me, hadn't you?"

So she slipped out the door and drew it shut behind her. Then she punched the doorjamb with a low growl.

Damn, damn, damn. In all her life, she'd never been so frustrated with herself. She'd just let slip the opportunity— the one single chance she'd ever have—to share a kiss, and most likely a bed, with the man she'd wanted since she'd scarcely understood what wanting meant. Not only that, but she'd given him the wrong impression with her refusal. Now he thought she found him unattractive and unkissable, when nothing could be further from the truth.

Gideon was still downstairs in the bar. She needed to see his wagonload of goods stowed safely in the horse barn. Not to mention, finish serving her customers without losing more furniture in the process.

But Rhys would leave tomorrow. She would never have this chance again. She worked so hard for this place. Every day, all day. Didn't she deserve one night for herself?

She rapped firmly on the door.

When he opened it, she spoke quickly, before she could lose her nerve. "You could," she said. "You could kiss me. I wouldn't mind."

"You wouldn't?"

"No."

He cupped her jaw in his hand and tilted her face to his. It was only then that she realized she'd addressed her fearless speech to his coat button.

His thumb stroked her cheek tenderly, and she let her eyes close. He did it again, dragging his thumb from her cheekbone to her jaw. Just that gentle brush of his skin against hers had her whole body humming.

Unable to bear the anticipation a moment longer, she opened her eyes.

He didn't kiss her.

"Thank you for that." He touched a fingertip to the corner of her mouth before releasing her. "Good night, Mrs. Maddox."

Before she could bid him the same, he'd closed the door.

Chapter Three

If only stone could burn.

In the thin gray dawn, Rhys stood before the gutted shell of Nethermoor Hall. After such a long absence, he hadn't known what to expect. He'd fantasized about finding the place just a scar on the moor, a still-smoking pile of cinders and lime. But those hopes had been disappointed. For unlike the roofbeams, floors, and passageways, Nethermoor's exterior walls had been built of stone. And damn it all, stone didn't burn.

Much of the once-great house's masonry had disappeared into the Dartmoor mist, no doubt scavenged for new construction. But here and there, an orderly stack of stones persisted—the corner of a room, an arched doorway leading from one nowhere to another. Fourteen unforgiving winters had scrubbed the remaining rocks of soot, and they appeared as weathered and permanent as so many granite tors pressing up through the moor's endless swaths of gorse.

Time and rain could do their worst for centuries. A conflagration could consume the surrounding heath. But Nethermoor Hall would never completely go away, because it was made of stone, and stones were forever.

Turning away from the house, Rhys walked the short distance to where the stables had once stood. Where the fire had begun. Little remained to mark the site, save a low border of rocks outlining the foundation. The place had grown over with moss and sedge. He kicked at a blackened piece of metal on the ground. An old bridle loop, perhaps. Or maybe a bit. An icy shiver crawled over his neck.

Behind him, his gelding whickered uneasily. The horse didn't like the place any more than he did. Maybe he should have given more credit to Darryl's tales. Maybe the scent of singed horseflesh did linger on the breeze. Did the perk of the horse's ears mean he caught the faint echoes of equine screams?

Rhys shuddered. In the years since leaving Nethermoor, he'd heard the death cries of many creatures, human and inhuman. But none were as eerie or chilling as the sounds this place had etched on his memory—the crisp, rhythmic crack of a whip kissing hide, the whoosh of a wind-fueled blaze, and those panicked screams of trapped horses.

Darryl Tewkes was right. Rhys *should* have died with those beasts fourteen years ago. He'd been courting death every day of his life ever since. But he was the human equivalent of a goddamned boulder. Huge, hard, indestructible. He'd weathered the daily beatings in his youth, the countless schoolyard and tavern brawls, the ravages of battle. He was starker, meaner, and scarred for his pains, but still here.

Still here. Standing in front of this hellish pile of rocks and misery he'd inherited.

If only stone could burn.

A bitter taste filled his mouth. He turned his head, intending to spit, but found himself doubled over and retching instead. God damn it. Eleven years in the infantry, and he'd never once vomited in battle.

Get up, the voice inside him said. The cold, commanding voice he'd never been able to silence, even with a hundred cannons thundering in his ears. *Get up*. No matter what struck him down—fist, shot, bayonet—he somehow always staggered to his feet, ready to take more. *Get up. On your feet. Stand, you miserable piece of filth.*

Rhys stood.

Slowly turned.

And left, without looking back.

He was tempted to ride straight on to Lydford, leaving Buckleigh-in-the-Moor behind him without so much as a farewell. But he had to return. He'd left his bags at the Three Hounds, for one. His horse hadn't been fed, and neither had he.

Most of all, he needed to see Meredith again.

He owed her an apology for that boorish proposition last night. Simply because she'd been the only soul in the village to greet him with civility, it didn't follow that she'd eagerly fall into bed with him. He couldn't think what had possessed him to even suggest it. He'd been so tired and bleary-eyed, and just a bit drunk on those soft, shy glances. He'd simply wanted to get close to her and stay there for a while, and learn if her hair smelled as lovely as it looked. And afterwards, sleep. Sleep and forget, instead of spending the night tossing and cursing the rafters.

Naturally, she'd refused him. As well she should. And she'd mustered the generosity to knock on his door and grant him a sort of absolution, but she hadn't been brave enough to look him in the face as she gave it. Still, he couldn't resist stealing a touch.

God, her skin was pure joy to touch. Fresh and smooth, like the underside of a leaf.

One glance in the washstand mirror this morning had revealed his lunacy. He was a hideous, cut-up wreck of a man. What could a woman like her possibly want with a fellow like him? Except money, perhaps. Not that she was the type to accept coin for her favors, but he didn't want her thinking he was the type to pay for them. He didn't use women that way anymore.

No, she deserved an apology. He wasn't especially good at making amends, but he'd do what he could. Greet her with a civil good morning, thank her for her hospitality, and pay her triple what he owed. And then he'd ride straight out of the village and never trouble her again.

The gelding picked its way along the narrow, well-trod path. It wasn't the most direct route back to the village, but it was the safest, as evidenced by the cross-shaped stone markers placed by monks centuries ago. A man who wandered off the safe path risked stumbling into a bog and becoming trapped in waist-deep peat and muck. As a child, Rhys had known the lay of these slopes better than he'd known his ciphers, but he didn't trust his memory enough to risk miring his horse today.

It was full morning by the time he descended into the small valley that cradled Buckleigh-in-the-Moor. Sunlight chased the mist into dark hollows and nooks. Considering the harshness of the surrounding terrain, this truly was a well-favored spot. A brisk stream had carved this gorge over millennia, and aside from the ready water source, the valley offered some protection from the brutal Dartmoor winds. The village even claimed a few dozen trees to its name, and they grew reasonably straight—an unusual occurrence on the windswept moors.

As he reunited with the main road and entered the village proper, however, Rhys noticed what he hadn't been able to see last night. Very little had changed in this village. Too little had changed, as a matter of fact. There were no new buildings. Neglected cottages had fallen into disrepair. Just as Meredith had told him, the village had not prospered in the Ashworths' absence. A thorn of guilt pricked him deep inside.

He turned toward the inn. Like most buildings in town, its foundations were stone, but its walls were fashioned from cob, a cured mixture of earth and straw. Slate shingles gave it a sounder roof than the usual thatch. With a gleaming coat of fresh limewash and green-painted shutters, the inn was by far the best-kept structure in the town, and the largest. Even at this early hour, the courtyard buzzed with activity. It was clear to Rhys that the Three Hounds was not only the physical center of the village, but its social and commercial center as well. And little Merry Lane now managed it all. Remarkable.

In the courtyard, he dismounted and walked his gelding toward the stables. A hunched figure rushed to meet him, hobbling with the aid of a wooden crutch.

"Lord Ashworth! By God, it is you. Merry told me you'd come back, but I could hardly believe her." The old man leaned on his crutch and tipped his hat, revealing a flash of silver hair beneath.

"Mr. Lane," Rhys said, catching his breath. "It's . . . it's good to see you."

Only it wasn't. It was hell to see George Lane as he was now—bent, aged, crippled and scarred. In Rhys's memory, he'd remained a man in his prime of life, an expert horseman gifted with an even temper and a steady hand. The Nethermoor stables had been Rhys's refuge in his youth, and Lane had always been kind to him. When fire broke out in the stables that night, it was George Lane who dragged Rhys's barely conscious form from the blaze. Once Rhys was safe, the stable master worked valiantly to save the horses. He succeeded in a few cases, but failed in most. During his last rescue attempt, a burning rafter had fallen on his leg.

Rhys had been sent to relations in Yorkshire immediately following the fire, and in the years since he'd never so much as written to inquire after his old friend's condition. Probably because he'd suspected, rightly, that his friend's condition would be just this. He was maimed for life.

That little thorn of guilt was swiftly growing tendrils and vines, twining his innards in a stranglehold.

"I'll take the horse in." Smiling, the old man balanced his crutch under one arm and reached for the reins with the other. "You go on in and have breakfast."

Rhys reluctantly handed him the reins. He wished Lane would allow him to do the labor of unsaddling and grooming the horse, but he wouldn't insist. He'd known many soldiers crippled in battle, and he'd learned to never second-guess their abilities.

Besides, George Lane couldn't be too hampered by his injuries. He still kept an immaculate horse barn, from what Rhys could see as he followed him to the stable door.

"No need to come in," Lane called to him, holding him off with an outstretched hand. "You know I'll take excellent care of him."

"I know," Rhys said, wondering why the man didn't seem to want him in his stables. Well, it could have something to do with the fact that his last stables had burned to the ground. If he were George Lane, Rhys wouldn't trust himself in there either, come to think of it.

He propped his shoulder against the wide post of the doorway and spoke into the darkened interior. "It's a large barn you've got here. Your daughter told me it's mostly pack ponies you keep."

"That's right," Lane replied. "I started breeding them a decade ago, from a few wild ponies I brought in off the moor. They're well-trained now, and hardy. We rent them out as they're needed, to local farmers and such."

Rhys shook his head. What a waste of the man's skill. "I wonder that you don't keep posting horses." To expedite travel, private and public coaches changed horses frequently. If the Three Hounds offered posting horses for hire and exchange, the inn could draw a great deal more business.

"I'd like to," the man answered, "but I've no suitable breeding stock. Hard to gather that kind of coin, especially in a village where folk pay their debts with eggs more often than shillings."

"I can imagine." Rhys startled as something prodded the back of his knee. He wheeled to find a pair of long-eared hounds nosing at his boots. "Go on," he told them, feinting a kick. "I've no scraps for you."

Though oddly, he could have sworn he smelled fresh-baked bread.

"They're just being friendly," a feminine voice said. "It's me they're after."

Meredith stood before him, both arms wrapped around a large woven basket. A bounty of yeast rolls peeked out from beneath a printed muslin cloth. Rhys's stomach churned with awakened hunger.

Damn, his whole body was churning with awakened hunger.

"You're still here," she said. "Thought perhaps you'd left."

"I did. And then I came back."

"I don't know how this inn got its name," she said, watching the dogs nip the tassel of his boot. "Maddox only ever kept two hounds. When he was drunk, he used to tell smart-mouthed travelers the third hound was in the pie." She spared him a fleeting glance before calling past him into the stables. "Father, I've told you, leave that work to Darryl. You're not supposed to be straining your heart."

"I'm brushing down the finest gelding in Devonshire. It's a pleasure, not a strain. And Darryl's gone to fetch water."

Rhys heard her release a frustrated sigh. Her brow creased with concern. "Father, you can't—"

Rhys laid a hand to her shoulder and drew her away from the door. "Don't," he said quietly. "Don't tell a man what he can't do. He'll only be more determined to prove you wrong."

Her face couldn't decide what expression to take. Her brow was more than a mite annoyed with his interference, and her cheeks were turning an embarrassed pink. But her lips twitched at the corners as though she might cry, and her eyes . . .

Her eyes were just beautiful. They made him too stupid to hold his next thought. If it hadn't been for the mountain of bread between them, he would have embraced her then and there.

Embraced her, of all things. What an idea. Where were these fancies coming from? Meredith Maddox was a beautiful woman, and there was no denying that he craved her body more than he craved a peaceful night's sleep. Any man with a pulse would feel the same. But this wasn't just lust. He'd never experienced such longing simply to take a woman in his arms and keep her there. He'd wanted to kiss her last night, and he'd never been much for kissing at all. It smacked of romance and innocence and all those other things that had nothing to do with him. His past encounters with women had borne a remarkable resemblance to his fights—impulsive, brutish, and never very satisfying.

What he wanted with Meredith was different. This strong, self-sufficient woman had awakened a tender impulse inside him. He was responsible for the state of her life. For the state of this village, in fact. It was his fault that it was barely dawn, and she'd already been working hard for hours. His fault that she had to play caretaker to an invalid father by day and constable to a band of unruly drunkards by night. Every hobbled step her father took, each tiny callus on her hand, every spot of blood on her dainty white tablecloth . . . all of it was his own damn fault.

"There was a doctor last year, passing through," she said softly, gazing unfocused at the bread. "He examined Father in exchange for free room and board. His heart's weak, the man said. If he doesn't slow down . . ."

Rhys gave her shoulder a light squeeze. "I've known your father almost as long as you have, Merry. Horsemanship is in his blood. It *is* his life. He'd rather die than slow down."

"I know. I know it, but . . ." She looked up at him and gave a one-shouldered shrug, as though he'd understand without any words.

And he did. Suddenly, Rhys understood *everything*. The reason he'd survived the past fourteen years and finally made his way back to this village. The reason he couldn't leave it now. The way to redeem his whole wasted life.

It all made perfect, unquestionable sense.

"Isn't it Sunday?" he said.

"Yes," she replied in a bewildered tone.

He looked about the courtyard. "Why aren't the people in church? Where's the vicar?"

"There's no vicar anymore. He left twelve years ago, when your father ceased paying his living. A curate comes out once a month from Lydford to hold services."

He swore softly. This made things a touch more difficult.

She gave him a cheeky smile. "What is it? Feel the need to confess your sins?"

"Bloody hell. That would take years." And he didn't particularly want forgiveness. No, he just wanted to make things right. "Confession isn't required, is it?"

"Required for what?"

"Marriage."

A roll tumbled from her basket, and the hounds scrabbled over it at their feet.

When she spoke, her voice was strangely brittle. "You're engaged to be married?"

"Not yet. I will be, soon." Before breakfast, he hoped. God, he was hungry. If she lost another roll from that basket, it would never reach the hounds.

"And you intend to marry your bride *here*? In Buckleigh-in-the-Moor?"

"I know the village church isn't the grandest, but it'll do. Wouldn't make sense to go elsewhere, now would it? Travel would be hard on your father."

She gave him a look of utter bemusement. "You wish to be married here. In this remote village. Simply so my father can be a guest at your wedding."

"Well, I thought you'd want him there."

"My lord, why on earth would I care if my father attends your wedding?"

The corners of Rhys's mouth twitched with amusement. Hell, he suspected he was close to grinning, and he didn't grin. Ever. But he was rather looking forward to learning how it felt.

Awareness sharpened her gaze. "Oh no," she said.

Oh, no?

Oh no, indeed. That wasn't the reaction he wanted. This would all be much easier if she'd simply accept the rightness of it. The inevitability.

But it wasn't him she'd focused on. Her gaze trained on a spot somewhere behind his left shoulder. "Here comes your welcoming committee."

He turned around. Coming toward him were the two

brawling apes from last night—Bull and Beak to him; he couldn't remember their real names—surrounded by a dozen other men. Rhys recognized some of them from the inn yesterday, but other faces were new.

To a one, they all carried flaming torches.

"Ashworth," Bull said, "we've come to escort you out of the village. For good."

Inside the stables, Rhys could hear the ponies growing restless and uneasy. He was uneasy, too. He couldn't abide open flames this close to a horse barn. But the band of fools holding the torches . . . they inspired nothing in him but derision.

"Harold and Laurence Symmonds, what the devil are you doing with torches?" Meredith asked. "It's full daylight, you idiots."

"Go inside to your father," Rhys murmured to Meredith. "Make certain he's safe. I'll handle this."

She disappeared into the stables.

Rhys stepped toward the center of the courtyard. "Very well. You've got my attention. Now say what it is you mean to say."

Harold Symmonds spat in the dirt. "The Ashworths were a scourge on this village. Fire burned Nethermoor Hall to the ground fourteen years ago and drove your folk from the moors forever. You should have stayed away, too. Now we're here with these torches to show you, fire will run you off the moor again."

"Ah," Rhys said, scratching his neck. "And yet I seem to be standing in place."

A gunshot cracked through the air.

Rhys wheeled around, searching for its source. He didn't have to search hard. Gideon Myles stood in the doorway of the stables, smoking pistol in hand.

"You peat-for-brains idiots. I've a wagonload of"—he threw a glance at Rhys—"of dry goods in this barn, and

I'll put a lead ball in each of you before I'll allow you to burn it down around my ears."

The mob was abashed.

"It was all his idea." Laurence jabbed a thumb toward his companion.

"It was not, you lying cur!"

Here they went again.

Laurence made a sweeping gesture with his torch, sending men leaping backward to avoid being singed. The two faced off, circling one another in the middle of the courtyard. Their band of followers, who'd clearly come on this errand for its amusement value, seemed happy enough to attend another fisticuffs in lieu of a lynching.

This time, Rhys was not going to stand back and watch. He stepped between the two men and grabbed each of them by the shirtfront. He grimaced as the torches' greasy smoke assailed his nostrils. One flex of his arms, and he could bash their skulls together and put an end to the whole scene. But he couldn't keep addressing every problem with violence. He didn't want to live angry anymore. "All right," he said, easing his grip. "That'll be enough."

"Fire! Fire!"

The panicked shout rose up behind him. Before Rhys could register its origin, a wave of ice-cold water sloshed over his head, dousing him to the skin. The shock of it froze him in place for a moment. An icy rivulet crawled down his back, and he shivered.

"I'm sorry," a meek voice behind him said. Rhys recognized it as belonging to Darryl Tewkes. He turned around, and there the youth was, twitchy eye and all.

"So sorry," he stammered again. "I was aiming for the torches, you know."

With a gruff sigh, Rhys shook himself. Water droplets flew everywhere. He took the fizzling torches from the two men, turned them wrong-end-up, and stubbed them in the dirt.

"Listen up, every one of you." The sound of gunfire had drawn gawkers, and had the whole village listening now. Damn it, he hated making speeches. He tried to keep his voice even. "You can bring your torches and your guns and your"—he rolled his eyes and flapped a wet sleeve at Darryl—"pails of cold water, and whatever else you please. You can't intimidate me. Fire, gunshots, drowning . . . I've been through each, and I've survived them all."

He stared down Harold and Laurence. "You fancy yourselves good in a fight? I fought for eleven years with the Fifty-second, the most decorated regiment in the British Army. Light infantry foot guards, the first line to attack in any battle. Fought my way through Portugal, Spain, France, Belgium. At Waterloo alone, I personally gutted seven members of Napoleon's Imperial Guard. And those are just the ones I killed up close."

Calmly, he turned to Gideon Myles. "You want to play with guns? I can do that, too. Rifle, musket, pistol . . . take your pick. I can clean, assemble, and load any one of them in under a minute. I don't waste black powder, and my aim is true."

And since he had the town's ear, he went on, "I'm also impervious to idiocy, I'll have you all know. A couple of Portuguese peasants once found me bleeding in a field, shot through the shoulder in a skirmish. Dragged me back to their henhouse and kept me there for the better part of a week, just sticking a poker between the slats every so often to jab me in the side and judge if I was dead yet." He turned to Darryl. "You there, with the bucket. Do you know how to say 'water' in Portuguese?"

Darryl shook his head no.

"Neither did I, damn it. And yet I'm still here. I'm

bloody well indestructible. Add to that, I'm Rhys St. Maur, your legendary living phantom, and you sure as hell can't scare me off my own cursed estate."

Silence.

Rhys had spoken all the words he intended to say. No one seemed to know what to do next. Harold, Laurence, Gideon Myles, Darryl . . . they all just stood there, gawping at Rhys, then gawping at one another. Band of bloody fools.

A yeast roll bounced off of Harold Symmonds's forehead, breaking the collective trance.

"Go home." Meredith was suddenly next to him, still holding her basket of bread with both hands. Her voice rang through the courtyard. "Go home, all of you."

One by one, the villagers turned and left. Myles disappeared back into the stables, presumably to resume keeping watch over his precious wagon. It struck Rhys that the man was inordinately protective of a load of "dry goods."

He released his breath slowly, feeling the tension in his muscles dissipate as well.

"Are you all right?" She looked him over from crown to boots. "I'm so sorry for that scene."

He wrung the water from his shirtfront, standing back so as not to drip on her bread. "Don't be. Wasn't your fault. And I needed a bath."

He looked up to find her frozen in place, her eyes riveted to his sodden shoulders and chest. He couldn't quite name the look in her eyes, but he suspected it was revulsion. With his shirt clinging to his body and his hair matted to his head—not to mention the fact that he'd just been met by a torch-bearing mob—he must have the look of a gothic monster.

"A bath," she said suddenly, shaking herself to life again. "Yes, of course. I'll have water drawn and heated."

"No, don't. The pump will do well enough for me."

"As you please, then." She turned to leave.

He caught her arm. "I . . . Merry, I'm sorry to bring you so much trouble. I'll make it up to you."

He'd make it up to all of them. To be sure, some of the residents of Buckleigh-in-the-Moor were right fools, and he'd never win any popularity contests here. But the majority of the villagers had to be decent, honest souls, and they had good reason to view him with suspicion. They'd all come around in time.

Meredith bit her lip. Her cheek dimpled with a fetching, lopsided smile. "You bring all sorts of trouble, Rhys St. Maur, and you always have done. But don't worry, I'll take care of Harold and Laurence and the others."

"I'm certain you will." She seemed to be taking care of the whole village. This inn, the travelers, her invalid father, the lives and fortunes of all these idiot men.

But who was taking care of *her*?

He asked, "Have you eaten your own breakfast yet?"

She shook her head no.

"Let's do this, then," he said, backing away. "I'll wash at the pump. You find us a morsel to eat. And then we'll sit down to breakfast together and fix our wedding date."

Chapter Four

As she laid the table for breakfast, Meredith refused even to think about Rhys's words to her outside. Surely her ears had deceived her. There was no way in Creation that he meant to propose marriage to her after a single night at the Three Hounds. Her accommodations were nice, but not that nice.

She didn't even have any ham or bacon. Until Mrs. Ware came in, there'd be no meat to serve except cold mutton pie. Just rolls and the whortleberry jam. And fresh cream and boiled eggs, and coffee made with cool spring water. Here was one consolation: The Three Hounds brewed the best coffee in England, or so a well-traveled guest had once proclaimed. Not that Meredith could know from experience. The farthest from home she'd ever been was Tavistock.

She'd just finished setting the table for two when Rhys entered the dining room, freshly bathed and dressed in a clean shirt and breeches. His hair was so short, it was already dry. She wanted to run her fingers over it, to see if it felt soft like goose down, or blunt, like clipped grass.

Lord, what was she thinking? That scene in the courtyard had made it perfectly clear that for Rhys's own safety and the harmony of the village, she needed to feed him and send him on his way. Today. No hair-stroking would be involved.

"Won't you be seated, my lord?" She tried for a breezy, casual tone. "Do you care for coffee?"

"I do. And please, just call me Rhys," he said, settling onto a wooden stool. "Not enough people do." He accepted the mug of coffee she handed him. Their fingers brushed in the exchange, and the sensation was electric.

He took a fearless swallow of the scalding brew. "So," he said, plunking the mug to the table, "when does this curate come into the village next? How soon can we be married?"

That electric tingle became a full-body shock.

"You can't be serious."

"Of course I can. I'm quite frequently serious. Do you think I'd enter into marriage lightly?"

A startled bubble of laughter escaped her. "What else can I think, when you've just walked through the door yesterday?"

"It's not as though I'm a stranger to you." He sipped his coffee again. "You've known me since you were a girl."

"Before last night, I hadn't laid eyes on you in fourteen years."

"Mm." A little smile crooked his lips. "That's what makes it destiny. We're fated to wed."

Meredith felt as though she'd been wedged into an old wine cask and set rolling down the rocky slope of Bell Tor. Rattled, disoriented. Just a bit drunk.

She crossed her arms over her chest. "Well, I don't want to marry you." And she didn't, not anymore. They needn't discuss the scraps of foolscap she'd covered with "Meredith St. Maur, Lady Ashworth" when she was twelve. "I don't want to marry at all." As a widow, she owned this inn outright. That wouldn't be the case if she took a husband.

He said calmly, "If there's one thing I've learned over the years, it's that fate doesn't care what we want."

"Well, I don't believe in fate." She hugged herself tighter still.

"Fate doesn't care whether we believe in it, either. That's the devil of it." He chuckled. "Meredith. Lay down that shield you're making with your arms and come sit with me." When she hesitated, he lifted a brow. "It's only breakfast."

Was it?

As she sat down, he picked up a knife and buttered a roll. "You'd understand what I mean about fate if you'd lived through a war in my boots."

The words settled like stones in her chest. "Was it true? Everything you said out there in the courtyard?"

"That and more." He bit into the roll, taking two-thirds of it into his mouth in one bite.

"That's . . ." *Heartbreaking.* "Remarkable, that you've survived." She felt in that moment how close she'd come, so many times, to never seeing him again. And it made her want to take him upstairs and pin him to the bed that moment. Make love to him just once, before he went away again.

"Ah, well." He swallowed. "Not so remarkable, really. Tried my best to leave this earth at every turn, but God and the Devil kept sending me back. Neither wanted me, I suppose."

Maybe I just wanted you more.

To avoid speaking the words aloud, she tore off an unladylike hunk of bread and chewed it noisily.

Pushing his coffee aside, Rhys reached into his coat pocket and withdrew two coins. He let them clatter to the table, where they lay like brass checkers on the blue-and-white gingham weave. On closer inspection, they weren't like any coins she'd ever seen. She picked one up and held it to the light, twisting it back and forth between her thumb and forefinger. The disc was irregular and crudely stamped. On one side a horse's head stood out in relief; on the reverse, she found a horse's tail.

She laughed at it. "Are these foreign money from your travels?"

"No. They're tokens that indicate membership in an elite gentlemen's society known as the Stud Club. Possession of one of those coins gives a man breeding rights to Osiris, England's most valuable stallion. The club rules state the tokens can't be bought or sold or given away. They can only be won or lost in a game of chance. There are only ten of them in the world, and at the moment I own two. Do you know how I came by them?"

She shook her head.

"Fate, pure and simple. Through no merit of my own, I was spared while other men—better men—fell." He propped an elbow on the table and cast a glance through the window. The bright morning sun made him squint, wrinkling the scar tissue on his temple.

Taking one of the coins in his hand, he said, "This one belonged to an officer in my battalion. Major Frank Brentley, from York. He was a good man. His wife traveled with the company, and she mended my shirts for me. He never drank, but he was a gambler through and through, always dicing or playing cards. Story was, he'd won this token drawing blind at vingt-et-un. Said he was blessed with good luck all his life."

He tapped the coin on the table. "Well, his good luck ended at Waterloo. We had the left flank of the line, and a *voltigeur* came out of nowhere. One moment Brentley was next to me, the next he was flattened by a rifle shot at close range, his gut ripped open at the seams."

Swallowing with great care, Meredith put down the bit of bread she'd been holding.

"Sorry," he said. "It's not proper breakfast conversation, I know. Anyhow, after I killed the French guardsman, I carried Brentley out of the action. Tried to make him comfortable. He pulled this token from his pocket. 'Have to play me for it,' he said. 'That's the rule. Heads or tails?' Then he died, and the coin rolled out of his hand, and it was too smeared with blood to make out the stamp on either side. But I'd won the coin toss, hadn't I? It's the way my life goes. It's like I've got a coin with 'Life' stamped on one side and 'Death' on the reverse, and no matter how many times I flip it into the air, it always comes up heads."

He reached for the other token. "This one belonged to Leo Chatwick, the Marquess of Harcliffe, the Stud Club's founder. Another good man. Had it all—youth, wealth, good looks. Universally admired. Murdered in cold blood almost two months ago now, while walking the wrong part of Whitechapel. Beaten and robbed by footpads. Or so most believe. His killers were never caught."

Meredith winced. "How dreadful. Was he a very close friend of yours?"

"No," he said. "I've learned that lesson. I don't make close friends."

The words made her ache with empathy, but they also twanged her pride. He'd take a wife, but not a friend? The compliment implied by his proposal grew fainter still. Whatever reason he had for wanting to marry, it seemed to have more to do with these queer brass coins than it had to do with *her*.

With his massive, scarred hand he picked up a boiled egg and tapped it with the edge of his spoon until a web of tiny cracks covered the brown speckled surface. The measured caution in his movements entranced her. She couldn't look away.

"I'm barren," she blurted out. "Most likely. I was married for four years and never conceived."

He frowned, peeling the shell from the egg. "Maddox was ancient. Doesn't mean—"

"It wasn't just him." She lowered her voice. "I've had lovers since."

His face shuttered. "Oh."

What would he make of her now? She lifted her chin, refusing to feel shamed. "Have I succeeded in changing your mind? Perhaps not so fated to be, after all."

"That wasn't my meaning. I'm just sorry you've been lonely. I'm a bastard for staying away so long. The fact that you're barren is of no importance. The last thing I want is a child. And you have my word, I'll not rush you into . . . consummation."

"What?" The breath left her lungs. She picked at the tablecloth. "Well, there went my prime inducement for accepting you."

He looked puzzled. "Truly?"

"Truly."

"So when you offered a kiss last night . . . you weren't just being generous?"

Her face heated as she nudged the saltcellar in his direction. "No, Rhys. Generosity had nothing to do with it. At all."

He studied her for a moment, then shrugged. "If you say so."

Why did he act so surprised? Surely he must be the recipient of a great deal of female attention, wherever he went. How could a woman not be attracted to him?

She watched as he picked up the naked, quivering egg he'd so painstakingly shelled. He halved it with a single snap of his jaws. The muscles in his cheek worked as he quickly downed the remainder. What an intriguing combination of tenderness and power he embodied. She imagined herself bared and white and trembling before him. So slowly, carefully revealed, and then . . . devoured. Just thinking of it made her a little bit afraid, and aroused beyond measure.

"If you don't wish to . . . to get children," she asked, "why on earth do you want to marry?" When men took an interest in her, bedding was usually foremost in their minds. And it wasn't as though she had money or influence to offer. Not enough to sway a peer of the realm, at any rate.

"I'm going to take care of you."

"I take care of myself. Quite capably."

"Yes, you do. And you take care of your father, and this inn, and the whole blasted village too. Things that should be my responsibility, now that I've inherited. I can't allow you to continue working so hard. I'm the lord of this place now, and I'm going to assume my role in the neighborhood."

She laughed. "Did you not notice the mob that greeted you this morning? The villagers don't want your help. They want you gone."

He shook his head. "That wasn't a mob, it was a band of fools."

"They may be fools, but they're big, strong fools. They could make real trouble for you, if they wished. And Gideon Myles is no simpleton."

"Gideon Myles." He snorted. "What is that man to you?"

Was that sudden edge in his voice jealousy? It shouldn't thrill her, but it did. Straight down to her toes.

"He's a business associate. And a friend." *And a smuggler who won't hesitate to use violence, if it suits his purpose.* She cleared her throat and continued, "Exactly what are your plans, Rhys?"

"I plan to marry you."

That thrill shot through her again. "Other than that."

"I plan to live up to my responsibilities as lord. Give

the village some means of support. It will take time, but I'll rebuild the estate."

"*Rebuild?* Rebuild Nethermoor Hall? Whyever would you want to do that?" She knew what kind of childhood he'd endured in that house. Why would he wish to rebuild it? Not to mention, no matter how much he wished it, Gideon Myles and his associates would never allow such a thing to occur. "And how do you think you'll accomplish the construction? The local men will never work for you."

"They will if I pay them enough."

She shook her head. "The older ones still hate your father. The younger ones, what few there are, have grown up hearing all manner of superstition and tales. They'll be afraid of you."

"Well, if I can't find local labor, I'll just have to bring in workers from Plymouth or Exeter, I suppose."

"That will cost you dear."

"I've some lands in the North I plan to sell. And I've lately come into some money. Not enough to restore Nethermoor Hall to full grandeur, but wisely invested it'll put a house together and leave enough left over to live on."

And if the investments weren't wise and they failed, what then? He'd be bankrupt with no source of rents or income. He'd leave again. Somehow every possibility ended with him leaving again.

"You won't need to do this anymore when you marry me," he said, looking around the room. "Work, I mean. I'll provide for you and your father both."

At the mention of her father, she felt a sharp twist in her chest. Drat him, he was making this so difficult.

"But I like the work here," she protested. "I'm proud of what I've done with this place, and I've plans to do more still."

"You could do far more as the lady of the manor."

"Rhys . . . you're being so naïve."

His eyebrows rose. "Me, accused of naïveté. I must say, I never thought that day would come. I've a mind to engrave the date on a plaque."

"You've forgotten what life's like out here. Right now it's a pleasant summer's morn, but you must recall how winter gets. It's harsh, lonely, desolate. You can't actually want to live here again. And we've learned to survive without a lord. Just go."

"I'm not going anywhere."

"Why the devil not?" Meredith certainly would, if she were Rhys.

"Circumstances would only pull me back. It's fate."

With a low groan, she propped her elbows on the table and buried her face in her hands.

"You don't believe me," he said, leaning forward. "I know. But when a man treads the border between this world and the next as often as I have, he starts to see the hand of fate everywhere. Sometimes in bright flashes, other times subtler shades. It's like discovering a whole new color, one most people just can't see. But I see it." He pulled her hands from her face. "When you look at me, your eyes shine with it. I'm telling you, this is meant to be."

Her heart fluttered. "And what makes you so sure of that?"

"This." He gestured at the breakfast laid out on the table between them. A few rolls, small earthenware crocks of butter and preserves. Two mugs of coffee and a dish of fresh cream. The plates were scattered randomly; crumbs dotted the checked tablecloth. The scene hardly looked like an omen of fate to her, but then—she thought she grasped his meaning. The warm light shone on them both with familiar intent, leaving them nowhere to hide their imperfections from each other. She hadn't even pinned her hair properly this morning.

To any casual observer, they would look like a couple having their thousandth breakfast together, instead of their first.

His warm gaze caught hers. "It just feels right, doesn't it?"

It did. It did. It was the rightest thing she'd ever felt, and utterly terrifying.

"Don't fight it," he said. "Marry me."

Don't fight it? But he wasn't fighting fair. He'd been gone for fourteen years, and now he strolled in one morning making promises to fulfill all his responsibilities and never leave again? Asking her and the village to abandon their hard-won security and place their futures right back in Ashworth hands? He offered a dream, but he'd force her to give up her safe reality to grasp it.

She just couldn't take that chance. Not on the basis of one almost-kiss and some invisible glimmer of "fate."

She forced herself to say the words. "No, Rhys. I can't marry you."

His eyes flared, and his hand balled into a fist. For a moment, he almost looked angry. Strange, after he'd remained so cool and collected before the riled-up villagers. Here was a flash of the Rhys she remembered from all those years ago: wild, angry, untamed. Irresistible.

Just a few seconds later, he'd suppressed that hot flare of emotion. His jaw relaxed, and he smoothed the tablecloth with his palm.

Of all the reasons why he needed to leave Buckleigh-in-the-Moor, this was the most compelling. She couldn't bear to see this place beat the spirit out of him forever.

"Well." She stood on weakened legs. "You'll have a long day ahead of you."

"That I will, Mrs. Maddox." He looked resigned as he rose from the table. "That I will."

"Shall I have Darryl saddle your horse?"

"No, no. I'll let him rest today."

She frowned with confusion. "So . . . you mean to stay another night, then?"

"I mean to stay permanently."

Flustered thoroughly now, she sat back down. "Did you not hear me, my lord? I'm sorry if I was unclear, but . . ." God, did she even have the strength to refuse him twice? Once had been difficult enough.

He smiled and headed for the door. "Don't worry, Merry Lane, I heard you. I know you said you can't marry me. But I also know you will. Just not quite yet."

After Rhys disappeared upstairs, Meredith kept herself busy. It wasn't difficult. There was always work to be done, and this morning, the more mindless the task, the better. She'd only just cleared the breakfast table when Mrs. Ware came in to start the day's cookery. There were tablecloths to iron and pewter mugs to scrub. Tomorrow afternoon the mail coach came through, and depending on the weather and condition of the roads, sometimes the driver stopped at the Three Hounds to rest the horses and allow passengers to take refreshment.

Before the noontime rush, she took a moment to rest. She picked up one of the newspapers Gideon had brought in the night before and opened it, smoothing the creased paper against the bar counter. Ostensibly the papers were for the inn's guests, but Meredith was the only one who read them. She read them all, every page. All those years of the war, she'd scoured them for any mention of Rhys. In the weeks following a battle, she would sometimes find an account of his regiment's bravery or a list of casualties that mercifully did not include his name.

Today, it felt as though she should snap open the paper and find the headline RHYS ST. MAUR RETURNED

TO DEVONSHIRE. Perhaps if she saw the words in print, she'd start to believe it was true. Though she doubted even the reporters of *The Times* could find a logical explanation for that scene over breakfast this morning. Perhaps the headline ought to read: IMPOVERISHED LANDLADY REFUSES LORD'S OFFER OF MARRIAGE.

Underneath that, in smaller letters, BOTH COMMITTED TO BEDLAM.

"Left your cask of Madeira in the storeroom." Gideon Myles appeared. He plunked a ceramic figurine on the counter. "And this washed up in a cove near Plymouth."

"Did it now?" Meredith took the china shepherdess in her hand and examined it in the light. It was finely made and carefully painted. Exquisite.

Fragile.

"Astonishing," she said, "that such a thing would survive being tossed about the waves and thrown up against a rocky shoreline."

"Is it?" Gideon said innocently, his mouth tipping in a grin. The man was devilish handsome, and he knew it. Not only knew it, but made use of it. As an intermediary between Devonshire's coastal smugglers and the markets of Bristol, London, and beyond, Gideon used that roguish charm to line his pockets, warm his nights, and generally have an ungodly amount of fun.

"Rather a miracle," she said.

"Thought she would look well in one of your redecorated rooms. Add a touch of class, you know."

"That she will." She smiled down at the shepherdess. "Very thoughtful of you, Gideon. I'm grateful."

His brow quirked. "How grateful?"

Impossible flirt. "Pint-of-ale grateful."

"Damn. Was hoping for straight-to-bed grateful. But I won't turn down the drink. Next time, I'll bring a string of bloody emeralds."

"I don't expect those wash up in coves too often," she said, sliding him a tankard of ale.

He gave her a devious smile. "Just have to know where to look." He threw back half his ale in one draught, and when he lowered the drink, his demeanor had changed. He stacked his arms on the bar. "What's Ashworth doing back in Devonshire?"

"How should I know?"

He stared at her, silently letting her know he didn't believe her ignorance for one moment.

Meredith shrugged. "Well, he's inherited the lands now, hasn't he? Only natural that he'd stop by to have a look at them." With a careful air of indifference, she added, "Perhaps he wants to start fulfilling his role as Lord Ashworth."

Gideon coughed. "Why would he want to do that? I might just as soon take up the old vicar's legacy."

He forced a chuckle, but Meredith caught the wounded glint in his eyes. Gideon Myles had been orphaned as a small boy when his parents fell victim to a fever. The vicar had taken him in, sheltered and educated him for many years. But when the living dried up, the clergyman left the village and abandoned Gideon to fend for himself at the age of thirteen.

"Shouldn't you like to be a vicar?" she asked. He laughed again, and she protested, "No, I mean it. I think you'd be better suited to the clergy than you credit. For all you cultivate that roguish image, you've a good heart beneath." She laid a fingertip on the ceramic lamb kneeling at his mistress's feet. "And a quick mind, as well. You're far too intelligent to be engaging in petty crime as a profession."

He looked away, and she thought she caught a blush rising on his throat. "Options are limited in these parts, aren't they?" He shook his head. "No, it's a devil's life for me. But lately I'm becoming far too acquainted with celibacy."

She laughed off his suggestive glance, knowing the words were just idle flirtation. As she'd told Rhys, Gideon was a business associate and a friend. Nothing more. Granted, he was a strapping man with a natural drive, and he probably wouldn't refuse an invitation to her bed. But she liked him too much to risk ruining things for a night or two of pleasure. That's why the few lovers she'd taken since Maddox died were all travelers passing through. No risk of emotional attachment.

Looking back, maybe that's why she'd always been so drawn to Rhys. He was always in motion—running, riding, brawling, fighting his way across the Continent. He was a man who'd never allow anything to hold him in one place.

Except now he was back, vowing to do just that—stay in one place.

"He said he wants to rebuild Nethermoor Hall." The words slipped out.

With a violent curse, Gideon plunked down his tankard. "Why the devil would he want to do that? It's worthless moorland up there."

"I know it, but Rhys said . . ." Her voice trailed off as she realized her slip.

His eyes flashed. "Oh, *Rhys* said? On cozy terms with him, are you?"

"Not like that," she replied tartly. "Not that it's any of your business."

"Damn right it is my business." He lowered his voice. "My *business*. My livelihood. I can't afford his presence here, Meredith. Neither can you. Ashworth's already put me a day behind schedule. If he stays in the neighborhood, my trade is finished. If I can't keep up my trade, you won't have cheap stores for this inn. If the inn suffers, the whole village suffers. That man is nothing but trouble for Buckleigh-in-the-Moor."

"I know, I know." She frowned, scrubbing at a water spot on the countertop that had been there for years and wasn't likely to go away anytime soon. "And I tried to tell him as much, but . . ."

She couldn't complete that sentence. *I tried to tell him as much, but he insisted it was destiny that I marry him.*

Mistaking her silence for genuine concern, Gideon stayed her wrist with his hand. "Don't you worry. He won't be in the village long. One way or another, I'll see to it."

She nodded, knowing he would. And his protective touch was kind, she supposed, but it did nothing for her. Not like Rhys's touch last night. She still felt that light caress tingling on her cheek.

It feels right, doesn't it?

She shook herself.

Gideon said, "If no man in the neighborhood will work for him, cart for him, or sell to him, he'll be forced to give up soon enough. And if he doesn't . . . well, there are other ways of convincing him."

"Like those torches this morning?"

Cursing, he cocked his head and rubbed the back of his neck. "I meant ways that involve real men and real weapons. Not a pair of inbred apes and a simpleton stable boy with his water pail."

She pointedly ignored his mention of violence and weapons. "Speaking of Darryl, I'd best call him and Father to their noon meal."

"Can you call all the way to Nethermoor, then? Always knew you were a clear-spoken woman, but that would astonish even me."

"What do you mean? Darryl's not up at Nethermoor. I just saw him, not ten minutes ago."

"Not Darryl. Your father." He raised an eyebrow.

"My father? Up at Nethermoor? What's he doing up there?"

Gideon shrugged and tipped his ale. "Better ask him that, hadn't you? Or your friend *Rhys*. It's the two of them up there together. My man just brought me the news."

Meredith put aside her rag.

"Not that I mind. The Symmonds boys are loading the ponies as we speak. We'll take them out toward Two Oaks and then around the long way. Ashworth and your father can stay out there all day, so far as I'm concerned."

"Not if I have something to say about it." She jerked at her apron strings, her fingers clumsy with nerves. Her father should not be out on the moor in the midday sun. That sort of exertion could endanger his health.

Gideon was right. Rhys's presence here was nothing but trouble for them all. She would go tell Rhys St. Maur to let her father be, pack up all his silly proposals, and leave the village today. And then she would somehow excise him from her imagination and get on with her life.

He had to move on, and so did she.

Chapter Five

Straining under the midday sun, Rhys hefted a chunk of lichen-crusted moorstone from its bed of gorse. A bead of sweat trickled down his bare back as he carried the rock up the sloping grade, then tossed it to the ground with a grunt, nudging it into place with his boot.

"Do you think it's big enough?" he asked, wiping his brow and squinting at the ground. The stones formed almost three sides of a rectangle now. A few more hours' work, and he'd have a completed outline for the foundation. "Maybe I ought to make it wider."

"It's already near as big as the inn," George Lane said. "Thought this was meant to be a cottage."

"It is." *The finest damn cottage ever built.*

And once Meredith saw it, she'd know he was serious about being here to stay. About marrying her. Not that he could claim to be surprised by her initial reluctance. As a suitor, he had little to recommend him aside from a bit of money in the bank. He surely wouldn't convince her on the basis of his fine looks and pretty manners. But once she saw the proof of his commitment to rebuilding the Hall and the village, she'd change her mind. She was a clever woman, and she understood when a situation would work out to her benefit. She'd married Old Maddox, after all, and Rhys would never believe *that* had been a love match.

"Where do you plan to put the door?" Lane asked, limping his way around the nearly finished rectangle.

"Over there." Rhys jerked his head as he hefted another stone. "Facing northeast."

"Away from the ruins, then? Well, I don't blame you for keeping that sight at your back."

"Away from the wind," Rhys countered.

The old man's eyebrows rose. "As you say."

Rhys chucked his stone in line with the others. He knew superstitions ran deep as granite here on Dartmoor, but surely George Lane didn't believe any of Darryl Tewkes's absurd ghost stories? "I mean it," he said, wiping his brow. "That flat there"—he pointed to a level area nearby—"is the most logical place for new stables. The stable master's cottage ought to face it, don't you think? And I'm guessing you'd rather be upwind."

"Stables?" Leaning on his crutch, Lane slid the soft felt cap from his head and twisted it between his old, scarred hands. "You mean to rebuild the stables?"

"I mean to rebuild it all," Rhys told him evenly. "Starting with the stables. I'm a member of a club, you see. It's called the Stud Club. Membership includes breeding rights to a stallion called Osiris."

"Osiris." The old man's hands began to shake. "*The* Osiris, the great thoroughbred champion?"

"So you've heard of him."

"Heard of him?" Lane laughed. "In his prime, the sporting papers were filled with nothing but talk of that stallion. I heard he'd been sold to a lord, though, some time back." He scratched the back of his neck. "What was his name . . . ?"

"Harcliffe. Leo Chatwick, the Marquess of Harcliffe. He's dead now."

"Oh. Did you know him?"

"A little."

"I'm sorry for the loss of your friend, then."

Rhys shrugged. "We weren't close. Be sorry for him, not me." He walked some distance away and propped his boot on another chunk of stone, rocking it back and forth to work it loose from the soil. This one was rather square, he noted, and not too firmly stuck—he'd wager it belonged to the old house. Must have tumbled this way after the fire.

He decided to leave it be.

He moved on to another rock instead and gave it a swift kick, jarring it loose. "Anyway, as fate would have it, I now control a one-fifth share in that stallion, and I plan to breed a few mares to him next year. I'll be needing stables. And a stable master."

"Do you . . ." Lane paused and sniffed. "Do you mean me?"

"Are there any other candidates around?" Rhys made a show of turning his neck, surveying the barren landscape.

Releasing a slow, wheezing breath, George Lane picked the largest boulder available and sat down, sliding his crutch to a rest beside him. "I'm crippled."

"Yes, I know." Of course he knew. That much was Rhys's own damn fault. "I mean to hire grooms, of course. You won't need to do the heavy work, merely supervise. There's no one else in these parts experienced in keeping and training horses of that caliber."

Lane swore softly under his breath. But when Rhys stole a glance at him, he could see the old man was smiling.

"Posting horses," Lane said suddenly. "Don't suppose you'd be of the mind to breed some of those? 'Twould be a great help to Merry, with the inn."

"Don't see why not." Rhys ceased working at the stone and crossed to sit near the old man. "But you won't have to worry about your daughter any longer, either. That's why I'm making the cottage so large."

The old man frowned. "Must be the old age, Rhys. I'm not following you."

"This house is for you, eventually. But in the short term, all three of us will have to call it home. While the Hall is being rebuilt."

"The three of us?"

"You, me, and Meredith." Best have out with it now, Rhys figured. The old man would find out soon. "Mr. Lane, I'm going to marry your daughter."

He had to hand it to fate. Wedding Meredith was a perfect solution. Beautiful in its simplicity, just like the cloudless sky above. With that exchange of vows, Rhys would take responsibility for not only Meredith's well-being, but that of her father and the village, too. He could see it all now. With the stables, they'd raise both racing and draft horses, to be sold for a profit. Once he rebuilt Nethermoor Hall, he'd be able to provide employment for half the village and give custom to the rest. The inn could continue, he supposed . . . they'd simply hire an innkeeper to look after it.

Rhys had so many plans spooling through his mind—years' worth of them. Perhaps enough to fill decades. It was a foreign sensation, planning more than a day in advance. It felt good. He'd heard gentlemen of his station, fellow heirs to the peerage, refer to their estate responsibilities as burdens. Oddly enough, today Rhys felt markedly lighter.

Lane stared at him in silence for some time. First one bushy eyebrow rose, then two. "*Marry* her. You plan to make Meredith your wife."

"Yes." It was more like the universe had planned it for him, but Rhys wouldn't quibble.

"Have you told Merry that?"

"I have."

"Well, then." Lane cocked his head, peering into the distance behind Rhys's shoulder. "That would explain why she looks so flummoxed."

Rhys turned on his heel to see Meredith cresting the rise, striding purposefully toward them with a basket threaded over her arm. The wind pulled strands of her dark hair loose, whipping them in all directions. As she drew near, she impatiently brushed the stray locks aside.

"Just what is going on here?" She addressed her question to Rhys.

"I'm building a house."

"A house? Whose house?"

"*Our* house. Well, at least a temporary one. Just a stone cottage. It'll take time to rebuild Nethermoor Hall. Years, maybe. I'll need to hire an architect, master craftsmen. So I reasoned we'll live here while it's under construction, and afterward, it can be your father's." He jabbed a thumb over his shoulder in the direction of the flat. "We'll be building the stables just over there, you see."

She stared blankly at the direction he'd indicated. Then her gaze fell to the unfinished rectangle of stones.

Perhaps she didn't see.

He said defensively, "I know it doesn't look like much yet. Just give me a few days. Once I start on the walls, you'll have a much better picture."

"You're planning to build an entire house by yourself? With your own two hands?"

"Well . . . yes. If I have to. I'd prefer to hire local men to help, but after that display this morning, I gather they won't be too eager to accept."

Not at first, at least. But just like Meredith, once they saw that Rhys was here for good, in multiple senses of the term, the villagers would welcome his presence in the neighborhood. Or at least they'd welcome the wages he could pay.

In the meantime, he'd work alone. This was how he'd gained his men's respect in the infantry—he'd never asked an enlisted soldier to do anything he wouldn't do himself. Not polish a buckle, not dig a grave. And he'd certainly never hesitated to lead a charge into battle.

"Listen," he told her, "I'm glad you're here. How much of a kitchen do you think you'll need? Do you want it facing the hillside, or the downslope? Considering the winds, it might make more sense to have the hearth on the hillside. Less heat lost that way. But then the downslope is nearer the leat, and you'd be that much closer to the water source."

She put a hand on his arm. He stopped talking, instantly. The pressure of her hand on his bare skin . . . he liked it. He liked it far too much.

"I said I can't marry you," she said.

"I recall it."

"Do you think you'll convince me to change my mind, simply by wooing my father?"

He shrugged.

George Lane called out, "Merry, we're going to breed prize racehorses! And Rhys here has plans to breed posting horses for the inn."

"Oh, really? Is that what 'Rhys here' said?"

She gave him a cool, flinty glare that was no doubt meant to be intimidating, but Rhys had seen and laughed in the face of too many intimidating glares to be affected.

What did affect him, greatly, was the firm squeeze she gave his wrist.

"We need to talk," she said quietly, her gaze flitting toward her father. "Alone."

"Certainly."

Meredith's body hummed with sensation as Rhys steered her aside, laying a hand to the small of her back.

To be accurate, his hand was so big it covered more than the small of her back. His thumb lodged just under her shoulder blade, and his little finger rode the swell of her hip.

Once they were a few steps away, he turned to her and asked, "Now what did you want to discuss?"

Good Lord, how was she supposed to think clearly, with him looking like this? Stripped to the waist, sweating, his muscles bulging from use and his skin burnt to a reddish-bronze by the sun. She tried dropping her gaze, but that was a mistake. His buff breeches clung to his hips and thighs like a coat of limewash.

With great effort, she pulled her attention back up to his eyes. The sun was so strong today, she had to squint, so she shaded her brow with one hand.

"Rhys, what are you doing?"

"I told you, I'm building a house. Laying the foundation."

She looked over at the carefully aligned rectangle of stones. In the background, the ruined remains of Nethermoor Hall stood sentinel on the hillcrest. How could he truly wish to build a new house here, in the shadow of that awful place?

"This isn't good for my father," she said. "He's an old man, and he's been hobbled for fourteen years. He's not supposed to engage in strenuous activity."

"I'm the one doing the strenuous activity. He's only advising."

"It doesn't matter—you're keeping him out here under the hot sun all day. That alone is a strain. Not to mention, you're filling his head with talk of stables and racehorses . . ."

"I believe he's excited about it."

Meredith had to admit, her father did look happier and healthier than he had in months. Enthusiastic, even.

But if this horse breeding scheme fell through, he'd be devastated.

"I'm certain he is excited, and that's the problem. You're getting him all agitated about things that may never come to pass. It's not good for his heart."

And it's not good for my heart, either.

"I'm not setting him up for disappointment. I'm preparing him for eventualities. You're the one becoming agitated about things that won't come to pass." He chucked her under the chin. "I'm not going anywhere, Merry Lane."

"Please . . ." When he said such things, with sincerity in those warm brown eyes, he made her want to believe him so desperately she could barely stand. "Please don't call me that."

"You don't like it?"

Not even Maddox had called her Merry, nor her lovers since. Her lovers hadn't called her anything at all. Well, the one nice gent had called her "love," and then there'd been that haunted-looking soul who'd called her "Sally" over and over again, then wept noisily in her arms for an hour afterward. That had been awkward. He'd put her off the whole business for a year.

It had been a long time since she'd felt a man's arms around her. And Rhys had some very fine arms. They could probably wrap around her twice.

Focus, Merry Lane.

"It's too familiar, and you know it," she said. "I don't even answer to Lane anymore."

"You're right," he said, nodding. "We should do this properly. I'll not call you by your Christian name till we're married. And even then, only after the novelty of calling you Lady Ashworth wears off." He smiled. "Might take a month or two."

Who would have guessed it? The man could be down-right charming when he wished to be.

And all too often, she could be a complete fool. "Y-yes, but . . . That is, I mean . . ." She stammered a bit, dropping her eyes in an effort to gather composure. The effort failed.

A puckered scar on his chest snagged her attention. Near his right shoulder, about the size of a shilling and just as round. It must have been a musket ball wound. She got lost in that scar for a moment, wondering what had become of the ball. Was it still lodged somewhere within that dense, powerful shoulder? Or had it ripped straight through? In either case, it was a miracle his arm hadn't separated from the rest of him, and that he still had the use of the limb at all.

Abruptly realizing she was being rude, Meredith lifted her face to his. With relief, she noted he wasn't looking at her, either. He was staring intently, thoughtfully—perhaps almost wistfully?—at something beyond her. Which was odd, because she knew there was nothing behind her but rocks. For a moment, she resisted the urge to turn around.

But then she gave in to temptation and turned away. Just as she'd suspected, there was nothing to see but the same eternal moorland—sloping gorse mottled with boulders. A harsh, endless landscape in shades of gray and brown and muted green, capped by a sky so endless and blue, she imagined an ocean couldn't rival it for depth or hue.

Not that she'd ever been near an ocean.

"What is it?" she asked. "What's the matter?"

"It's pretty." He sounded surprised. "This place. Over the years, I've never remembered it that way, but it's . . ." He sighed roughly. "It's beautiful."

Meredith stared, trying to imagine this vista through the eyes of someone who hadn't grown up looking at it every day of her life. She thought of the adjectives travelers used: forbidding, eerie, lonesome. Even some of the villagers avoided the high moorland for years at a time. Up here, there were no trees, no shelter from the wind and sun. No mercy. There was a reason they'd built the war prison not twenty miles away. Despite the brilliant colors and vast expanse, to most this place resembled a jail made of emptiness rather than walls.

It took a certain courage, to look on this landscape and call it beautiful.

"It *is* beautiful," she said, turning to face him. And so was he. Rugged, scarred, wild . . .

"I'm glad you think so, too. Since you'll be looking on this view the majority of your days, once it's finished." His smile was a flash of white in his tanned face.

Beautiful. He was a beautiful, enormous, impossible fool of a man.

"You know," he said slyly, "if I had a few laborers, I wouldn't need your father out here at all. Surely you have some influence with the local men."

She did. But that wasn't the point. "I know you mean well. But you can't expect to simply ride back into Buckleigh-in-the-Moor one night and have the village on your side the next morning. The name Ashworth is a curse in these parts. People still remember your father's misdeeds, even if you've forgotten them."

He grew pensive, tight. "I haven't forgotten them."

She cursed herself silently. Of course he wouldn't have forgotten them. They'd been beaten into him but good. Even now, he probably still bore marks from them, somewhere under all those battle scars.

He said, "I promise you, I remember my father's misdeeds as clearly as I recall my own. And that's why I've been spared all these years, so I can return and set accounts to rights."

Suddenly, his mood lightened. He smiled and stretched. The muscles of his abdomen rippled, drawing attention to the line of dark hair dividing them, like the old Roman leat scored the rock-solid moor. Meredith's mouth went dry.

He said, "I ought to be working. Come now, Mer—" He raised an arm, his biceps flexing as he scratched the back of his head. "Mrs. Maddox. Surely you can—"

"Oh, for goodness' sake," she blurted out. "Would you please put a shirt on while we're speaking?"

His face went red. "Of course. I beg your pardon." Loping a few yards up the incline, he crouched to gather a scrap of white. As he bent, she noted a larger, uneven scar on the back of his shoulder. The answer to her question. Evidently that musket ball had ripped straight through.

A little shudder passed through her as Rhys strode back, yanking the shirt over his head and letting the linen drape loose about his waist.

There, now maybe she could think. Maybe. The sun was beating down on them both, but she knew she had only him to blame for her overheated condition. There was nothing to do but retreat and regroup.

"We'll discuss this further tonight," she told him. "Back at the inn. Dinner will be at six. See that you're not late. I've brought you a packed luncheon in the meantime." She thrust the basket at him, and he took it, surprised. "Be certain my father drinks enough water and finds some shade, or I'll have your hide. The weather's fair, but if there's a mist or a storm, you're both to stay right here, do you understand? I'll send men out to you. You've been gone from these moors far too long to find your way in the dark. That's all I need, is for the two of you to go wandering into the bog."

He flicked a bemused glance toward the bright, cloudless sky. A chuckle rumbled from his throat.

"What?" she asked, her wits fraying at the edges. "What now?"

"You're speaking like a wife already."

She made a dismissive gesture. "You're impossible."

"See? And there you go again."

With a low growl of frustration, she turned to walk home.

"It wasn't a complaint," he called after her. "I rather liked it."

So did she. So did she. And that was the most impossible thing of all.

Chapter Six

That evening, Rhys was halfway through his third plate of stew before he paused to draw breath. The day of heavy labor had left him ravenous and exhausted, but in a good way. An honest, productive way.

With a pleasantly full belly, he sat back in his chair and watched Meredith as she went about the honest, productive business of running the inn. He shook his head. It wasn't right. His own day's labor was over, and she had hours yet to work. Had she even taken her own dinner?

Tonight she had a small group of travelers to tend— a middle-aged man and two younger ladies. Rhys supposed one was the man's wife and the other his wife's sister or cousin or some such. But just watching them interact, damned if Rhys could pick out which was which. The man didn't favor either lady with particular attention or regard. Pathetic. What a waste of matrimony. Once Meredith was his wife, he'd make certain every man in the room knew she belonged to him.

For this evening, however, he was forced to content himself with watching his future wife tend her customers— serving them steaming plates of food and mugs of hot tea, chatting briefly with them about their journey. He hated that she'd been forced to work so hard, but she clearly took some pride and enjoyment in it.

She gave him a smile as she passed his table on her way back to the bar. A sweet, fleeting curve of her lips— and an accidental one, if her quick correction to serious-ness was any indication.

As soon as Meredith left the travelers, down swooped Darryl Tewkes like a carrion bird. "Will you fine gentle-folk be staying long in the neighborhood?" He pulled up a stool to their table, crowding the ladies together. "We've all manner of fascinating sights here in Buckleigh-in-the-Moor. I'd be glad to tour you around, in the morning."

"Sights?" the man asked through a mouthful of beef. "What sights?"

"Why, it's a mystical journey through time, you see."

Rhys drowned his groan with a large swallow of ale. He listened to Darryl launch into his now-familiar speech: the tinners' works, the cairns, the stone crosses, the tors . . .

"And best of all . . ." The gawky youth lowered his voice. ". . . the haunted ruins of Nethermoor Hall."

"Haunted?" The two ladies echoed him in unison, then looked to one another wearing matching expres-sions of horrified glee.

They had to be sisters.

"Aye, the cursed house of Ashworth," Darryl contin-ued, leaning in close.

Rhys cleared his throat and pushed back, scraping his chair legs against the flagstones.

Darryl froze. The two young ladies went so pale, they might have been ghosts themselves. After a long mo-ment, Darryl raised his head and gave Rhys a chagrined, twitchy look, as if asking permission to continue.

With a quirk of his neck, Rhys picked up his ale and pointedly moved on, ignoring them all. Let Darryl

Tewkes tell his fantastic stories while he could. Soon the name Ashworth would mean something different to this village. Something other than a curse, or a macabre sightseeing attraction for travelers passing through.

He caught sight of Meredith at the bar. She was smiling and flirting with a hunched old man as she poured him a glass of gin. Her hair was falling loose from its braid again, and heavy locks dipped and swooped as she bent to retrieve a glass or stretched high to replace the bottle on its shelf.

God, she was a joy to watch. He'd grown accustomed to the idea of marriage very quickly, for a man who'd shuddered at the very notion for the whole of his adult life. That, more than anything, proved it must be destiny.

Even now, as he watched those dark strands working loose from her plait, his fingers ached to stroke her hair. He'd never taken time to do such a thing with a woman before. Perhaps he'd felt the lanky strands of a harlot's hair slithering over his bare skin a time or two, but he'd never wanted to touch it on purpose.

He wanted to touch Meredith *everywhere*. Caress her brow with the backs of his knuckles—the callused pads of his fingertips were too rough. Curl his fingers in that hair, bury his face in it. Wake early on a Sabbath morning just to lie abed for hours and count every strand. A man could do that with his wife, couldn't he? Sprawl out on the mattress, tuck her head against his chest, and stroke her hair for the sheer pleasure of it?

He'd just need to keep his shirt on.

He silently cursed himself for that mistake. What had he been thinking, letting her see his bare torso, all the scars he'd accumulated over the years? The look on her face as she asked him to put on a shirt . . . She must have been disgusted. He could tell by the guarded, wary glances she kept throwing him.

Meredith ducked behind the bar and lined up four glasses for filling. Rhys started toward her, eager to make a better impression tonight.

"Don't even think it."

Gideon Myles stepped in front of him. Rhys had to admit, the man had bollocks, to try that move with him.

"Leave her be. She's not for you," Myles said in a low voice. "There's nothing in this village for you."

"Oh, really? I've a title and a pile of legal papers that say otherwise."

"And I've a pistol." Myles's hand went to his waistband.

Rhys waved his hand dismissively. "Yes, yes. Saw it this morning. I wasn't impressed then, either." He eyed the man closely, taking his measure. Average height, lean, and probably about five years Rhys's junior. His eyes held the hungry gleam of ambition, and pure arrogance fueled his swaggering step.

Rhys didn't like him. At all.

"You're very protective of those dry goods you carry, Mr. Myles."

"My trade is none of your concern."

"Oh, I think it is. As the lord of this place, unlawful activity is my concern. And my concern . . . well, that's your problem, isn't it? You're transporting smuggled goods through this village, and you're worried I'll put a stop to it."

To his credit, Myles didn't even try to deny the charge. He coolly raised his eyebrows. "And . . . ?"

"And you're right. I will put a stop to it."

His jaw clenched. "Like hell you will. Stay out of my way, Ashworth, and I'll make no trouble for you. This is business, not personal."

"Oh, it's personal to me." Rhys took a small step toward him, forcing Myles to take a small step in retreat. "If you trafficked in French goods during the war, in even the smallest amount—it's personal, indeed. Your 'trade' could have purchased the lead that ripped through this shoulder." He thumped his hand over the old wound. "Missed my heart by inches."

The younger man set his jaw. "Can't blame that one on me. If I'd paid for that ball, it would have found its mark."

"Fair enough. Forget me. Let's speak of others, then. How many casks of brandy do you think it took to fund each bayonet or saber that skewered one of my men in battle?"

"I don't know." Gideon's eyes flashed. "About as many as it took to keep these villagers from starving to death after you left Devonshire."

Touché.

They stared at each other for a moment.

"Guess you were right," Myles finally said. "It is personal."

Rhys nodded in agreement.

"Very well, then. You have a week to get out of my village. Or I will *personally* make certain you leave."

Rhys just laughed and shook his head. "You and what army? Oh, wait—I forgot. Armies can't kill me, either."

"A week." Myles backed his way to the door, pausing just before he left to add, "I'll be back in a week. Don't let me catch you here."

The moment Gideon Myles left, Rhys ceased caring about him. As if he'd allow some petty smuggler to dictate where and when he could be on his own land. What a joke.

He strolled over to the bar and sat down on one of the stools. He watched as Meredith tapped a fresh cask of wine. The defined muscles in her arms made a stark contrast with her delicate features and small frame.

"Don't you have a girl to help you in the evenings?" he asked, looking about the room. "A barmaid?"

She shook her head as she poured. "Not at the moment. My regular girl gave birth not a few weeks ago. Don't know yet whether she'll come back."

"When does the post come through next?"

"Tomorrow."

"Might I beg a few sheets of paper and some ink?"

She didn't answer him, just shrugged as she left to deliver the glasses of wine. But a few minutes later, two leaves of heavy, cream-colored paper materialized on the bar before him, along with a quill and a small pot of ink.

"Who are you writing?" she asked, leaning both elbows on the bar. "A friend?"

"Not exactly." In fact, Julian Bellamy might very well be an enemy.

Along with Rhys and the Duke of Morland, Bellamy was one of the three surviving members of the Stud Club. He'd been the closest to Leo, and, by all appearances, had been devastated by his friend's tragic death. Since the murder, Bellamy had seemed a man possessed, determined to hunt down Leo's killers and bring them to justice.

In recent weeks, however, a new witness had surfaced. If the whore who witnessed Leo's killing could be believed, Bellamy might have had something to do with the death.

Rhys would have preferred to ask Morland to send his belongings out to Devonshire. He and Rhys had exchanged more punches than words as schoolboys, but he now counted the man as a friend, of sorts. But the duke was currently honeymooning at his Cambridgeshire estate, leaving Rhys no choice but to write Bellamy. Murderer or not, there was no one else in London he could ask.

He worked slowly; with his stiff fingers, he had to take care if he wanted his penmanship to be legible at all. After half a page, he dropped the quill and paused to shake out his hand.

"Why don't you switch to your left?"

He looked up to see Meredith back at the bar.

She nodded at his gnarled right hand. "Why do you still try to write with it? You favor your left, anyhow."

How did she know that? It was true, Rhys had favored his left hand from his youth. But he'd been beaten for attempting to write with it. So he'd switched to his right, and then he'd been beaten for his poor penmanship. So he'd practiced in secret, spent painstaking hours laboring over a paper and quill, until his awkward scratchings became effortless, flowing script.

And then he'd just been beaten for something else.

"Care for gin?" Meredith held the bottle poised above an empty glass.

"Thank you, no."

With a little shrug, she tipped the bottle and poured anyway. After filling the glass to halfway, she put aside the bottle and raised the glass to her own lips.

"Does it bother you much?" she asked from behind the glass, casting a pointed look toward the room behind him.

Rhys threw a casual glance over his shoulder, having formed a good expectation of what he'd see. He was right. Everyone in the room was staring at him. Their eyes were filled with hatred, fascination, fear, or all three. He recognized more than a few men from the torch-bearing mob that morning. Over by the hearth, Harold and Laurence Symmonds glared at him over tankards of ale.

"Are they brothers or cousins?" he asked, tilting his head to indicate the bull-headed, beak-nosed pair.

"Yes." At his obvious confusion, she explained, "Their mother took up with a pair of brothers. No one was ever able to sort out who belonged to whom. But yes, they're brothers *or* cousins."

"Explains a few things," Rhys muttered. He turned back to Meredith and shrugged. "The staring doesn't bother me. I'm used to it. They'll come around, in time."

She didn't agree or disagree, just sipped her drink.

"When we announce our engagement," he said, "they'll come around that much faster."

She sputtered into the glass.

Rhys resumed writing his letter. "Still so surprised? I told you, it's fate. As suitors go, I know I haven't much to offer you at the moment, but that's why I've started the cottage. Made good progress on the foundation today. It should be large enough for all three of us, if I build two stories." He scratched the back of his neck. "It'll take some time, though, collecting that much stone."

"What do you mean?" She raised her eyebrows. "You've a great pile of stone, just sitting there atop the hill."

She meant the remains of Nethermoor Hall, of course. And she was right—the crumbling heap was a ready supply of building material. But somehow, Rhys just couldn't stomach stealing rocks from his hellish past to build the house of his future. The cottage was meant to be a fresh start.

"I'd rather save that for rebuilding the Hall," he lied. "I'll gather moorstone for the cottage. Or quarry some granite out of the slope, perhaps."

She shook her head. "Why not just use cob?"

"Cob?" Odd, he hadn't thought of that. Down here in the village, most of the buildings were fashioned from the traditional walls of packed earth.

"Once you have the stone plinth, all you need for a cob house is soil and straw," she said. "It's easier, and cheaper by far. And built right, it will last centuries."

She looked up at the ceiling. "It's what I plan to use, when I have the chance to expand this place."

He looked up in surprise. "You have plans to expand the inn?"

"Oh, I have all sorts of plans for this inn."

He signed his letter, folded it, and shoved it in his pocket. "Tell me about them."

She gave him a mocking look. "I'm shocked you'd ask, seeing as how they're fated to never come to pass."

"Humor me. I'd like to hear them anyway."

"Very well." She set a second glass on the bar and filled it halfway. Despite his dislike of liquor, Rhys didn't object. It was beginning to feel awkward, letting her drink alone. He didn't want to interrupt her or argue the point, so he accepted the glass and took a cautious sip.

Fire ripped down his throat.

"Damn," he said, coughing. "This isn't Plymouth gin."

"No, it's a local brew. Cures all ills."

"Causes them, do you mean?" He took another slow sip and found it burned less this time. "Go on, then. You were telling me about your plans."

She refilled her own glass. "As I said, I plan to add a new wing when I have the chance. And by 'chance,' I mean funds, of course. Guestrooms on the upper floor and a proper dining room and parlor below. It'll adjoin the building just there," she said, indicating the direction with a jut of her chin. "Across from the stables. That way, the courtyard will be enclosed on three sides instead of two."

Rhys sipped thoughtfully as she went on, detailing her plans for quality furnishings and finer dining room fare. The Three Hounds was well-situated, she explained, positioned on the only road traversing this part of the moor. The inn six miles down the road currently took most of the travelers' business, but Meredith meant to change all that.

"With the war over, more people will be taking pleasure tours. There's no reason why the Three Hounds shouldn't have a slice of that pie." Her whole face became animated as she continued describing her plans. "With finer accommodations, larger rooms, some posting horses . . . this place could be a real *destination*. A stopping place for gentlefolk passing through on their way to tour points west. Why should they not break their journey here and explore Dartmoor, too? As you said earlier, the moor can be a pretty place."

"Beautiful. I believe I used the word beautiful."

"So you did." She gave him a shy smile. "Beautiful, then."

Their gazes tangled and held. Rhys took a deep, slow drink from those lovely eyes. They made him feel refreshed. Washed clean, as much as a man like him could ever be.

The longer he stared at her, however, the further the smile faded from her face.

In a nervous gesture, she moistened her lips with her tongue. Then she gave herself a little shake and announced to the room, "Home time, gentlemen."

The last few stragglers roused themselves from their stools and lumbered out the door, grousing as they went. One of them yawned, and Rhys could not help but do the same.

"You must be exhausted," Meredith said briskly, wiping her hands on her apron after straightening the last of the chairs and latching the door. "I'm sorry to have kept you up so late, blathering on about my silly plans."

"They're not silly plans. They're quite sensible ones."

Together they moved toward the back staircase. And even though they were plans she'd never need to put into action, he admired the cleverness and spirit behind them. He admired those qualities even more than he admired her lovely hair and eyes—and that was saying something. "You truly do have it all worked out, don't you?"

"I do. And I'm proud of that. I'm proud of what I've accomplished with the Three Hounds so far, but I know I could do so much more."

"I'm certain you could."

"So you see . . ." She swallowed hard as they stopped at the door to his room. "The village, the inn, my father, me . . . we'll all be just fine without you. You can leave, Rhys. Go live your life, and leave us be."

Ignoring her words, he leaned one shoulder against the doorjamb. He wasn't going anywhere. "God, you're beautiful."

The words just tumbled out, and Rhys had no idea where they'd come from. He didn't recall ever speaking those words to a woman before. Damn, everything with Meredith felt new. Or maybe he was just so green.

The gin. He blamed the gin. Liquor always made him maudlin and impulsive.

"Why, Rhys St. Maur," she said, grinning, "was that flirtation?"

"No. I don't know how to flirt."

"Come now, be truthful." She reached for the edge of his shirt collar and played with it coyly. Her voice husky, she said, "All this talk of marriage and destiny and fate—it's all just a ploy to get into my bed, isn't it?"

Was he really that drunk, or did she sound *hopeful*?

"No," he said honestly. "No, it's not."

Though Holy God, the very idea of taking her to bed had him reeling. Pictures filled his mind. Wild, depraved pictures, like the etchings soldiers carried in their boots and bartered for greater value than gold. And thanks to the damned flames of gin licking away inside him, Rhys was powerfully tempted to act those pictures out, in the flesh. In her flesh. He wanted to find her softest, most secret place and lodge happily there, all night long.

Vulnerability flickered across her eyes. "Don't you want me?"

Hell. Of course he wanted her. He wanted her so badly, his ears ached from clenching his jaw so tight. He wanted her so much, he could have pushed against this doorpost like Samson and brought down the whole damned inn.

But he'd made that mistake yesterday—pushing too hard, too fast.

He forced a casual smile. "I'm saving myself for the wedding night."

Her burst of surprised laughter drew his gaze to her mouth, and there his gaze gladly lingered. She had lovely lips. A dusky pink shade, richer red toward the center. The lower one plumper than the top. Hers was a pretty face, but not a soft one. Her cheekbones sat high and proud. She had a determined set to her brow and jaw, and her chin tapered to a decisive point. But her mouth was a soft, lush, vulnerable curve in the midst of all that strength and resolve.

He wanted—no, *needed*—to taste it.

"No," he whispered, standing straight and framing her delicate face in his big, gnarled hands. "I won't take you to my bed just yet. But I'll take that kiss tonight."

Chapter Seven

And take it he did, before Meredith even had time to draw breath.

He pressed his lips to hers quickly, as if she might change her mind if he gave her the chance, or as if he might change his. The timing was off, and their lips mashed together at the wrong angle, and her eyes were still open.

For a moment, she felt fourteen again. Awkward, uncertain. Painfully aware of everything *but* the joy of being kissed.

But then he tilted her face a degree, and his mouth shifted a fraction against hers. She remembered to close her eyes.

And suddenly, they fit. Suddenly, this kiss *was* everything. And she still felt fourteen again, but in that blissful, giddy way of tumbling headlong down a rocky slope with no thought for caution, no purpose but to chase exhilaration and joy.

Rhys St. Maur was kissing her.

And it was *wonderful*.

They remained that way for an improbably long time, mouths pressed together in tender innocence. He made no move to part her lips or explore her mouth with his tongue, though she would have gladly allowed it. If he'd wished, he could have taken everything. But he didn't even try. He just kissed her softly, over and over again. The corners of her mouth. Her top lip, then the bottom. Sweet little sips of gin and heat.

When at last he pulled back, she instinctively raised her hands to cover his, pressing them tight against her face and forbidding him to release her. The thought struck her that she could have been touching him all the while. She could have been stroking his hair, or smoothing her palms over the hard planes of his shoulders and chest.

Damn, she was a fool.

But she settled for this, dragging her thumbs over the back of his hands, tracing the delicate crooks between his fingers, and finally encircling his thick, corded wrists as she opened her eyes.

"That was . . ." He looked down at her with a strangely puzzled expression. "That was nice."

"Yes. Quite."

He slid his hands from her face. She reluctantly released his wrists.

With a self-conscious clearing of the throat, he reached behind him, groping for the latch. "Well, it's late. I suppose I'd better be . . ."

"Wait."

To hell with feeling fourteen again. And to the devil with "nice."

With decisive speed, Meredith grabbed him by the collar, hauled herself up on tiptoe, and kissed him, hard.

He stumbled back against the door, and the moment of shock jarred his lips apart. She slid her tongue straight through that window of opportunity. That was all it took. Now he really, truly kissed her back. Mouths open, teeth clashing, tongues tangling. Desire evident.

Yes, at last. This was what she'd been wanting—this frenzy of wild tastes and rough textures. The slick heat of his tongue, the scrape of his whiskers, his heady male scent. Rhys St. Maur, the man. And her body responding to his, all woman.

Growling deep in his throat, he slid his hands around her waist and fisted them in the back of her dress, lifting her up and against him. Her whole body pressed flush to his. Her breasts squashed flat against his chest, and she could feel every deliciously solid inch of him.

Until, with a regretful moan, he lowered her to the ground.

"Well?" Her voice was breathless, but she hoped her eyes communicated the proposition with greater success.

"Yes, I'm well," he said, nodding absently. "Very well indeed."

She laughed softly, clinging to his neck. There was no doubt that Rhys St. Maur was all man, but in rare moments he had this sweet, uncertain, boyish look on his face. It endeared him to her all the more.

She bit her bottom lip and swayed gently in invitation. "I meant, what do you think? About tonight."

"I think"—he unlaced her arms from his neck and squeezed her hands before releasing them—"that tonight, I'll have very vivid dreams."

To her disappointment, he found the door latch and slid it open. Before stepping inside his bedchamber, he dropped one last kiss on her cheek. "And for once, I might enjoy them."

Five mornings later, Meredith sat in that same bedchamber, watching Rhys sleep. The first rays of dawn seeped in through the window. Gray, watery light, not yet gold. The white linens reflected it with a fuzzy glow, but the rest of the room remained in murky shadow.

A cock crowed in the courtyard.

From the bed, Rhys answered with a low, soft snore.

Meredith released her breath and quietly adjusted her posture on the chair, just hoping the sun would rouse itself before Rhys did.

She hated resorting to this kind of spying, but she couldn't think of any other way to assess his . . . health. Over the past week, she'd developed a powerful suspicion that Rhys had suffered a war injury to his male anatomy. Why else would he have resisted that clear invitation the night they'd kissed? Not to mention the subtler ones she'd issued every evening since.

Part of her couldn't believe he was even still here. Contrary to all her arguments and the application of common sense, he'd forged ahead with this cottage plan. Every night she'd thrown him flirtatious glances in the bar. Surely he'd come to his senses and leave any morning, she reasoned. She wanted one night with him first.

Last night had been the final indignity. He'd come in from another day of hard work up on the moors. Damp from the pump, but still glowing with the day's exertion. Wildly attractive. He'd sat down at his usual table, eaten his usual three plates of food whilst enduring the suspicious glares and muttered curses of the villagers. Then he'd approached her at the bar to apprise her of the day's progress.

"Finished fitting together the plinth today," he'd said. "Now that the foundation's done, I'll start preparing the earth for cob. I'll need to hire ponies from you tomorrow to haul up a load of straw. If all goes well, tomorrow I'll be able to start the first rise." He'd yawned the grizzled, lazy-yet-lethal yawn of a lion. "I think I'll turn in early tonight, unless you need me."

Oh, she needed him, all right. She'd wanted to lean over the bar and kiss that sleepy mouth, right in front of the whole room. The sweet, bloody fool was building a house of stone and earth with his own two hands. For her father. How could she not want to kiss him? How could she not want to do far more than that?

Instead, she'd whispered shamelessly, "Shall I come to your room after I lock up?"

And though he'd sucked in his breath, and his eyes had fair blazed with desire, he'd bid her a polite good evening and retreated upstairs. Alone.

Something had to be wrong down there. Red-blooded men—and Rhys was a fine specimen of a red-blooded man in his virile prime—just didn't walk away from invitations that obvious.

Gradually, the room warmed with weak, yellow light. She blinked, bringing the picture before her into focus.

His huge frame overflowed the bed—the same bed that would have felt lonely and half-empty if she'd slept in it alone. He slept on his side, linens bunched about his legs and waist. From the glimpse of bare chest and leg, she could tell he was likely nude. But drat it, it was impossible to see what she needed to see from this vantage.

She rose from the room's single chair and crept toward the bed, hoping to get a closer look. Then she froze in place as he emitted a harsh, guttural sound. It was the sound of a man dealing a blow. Or taking one.

He thrashed suddenly, tangling in the bedsheets as his elbow jabbed the pillow. "No," she heard him moan. Then more forcefully, *"No."*

She stood there, immobile, not knowing what to do. Should she wake him? Did she dare? If he were reliving some fight or battle in his dreams, he might lash out at her in confusion. Perhaps she should just leave him. No one ever suffered long-term effects from a nightmare. If he woke on his own and saw her there, he might feel violated or ashamed.

His breathing came fast and shallow now. He ceased wrestling the pillow and flipped onto his back, his fists clenched at his sides. They were the size of millstones.

His teeth were gritted, the tendons strained and bulging along his neck. A low, inhuman growl rumbled from his throat and forced its way through his teeth.

Meredith's heart ached. She didn't know what form of agony he was enduring in that dream, but she knew she couldn't stand by and watch him suffer a moment longer. In her girlhood, she'd been witness to his pain and never done a thing about it. There'd been nothing she *could* have done, then. How exactly did a reedy waif of a servant's daughter protest the lord's maltreatment of his own son?

But she wasn't a girl any longer, and she could do something to ease Rhys's suffering now.

She crept to the bedside and crouched by his sleeping form. "Hush," she said quietly. "Hush. You're safe, Rhys. All is well."

She forced her fingers to cease trembling and laid one hand to his shoulder. At his sharp wince, she almost withdrew the touch. But she kept shushing and soothing in quiet tones and simply kept her hand there, pressed lightly against his heated flesh, until the tension in his body released. When his fists uncurled at his sides and his breathing steadied, she withdrew her hand and began to breathe again herself.

For a quarter hour or more, she knelt there, watching him return to a peaceful slumber and allowing her own heart rate to slow.

He released a soft sigh in his sleep, one that melted her deep inside, and his lips curled in a little half-smile. She wondered if she was in the dream he was having now. She hoped so. He gave a little groan—one that hinted at pleasure, not pain.

She couldn't resist any longer. Stealthily, she tugged at the folds of the bedclothes, drawing them loose from his midsection. And then she lifted the side of the sheet and bent her head to peek beneath.

No, no war injury. None that would inhibit his normal male function, at any rate. Whatever scars covered the rest of his body, these parts of him were healthy indeed. *Perfect.* As if his organ could sense her interest, it jerked for attention. Arousal rushed through her on the receding tide of anxiety. Just looking at him, she felt heat building in the hollows of her knees.

He made a sudden movement, and she dropped the sheet. She pulled her gaze back up to his face just in time to watch his eyes snap open—dark, intense, furious, dangerous. The hairs on the back of her neck lifted, and her heart battered her ribs. She had the suspicion a fair number of Napoleon's soldiers had witnessed this very same look in Rhys's eyes, and it was the last thing they'd ever seen.

"It's me," she said quickly. "It's Meredith."

He blinked a few times. Comprehension drove the violence from his eyes. "Christ," he muttered, sitting up on one elbow and rubbing a palm over his face, then over his shorn hair. "You surprised me. Is something wrong?"

"No. Nothing's wrong." She almost laughed, remembering her reason for the visit. "Everything is perfectly well. I'm sorry to wake you, I just . . . heard noises, and I was concerned."

"Damn nightmares."

"Do you want to talk about them?"

"No." With a glance at his exposed chest, he swore again. He shrugged to the far side of the bed, diving under the bed linens and jerking them up to his chin.

And now she did laugh. She couldn't help it. "Have I offended your modesty?"

"No. No, I'm offending yours. I don't want to disgust you."

"Disgust me? How could that be?"

"The other day. You asked me to put on a shirt." He

drew the sheet tighter about his chest. "I know it must look repulsive . . . you know, with all the scars."

"Oh, Rhys." She buried her face in her hands for a moment, then removed them and decided to just be honest. "I asked you to put on a shirt because you're the most distractingly attractive man I've ever seen, and I could barely speak two words of sense for the sight of you. I don't find anything about you repulsive."

He blinked some more. "Oh."

She sat on the edge of the bed, in the empty space he'd created by moving over. "As for scars . . ." She reached for the top of the bedsheet and pulled. He allowed the linen to slip from his grasp, and she drew it down to reveal his chest, marked by battles of various sorts. "Surely you can't believe they're disgusting. Don't you know how women feel about scars, Rhys? Haven't your lovers been fascinated by them?"

His breathing grew thready as she drew a fingertip across his collarbone.

He said, "There haven't been any lovers. Not for some time."

"How much time?"

"Years."

"So long?" Emotion rose in her throat. She swallowed hard, trying to keep her heart down in her chest where it belonged. Rhys was one of the most intensely sensual men she'd ever known. She'd sensed it even as a girl. It was what had drawn her to him, at an age where her own feelings of desire were just beginning to stir and coalesce. She'd always been fascinated by him, but more than ever in her fourteenth summer. That year he'd left for Eton an overgrown boy and returned a young *man*. She couldn't help but marvel at his wildness, his strength, his body—these same broad shoulders she traced with her touch now. She let one fingertip wander the small valley carved between his shoulder muscle and his biceps.

What a grave injustice, that this beautiful man had been deprived of physical affection and pleasure for years. And yet, she could not deny the swell of possessive joy in her breast, to know he belonged to her in some sense. She would be his first, after so long. He would always remember her. She would make certain of that.

Flattening her hand, she swept a palm down his biceps, flipping her wrist to caress him with the backs of her fingers as she drew her hand back up.

"Meredith . . ." There was a warning in his voice. But none of the strength coiled in these formidable muscles marshaled to push her away.

"Hush," she told him, stroking his arm again. "Let me touch you."

He relaxed against the pillow, and his eyes fluttered closed.

Behind his eyelids, Rhys saw tulips. An endless field of red tulips, and a sky the brilliant blue of aquamarine. He'd spied that field on a pleasant spring morn, marching through Holland with the Fifty-second. A light breeze had teased his hair . . . almost as sweetly as Meredith now caressed his skin. That field of flowers had been the most beautiful thing he'd ever seen, so beautiful it made even his healed wounds ache. He'd led his men straight through it, unable to resist. Striding through that field of a million cheery blossoms all facing the sun at his back, he'd felt as though they were welcoming him into their midst. He waded knee-deep in that beauty, bathed in it—as if it could wash away all the ugliness of war. *This must be what heaven is like,* he'd thought. *I'd best look and breathe my fill of it now, because God knows I won't be enjoying it after I die.*

It was only when he'd halted and glanced over his shoulder that he'd seen the truth: the piercing glint of a hundred bayonets stabbing the blue sky in unison. His entire battalion of bedraggled soldiers, crunching through the field, mowing down the tulips with boots and blood-ied stumps of bare feet. He'd been welcomed by the beauty of God's creation, and he was leaving grim de-struction in his wake.

Because he was a violent brute, and that was what he did.

Meredith's caress . . . ah, *this* was pure heaven. And he knew the longer he allowed her to touch him thus, the further he was treading heedless into that pristine, allur-ing beauty, insensible of the damage he could cause. But he just couldn't bring himself to stop her. Not yet.

He kept his eyes closed. She swept her hand down his arm again, and arousal rushed through his body, gather-ing in his groin and clamoring for release.

"Women find a man's scars irresistible," she said softly. "We're drawn to them, to the mystery." Her fin-gers found the neat round entry wound where the ball had passed through his shoulder at Vitoria. She traced the puckered scar, pressed a thumb against it. A hint of humor lightened her voice. "Think of . . . think of nip-ples."

"Ni—" *Holy God.* "Did you say . . ."

"Nipples. Aren't men hopelessly fascinated with a woman's nipples?"

He could not have spoken for other men, but sud-denly Rhys could think of little else.

She said, "A man's scars are the same for us. We can't help but wonder about them, the color and texture. We long to explore them—not just with fingers, but with lips."

Her lips grazed his shoulder, and his eyes flew open. A loose lock of her upswept hair brushed his chest as she kissed his old, healed wound. He wanted to catch that dark ribbon of hair in his fingertips, but he couldn't move. If he dared move, she might stop.

Don't stop. Don't stop.

She trailed warm kisses across his chest. Sweet, tender, feminine. And so damned erotic, he was already hard as a gun barrel and primed to fire.

Pressing one last kiss to the scar at his temple, she lifted her head and straightened. He couldn't have imagined the expression on his face, but the smile on hers told him she liked it.

His gaze slipped downward, and he realized suddenly that she wasn't even dressed. Her thin linen nightrail slid down one shoulder. The graceful contours of her throat and collarbone drew his eye downward still. He glimpsed her small, firm breasts swelling beneath the sheer fabric.

He cleared his throat. "Like nipples."

Her smile widened. "Yes."

His fingers went to the ribbon tie at the neckline of her shift. Grasping one frail lace of satin, he undid the simple bow with a slow, agonizing pull. He let his hand fall back so he could enjoy how the fabric gaped to reveal a hint of flesh. Then she rolled her shoulder, and the muslin eased down to bare one breast.

He was stunned immobile for a moment, mesmerized by the milky perfection of her flesh and its rosy pink undertones. And by her lovely pert nipple, just a few shades darker than her skin. As he watched, her areola ruched and puckered, pushing her nipple into a tight bud. A bud that begged to be plucked, sucked.

A soft groan escaped him as he propped himself on one elbow and reached for her with his other hand. Her breast was so small and delicate, and his hand was so big and ugly—if he cupped her, he wouldn't see anything of her at all. Where would be the good in that? Instead, he brushed the back of one fingertip along the underside of her breast. Her skin shivered and rippled into gooseflesh. He almost drew back, but her soft sigh of pleasure encouraged him. He stroked the place again, then drew a wide circle with his thumb, tracing the outer edge of her areola. She was the softest thing he'd ever touched. His mouth watered.

As if she could sense his need, she leaned forward, meeting him halfway. "Yes," she urged. "Kiss me."

He pressed a kiss to the underside of her breast, tasting her skin with a furtive swipe of his tongue. And it was paradise. The stuff of a laudanum dream. Pleasure so acute it verged on madness. The spicy-sweet scent of her skin intoxicated him. Against his mouth she was cool and perfect, like honeydew. And it was a very good thing he was going to marry her, because he knew from just this one first taste that he would never, ever get enough.

"Take down your hair." He said it in an authoritative voice of command that really wasn't suited to use with his future wife, but damn—he wanted her to obey, and he wasn't taking any chances asking nicely.

She did obey, hastily pulling free the ribbon that tied her plait. Her bared breast jounced deliciously as she unbraided her hair, then shook it free. Those thick locks tumbled about her shoulders and chest, dark and sensuous as sable. A curve of creamy skin, capped by her pale, taut nipple, peeked out through the fall of hair draping her breast.

Add in that flirtatious smile and the tender invitation in her eyes, and . . . Jesus. Fields of tulips, aquamarine skies—they had nothing on Meredith. She was the most beautiful, perfect thing he'd ever seen.

He sat up in bed. "I should go."

"What? Why?"

"Plenty of work to be done today. I'll need to hire the ponies, remember."

"Rhys." She put a hand to his chest, stopping him dead. "It's early yet. And you've been working so hard all week. Take the morning to rest, enjoy yourself."

"I enjoy working on the house."

She gave him a coy look through lowered lashes. "More than you'd enjoy me?"

He scanned the room for his shirt and breeches. There they were, on a hook by the door. Damn it, why had he left them so far away? He nodded toward them. "Could you be so good as to hand me my clothes?"

She laughed. "No, I could not be so good. I'm beginning to wonder why I'm still wearing anything."

She moved to draw her chemise down the other shoulder. He covered his face with one hand and groaned into it, debating the wisdom of giving her exactly what she deserved and rising from bed naked, crude erection and all. Instead, he pulled the sheet free and wrapped it around his waist as he stood, throwing the tail over his shoulder so it draped like an ancient Greek's toga. It made him feel stately and philosophical, which helped in the battle to tamp down his lust.

He crossed the room to dress. "This isn't going to happen. Not this morning. I apologize for taking the liberties I did."

"Rhys," she said as he pulled the shirt over his head. "There's no need for apology. We're both adults. We want each other. There's no reason we shouldn't have some fun. It needn't mean anything more than that."

Whipping the sheet from his waist, he reached for his breeches and pulled them on with impatient tugs before turning to face her. "Meredith. You're my future wife. When I make love to you for the first time, it is damn well going to mean something. To me, at least."

She blinked, obviously surprised. Dropping her gaze,

she threaded her arms back through the sleeves of her shift and tied the ribbon with shaking fingers.

Rhys took a deep breath and composed himself. See? He was such a destructive brute. He'd barely touched her, and he was hurting her already.

"I'm sorry. I'm not angry." He grabbed his boots and sat on the opposite edge of the bed. "I . . . I'm just not especially good with words. I want to explain this, but it may not come out right. Will you let me try?"

She shrugged her acquiescence.

He began cramming his right foot into its boot. "I've torn apart a lot of things in my life. Too many. I've been in the business of death for years now, and there's only one thing I've never successfully managed to destroy. You're looking at it." He began on the left boot, working more slowly. His stiff knee made it tricky. "This body has survived blows, musket balls, bayonets, grenades, and whatever else God and Napoleon could find to hurl at it. I'm simply fated to live. There's no other explanation. And now that I've come to terms with that, I'm done tearing things apart."

He plunked his booted feet on the floor and turned to face her. "I want to build something now. Can you understand? Every day for years, I've woken up thinking, *this* is the day I die, or kill trying. Now I wake up and think, this is the day I start mixing the cob. I'm working myself to bones out there on the moor, sweating and piling rocks and digging in the dirt. Each morning I'm greeted by new aches and pains, heaped atop a lifetime of injuries. But it's all worth it. I'm going to build that house with my own hands, from the foundation to the roof. I'm going to do it for us, and I'm going to do it right, so it lasts forever. Can't go raising walls on a shaky foundation. Can't go slapping thatch over rafters so thin, they'll topple with the first winter storm. Do you know?"

She nodded. "I know."

He reached for her hand. "It's the same with us. I mean to build something with you. Something that will last. Much as I want you, I don't want to rush and bollocks it up. We're meant to be together, and—"

"Rhys . . ."

"And I know you don't believe that yet." He squeezed her hand. "It's all right. I'll keep building—stone by stone, plank by plank, kiss by kiss—until you do. And yes, I'll wake up stiff and aching for you each morning. But it's worth it." He reached out and tilted her face to his. "You're worth it."

Her eyes went wide. "You're unbelievable."

He stood and reached for his waistcoat. "What I am is indestructible. And I'm not going anywhere, Meredith. You're stuck with me now."

Chapter Eight

"Here you are. Coddled eggs and toast." Meredith laid the plate in front of her father.

He frowned at it. "Thought I asked for fried."

"Did you?" She propped her hands on the waistline of her green serge skirt and stared at the plate. "Are you sure?"

"I'm getting old, Merry. But not so old I can't remember what I said five minutes ago."

She plunked the salt down in front of him. "Just eat them. Eggs are eggs."

His bushy eyebrows rose as he lifted his coffee. "What's gotten into you this morning? You're not your usual self."

No. No, she wasn't. What a morning. Thank goodness Rhys hadn't shown his face for breakfast. She wouldn't have known what to say to him. And considering her state of distraction, she probably would have served him burnt porridge with a side of soap.

"I'm sorry, Father." She moved back to the stove and cracked two eggs into a buttered pan. "I'm just a little tired, that's all. Perhaps I'm not sleeping enough of late."

"You haven't slept enough in years, Merry. You're always working yourself too hard. Things will improve, now that Rhys is back."

"I'm not engaged to Rhys." Just how many times would she be forced to say those words before someone believed them?

"Even if you aren't. He'll give me a post, and I can support you for a change. The way it should be. You can rest."

Meredith shook her head. As if she would allow her crippled, aged father to perform manual labor while she sat idly by. "I don't want to rest. I want to keep my inn."

Rhys had truly moved her earlier, with his little speech about building the house, and constructing it to last. The excitement shining in his eyes had been wonderful to see. She understood just what he meant, because she felt the same way about the Three Hounds. No, she hadn't built it from the ground up, but she'd worked herself not just to the bone, but to the marrow to make the inn what it was today. She was damned proud of it, too.

This place represented independence, security, friendship, personal satisfaction . . . a home. Everything she'd ever wanted in her life, save one thing.

Rhys St. Maur.

And now, miracle of miracles, it seemed that Rhys wanted her, too. But only if she agreed to marry him. Only if she gave up the inn.

He simply didn't understand. Her responsibilities extended beyond caring for her father. The Three Hounds was the financial and social heart of the village. Everyone in Buckleigh-in-the-Moor depended on it, and depended on *her* to manage it.

She slid the fried eggs onto a plate, then placed it in front of her father, switching out the coddled ones for herself. After pouring herself a mug of coffee, she sat down across from him. For a few minutes, they ate in silence.

When the eggs had fortified her sufficiently and she felt up to addressing the subject, she said, "Father, listen to me. Please don't get carried away with wild ideas. We can't be sure Rhys is here to stay. He's a gentleman having a lark pushing stones about the countryside. When the amusement wears off, what then? He may decide his 'fate' lies elsewhere and leave."

"Why would he do that?"

"Why wouldn't he?" She lowered her voice and tried again. "Haven't you noticed, Father? Everyone who *can* leave this place, does."

His brow creased. "When did you become so jaded, Merry?"

Ten years ago. When I married a man several years your senior, just to put a roof over our heads.

"I'm not jaded. I'm being realistic. Someone has to be." Unfortunately, it seemed that someone must always be her. It certainly wouldn't be Rhys, with his strange insistence on destiny. Would fate get the laundry done?

She pushed back from the table. "Mrs. Ware will look after anything else you need. I'd best gather the linens for Betsy."

She went upstairs and gathered the bedclothes from each room, beginning with her own cramped, simple quarters, and continuing to her father's slightly larger room, then proceeding through every guest room, whether they had been occupied in the past week or not. Meredith knew that people of means typically traveled with their own sheets, but she made it a point to dress the beds in clean linens, as a matter of aesthetics and pride.

She saved Rhys's bedchamber for last, telling herself to invade the unoccupied room, whisk the sheets from the mattress, and make a quick retreat. But of course, the corner of one sheet snagged on the bedpost, and she had to climb atop the mattress to tug at it . . . and deuce it, the sheets were pitifully clean, when by all rights they should have been marked with passion.

And she was so very tired.

For a moment, she contemplated flopping onto the bed, snuggling into what lingered of his spicy male scent, and taking a long, luxuriant rest. She could all too easily imagine him lying next to her. She had a fair amount of practice imagining that. Except now, she had the benefit of much more information. She knew how his body fit against hers, solid in every place she was soft. She knew how his skin felt to the touch—weathered and sun-warmed atop his forearm, supple as kid on the inner side of his wrist.

She knew the taste of his kiss.

Oh, Rhys.

With a sharp yank, Meredith pulled the stubborn sheet free and roused herself from her fantasy. She understood dreams, sometimes even reveled in them. She wasn't jaded, like her father had suggested. But she knew where to draw the boundary between dreams and reality.

The familiar titter of the washerwoman's laughter floated up from the courtyard. Meredith tied the dirty linens in a bundle and went to the window, calling to catch Betsy's attention. She stuffed the heap of linen through the window, and Betsy swooped quick to catch it in her basket—a move that earned her appreciative calls from a few of the men nearby.

"Excellent aim, Mrs. Maddox!" Darryl waved to her from the stables. The hounds yipped and wrestled at his feet.

Meredith smiled in return, but didn't linger to join the fun. Instead she left the window to hurry downstairs. She'd caught sight of Robbie Brown rolling into the courtyard with his wheelbarrow of peat for the fires.

She'd need to assemble his payment in coin and bread. After that, she'd speak with Mrs. Ware about the day's meals, depending on what sort of meat the Farrell boys brought in.

She had an inn to run and a village to support.

When she entered the public room, she found it near full already, despite the early hour. A few travelers were taking a light meal before continuing on their journey. Village men were meeting over coffee to gossip and discuss trade. Even Harry and Laurence were here, eating breakfast.

She stopped in her tracks. What were the Symmonds boys doing here? The two of them never saw this side of noon, unless they'd been up all night keeping watch for Gideon. And last night, she hadn't even needed to chase them out at closing time. They'd gone home unusually peaceably, at the early hour of half-ten.

"Rough night, boys?" Hands propped on her hips, she approached their table.

Harry looked up from a plate laden with eggs, bacon, rolls and jam. "Suppose you could say that." He exchanged glances with Larry, and the two began chuckling.

Their laughter was echoed from a few other tables. Meredith slowly pivoted, taking the measure of her clientele. Now that she noticed it, a fair number of these men never darkened her door before midday.

"What?" she asked sternly. "What is it?"

The laughter only grew.

"Rough night indeed, Mrs. Maddox," Larry said around a mouthful of eggs. "But the rough morning . . . now that belongs to your friend Ashworth."

Dread seeped through her limbs. "What have you done?" Her voice shook a little, and she firmed her jaw to compensate. "Harold and Laurence Symmonds, tell me this instant. What have you done to him?"

"Easy, Mrs. Maddox," Skinner said from the next table over. He winked at her over his coffee. "We didn't hurt the man none."

Harry muttered, "Not this time."

The room broke into laughter again, but Meredith didn't wait to sort it out. With a hasty word to Mrs. Ware as she passed through the kitchen, she tore out the back door of the inn and made a straight path up the rocky slope—the most direct route to the ruins of Nethermoor. If Rhys had hired the ponies, he would have to lead them up the circuitous footpath. Perhaps she could beat him there and intercept whatever unpleasant surprise Harold, Laurence, and the others had planned for him. How long had it been since he'd left that morning? An hour, perhaps? She would have to hurry.

After twenty minutes of hard walking and scrambling over uneven ground, she reached Bell Tor and skirted the ancient stacks of granite. Despite the warming sunlight, she shivered as she neared the ruins of Nethermoor Hall. Just over this crest was the flat where Rhys was building his cottage. Panting for breath and clutching her side, she climbed up those last few steep, rocky yards . . .

And found heartbreak waiting for her on the other side.

A half-dozen dappled ponies roamed the shallow depression, grazing happily on sedge and gorse. Their unloaded burdens of straw were stacked neatly in a pile, ready to be mixed with earth. And the foundation of Rhys's cottage—the stones he'd spent a week hauling from the surrounding area and painstakingly fitting together to form a level, unshakable plinth—completely destroyed. Scattered to all corners of the moor.

Her heart twisted in her chest. So hard, she forgot all about the cramp in her side.

Rhys was there, stripped down to his shirt and

breeches, clearing the area. Methodically picking up the stones one by one, then sorting them into piles by size. Preparing to build it all again.

She watched him in silence for a few minutes. When she approached, she could tell he sensed her presence. He didn't greet her, however. He refused to meet her eyes.

"Oh, Rhys. I'm . . ." Her voice caught. Really, what could she say? "I'm so sorry this happened. I know you put so much work into it."

So much work, and so much heart.

He gave a diffident shrug as he kept right on working. "I was worried I'd made the thing too small, anyhow. Now I can enlarge it."

"Aren't you angry?"

"What good would it do to get angry?" With a low grunt, he plucked a small boulder from the ground.

"I don't know if it would do any good, but it would certainly be natural."

He tossed the stone aside easily, as though it were an apple core. It landed with a resounding thud. "I've wasted most of my life being angry. Never changes a damn thing. I just end up hurting everything around me."

Meredith hurt *for* him. She watched as he continued clearing and sorting the stones. His motions were brutish, and barely controlled. It couldn't be healthy for him, holding his emotions in like that. If his unleashed anger inflicted damage on everything around him, what damage was it doing to *him*, when he kept it inside?

"Rhys . . ."

With a rock balanced in either hand, he strode over to confront her. His eyes burned into hers. "Tell me one thing."

She mutely nodded her acquiescence. As if she could refuse.

"Did you know they were planning this? Is that why you came to my room this morning, tried to keep me in bed?"

"No," she said quickly. "God, no." Of all the horrid notions . . . no wonder he couldn't bear to look at her. "Rhys, it wasn't like that. I had no idea. You must believe me."

With a rough sigh, he heaved the rocks aside. First one, then the other. "I believe you. Just had to ask."

Before he could turn away, she caught his wrist. "Stop for a moment. Please?"

He stopped.

The wind gusted, tangling her skirt around her legs and forcing her to raise her voice. "I had no idea they'd do this last night, but I suspected they'd try something soon. You must understand, they're concerned. I'm concerned, too. I heard what you told me earlier, about needing to build something here. And I understand, more than you could know. To you, this rebuilding plan is some kind of redemption, but to everyone in the village . . . it's a threat."

"A threat? How can it be a threat?"

"We've built a livelihood here, just barely. Mainly due to the inn, and Darryl's little business touring the travelers, and . . ."

"And Gideon Myles's smuggling ring."

Her voice failed her. He knew about Gideon?

"Yes, I know. Myles and I had a not-quite-friendly chat just before he left town last week. Just how involved are you with that business?"

"I'm not—" She swallowed hard. What use was there denying it? "Not very."

He gave her a queer look as he backed away, returning to his pile of stones. "That's what I'd hoped. But this morning made me wonder."

A queasy feeling churned her innards. She recognized

it as guilt. And why should she feel guilty, simply because she'd done whatever she could to ensure the village's survival?

"Rhys, try to understand. Our livelihood as a village . . . it's a delicate balance, and you're threatening to topple it."

"Topple it? I want to rebuild it, on something more solid than ghost stories and smuggled brandy. My ancestors supported this village for generations."

"Yes, but *this* generation doesn't understand. There's already a betting pool down at the tavern. The men are all laying wagers on how long it'll take you to leave."

"Oh, really?" His voice went dark. "What date is your money on?"

"I'm not a gambler," she said, hoping a little smile would lighten the mood. "You've been gone for so long. It's hard for people to believe you're serious when you say you're here to stay."

"Well, I don't know what else I can do to convince *people*"—his pointed look told her he meant the one particular person standing before him—"that I'm truly here to stay. Other than to stay. And keep building up these stones, no matter how many times they knock them down."

"You truly mean that? No matter what they do, you'll remain here on the moor?"

"Like a damned boulder." An ironic smile quirked his lips. He ran a hand over his hair, then wiped his brow with his sleeve. "Let's put it this way. It's not like I have something better to do."

Was that meant to reassure her? It didn't. Perhaps it helped convince her he wasn't leaving anytime soon, but it certainly didn't make her any more inclined to marry him.

Marry me, Meredith. It's not like I have something better to do.

"Just the same," he said, "I'd rather not rebuild this foundation a dozen times. I suppose I'll start camping out here to guard it. You've need of your guest rooms anyway."

"Out here? At night?"

"I'm a soldier. I've camped in worse conditions than these." He looked around the rubble. "Much worse."

Her gut told her he wasn't exaggerating. But even if he *could* endure it, she hated the thought of him staying out here in the cold when she had warm beds and hot food at the inn. Not to mention, the open moor was danger-ous at night. Dark, damp, perilous. In protecting the cottage, he'd only be endangering himself. Next time Gideon's supporters got up to their mischief, the house wouldn't be their target. Rhys would.

"There has to be another way," she said.

"Perhaps. If there is, I'm certain you'll think of it. You're cleverer than I am."

And with that he went back to work, lifting stone after stone. He began to arrange some of them into a line.

With a defeated sigh, Meredith sat down on one of the largest boulders. She didn't feel up to walking back just yet. She was fatigued and frustrated and boiling angry on Rhys's behalf. Those Symmonds boys had better have cleared out by the time she returned, or she'd be breaking bottles over both their heads.

For the moment, she simply sat and watched Rhys, and the controlled wrath in his movements as he hefted and slung the rocks from one place to the other. Beneath his shirt, his muscles bulged and flexed. His face was a mask of grim determination. When stone cracked against stone, Meredith felt the echo reverberate in her spine, but he didn't even flinch.

What must it be like, to possess that kind of power? If only she had the strength to build walls with her own two hands . . . She'd have already built her new guest wing for the inn.

An idea began to form in her mind.

"If you're building with cob," she said thoughtfully, "there's a great deal of waiting involved. You have to build it in rises, you know. So the walls don't buckle or crack. Just a few feet of height at a time, and you'll need to let the walls settle between each rise. A week, at least."

"I'm certain I'll find ways to keep myself busy here-abouts."

"Perhaps. But the ideal would be to have two build-ings going up at the same time. While one rests, you add a layer of cob to the other. And the reverse."

He propped one boot on a stone and looked up at her. "Are you saying I should build two cottages?"

"No." She leaned forward, suddenly excited at the brilliance of the scheme. "I'm saying we should become partners."

One eyebrow rose. "Isn't that what I've been suggest-ing?"

"Business partners, not . . ." Her hands fluttered. "Just hear me out."

Purposely mute, he made an expansive gesture of invi-tation.

"You want to build your cottage, but you don't have laborers. I want to add on to my inn, but I lack the funds. We'll work together and build both at the same time." She rose from her stone perch and began pacing back and forth. "I'll convince the men to work for us, and I'll provide all their meals during construction. You'll pay the wages and material costs. Once they've completed a rise on one building, they'll switch to the other while it settles and cures."

He scratched his neck and peered toward the horizon.

"What's the advantage to me, financing an addition to the inn?"

"It's a gesture of good will." She ceased pacing and went to stand before him. "Don't you see? The villagers are afraid you're going to disrupt their lives with these plans to rebuild Nethermoor Hall, and then leave them in worse straits than ever. If they see the improvements to the inn occurring at the same time . . . well, they won't worry so much. No matter what happens with you and your house, Buckleigh-in-the-Moor will have come out for the better. And if the two of us are working together, they'll stop fighting you every step of the way."

"They?" He cocked his head and looked her up and down. "Am I truly to do this because 'they' won't worry so much? Or are we talking about you and your own concerns?"

She inhaled slowly. "I . . . I don't know. Both, I suppose. Does it matter?"

"Maybe not." He studied the grit under his fingernails.

"Please, Rhys." The wind whipped a strand of hair into her mouth, and she drew it back with one hand. "Either way, it's going to take you just as long to build a cottage. But if you'll allow me, I think I can persuade the local men"—and Gideon too, if she played it just right—"to give you a chance."

"You really think they'll take work with me?"

"If I approach them about it? Yes. This village is more than those dozen brutes who camp out in the tavern each night. There are several cottagers in the area scraping out a living from the moor, supporting families, many of whom have been here since your father's day. They'd jump at an offer of work, if it's presented favorably."

He released a deep sigh. "Very well, then. You have me convinced. We're partners."

"*Business* partners."

He didn't reply—just gave her a knowing half-smile and stuck his big, powerful hand into the gap between them.

Meredith did the same, and they shook hands in a brisk, very businesslike manner. And then, for an extended moment, neither one of them let go.

"Walk with me," she heard herself say, in an embarrassingly wistful tone. When his chin ducked in surprise, she released his hand and continued, "I mean . . . I'll see about assembling a workforce tomorrow. For today, why don't you rest? Walk back down to the village with me. We'll take the long way, along the stream. It's a fine day for a walk, and it will give us a chance to talk." She added swiftly, "About the construction."

"What of the ponies?"

"I'll send Darryl for them later. They'll be fine."

After a moment's hesitation, he wiped his hands on his breeches and picked up his coat where it lay nearby. Slinging it over his arm, he said, "All right, then. Lead the way."

She set an unhurried pace across the ridge, and he followed.

"Mind the path," she told him, guiding him around the edge of the bog. He'd been away so long, she worried he might forget where to step. On the surface, it merely looked like a patch of damp land, dotted with scrubby patches of heather. However, beneath the unthreatening wreath of loam lay a spring—the source of the stream that flowed down these slopes and straight through the heart of Buckleigh-in-the-Moor. Peat and muck covered the spring two yards deep, and this bog was the sad end of many an unsuspecting creature with the bad fortune to misstep and become mired.

As they turned down the slope, the waters gathered and funneled into a steady trickle, draining the layers of surrounding peat. The ground was firm and safer now, and they walked two abreast as they followed the winding, ever-widening stream.

From his easy gait, Meredith could sense that much of the angry tension in his body had dissipated. Good. Back at the cottage site, he'd been so tightly wound and obviously hurting, she'd been afraid for him. Or afraid for the rocks.

"It's been years since I walked this way," she said. "But it looks the same as it ever did. Has it changed any, in your view?"

"The landscape? No." He gave her a playful look. "But my companion's a damn sight lovelier than before."

Her cheeks blazed with a blush so fierce not even the cool breeze off the stream could soothe it. To say her adolescence was awkward rather understated the matter, but still . . . it burned her pride to know he remembered. "I know, I know. Back then, I was all freckles and bone."

He laughed. "You were, but that's not what I meant. Even freckles and bone, I'm certain you were lovelier than my horse."

"Oh! Different companion. Yes, I see." To disguise her embarrassment, she forced a laugh. "But that was a beautiful horse. My father still reminisces about that gelding. Finest beast he ever kept, he says."

Rhys lapsed into silence.

Meredith breathed with relief. It seemed her secret was safe, then. She'd followed him along this route many times as a girl, always taking great pains to remain hidden from view. It hadn't been too difficult—she'd been a reedy little thing with wild hair, always dressed in faded homespun. She'd likely blended right into the moor like a clump of gorse.

Even as they followed the path, she measured the distance by the old landmarks that had been her hiding places. The boulder standing sentinel atop a crest, the bowl-shaped depression where the river took a sharp curve, the twisted hawthorn tree surrounded by heather in its full violet bloom.

Skylarks spiraled in the sky above them. The further they walked, the closer they drew to a destination familiar to them both: the waterfall that tumbled into a steep gorge, gathering in a secluded pool beneath. That pool had been Rhys's escape in his youth, during his breaks from school. Meredith's escape, too, though little he knew it. She'd followed him many a summer afternoon, watching in secret while he stripped bare and plunged into the cool, clear water. At the time, the pull had been youthful infatuation and simple curiosity. But she'd grown into a woman since those days. As they drew nearer to that hidden pool, true desire swirled and eddied in her blood.

"Enough about me," he said. "Tell me more about you."

This was a new development, too. Logically, a vigorous young man on the brink of seventeen had taken no interest in a spindly, underdeveloped pest of a girl. But Rhys noticed her now. As they walked, he asked her questions about her father, the inn, her life over the past fourteen years. Meredith wasn't used to talking about herself. While tending bar, she was always the one listening. She would have thought there little to tell, but nerves loosened her tongue, and somehow she found plenty to rattle on about. Rhys walked beside her, silent and attentive, taking care of her in small ways. Steering her around a rock, helping her over the crossing when the first bank grew too steep to navigate.

"And Maddox?" he asked.

"What of him?"

He kicked a small stone out of their path. "How did that happen?"

"How did I come to marry him, you mean?"

He nodded.

"After the . . ." She paused, then decided there was no use talking around it. "After the fire, my father's convalescence was prolonged. For several years, the Ashworth estate paid him a pension. I took care of Father, and we lived well enough on the annual amount. But then the money stopped coming, around the same time the vicar's living dried up. I was eighteen and frantic. I didn't know what to do, but I needed to find some way of bringing in food, or we'd starve."

Meredith didn't like remembering those desperate times. A lump formed in her throat, like congealed porridge—which was what they'd eaten, sometimes twice a day. In her distraction, she neglected to choose her steps carefully. Her foot landed awkwardly on the path, and she stumbled.

Rhys's hand shot out to grip her elbow.

"I'm all right," she told him, steadying herself. "Thank you."

He didn't release her arm, however. Rather, he slid his hand down to capture hers. When she gave him an inquiring look, he merely said, "Go on."

So they walked on hand-in-hand, wading through a bank of ferns. The whole moor greened up around the stream, and the banks were saturated with rich color, slick with moss. The fertile aroma of wet earth clung heavy here, too strong for even the wind to scrub away.

"I went to Maddox," she said, "to offer my services as a groom in the stables. I knew how to do a stablehand's work, of course. You know I practically grew up in the Nethermoor stables, and Father taught me everything.

To show Maddox I could do a man's work, I went dressed in men's clothing—breeches, boots."

Rhys chuckled. "And how did that work?"

"Not as I'd hoped." She smiled to herself, remembering the way Maddox had searched her appearance with those rheumy blue eyes of his. As though he were mentally sifting through decades' worth of life as a male, trying to recall the perspective of a virile man in his prime.

"He wouldn't take me on as a stablehand," she continued, "but he offered me a post as a barmaid. Thought my pretty face would help sell pints." Perhaps she should have been offended, but she hadn't been. For the first time, she'd tasted the power inherent in womanhood. She recalled it had felt oddly gratifying, to find some use for the slight breasts and hips she'd been growing.

"And . . . ?"

"And I told him I'd rather not be a barmaid, but I'd marry him if he liked."

Rhys coughed. "You proposed to *him*?"

"Yes," she answered, matter-of-factly. "Father and I needed more security than a barmaid's wages would provide. And I've never regretted it. Maddox was kind to me, and I was a help to him."

"And when he died, he left you the inn."

"He did. And in the six years since, I've made the inn my own. In the end, it worked out well for everyone."

They heard the falls before the ridge came into view. Meredith felt it as much as she heard it: the low, dramatic rush of sound. This was not the trickling melody of the stream, but rather its ominous percussion. The sound of water forced to a crisis, hurtling into the unknown.

Rhys made a contemplative noise. "I suppose that's fate for you."

"Fate?" Meredith laughed. "You sound like the old

moorfolk, so superstitious. How can you believe in that nonsense?"

"How can I not? Do you think it's all just random, then? No rhyme or reason to the world?"

"No. I believe in hard work and hard choices. I believe people reap what they sow."

They came to a halt as they neared the falls. The drop was so steep and unexpected. From their vantage upstream, it looked as though the stream simply hit a wall of glass. Still holding hands, they advanced onto the rocky outcropping that bordered the falls.

"Looks much as I remember it," he said, peering down over the edge.

Edging forward until her toes met the lip of stone, Meredith followed his gaze. The water plummeted straight down, pounding into a circular pool some ten feet below. A lush oasis of greenery encircled the water—trees, shrubs, ferns. Leafy branches hung over the pool, shading all but the center, where a round column of sunlight pierced the darkness.

Even in full daylight . . . even to a woman nearing thirty, with a dozen menial tasks awaiting her at home and precious little energy for fancies . . . it looked enchanted. This pool was like a sparkling, precious gem, sewn into the seam of the earth's foundation garments. From her girlhood, the sight had never failed to stir Meredith's imagination and emotions. Her heart began to beat a little faster.

Rhys seemed affected by the beauty, too. His voice became husky. "You say you believe people reap what they sow?"

She nodded.

"Well, look at this place," he said, gesturing down at the secluded pool. He turned to her, raising his free hand to cradle her cheek. "Look at *you*."

Before she could protest the utter impossibility of his

directive, he dropped a light kiss on her lips. Then another.

When he spoke again, his voice came from somewhere deep. Well hidden. "This very moment has to be the work of fate. Because I swear to you, there's nothing I've done in my life to deserve it."

He kissed her again, and she clung to him, dizzied by the height of the drop, and the pounding of the falls, and the soft, delicious heat of his lips on hers. How did he do this to her? She'd been mad for him as a girl, but she'd chalked that up to youthful infatuation. She'd tracked the events of his life religiously for a decade, but she'd told herself that was idle curiosity. And now . . . now she desired him so much she could scarcely stand, but surely that was only lust. Wasn't it?

"There's no such thing as fate, Rhys."

"Yes, there is," he said. "You're mine. And I'm yours."

Her world started to spin. She pulled away from his embrace. "You can't honestly claim to live by such a belief. Just waiting to see what destiny brings?"

He shrugged, picking up a pebble at his feet and lobbing it into the pool. "This is what I've learned, over the course of my life. Fate is fate. Things will happen the way they're meant to happen. It's pointless to resist."

"Pointless?"

Meredith blinked at him. His argument was starting to chafe her pride. She didn't appreciate the insinuation that all her work and sacrifice over the past ten years had been pointless. That no matter whether she'd married an arthritic innkeeper or spent her days foraging for roots and slugs, she would still be standing here, with Rhys, at this moment. She wanted him to recognize the effort she'd made to hold this village together. Not only recognize it, but respect it. And she wanted him to see that he could make his own fate anywhere. With his strength, determination, rank, and wealth, he could have so much more than the rural life he envisioned in this place.

Somehow, she needed to shock him out of this blind, persistent belief in destiny.

She cast a brief glance sideways, over the edge of the outcropping. "Perhaps it's my destiny to fall into that pool."

"Don't be ridiculous."

"What's ridiculous about it? You said yourself, if it's meant to happen, it will happen. I'll fall into that pool. And what then?"

He retreated a pace, running a hand through his hair. "That's not what I—"

"What then, Rhys?" Her eyebrows rose. So did her voice. "Should I just be still and wait for my destiny? Would you just sit back and wait to see if I'm fated to drown?" She inched away from him, closer to the edge. "After all, it's pointless to resist."

Recognition flashed in his eyes. "Merry Lane, don't you dare—"

"Fate is fate," she said.

And then she took a large, retreating step . . . into nothing.

Chapter Nine

Meredith wasn't there anymore.

Rhys's bones weren't, either.

And what he rationally knew must have passed in an instant, seemed a bloody eternity. An eternity during which, of all absurd things, he found himself pondering science.

He'd never understand the principle of gravity. How was it that his heart soared into his throat, at the same time the earth was tugging her body down?

For that matter, the earth was taking its damn sweet time with the tugging.

Splash.

Finally. Oh, thank God. *Splash* was good. *Splash* was much, much better than *thud*. Or *crack*.

He was jarred into motion. Maddeningly, his first motion was to sink to his knees with relief. But a half-second later, he'd scrambled to the edge of the overhang and stuck his head over, scanning for a glimpse of her in the darkened pool. If she'd drifted left, been caught beneath the falls . . . she'd be churned and tumbled by the force of the cascade, with no escape.

But no. He caught sight of her to the right. The light fabric of her dress billowed beneath the clear surface, like the reflection of a cloud. She'd been spared the rocks and falls. But the pool was deep there.

Damn teasing woman. She knew how to swim.

Didn't she?

Without tearing his eyes from the pool, he tossed his coat aside and began yanking at his boots. Surely any moment now he'd see her break through the surface. She'd smile up at him, taunting and triumphant, those silver eyes flashing like flints.

Any moment now.

"Meredith," he bellowed, pulling his right boot free. "That's enough. You've made your point. It isn't funny." He faltered with the left boot. Damn stiff knee always made it harder. Still she didn't surface. Perhaps she was tangled in weeds. Or maybe she'd hit her head on the way down.

He wanted to curse, but he didn't. No breath to waste. By the time he finally had off with both boots, exertion and panic were driving the air from his lungs. With a ragged gulp to refill them, he dove after her.

The cold smacked him first. Then the wet seeped in. He fought the impulse to flail about the surface, instead letting the weight of his body pull him deeper.

Into the dark.

He opened his eyes to the stinging water, straining to make sense of the murky shadows. With Herculean effort, he forced himself to be still and turn a slow circle in place.

Rocks.

More rocks.

Shaft of sunlight, bubbles from the falls.

Empty darkness.

Meredith.

In one stroke, he was at her side. Throwing an arm about her waist, he powered their way up with the other, until they broke the water's glassy surface from beneath.

From her first splash to their surfacing, the entire ordeal had probably lasted thirty seconds. Rhys felt like thirty years had been added to his age.

Kicking fiercely, he pushed them to the pool's edge, where it was shallow enough for him to stand. He set Meredith on a boulder submerged just below the water's surface, cradling her head and shoulders in his arms while the water did what it would with her billowing dress.

She did not move. Her eyes were closed.

Sputtering, he pushed the hair back from her face and bent his head to check for breath. Warmth puffed against his cheek.

"Meredith." He gave her a shake. "Meredith, wake up."

Some vestige of his battle mentality asserted itself. There was once a time when he'd been cool and collected in such situations. He checked her for obvious signs of injury, looking in vain for signs of swelling or blood.

When that yielded no discoveries, he resorted to frantic shaking again. "Jesus, Meredith. Don't do this to me."

Her eyes fluttered open. Straightening her arms, she brought herself to a sitting position on the boulder. Her legs dangled free in the water.

A faint smile nudged the corners of her lips. "If that was a test of faith," she said evenly, "I think you failed."

"You . . . You . . ." Rhys shook a finger at her. "Damn it, you know that was—"

"Fate?"

And now he swore. Violently, crudely, punching at the water as he did. Rhys knew anger. He'd lived angry, to one degree or another, nearly all his years. But never before had he felt so enraged and so relieved in equal measures. The combination was so dizzying, so confusing . . . he couldn't even speak, or think.

Only act.

When she laughed at his rage, he wedged between her floating legs, pulled her lithe form flush against his angry bulk, and quieted her mouth with his own. No tenderness. No caution. Just raw emotion and need.

Now then, Merry Lane, he thought as he drove her jaw wide and made his best attempt at possessing her with his lips and tongue and teeth, *just you try to laugh at this.*

She didn't laugh. No, she moaned with pleasure and clutched him to her shivering body. Gave back as good as she received, catching his tongue and pulling him deeper into the kiss. They battled with lips and teeth, each working to persuade the other. Eventually the argument slowed, deepened, became more of a thoughtful discussion, and then . . . and then, delicious accord. They moved in a rhythm, his tongue stroking hers, and she clung to him, throwing her arms around his neck and wrapping her legs around his hips. They fit together so perfectly, as though they'd been fashioned just for this. Even she couldn't deny it.

He let her up for a quick breath, as a test.

"Rhys," she breathed. "Yes."

And then he kissed her again, triumph surging through his body and centering in his groin. He was hopeless with words, couldn't sing worth a damn. Even the way he ate his food sent women fleeing. But when he kissed her, she went pliant in his arms. This mouth was good for *something.*

Their garments were soaked through, matted to their skin. He could feel every contour of her body, every rib and nipple and fingertip. And by the way she ground her pelvis against his, he assumed she could feel every hardened ridge of his. Despite the coolness of the water, heat smoldered between their bodies. Her thin muslin skirt and petticoat swirled around them on the water's surface, leaving her bared beneath.

Her leg twined around his, and he thrust his hand under the water to grip her thigh. Encouraged by her soft moan, he slid his palm up the underside of her leg and cupped her backside. And once he'd gone that far . . . he couldn't stop himself. He reached between her thighs to touch her sex.

Their kiss slowed now. He took his time, exploring her mouth gently with his tongue. Tracing her folds lightly with his fingertips. She shifted in his arms, giving him freer access, and he slid a finger inside her heat.

God, more mysteries of science. How could she possibly be wetter than water? But she was. Wet, warm, slippery, inviting. For him.

For *him*.

Gasping, she tore her lips from his. "Can you feel that?" she whispered, pressing kisses to his jaw and ear. "Can you feel how much I want you? I've wanted you for so long."

If the evidence weren't currently sheathing his finger, he could hardly have believed that she wanted him at all. But what did she mean, for so long? He'd barely been back in town a week. Though he'd give her that—it had been a damn long week.

Releasing his neck, she burrowed one hand in to the space between them, cleaving his waistband from his chilled abdomen. The wet fabric didn't have much give, but her agile, slender fingers slipped into the gap and worked slowly downward. He froze, one finger still buried inside her. Her breath came hot against his ear. At last, her fingertips grazed the swollen head of his cock.

"Jesus."

She swirled a finger around the tip, and pleasure exploded inside him. He bit her shoulder to hold himself back.

"I want you." She licked his cheek. "I want you."

"Merry . . ." The word struck a chord in him. "Say you'll marry me." He knew she was reluctant, but he had this one advantage. She wanted him. Against all sense and reason and laws of nature, she wanted him. He'd intended to wait for marriage, but he'd settle for a betrothal. Hell. Right now, he'd settle for just about any syllable out of her mouth that rhymed with "yes."

He drew his finger out of her sheath, then plunged it deeper. "Say yes. Say it now."

Now. Please let it be now. And then he could take her, right here. Slide straight into that slick, inviting heat. And for once in his life, it might feel right.

"Say yes." He added a second finger, pushed deeper still.

"I . . ." Panting, she let her head fall to his collarbone. "I can't marry anyone. My father. The inn. The village . . . They all depend on me."

"Let them depend on me." He cinched his free arm about her waist. "I'll take care of everything. I'll protect you, and your father, and the village. I'd never allow you to come to harm."

"Rhys . . ."

He nudged back, forcing her to lift her head. The doubt was plain in her eyes. Why couldn't she believe him? Perhaps it was too much to expect, after only a week—but damn. It still hurt that she didn't.

And then, a horrible thought struck. Maybe she didn't believe him because she knew it was a lie. He *had* allowed her, and her father, and the entire village to come to harm, long ago. He'd allowed them to suffer for the fourteen years since.

Could it be she knew something of the truth? He'd never spoken about that night, not to anyone.

With deep regret, he withdrew his fingers from her body and took her by the waist, setting her back on the boulder. She bit her quivering lip, and he rubbed his hands up and down her arms to warm them. He tried, very hard, to ignore the tight knots of her nipples, thrown into stark relief by her wet gown.

"Merry . . ."

"I'm not looking!" The voice came from somewhere above.

Rhys started. "What? Who the—"

"Hullo!" the call came once more. "Hullo, down there! I'm up here. But don't you worry, I won't peek!"

"It's Darryl," she muttered through chattering teeth. "I'd know that voice anywhere."

Sure enough, Rhys looked up to see Darryl Tewkes edging his way along the overhang, both hands pressed to cover his eyes.

"I'm not looking!" he repeated. "I know you may very well be indecent, so I'm not looking. I swear it."

The youth took a step closer to the edge.

"Look!" Meredith and Rhys shouted as one.

Darryl froze.

"For God's sake, Darryl," she said. "Open your eyes. We're clothed, we just had a . . ." She gave Rhys a wry smile. "A mishap."

That was one way to put it.

"Oh. All right, then." The youth uncovered his eyes. He glanced down at his feet, mere inches from the edge, and jumped back with a shout.

Rhys shook his head, chuckling. The fool would be twitching all day now.

Grasping a mossy stone for leverage, he hoisted himself out of the pool. Thanks to the cold water, his arousal had flagged rather quickly, all things considering. In fact, he suspected his bollocks might have drawn up into his ribcage.

He extended a hand to Meredith, and she took it. Pulling her out was no easy task, with the weight of her sodden petticoats and gown complicating matters, but they managed it together, and soon enough she stood dripping on solid ground. The sprigged muslin of her gown was all but translucent, hugging her every bump and curve.

Confronted with this sight, poor Darryl Tewkes just didn't know what to do with himself. He raised a hand to his eyes again, then thought better of it and forced the hand back to his side. Eventually he settled for staring up at the sky.

"My coat's up there on the outcropping," Rhys called. "Give it here, will you?"

"Oh. Certainly." Darryl did as asked. Except that he nearly tossed the coat straight into the pool. Only a quick, acrobatic snag from Rhys saved it from a watery end.

He exhaled with limited forbearance. "Tewkes, I'm assuming we're all headed back to the inn. Why don't you walk around the falls and meet us down here? And bring my boots."

"Absolutely, my lord."

The youth disappeared once again, and Rhys took the opportunity to drape his coat securely about Meredith's shoulders.

When Darryl emerged through the trees, she asked, "So what's this about? Why are you after us?" Her complexion went to ash in an instant. "It's not Father?"

"No," Darryl assured her. "No. But Lord, I've been walking all over this moor, looking for the two of you. There's a man down at the inn. Quite fancy sort, just come in this morning from London." A twitching eye turned on Rhys. "He's looking for you, Lord Ashworth."

When they reached the Three Hounds after another quarter hour of walking, Rhys was fairly certain who they'd meet. So it was no shock to enter the tavern and spy Julian Bellamy occupying the corner table.

What was a surprise, however, was Bellamy's companion. He had a girl with him. A very pretty girl, who couldn't be older than twenty. She had curled yellow hair and an innocent blush that seemed at odds with her lush figure. On closer inspection, that blush looked to be painted on.

Strange. Rhys wouldn't have figured Bellamy to be traveling with a doxy. From all evidence a few weeks ago, the man was in unmitigated, unrequited love with Lady Lily Chatwick, the Stud Club founder's grieving sister.

When Bellamy caught sight of Rhys, he rose from the table and met him in the center of the room, directing his friend to remain seated. From the table, the girl gave Rhys an uneasy look.

He was used to those looks. And with his still-damp breeches, muddied boots, and bits of moss clinging to his coat, Rhys supposed he must look a fright. Even more so than usual.

"I know I asked you to send my things from London," he said, greeting Bellamy with a nod. "But I didn't expect a personal delivery."

"Arrived not a moment too soon, it would seem." Bellamy cast a disapproving glance at Rhys's bedraggled attire. As always, the man himself was turned out in stylish, tailored velvet. "Good Lord, what have they done to you out here?"

"I've been working. It's what we simple country folk

do. Not all of us can afford to spend our time swanning about London in the latest fashions."

"Welcome to the Three Hounds, sir." Meredith appeared at Rhys's side, surprising him with her speed. She'd entered by the back way to discreetly change into dry clothing, and she'd certainly done so with haste. She'd woven her damp hair into a single plait hanging down her back, and she wore another of her simple frocks, this one a cinnamon color.

Beneath that dress, her skin would still be cool to the touch. She would taste of spring water, crisp and sweet. Perhaps she was still wet for him, even now.

As if she could hear Rhys's lascivious thoughts, she cleared her throat in rebuke. To Bellamy she said, "Can I bring you and your lady friend some refreshment?"

"Brandy for me," Bellamy said. He spoke over his shoulder. "What are you drinking?"

"Oh!" The yellow-haired girl perked, abandoning her examination of her fingernails. "Raspberry shrub would be lovely."

Meredith choked on a laugh. "As a general habit, we don't do pink and bubbly in this establishment, but I think I've a bottle of cordial somewhere. Will that do?"

"Yes, please."

Meredith gave Rhys an amused glance as she headed for the bar. "Do have a seat, the three of you."

By the time Rhys and Bellamy settled themselves at the table, she was back, bearing a tray with a tumbler of brandy, a skinny glass of cordial, and a pint of ale, which she set before Rhys. He loved that she knew what he'd drink without asking. But he hated that she was serving them, when by all rights she ought to be a lady, with a fleet of servants to wait on *her*.

And damn, what kind of gentleman was he, allowing her to serve him this way? Belatedly, he pushed back from the table and stood. It was a meager gesture of respect, but it was something. As she lingered over the task of distributing drinks, Rhys could tell she was curious just what this conference was about. So was he, for that matter.

"Join us." Rhys offered the chair next to his. "Mr. Julian Bellamy, this is Mrs. Meredith Maddox. She's the proprietor of the Three Hounds."

"We need to speak privately," Bellamy said. He shot a glance at Meredith. "With all due respect."

"She's also my future wife." Rhys pulled out the chair. "And if this is about Leo Chatwick's murder, she already knows as much as I do."

He chanced a look at Meredith. Her eyes had gone the dark gray of thunderclouds, and they were twice as agitated. He shrugged, well aware that he wasn't playing fair. Now she had a choice: Accept the label of future wife, or abandon all curiosity about the conversation.

He stood there, poised with the empty chair, awaiting her decision.

"It's my inn," she said finally, taking the chair from Rhys's grasp. "I'll sit where I please."

And sit she did.

"Fine," Bellamy said. "This is Cora Dunn. She's the one who found Leo after the attack and brought him to my home."

Ah, so this was the prostitute who'd witnessed the murder. And she'd found more than Leo's senseless form, if Rhys remembered the story right. When they first learned of the murder, it had been assumed Leo was alone when he was attacked. There was no way to confirm it, however, since the whore who recovered his body had disappeared.

But just two weeks ago, the remaining members of the Stud Club had all been together in Gloucestershire when a stunning revelation was made: Not only had the prostitute been found, but she reported that Leo had been with another man when he was attacked—and his companion's appearance closely matched that of Julian Bellamy.

"So," Rhys said to the girl. "Who was Leo with that night?"

She twisted her glass of cordial by the long, slender stem. "Well, I don't know, do I? A man who looked a great deal like Mr. Bellamy here."

"But he wasn't me," Bellamy interjected.

"Could have been," Cora said, sipping her cordial. "I saw him in a darkened alley, you know, and his face was smeared with blood. Don't know as I'd recognize the gent now, were we sitting face to face."

Bellamy swore under his breath. "We've been through this. I set the fashion for brainless young bucks of the *ton*. They ape my hair, my attire, my mannerisms. Lots of young men look like me. This one wasn't me."

"Well, of course I don't believe so." The girl bit her lip. "But the two of you do look remarkably like. And his clothes were beautiful." Propping her chin in her hand, she went on wistfully, "Had a waistcoat of velvet with gold stitching. That stitching glittered, even in the dark. What I wouldn't give to have embroidery half so fine."

A fit of coughing overtook Meredith. She reached for Rhys's ale and helped herself to a long draught.

When she attempted to slide it back, he told her, "Keep it." To Cora, he said, "Why don't you start again. Tell us everything that happened that night, from the beginning."

"Well, I was in Covent Garden, in my usual place for the evening. Each lady has her usual place, you know. A hackney stopped right in front of me, and this splendid-looking gent beckoned me inside. Fair hair, light eyes, fine features. I'll tell you," she said, directing the comment at Meredith, "it's not often we get one so handsome as that."

Meredith looked completely nonplussed by the "we" in that sentence, but she merely tilted her head and said, "Go on, then."

"Anyway, he complimented my bonnet, which I *was* quite proud of. I'd just replaced the ribbons a day before. When I said, 'I thank you, sir,' he told me to call him Leo. And then he asked me if I'd like to see a boxing match over in Whitechapel. He'd made plans to attend with a friend, he said, but the friend cried off."

Bellamy gave a low groan of culpability. "That would be me."

"Normally, I told him, I stay far clear of the East End. That's for low-class girls, the ones what work the docks. But he was so handsome, and he asked so prettily. And I'd never seen a boxing match, not a real one, so . . ." She lifted her eyebrows. "Off we went. On the drive, he was ever so kind to me. Let me drink brandy from his flask. I didn't even know then that he was a lord, but I could tell he was true Quality. Not from his clothes or his accent, but just his manners." Cora's eyes fell, and she traced a groove on the tabletop. "He treated me like a person, Leo did. Like a sweetheart even, not just a whore. Sometimes I still can't believe he's dead. Like to broke my heart, though I'd scarce known him a few hours and we hadn't even . . ."

She didn't finish the thought. No one at the table needed her to.

Bellamy cleared his throat. "Yes, that was Leo. Always considerate of others, regardless of their station. Most fair-minded man I've ever known."

"So you went to Whitechapel," Rhys prompted.

"Oh, yes," Cora went on. "And that boxing match was a sweaty, smelly business. All the men shouting and shoving and carrying on. Didn't like it at all, but at least it was finished quick. Afterwards, the whole crowd was milling about. Leo was foxed on brandy and giddy from the fight." She turned to Meredith again and murmured low. "You know how men are. They get riled up by the violence. Makes 'em randy."

Meredith gave the girl a patient smile. Behind it, he could tell she was chewing a mouthful of unspoken remarks. Rhys wished he could look forward to going to bed with her tonight, just to hear all the thoughts she was so obviously keeping to herself.

Of course, that wasn't the only reason he wished they were sharing a bed tonight. Nor even the main reason.

"Leo took me round the corner. He started talking very sweet to me. What a lovely girl I was, and how lucky a man would be to enjoy my favors." She laughed a little. "I told him he didn't need no luck with me, just a shilling or two. He laughed and kissed me on the cheek and promised to give me three. Well, I thought he meant to just duck into a dark corner and lift my skirts, like most of them do—but no. He said he wanted to take me home with him, and would I be lovely to him there? A real bed, he wanted!"

"Fancy that," Meredith murmured.

"Leo sent a boy to call the hack. While we were waiting there, a gent called out to him from the shadows. Leo seemed to recognize who it was. He told me to wait right under the streetlamp, and he'd be just a few paces away. The two of them went round the corner to discuss."

"Discuss what?" Bellamy asked.

"I don't know, do I? Couldn't make out the words. But they were discussing it angrily, I could tell that much. Then it got very quiet, and I started to prickle all over. Thought perhaps they'd forgotten me, and I'd be lost all alone in Whitechapel. All I had to my name was the half-crown sewn into my stays for emergencies." She drained the rest of her cordial, as if for courage. "Seemed like ages I stood there, not knowing whether to follow after them or not. And then suddenly I heard sounds. Horrid sounds. Punches, blows, cries. Worse than the boxing match."

She gave a little shudder. "Were it anyone else, I would have run home that instant. But I'd grown so fond of Leo, and I was ever so scared . . . I turned into the alley and let loose with a scream."

Everyone went silent. Rhys supposed, like him, the others were waiting to see if she'd demonstrate.

Fortunately for Meredith's cordial glass, the girl didn't.

"It took a few moments before I could make out a thing, what with the dark and shadows. But there were two big, coarse-looking men standing there. And at their feet, Leo and his friend were moaning on the ground. I screamed some more. The two men took off running the other direction, disappeared at the end of the alley."

"Could you recognize them if you saw them again?"

She shook her head, and a blond ringlet bobbed against her cheek. "They ran away so fast. All I know is that they were big and brutish and fearsome, like . . ." Her gaze darted toward Rhys, then quickly away. She cleared her throat. "Oh, and one was bald—I remember his head gleaming in the moonlight. And the other . . . well, I heard him shout to the first as they ran away. Sounded Scottish. That's all I know.

"Besides, all my cares were for Leo. I went to him. He was knocked cold. His friend looked to be in bad shape, too, but he could speak. He told me to go for a hack, and then he gave me an address." She looked to Bellamy. "*Your* address."

Rhys and Bellamy exchanged a look.

She sniffed. "So I ran back to the street, and as luck would have it, Leo's boy had just returned with the hack. I made the driver come help me. Told him there were two gents as needed a doctor and quick. But by the time we rushed back to the alley, the dark-haired man had vanished. Only Leo was there."

She sniffed again, and a tear streaked down her cheek, trickling through the fine dust of face powder. Bellamy pulled a square of white linen from his pocket, and she accepted it wordlessly.

"We brought him to the cab, and I tried to keep him warm. He was shivering and so pale. His breathing was all rattled. 'Don't die,' I told him, over and over. 'Don't die, Leo, please don't die just yet.' " She sobbed into the handkerchief. "But he did. He died right there in my arms. And I kissed him, I couldn't help it. I tell you, it broke my heart clean in two. Only a few hours, and I was half in love with the man."

She cried noisily.

Rhys averted his eyes. Perhaps it was all the lingering arousal and emotion from their encounter at the pool, but he was strangely moved by Cora's story. He was glad Leo had some tenderness as he went, even if from a stranger. Charm and fine looks helped him to the end. Most men who died by violence weren't so fortunate. How many times had his own wounded, broken body been dragged from a tavern floor or battlefield? And never once had he awoken to find a little blond angel hovering over him. Hell, Cora couldn't even look at Rhys without flinching. The thought of her weeping over his battered form . . . it made him laugh.

The laugh stuck in his throat, and he harrumphed around it.

He risked a look at Meredith. She caught his gaze, and her knee grazed his beneath the table. Then stayed there, lightly pressing against his leg.

It could have been an accident. But he didn't believe in accidents.

"Oh, yes," Bellamy said. His suspicious expression was at war with red-rimmed eyes. "You were so in love with Leo. But you didn't neglect to strip his pockets, did you?"

Cora wiped her nose. "Well, I needed coin for the hackney. And he *had* promised me three shillings, and . . ." She shrugged away a great portion of her sentiment. "I'm just a whore, aren't I? Alive or dead, he could spare a few coins."

"Except," Rhys said, reaching into his coat's breast pocket, "one of those coins wasn't a coin at all."

From his pocket he withdrew one of the brass tokens that represented membership in the Stud Club. He laid it on the table, then slid it toward Cora with one fingertip. "You recognize it?"

"Of course." She picked it up, peered at it, laughed at it a little. "Queer little thing, isn't it? At first, I didn't know what to make of it. Didn't figure it was worth anything. I just held on to it in my purse until Jack offered me a guinea for it in trade. I grabbed at the chance, took the next coach home to see my mum in Dover. That's where your friend found me again."

Jack d'Orsay wasn't precisely a friend, but neither Rhys nor Bellamy argued the point.

"After that night with Leo . . ." Her gaze fell to the token, and her voice went soft. "I wanted a change from that world, you know? Working as a Covent Garden girl . . . it wasn't how I planned my life to be."

All four of them stared at the table in awkward silence.

Finally, Rhys said, "That's the way of things. Fate laughs in the face of all our plans."

Bellamy banged the table with the side of his fist. "We have to find that man who took Leo into the alleyway. Obviously he was lured into an ambush."

"You don't know that. Sounds as though this stranger

and your friend were both victims." This came from Meredith. "They were both injured."

"He was clearly feigning," Bellamy said. "And culpable to some degree. Otherwise, why would he have disappeared?"

"I don't know," Meredith replied, unintimidated. "I agree, you'd best find him and ask. But I doubt you'll find him here on Dartmoor."

"I doubt it, too. That's not why I'm here." He turned to Rhys. "I'm going back to London to see what I can learn. I need a place for Cora to stay. A safe place."

"You mean here?" Rhys asked.

Bellamy nodded.

"Now wait a minute," Meredith said. "I run a respectable establishment. The Three Hounds isn't that kind of inn."

"I'll pay all her expenses," Bellamy said. "She won't need to ply her trade. She just needs a place to stay. If Leo's killers knew she was a witness, she could be in danger." He turned to Rhys. "I thought the inn would be ideal, unless you have someplace else in mind. Have you a personal residence?"

"She'll stay here." Meredith rose to her feet, suddenly every inch the welcoming landlady. "Come along then, Cora. You must be fatigued. We'll find you a room and leave the men to their conversation."

Cora rose from the table, and Meredith beckoned her with a motherly hand. "Mr. Bellamy, will you be needing accommodations as well?"

"Just for the night."

"Very good, then. The Three Hounds is delighted to welcome you." The tone in her voice, however, was not a very convincing rendition of delight. "I'll prepare a room for you, too."

"He can have mine," Rhys said. To her confused frown, he added in a low voice, "I'll be camping out on the moor from now on. To discourage a repeat of this morning's events."

"Which events?" she whispered. "The ones at your building site, or the ones . . ." Her eyes flashed up toward the bedchambers.

"Both," he said simply.

Her frown deepened.

After the ladies left them, Bellamy shot Rhys a strange look. "You're marrying? After Leo's death . . . when we discussed Lily's future, you said you didn't want to marry."

"I didn't. Not then." And he still had no interest in marrying Leo Chatwick's grieving twin sister. Lily was a refined, elegant lady—in the royal line, if he correctly re-called. Rhys wasn't the man for her.

Neither was Julian Bellamy, a fact that explained the man's persistent ill humor. If ever there was a man who discussed his childhood less willingly than Rhys, it was Bellamy. No one knew where he'd come from, and Rhys himself couldn't have cared less. But where a lady of Lily Chatwick's rank was concerned . . . even Rhys knew such things mattered. Greatly.

"So you're telling me that in the past week, this wid-owed landlady has somehow changed your mind?"

"Aye."

Bellamy riffled his unkempt shock of hair. "Don't get me wrong. She's a comely enough bit of goods, but . . . a trifle hard around the edges, don't you think?"

"What makes you say that? Because she challenged you?" Rhys chuckled. "She's a strong woman." And sweet, and soft, and secretly vulnerable, and like hot silk between her thighs. But he preferred to keep those sides of Meredith to himself. "She works hard, and she won't brook any nonsense."

"I could see that."

Rhys flexed his hand until his knuckles cracked. "A man like me has no use for delicate porcelain types."

"Point acknowledged."

"How's Lily?"

Bellamy sighed roughly. "Delicate. As porcelain. Leo's heir will arrive from Egypt in a matter of months, and she'll have to vacate the house. I don't know what Lily expects to do then, but she refuses to discuss it. Says she'll deal with it on her own." He finished off his brandy with an angry draught. "On her own. What is the world coming to, with these modern women? A man can't tell them what to do."

"Don't I know it," Rhys muttered, still thinking of Meredith's frown. If she was unhappy about his decision to stay on the moor, she could easily change it by marrying him. After that incident in the pool, he knew he'd never make it through another night under the same roof without bedding her.

"Lily's after me to cease hunting for Leo's killers. Says it's useless." Bellamy shook his head. "There's no way I'll stop. Not until I find the men responsible and see them hanged. Or worse." He looked to Rhys. "That's where you come in."

"Let me guess. I'm the 'worse.' "

He nodded. "I'll admit, these past weeks *have* been fruitless. I've been searching for two nameless, faceless brutes . . . not an easy task. Cora's story has given me new hope. It's much easier to find a dandy than two common ruffians. There are fewer of them, to start, and gold embroidery does stand out in a crowd. I'll find him, mark my words. And when I do, I'll send word to you. We'll need to get the truth out of him. And you promised to lend muscle, if you recall."

"I recall." He tapped his stiff finger against the tankard. When he'd made that offer, he'd have picked a fight with anything big and angry, just in hopes of losing for a change. "But things are different now. I have responsibilities here. And I think I'm done with brawling."

Bellamy leaned over the table and drilled him with a look. "Well, you'll come out of retirement for this. You're a member of the Club, and Leo was our founder. You owe him that much, to avenge his death."

Uncertainty quirked the corner of Rhys's mouth. Just what did he owe Leo Chatwick? This Club of his had done nothing for him. But it was Leo's murder that had finally convinced Rhys of the futility of chasing after death. If Leo hadn't been killed, Rhys might not have returned to Buckleigh-in-the-Moor for years. This one chance at redemption might have been a long time coming.

Perhaps he did owe Leo a great deal.

"Find the man first," Rhys said. "Then we'll talk."

Chapter Ten

During his brief stay at the Three Hounds, Mr. Julian Bellamy did precisely one thing to endear himself to Meredith.

He left before dawn.

By contrast, she'd expected Cora to sleep until noon—wasn't that what ladies of the night must do? So the girl's appearance during morning baking was a true surprise.

"Good morning, Mrs. Maddox."

Meredith lifted a board lined with risen yeast rolls and sneezed at a puff of flour. "Mr. Bellamy has already left for London."

"Yes, ma'am. I gathered as much."

Cora was all fresh-faced innocence this morning. No paint or powder to obscure her fair complexion, and her blond hair was styled in a simple knot. Her china-blue muslin day dress was low-cut and in want of a fichu, but otherwise unremarkable in style or quality.

And despite all this, she was still a very pretty girl. Perhaps prettier than she'd been yesterday. Which made Meredith think the girl would be trouble.

She didn't like having Cora in the inn, but she liked the alternatives less. There was no way this harlot was staying in any private residence—be it a London town house or moorland hovel—belonging to Rhys. Meredith might have refused the man's offer of marriage once or twice, but she wasn't resigning all interest in him. Not after yesterday at the pool, when she'd been inches away from making years of fantasies come true.

She wrenched open the oven door, and a wave of heat swamped her. Sweat beaded instantly on her brow and neck. Her defenses were momentarily stripped. Memories rushed in.

His strong arms anchoring her in the pool. Their tongues, mating with wild abandon. The hot, swollen tip of his arousal gliding under her touch, silky as twice-milled flour.

His fingers, so thick inside her . . .

She thrust the bread into the oven and banged the door shut. *Focus, Meredith.* Her torrid daydreams had already scorched the first batch of rolls.

"Breakfast is over," she told Cora, wiping her hands on her apron. "And the noon meal will be awhile yet. But there will be fresh bread in a few minutes. Do you take coffee or tea?"

"I don't suppose there's chocolate?"

A pretty face *and* a taste for sweets? Trouble. "I'm afraid not."

"Then tea, please."

When Meredith moved to put the kettle on, the girl intervened. "Oh, let me do it, ma'am. When I lived in London, I always made tea for the girls in the house. I've a knack for it."

Meredith surrendered the kettle. As she watched the girl fill it with water and place it on the hob, she cleared her throat and brought out her sternest voice. "Listen, Cora. We both know this discussion is coming, so we may as well have it over with now."

The girl's eyebrows arched in surprise, as if she'd no idea what Meredith was going to say. "Yes, ma'am?"

"This is my inn, and it's a respectable establishment. The local men who come in here of an evening—they're going to take quite an interest in you. But even if you are a friend of Lord Ashworth's, I warn you now, I won't abide any mischief."

"Oh, yes, ma'am. I'm not wanting any mischief. I know Mr. Bellamy said he'd pay my account, but I'd rather work for my keep."

Meredith narrowed her eyes. "I thought I just told you—"

"Oh, not *that* kind of work." The kettle rumbled. Cora plucked a towel from the table and wrapped it about her hand before removing the kettle from the hob. "That life was never what I wanted. I hardly know how it happened. I was living in Dover—that's where I was raised. My mother worked as a seamstress there, and one day she sent me to the market. I was dallying with friends on my way home, and a fancy gent drove by in a splendid coach. Handsome as anything, he was. He opened the door and called me a pretty little thing and asked, would I like to ride with him to London? Why certainly I would. Always wanted to see London, what girl didn't?" She frowned. "Where's the tea?"

Meredith motioned toward the tea caddy.

Biting her lip, Cora measured tea leaves into the pot with childlike concentration. She was such a strange mix of girl and woman. Meredith couldn't decide which she was feigning: the innocence, or the worldliness.

"So you went with him to London . . ." she prompted, vaguely wondering why she was even taking an interest.

"I went with him to London. And when I arrived there, I was a whore. The handsome gent shoved me out in Covent Garden and tossed me a shilling." She gave a matter-of-fact shrug as she covered the tea leaves with steaming water and set them to steep.

"How old were you?"

"Thirteen."

Meredith gasped. "Oh, no."

"Oh, yes. Thirteen and alone in the world, with no other way of earning bread, no coin to go home . . . I didn't think my mother would even want me back." A little smile curved her lips as she stared down at the tea. "But she did. When I went to see her just last month, she told me she'd prayed for me every single day."

"Of course she had." Meredith poked at the fire. Smoke stung her eyes, giving her a convenient excuse to blink away a tear. The girl's story was undeniably moving. Stirring enough to blow years of accumulated dust off her maternal instincts. She might be barren, but the Three Hounds worked like a magnet for unwanted adolescents in need of a friend. First Gideon, then Darryl. Now this girl, too.

She took the towel from Cora's hand and prepared to remove the rolls from the oven. "And how old are you now?"

"Eighteen, ma'am. And I don't want to go back to that life, I don't. Please let me work for you, Mrs. Maddox. By the time I leave here, mayhap I'll have prospects for better employment. Perhaps Mr. Bellamy or Lord Ashworth would see fit to furnish me with a character reference, and I could find a post in service. Could send my mother some money from time to time, and she wouldn't have to worry where it come from."

"Well, I can see you've thought it all through."

"Lay awake half the night, ma'am. I suppose that's why I overslept."

Meredith offered her a fresh roll, and Cora accepted it eagerly, crying out in alarm when it singed her fingertips. Meredith smiled at the ensuing juggling act, and at Cora's bubbly, girlish laugh.

"Is there jam?" she asked hopefully, her cheeks flushing pink.

"Yes. Yes, there is. And honey too." And the next time she saw Gideon, Meredith would ask him to bring round some chocolate.

As she retrieved the pots of sticky sweetness, Meredith thought of herself at Cora's age. She'd already been caretaker to her invalid father and the family's only potential wage-earner. All that, plus desperate and hungry. Fortunately, thanks to her father and dear late mother, she'd had some skills and education. Sometimes she'd suspected Maddox of marrying her out of pity. Or perhaps simply because she knew how to read and write and do sums better than most anyone in the village. Certainly better than Maddox himself.

She'd been lucky. By contrast, Cora had found herself friendless, penniless, uneducated, and transplanted to an unfamiliar city at the age of thirteen . . . after being crudely indoctrinated into womanhood by some passing "gentleman" with a high-sprung carriage. It was remarkable that she'd survived at all, and her tale certainly explained why she acted like a girl who was thirteen-nearing-thirty.

It made a tragic sort of sense that a child stripped of innocence might cultivate another, more willful naïveté to replace it. She thought of Rhys, and his stubborn belief in fate. What lies would an abused boy tell himself, rather than believe he'd somehow earned such vile treatment?

Cora poured two cups of tea, and Meredith took a cautious sip. "Not bad at all," she said, savoring the rich warmth spreading down her throat. "I'll teach you coffee next. There's an apron hanging on a nail, just the other side of the onion bin."

The girl clapped her hands together. "You'll allow me to work for you?"

Meredith nodded as she took another sip of tea. She wanted to give the girl a chance, and there was no doubt she could use the extra help. Once the new construction started, she'd have a crew of hungry men to feed. And those hungry men would be earning wages, a portion of which they'd slide right back across the bar at the end of the day.

"You'll be my new serving girl," she said. "Your day starts at breakfast, and then you'll help Mrs. Ware with the cooking until the noon meal. Your afternoons will be your own from two to five, and then it's back to tend the bar until close. How does that sound?"

"Oh, it sounds lovely."

"Lovely?" Meredith chuckled. "We'll consider this first week a trial. Innkeeping is difficult labor. You may not take to it."

"Oh, I will." Cora's cheeks dimpled with a grin as she looped the apron over her arms. "I'm stronger than I look."

"I don't doubt it. We women usually are." She slid a bowl of risen dough in the girl's direction and demonstrated the way to form rolls. "But mind you, this isn't London. Some of the men hereabouts are of a rough sort. If they give you any trouble, you're to tell me."

"Yes, ma'am."

"And don't go wandering the countryside on your own. The moor can be dangerous if you don't know your way. If there's anywhere you need to go, the stable hand will take you."

"Not at the moment, he won't." A deep voice interrupted them. "Darryl's occupied putting up my mare."

Meredith turned to spy Gideon standing in the doorway between kitchen and tavern. Leaving the rolls to Cora, she hurried to meet him. God, she hoped he hadn't . . .

"No. No wagon today," he said, answering her unspoken question. "I've come on horseback, just to suss matters out. Brought your newspapers, though." He held them aloft. "There's a fine bottle of port in my saddlebag, and . . ." His gaze drifted over her shoulder. "And bloody hell, who *is* that?"

She looked over her shoulder at Cora. The girl was covered in flour to her wrists, industriously pulling the yeasty dough and shaping it into knots. The lumps of risen dough bore a marked resemblance to her pale breasts, overflowing her bodice in two healthy scoops as she leaned over the table.

"That's Cora," she said, turning back to Gideon.

His unshaven throat worked. "She looks like a harlot."

Meredith pulled him through the doorway, out from the girl's hearing. "Well, she was. Until recently. Now she's my new barmaid."

He scowled. "You're taking in whores? I thought this wasn't that kind of inn. You're always talking about making the Three Hounds a respectable establishment."

"It is respectable. As I said, she's not working that trade anymore."

"Oh, I see. So this is your new charity project, rehabilitating fallen women?"

"No. She's a friend of Lord Ashworth's, and she needs a place to stay."

His jaw clenched. "Ashworth's still here?"

"Here in the inn? No. Here in the neighborhood? Yes."

Gideon swore. "So he's moving his personal whore into the inn. And what's next? Don't let him get cozy here, Meredith."

"She's not *his* whore." She sighed. This wasn't how she'd hoped to break the news of the construction partnership. "Sit at the bar," she told him. "I'll bring you something to eat, and we'll talk."

Back in the kitchen, she praised Cora's progress as she poured a mug of tea and heaped a plate high with hot rolls and a cold leg of chicken from the night before. She set both mug and plate before Gideon on the bar. As was the case with most men, his mood usually improved after a meal.

"Now listen," she said as he fell on the food, "I won't hear anyone speaking that way of Cora. She had a bad lot of luck when she was younger, and circumstances forced her into a less-than-honorable occupation. Which makes her not so different from some smugglers I know. Anyhow, she won't be taking any customers here."

"Are you certain?" He washed down his third roll with a gulp of tea. Craning his neck, he curved his gaze around Meredith to gawk through the kitchen doorway. "Old habits and all that. With looks like hers, she won't lack for offers. What if she just gets bored? What if she takes a fancy to some traveler who pays her a few compliments, and takes him to her bed?"

"Then she wouldn't be much different from me, now would she?" Side-stepping to block his view, she said icily, "For a man with no aspirations to the clergy, you're frightfully judgmental today."

"I just don't like it. She's trouble."

"Most of my favorite people are."

When he failed to respond, she studied him close. He'd downed four rolls and the chicken now, and he still had that gleam of hunger in his eye. So here was the explanation for his ill humor. He wanted Cora. He desired the girl, and he was annoyed with himself for it.

To be truthful, Meredith was a mite annoyed with him, too. She was used to Gideon making eyes at *her* over his mug of tea. But Cora was younger, prettier, and decidedly more buxom. She supposed a man couldn't look at her without his mouth watering, any more than he could stand dry-mouthed before a juicy, well-seasoned roast of beef.

Still, it hurt her pride a bit.

"The men will be brawling over her every night," he said, a mulish set to his jaw. "If both Symmonds boys survive the week, I'll be shocked."

"They'll be too worn out to brawl."

"What do you mean?"

"They'll be working."

He made a dismissive snort. "Not likely. While Ashworth's still in the area, I can't resume with the wagons. The men are on furlough."

"They'll be working for me. And for Lord Ashworth."

"Meredith," he growled. "Tell me you're joking. And do it fast."

"It's the truth." She told him of the building scheme, all the while enduring his cool glare—one that only grew colder by successive degrees, the more she explained the plan. By the time she finished, she would have sworn frost had crystallized on his eyelashes.

"You must understand," she pleaded. "I've been saving money for years now, both thick and thin, and it would have taken me another decade to raise the funds Lord Ashworth can pull from his coat lining. I have to take this chance, can't you see? This is my one opportunity to improve the inn."

"He's rebuilding Nethermoor Hall, for Christ's sake. What'll become of my goods up there?"

"He's not rebuilding the Hall. He's building a cottage nearby. During construction, we'll be able to give you honest work, hauling legitimate supplies. As for the other . . . well, the man can only be in one place at a time. When they're busy putting a rise on the inn, you'll be able to come and go from the moors as you please."

"With whom? You've stolen my workforce."

"I know it will take some doing, but you'll make it work. Gideon, you don't have a choice. Lord Ashworth's not going to leave easily. He's determined to see that cottage built." She twisted an apron string about her finger. "He's building it for Father. I can't say no."

She wouldn't tell him Rhys was also ostensibly building the cottage for *her*, as his bride. No point in mentioning it. To that much, she'd already said no.

"And once these little construction projects are finished? What then?"

"He'll leave." The truth of it sank in her gut and weighed heavily there. "I'm certain of it."

"Good. Because it's a certainty. The man's been absent fourteen years. A whim brought him back, and the next fickle breeze will chase him off again. I just hope your building's raised before it happens."

"It will be," she said, shifting defensively. "With the amount of money he's spending, I don't know that I'd call it a whim."

"He's an aristocrat. Their whims may be expensive, but they're whims just the same."

Sniffing, she reached for his plate, stacking the silver and mug atop it. He wasn't saying anything she hadn't been telling herself since the night Rhys walked into this bar. But he said it very convincingly, and it was only just now she'd let herself realize how very much she wished they were both wrong.

Gideon leaned on the bar. He spoke with quiet intensity. "There are two kinds of people, Meredith. Ones who are made to stay in one place, and ones who aren't. We're the first kind, you and me. God knows, we could have left this village in our dust and gone on to bigger things, better things. But we didn't, either one of us. Because we care about this godforsaken place, even if it never gave a damn for us. We'll cling to the breast that weaned us, trying to wring milk from a granite teat, and don't try to tell us it's futile, because we already know. But we're here."

She swallowed hard.

"As for Ashworth . . ." He made a gruff sound in his throat. "He's the other kind, Merry. The leaving kind. You'd do well to remember it." He looked over his shoulder at the tavern, glancing from roofbeams to hearth. "You've poured years into this place. Work, sweat, blood, tears. What would you do to protect it?"

"Anything." She didn't even think the word, just spoke it. "Anything in my power."

"Aye," he said ominously, "I know you would. And you know I feel the same about my trade. To protect my livelihood, I'd do anything in my power. The only difference between us is, I travel armed."

The door creaked open.

"Well, if it isn't the famous Gideon Myles. And his much-touted pistol."

Rhys stood in the tavern entrance. He took up so much of the doorway that only a few meager scraps of sunlight framed his imposing silhouette. Slow, heavy strides carried him into the room, and Meredith's heart bounced with each one.

"You know, Myles," he said, propping one elbow on the bar, "it's my experience that men who are always bragging about the size of their firearms are compensating for other"—he raked Gideon with a derisive glance—"deficiencies." He turned to Meredith. "Good morning, Mrs. Maddox."

"Yes," she replied stupidly.

Yes. It was a very good morning, now.

Rhys looked magnificent. Fresh-scrubbed, clean-shaven, and turned out like a gentleman from head to toe—topcoat, cravat, waistcoat, trousers, boots. How had he managed it, camping out on the moor? She had visions—delicious visions—of him bathing in the stream, shaving in the glassy reflection of the pool. But why? For what earthly purpose?

Though her brain puzzled over the mystery, the rest of her had no question. She knew in her blood he'd made the effort for her. And that made him the most powerfully arousing sight she'd ever beheld. He smelled of soap and wild sage and clean male skin. She stared hard at the snow-white tangle of linen at his throat. Her fingers itched to get at that knot, wrest it open, wend inside his shirt, and lay claim to all within. He was like one big elaborately wrapped gift that she longed to tear open.

She laughed silently at the irony. All that care he'd put into his dress, with the ultimate result that she wanted him immediately, completely naked.

His fingers, so thick inside her . . .

"Are you ready for church?" he asked.

The word jarred her. "Ch-church? Did you say church?" And no. She was absolutely ready for something, but church wasn't it.

"It *is* the first Sunday of the month, is it not?"

She nodded in disbelief. *This* was the reason he was all dandied up? For church?

As if in confirmation, the church bell began to toll.

"If you're ready," he said, "I thought you might walk over with me."

Meredith drew in her breath with an audible hiss.

A lazy, lopsided smirk eased its way across Rhys's face.

Oh, he was a sly devil. Dressing to seduce, and then tempting her with the one chaste activity that would make them an official pair in the eyes of the village. Walking to and from church together was something courting couples did. Hereabouts, it was tantamount to announcing an engagement.

"You don't need me to walk with you," she protested. "You can see the church from the front door. It's paces away, just across the road. You can't get lost."

Gideon spoke up. "You heard the lady. She's not

walking anywhere with you. Why don't you walk straight out of town?"

Perfect. Just what she needed, a contest between Rhys and Gideon to see who could piss the farthest. "I don't believe I'll go this morning. I . . ." She put a hand to her temple. "I have a touch of headache."

Rhys didn't answer, just slowly circled the counter to her side of the bar. Meredith braced her hands on the polished wood as he came to stand behind her, a little closer than was friendly. A long, silent moment passed, and the tempo of her pulse doubled. What did he mean to do?

She wasn't even certain she'd felt it, at first. The sensation was more quiet than a whisper, more subtle than insinuation. Just the ghost of a caress tracing her lower-most left rib. The feeling intensified as it scraped over the vulnerable notch between waist and hip. Then snaked over the small of her back, insidious and tanta-lizing.

With sudden clarity, she realized what was happening. This storm of wicked sensation was all the result of one simple, deceptively innocent act. Rhys had her apron string between his fingers, and he was giving it a tug.

Slowly, surely . . . with an unwavering purpose she felt from the arches of her feet to the tingling roots of her hair . . . he was pulling the string loose.

There was a moment of tension. The length of rolled muslin drew taut. Quivered, resisted. At last, the knot surrendered.

And she was completely undone.

Confident hands rose to her shoulders. Hooking a fin-ger under each strap, he drew the untied apron down her arms. She began to tremble by the time he reached her elbows. To disguise it, she took the task from him, shrugging the apron over her wrists.

Her tongue was thick as she swallowed around it. Awareness prickled over every inch of her flesh.

"Meredith." His deep, insistent voice fell on her nape. "Walk with me."

"Mrs. Maddox?" From the kitchen, Cora's bright voice clashed through her desire. "Was that the church bell?"

Meredith clutched the discarded apron to her chest, as if she needed to cover herself for modesty's sake. He'd removed nothing but this scrap of flour-crusted muslin, yet she felt bared to the skin.

Cora walked out from the kitchen, and drew up short when she came face-to-face with Rhys. The girl swallowed hard. "Good morning, my lord," she told her slippers, apparently unable to look him in the face. "I . . . I didn't mean to interrupt."

Bless him, Rhys tried not to look offended. But Meredith—who had no problem looking him in the face for hours on end—thought she caught a fleeting wince.

"Good morning, Miss Dunn," he said gently. "That was indeed the church bell. I was just preparing to walk over. If Mrs. Maddox will join me."

Meredith twisted the apron in her hands. "But the baking . . ."

"Is all finished, ma'am." Cora smiled.

"Is it now? That's convenient." Rhys cocked an eyebrow. "The resourceful Miss Dunn has finished the baking. You're free."

He offered Meredith his arm.

She stared at it.

A tense silence filled the room, expanding like a bubble until it encompassed them all—Meredith, Rhys, Gideon, Cora. No one seemed willing to prick it.

"I'm new to the village," Cora finally put in, even as her voice faltered. "I'd be obliged if you'd show me the way to the church, my lord. That is . . . if you reckon they'd allow a girl like me inside."

Meredith wanted to bury her face for shame. A whore–turned–serving girl was correcting her manners.

"Well," Rhys said, clearing his throat. He offered Cora the same arm Meredith had declined. "We'll do this, Miss Dunn. I'll step over the threshold first. If the ground doesn't open up and suck me down to hell straightaway, it ought to be safe for you."

With a brave smile, Cora cautiously linked her arm with his. "Thank you, my lord. That's very good of you, I'm sure."

The two of them started for the door.

"We'll all walk together," Meredith blurted out. Hurrying round the bar, she nudged Gideon from his stool and jammed her arm through his. "All four of us."

When he tried to withdraw his arm, she dug her fingernails into his sleeve. She knew he hadn't darkened the church door since the old vicar left, but he would fall to his knees in prayer today. Even if she had to knock his legs out from under him.

Tugging Gideon forward, Meredith shut up the tavern, then hurried to keep step with Rhys and Cora as they entered the courtyard. What a party they made: a lord, a whore, a smuggler, and a widow, all walking to the church. It was like the prelude to some bizarre, blasphemous joke that would only sound more humorous with successive pints of cider.

As it was, Meredith had a hard time not releasing a drunken giggle as they stepped through the entrance. Surprisingly enough, the earth did not open to swallow them all in one efficient gulp. As had been the custom in Buckleigh-in-the-Moor since long before Meredith's time, the men occupied one side of the church, and the ladies sat opposite. She took it upon herself to separate Cora from Rhys's arm and herded her down a narrow wooden pew. Across the aisle, her father and Darryl sat in one of the first rows. Father caught her eye and gave her an approving nod.

When Rhys took his seat at the end of the same pew, Meredith worried for a moment that his colossal bulk would act as the trigger for a catapult, launching Father and Darryl into the air.

It didn't, but there was a creaking moment of concern.

Gideon didn't join their group. He eased into the row behind, crossing his arms over his chest. His surly expression matched his posture of disrespect.

It did something strange to her insides, just gazing at them all, seated so close together. Despite their differences and their ambivalence toward one another, she cared for all four men, in different ways. She liked having them all in her sights at one time.

Darryl drew her attention with a frantic wave. His eyes shilling-wide, he pointed at Cora. "Who's that?" he mouthed.

"Cora," she said back. "New barmaid."

The youth stared, his jaw gone slack with sentiments that had no place in a house of God.

Darryl's weren't the only eyes fixed on Cora, either. Throughout the sanctuary, every man's eyes held a look of fascinated rapture. Every woman's gaze burned with envy. Church *and* tavern attendance were likely to go up during Cora's stay, she'd wager.

When the curate took the pulpit, she noticed that he and Rhys exchanged little nods of greeting, as though they'd been already introduced. Perhaps Rhys had taken it upon himself to greet the clergyman earlier—it would make sense that he had, if he were determined to start fulfilling the role of local lord.

Perhaps he truly did mean to stay.

Gideon's words echoed in her ear. *He's the other kind, Merry. The leaving kind.*

Despite all the excitement and confusion of the morning, as the service began, she remembered why she so rarely attended anymore—for the same reason she read her newspapers standing up. As hard as she labored day in and day out, if she sat still for more than three minutes at a stretch, her body interpreted it as an invitation to doze. During the first reading, somewhere between "begat" and "spake," it was as though her chin grew a thick coating of lead. Her neck muscles simply refused to hold it up.

"Meredith Maddox."

She jolted awake. Was that *her* name she'd just heard? Surely this curate hadn't developed the habit of chastising sleepy congregants from the pulpit.

"And Rhys St. Maur," the curate went on, "both of Buckleigh-in-the-Moor. If any of you know of any cause or just impediment why these two persons should not be joined together in holy matrimony, ye are to declare it. This is the first time of asking."

Chapter Eleven

❧

The entire assembly went dead silent. No one was sleeping now. And Meredith had never been more awake.

Banns. He'd told the curate to read the banns, announcing their intent to marry in front of the entire village. In front of her father. In front of Gideon Myles. Of all the presumptuous . . .

With a loud harrumph, the curate turned the page of his liturgy and began to intone the psalm in a low, sonorous voice. No one stood. No one sang. When the curate paused, no one joined the response.

And since they were all so clearly waiting for her to make a scene, Meredith decided to oblige them. She rose in her pew and confronted Rhys across the aisle. "You had him read the banns? What on earth would possess you to do that?"

Did he mean to simply circumvent her? Persistence in a suitor was one thing. Complete disregard for a lady's willing acceptance was another.

"They have to be read three times," Rhys said, as if it should be obvious. "He only comes here once a month. If we're to be married with any sort of reasonable speed, I thought . . ."

"What are you on about? We aren't engaged!"

"Perhaps not," he said calmly. "But we will be married. Call it faith."

"You . . ." Her hands balled into fists at her sides. "You are impossible."

He pointed to his prayer book and read with beatific calm, " 'With God, nothing shall be impossible.' "

Meredith turned into the aisle. She couldn't remain there a moment longer without profaning the place.

She stormed straight out of the chapel, and the entire congregation followed in a thunder of footsteps. Not surprising. Church service happened once a month, but melodramas like these were the stuff of the annual fair.

"Meredith!" Rhys called to her as she hurried down the church steps and turned into the road. Unfortunately, his strides were worth three of hers. He caught her arm and wheeled her to face him. "You can't run away from this."

"What's he talking about?" Gideon appeared at her side, breathless. "Have you agreed to marry this man?"

"No," she insisted, snatching her hand from Rhys's grasp.

"Do you want me to kill him for you?"

"No!" Once she'd mastered her voice, she repeated. "No, there is no violence necessary. And no, I have *not* agreed to marry him."

"Ah, but she will," Rhys said with a saintly expression. "So it has been written." He looked down at the open prayer book he still carried in his hand and flipped a page.

"Quote to me one more time from that book," Meredith said, leveling a finger at him, "and you invite its desecration."

His mouth snapped shut. So did the book.

By now the entire village—churchgoers and the rest— had assembled in the road to watch the commotion.

"La!" exclaimed Cora, watching from a few paces away. "This is so romantic!"

"This is nothing," Darryl whispered to her. "Just wait until I take you on a tour of the moors. We've ancient burial cairns and haunted ruins . . . It's a mystical journey through time."

The girl cooed softly. "You don't say."

"Nothing about this is romantic!" Meredith cried, running a hand through her hair. "It's oafish, and . . . and overbearing. Not to mention, insulting."

"Insulting?" Rhys echoed. "How so?"

"To be proposed marriage as some sort of eventuality of fate, regardless of how I might feel about the idea? Simply because the man in question has nothing better to do with his time?" She turned to Cora. "Perhaps that meets your definition of romance, but it doesn't square with mine."

Rhys cocked his head. "So that's the problem," he said wonderingly. "You're holding out for romance."

"That is not what I said."

"It's what you meant. You want romance. You want to be wooed." He looked to the horizon, whistled softly, and muttered an oath that surely wouldn't be found in the pages of his prayer book. "I'm no good at that."

Gideon arched a brow. "Too bad for you."

Thoroughly exasperated, she looked from one man to the other. "Listen, the both of you. I don't intend to marry anyone. That inn across the road is the heart of this village. And my heart is in that inn."

"I know it," Rhys said. "That's why I've pledged to fund improvements to the Three Hounds. A new wing of guest rooms, no less. And in time, a stable of posting horses."

A murmur of interest swept the crowd.

Rhys continued in a voice for all to hear, "There'll be work to be done, wages to be earned. With Mrs. Maddox's help, I plan to ensure the well-being of the inn, and of the village."

"I beg your pardon," Gideon seethed, "but I've been doing both those things for some time now. Looking after the inn and the village. With Mrs. Maddox's help." He puffed his chest. "No one wants you here."

"They may not want me, but they've got me. Which means this town has no more need of *you*."

The crowd hushed.

Red surged up Gideon's throat, spreading up his face, all the way to his hairline. "Don't you—"

Rhys said, "You can go, Mr. Myles."

But he couldn't, Meredith wanted to protest. It didn't matter whether or not the place needed him; Gideon needed this place. The smuggling trade wasn't the half of it. Even though he'd grown to a man, that abandoned boy still lived inside him, craving family, friendship, acceptance. He didn't believe he'd find them anywhere else. If Rhys backed him into a corner . . . there was no telling what he'd do.

Gideon's hand went to cover the pistol jammed in the waistband of his trousers. His index finger tapped in an ominous rhythm.

"Gideon, no. You're better than that."

"Am I?" He flicked Meredith a glance. "Let's have her decide, shall we? She knows best what—or whom—this village needs. Who will it be, Meredith? Lord Ashworth? Or me? Seems this place isn't big enough for the two of us."

Wonderful. How could he put her in such a position? The eyes of the village were on her now. This wasn't the time to appear hesitant or unsure. Meredith drew a shaky breath and clasped her hands together to keep them from trembling.

"This village needs an inn," she said, speaking to the crowd. "A respectable establishment, fit for quality guests. Men may come and go. But this road we're standing on will always be here. It's our one resource, and it will bring us a steady stream of travelers with coin to spend. We just need to be ready to serve them."

Many of the assembled villagers began to nod.

She tilted her head toward Rhys. "We need Lord Ashworth to fund the improvements." She gestured at Gideon. "We need Mr. Myles to haul the supplies and stores. And we need every willing, able-bodied man to join in the labor."

Lowering her voice, she turned to Rhys and Gideon. "Gentlemen, if this village isn't big enough for the two of you . . . I suggest you begin the work of enlarging it."

She turned and walked briskly toward the inn.

"How long?" Gideon caught up and grabbed her by the elbow. "How long will it take, this building scheme?"

She looked skyward for the answer. "I don't know . . . two months?"

"Two months."

"Give or take."

"Very well, then," he said through his teeth. "Because I know this is important to you, I'll give you two months. See that Ashworth is gone at the end of them. Or it's God's truth, Meredith . . ." His eyes went gunmetal gray. "I'll kill him."

He turned on his heel and stalked off to the stables, leaving her with nothing but a cold certainty that he meant that threat. At the horse barn door, he stopped for a moment before disappearing inside. "Two months."

Rhys came to stand beside her, laying a hand to the small of her back. "Well, glad to know that's all settled. Good. He'll be here for the wedding."

"What?" Meredith was seriously beginning to wonder if he hadn't taken a grenade to the head during his time on the Peninsula.

"Two months. That's what Myles said, wasn't it? We'll be married in two months. Next month will be the second reading of the banns, and then a month after that, the third. We can be married that very Sunday."

She gaped at him. "For the tenth time, I haven't agreed to marry you. And didn't you hear Gideon just now? He will kill you."

He made a derisive sound. "He might *try*."

"You're impossible."

"So you've told me."

"And . . . and infuriating!"

"Don't forget indestructible. And here's something else. I'm your future husband." He cast a glance around the crowded courtyard. "All of Buckleigh-in-the-Moor knows it now, so you might as well get used to the idea. In the meantime, I'll do my best with the romance."

He lifted her hand and brought it to his lips, pressing a warm kiss to her knuckles. And despite all her attempts to keep a disapproving expression on her face, below the neck she melted to mist.

"I don't want to be wooed," she said feebly. And completely unconvincingly, even to her own hearing. "Go away, damn you."

"Oh, I'll go." He backed away, grinning ear to ear. "I'll go. But I'll be back. With flowers."

Chapter Twelve

After three weeks of camping on the moor, Rhys had learned to enjoy the solitude at night.

In the army, there had always been men about. Even though officers slept in tents, he could always feel the bodies crushed around it, hear the noises of men snoring, coughing, frigging themselves to sleep. Truthfully, it hadn't bothered him. The alternative was to be left alone with his memories, and those were far less pleasant than any rude sounds created by men or war.

But now he kept vigil with something other than memories of the past: plans for the future. And as such, Rhys didn't mind being left alone at all.

There were still sounds enough to fill the night. The soft howl of the wind, the screeches of ravens and owls, the strangled hiss of the peat fire. Once asleep, he probably added his own nightmare-induced cries to the chorus, but here was another benefit of isolation: There was no one around to hear.

He and the men had completed two rises on the cottage now. The walls stood two feet thick and five feet high, so far. They formed a solid box with no entrance or window. The holes for doors and window glass would be sawed once the house was complete. After they laid the next rise, Rhys wouldn't be able to vault in and out of the structure any longer. He'd have to get a ladder, he supposed, or make his bed on the ground nearby.

But for now, he slept inside his house. Tonight he lay face-up on his pallet of blankets, staring at the four earthen walls rising up around him and the empty gray sky overhead. It was one of those strange, misty nights where a thin fog trapped the moonlight close to the earth, but no stars shone through.

To others, he supposed the unfinished cottage might resemble some sort of mausoleum, but Rhys had never felt more alive. He could scarcely sleep at night for the plans tumbling through his mind. Plans for cottage furnishings and plans for the new stables, and some disconnected wonderings about whether the Duke of Morland would sell him a mare suitable for breeding with Osiris. And all sorts of plans for Meredith.

Which parts of her body he'd like to stroke, and which to kiss. Which parts might respond more favorably to a lick . . .

Just as that pleasant image was carrying him off to sleep, Rhys was startled awake by a loud sound. A new sound.

There it was again. A noise like rocks clacking together, or the scraping of chain. Too clumsy to be the work of any nocturnal creature.

He rose from his pallet and strode over to the corner where he'd left an old crate. Planting one boot on the crate, he grasped the top of the wall with his hands and vaulted up to sit on the packed-earth wall. He scanned the darkness. Nothing caught his eye, but the sound reached his ears again. This time, more like a distant bang. And was that an inhuman howl, or a trick of the wind?

Finally, he turned toward the hillside and looked up to the rise where the ruins of Nethermoor Hall could still be glimpsed, presiding over the gloom. A strange wisp of white light came into view, bobbing briefly on the crest of the hill before it disappeared again.

With a rough grunt, Rhys shoved himself off the wall. His boots punched the ground, and he hit the trail a moment after. Most likely, he'd find nothing but wind and mist, or perhaps some bats making mischief. But he knew he wouldn't be able to sleep until he'd investigated.

His long strides ate up the rocky slope, and soon he'd reached the top of the rise. His view of the ruins was unobstructed now—at least, not obstructed by rocks anymore. A frothy mist still swirled about the place, weaving through the arches and spiraling up the lone remaining chimney.

"Hullo!" he called out as he reached the edge of the burnt-out hall. "Someone there?"

No answer. Not that he'd been expecting one.

And there it was again—the light. Darting and dancing in the mist, like a mischievous little piskie. That sight would have been enough to send most moorfolk fleeing for their snug thatched-roof huts. Local legend told of many an unsuspecting fellow being "piskie-led" into danger.

But Rhys didn't believe in piskies or ghosts. If anything was playing tricks on him, it was just the fog. Or perhaps his memory. A lot of bad memories lived here.

Crouching, he threaded his body through the remains of a window and entered the ruin. Despite the glow of the moonlight, he wished he'd brought a torch. It was darker here, inside the old walls. As though the stones sucked all the moonlight into themselves and devoured it.

Intrigued by another flash of light, he entered a mostly intact corridor. He searched his mind in vain for any memory of this place—it was long and narrow, with no doors opening off it, save the two on either end. Most likely it had connected the main house with the servant quarters. He'd never wandered there, never been friendly with the servants. With the exception of George Lane, he'd spoken to the servants as little as possible, save the occasional churlish word when absolutely necessary. If they didn't know him, or didn't like him, his boyhood logic had argued, they wouldn't ask inconvenient questions or try to interfere.

Suddenly the wind picked up, gusting through the narrow tunnel with an almost human scream. Rhys picked up his pace, spurred by the wind's icy bite on his neck.

He stumbled a little on a bit of rock, and he swore. Why was he letting this place spook him? After all, wasn't *his* the spirit supposedly haunting the place? He should find nothing here to scare him, not anymore.

But against all reason, his head began to spin. He put a hand against the wall to steady himself, closing his eyes to the dark.

The more the wind blew and echoed through that corridor, the higher his hair raised along his scalp. He heard the echoes of his father's shouts, his mother's keening wail, his own startled cries. And those horses . . . God, the screaming horses. Nausea churned in his gut.

Enough of this. Enough. Mysterious piskie lights be damned.

Rhys turned on his booted heel and started back down the corridor the way he'd come. At some point his determined stride became a jog. He tripped over the same damn stone he'd stumbled over before, this time sprawling to the ground. His knee skidded on gravel, and grit dug under his fingernails.

Stand, the voice inside him said. *On your feet, brat.*

Just like always, he obeyed, scrambling to his feet and running for the entrance of the corridor. Only when he reached open air did he let himself slow. He stood doubled over, hands braced on his knees, drinking great lungfuls of moorland mist. Why had he ever returned to this cursed place?

A loud clanging behind him made him jump.

"Who is it?" he demanded, whirling around. "Who's there?"

No answer. No lights. No more wind, it seemed.

Just a sudden, sharp blow to the back of his head.

The night suddenly had stars.

And the old bastard kept after him, even as he slumped to the rocky ground. *Up. Get up. Stand and take another, you sniveling son of a whore.*

As he spun into unconsciousness, the voice mercifully faded. And even the stars behind his eyelids went dark.

The Three Hounds was enjoying another profitable night. Meredith smiled with satisfaction at the sight of the packed public room. The men had finished the second rise on the inn's new wing today, Rhys had paid out the weekly wages, and tomorrow was Sunday, a day of rest. All were in good spirits. And with Cora behind the bar, the spirits were flowing freely.

As for Cora herself, she was laughing at something one of the men said. Her back was to Meredith, and the room was too noisy to hear, but those blond ringlets dangling from her upsweep shook merrily.

All good, all good. Meredith was very pleased with how Cora's employment was working out. The girl was a bit childlike and dreamy, perhaps. But she'd revealed herself to have a surprisingly good head for sums and a cheerful, friendly manner with the travelers.

And of course, she had a way with the men.

Cora possessed a soft, feminine allure that acted like a lodestone for every pair of bollocks in the vicinity. Even Meredith found herself captivated, trying to understand just what it was about the girl. It wasn't simply her pretty face. No, it was that air of wonderment she carried. She received every word a man spoke as *the* most fascinating bit of information imparted to humankind since the Ten Commandments, greeting the news with wide, round eyes and those slender bronze arches above them, and—most importantly—that breathy, feminine coo of interest.

It was a talent, that. One Meredith had never mastered. And Cora seemed happy to discover that this talent had more honest applications than whoring.

A few reedy strains of music wafted over the din. As she made her way to the bar, Meredith spied Darryl in the corner, sawing away at his fiddle with more enthusiasm than skill.

Music, friendship, merriment, drink, flirtation—the Three Hounds was a nightly party of late. The community spirit pleased Meredith greatly, as did the influx of coin. The only thing missing from the scene was Rhys.

True to his words after church three weeks ago, Rhys had indeed been wooing her. In his own gruff, rough-hewn way. Though by night he camped out at the cottage site, he came down to the inn for dinner every evening, always bringing her some small treasure from the moor. Wildflowers were hard to come by in September, but somehow he'd conjured up a few. Other days he'd brought a sleek raven's feather, or a polished stone from the stream. Once, during the turning of earth for cob, he'd found an odd little bronze clasp that looked worn by centuries. From the Romans' time, they'd decided as they hunched over it in the light, turning it this way and that. If not earlier.

And then one night he'd come in late, well after dark, plainly exhausted from a long day of labor. He'd grasped her by the shoulders and pressed a warm, firm kiss to her forehead.

"Sorry," he'd said. "That's all I have today."

That kiss had been her favorite gift of all.

And oh, how it made her yearn for more. But for all that his hard work and sweet gestures were chipping away at her own reluctance, she'd yet to make a dent in his. No matter how she tempted him, directly or indirectly, after his dinner he always left and retreated to the high moor. It disappointed her, and not only because she'd much rather have him sleeping in her bed. Rhys was missing out on all this nightly camaraderie. He would never truly become a part of the village and be accepted by the locals if he didn't mingle with them outside of work. Give them a chance to take his measure, not just his coin.

Was he even giving her that chance? Even in their private conversations, Meredith realized, he always encouraged her to do most of the talking. It was only just becoming clear to her that for all she knew *about* him, Rhys was a difficult man to truly know. What was it he'd said?

Like a damned boulder.

She'd yet to find his cracks.

"How are you faring?" she asked Cora as she reached the bar. "Why don't you go have a cup of tea in the kitchen? I'll do the serving for a bit."

"Are you sure?" Cora blew a stray hair from her face. "Shall I make enough for you, too?"

Meredith shook her head. "No, but my father might like a spot of tea brought up to his room. And a slice of buttered toast, perhaps."

"I'll be glad to, Mrs. Maddox."

Someone opened the door, and a cool burst of wind swept through. Meredith thought, not for the first time that evening, about Rhys sleeping out alone on the barren moor. Was he cold? Was he hungry? Was he safe? She couldn't help but worry about him.

"Oh, Lord," Cora muttered. "It's *him.*"

A cheer rose up from the assembly. Meredith glimpsed Gideon by the entrance as the crowd parted around him. True to his word, he hadn't interfered with the construction plans—he'd even helped on occasion, hauling wagonloads of lumber and straw, along with increased amounts of ale and foodstuffs to keep the workers fed. But Meredith suspected his increased presence in the neighborhood was mostly selfish in motivation. Gideon wanted to keep a watchful eye on his smuggled goods and his enemy.

Tonight, however, he appeared to be here to have fun. Wearing a devil-may-care grin, he worked the crowd with his usual charm.

"Don't you like Mr. Myles?" she asked Cora.

"Doesn't matter what I think of him. I can tell he doesn't like me." She wiped her hands on her apron. "Struts around, orders me about."

"You, girl," Gideon called from across the room. "Look lively and pour me a brandy."

"See?" Cora whispered. "And the way he stares at me . . ."

"They all stare at you."

"Not like he does. I think he knows what I was. You know, before."

Meredith bit her lip, wishing she'd never said anything to Gideon about Cora's past. "Trust me," she soothed, "it's not that he doesn't like you. He likes you too much, that's all. You have the poor man turned arse over ears, and he's scrabbling to pretend he's still in control."

Gideon approached the bar, eyeing Cora with a lustful gaze.

"What brings you in tonight?" Meredith asked.

"For one cause and another, I feel like celebrating." His eyes never left the barmaid. "Thought I ordered a brandy."

"I'll pour it for you," Meredith interjected. "Cora was just going off for her break."

"Oh, was she now?" His jaw slid back and forth, as though he were chewing on a decision. "In that case . . ."

He turned, went to the largest table in the center of the room, and upended it with a spectacular crash. Meredith gasped, and Cora gave a little shriek. The men who'd been huddled on stools around it all leapt to their feet. Of course, this being Gideon, they didn't argue back. But no one in the tavern—Meredith included— knew what the devil he meant to do.

Gideon shoved the now-vertical table to the far edge of the room, kicking the vacated stools to the sides as he went. Then he strode back to the bar. His boots echoed off the flagstones with each swaggering step. Meredith had known the man from childhood, but she'd never seen such determination in his eyes, nor such raw, open yearning.

"If Miss Dunn isn't tending the bar"—in an explosion of agile strength, he vaulted the countertop and slid over to their side, landing between Meredith and Cora—"then she's free to dance." He swept her into his arms.

"Oh, *la*." Cora's cheeks blazed red.

Well, Meredith thought to herself. Wasn't it romance the girl had been wanting?

"Tewkes!" Gideon called, his eyes never leaving Cora's face.

In the corner, Darryl startled. "Aye, Mr. Myles?"

"That fiddle you're holding. Play it."

And play it he did, lurching into a wild reel of dubious melody.

"Now, then. Let's see if you can keep step." With a wide grin of encouragement, Gideon danced Cora right out from behind the bar and into the space he'd cleared at the center of the room.

The men crowding the perimeter roared their approval, hiding their envy with varying degrees of success. Meredith knew they were probably all wondering why they hadn't come up with the idea themselves. Because they weren't Gideon, of course. And even if they had thought of it, none of them were so ingenious, so crafty, or so devilishly arrogant as to try.

Gideon and Cora hadn't made but a few sweeping twirls of the room, however, before the men's collective intelligence drew a new conclusion. Cora might be taken as a partner, but there was one other woman in the room.

Several pairs of ale-merry eyes turned on Meredith at once.

"Oh, no," she laughed as Skinner came toward her, his huge mitts outstretched. "No, I don't dance."

But Gideon's outlandish display had emboldened them all. Despite her protests, Meredith found herself swept out from behind the bar and spun from partner to partner as Darryl's frantic fiddling went on. The faster they turned her, the more gaily she laughed. In the center, Cora looked similarly flushed and breathless with enjoyment. Those who weren't dancing clapped and stomped. Meredith began to fear the uproar would bring down the roof.

But then, Darryl's fiddling died a quick, mournful death, and a fresh gust of night wind froze them all in place.

Rhys stood in the tavern door. Meredith briefly wondered if the man was capable of making anything other than a dramatic entrance. Was it his sheer size, or the intensity he exuded? It certainly wasn't her imagination. Everyone in the room was transfixed.

Meredith rejoiced. His timing couldn't have been better. Rhys could join the party, socialize with villagers, and perhaps even smooth things over with Gideon. Thanks to Cora, the smuggler was in good spirits tonight.

"Good evening, my lord." Though everyone else in the room remained frozen, Meredith put out her hand and crooked her finger in invitation. "Come dance with me?"

"Another time perhaps."

He staggered in from the night, wearing a strange expression on his face. His complexion was unnaturally pale. He looked just like the living phantom of Darryl's stories.

With one hand pressed to the back of his head, he reeled to a halt. His glassy eyes shifted from Meredith to Cora and back. "Are either of you ladies handy with a needle?"

"Why?" Meredith asked.

"I've something that needs stitching up." He pulled his hand from his head. In it, he grasped a wad of torn fabric, soaked through with blood.

At the sight, Cora shrieked. Gideon slipped a protective arm about her waist.

Rhys just stared at the bloodied rag for a moment, blinking.

Meredith started toward him. She knew that expression. Any tavernkeeper would.

He was going down, hard.

And before she could reach him, he did. His eyes rolled back in his head, and he slumped to the floor, landing with a thud that rattled the candlesticks.

Chapter Thirteen

When Rhys came to for the second time that evening, he found himself slumped over a chair. The chair was backward. His legs straddled the seat, and his bare chest rested against the back.

Another moment, and he'd recognized his surroundings as the kitchen of the Three Hounds. He looked down to see two of the eponymous animals curled at his feet.

He blinked, and they became four.

"Ah."

The dogs' ears twitched at his low cry of pain. All eight of them.

Someone was digging a needle into his scalp. His eyes told him it couldn't be Meredith, because two of her were currently adding peat to the fire.

The heat from the blaze swam before his eyes and warmed his bones, but the smoke made him gag. Rhys swallowed hard. The last thing he wanted was to retch in front of her.

"Oh, Rhys. Thank God you're awake," she said, noticing his next wince of pain. She took a cup from the table and waved it under his nose. "Local gin? Cures all ills."

At the smell, his stomach clenched. He declined with

a careful shake of his head. "Just a drop of water, if you would."

She offered him a battered tin cup, and he managed to take it in one shaking hand and lift it to his lips. "Sorry I interrupted the party."

Meredith pulled up a stool and sat next to him. "You gave us a fright. What happened?"

"Thought I saw a light up at the ruins. I went up to investigate."

"Alone? Unarmed?"

He nodded and took another sip.

"And . . . what did you find?"

Was it a trick of his bashed-in brain, or did he discern a strange note in her voice? As though she already had in mind the answer to her question.

A jab to his scalp sent the thought right out of his head.

"Just one more, my lord." Cora's voice, thin with concentration. "Hold very still, if you please."

Rhys gritted his teeth against the pain. He'd known enough pain in his life that it was sort of like crossing paths with an old acquaintance in the road. The hurt came, he acknowledged it with a jerk of his head, and then they parted ways. "Found nothing but shadows, and caught a rock to the head for my trouble."

"Did you see who did it?"

He laughed a little. Only a little, because laughing hurt like the devil. "Can a man see the wind? Could I grab hold of the mist? A gust of wind must have knocked a stone free. Those old walls are crumbling more with every gale."

"Are you certain there wasn't someone there? Someone purposely trying to harm you?"

"And who would that be?"

"I don't know," she said, avoiding his gaze. Her lips

quirked. "A ghost, perhaps? The moorfolk have their suspicions, you know."

"Yes, and Gideon Myles has a passionate wish to see me dead. I know that's what you're thinking."

Meredith circled behind him. "You do have a nice hand with stitching," she told Cora.

With a hint of pride in her voice, Cora replied, "My mum was a seamstress."

"The bleeding's stopped. Well done. Cora, you may go close up the tavern."

"Yes, Mrs. Maddox."

Once Cora had left, Rhys heard the trickle of water. Then he felt a cool cloth pressed to his aching pate. Her fingers teased through the hair at his brow, creating ripples of sweet pleasure to counteract the pain.

"Why do you keep your hair cut so short?" she asked. "You used to wear it long."

"Started shearing it close in the army. Because of the lice. Now I'm just used to it."

"Oh." Her fingers stilled. "Well, it made Cora's work easier tonight. No amount of stitching could save your shirt, though. Went straight into the fire." She removed the damp cloth and applied a fresh one. "When did this happen? Gideon came in tonight just a short while before you did, and he was in an unusually good mood. That is, until you stumbled through that door. He seems to have disappeared now."

"I don't know how long I was unconscious. Could have been seconds, could have been hours. But I doubt Myles had anything to do with it. If he'd been responsible for this"—he raised his hand and gingerly explored the wound—"something tells me he would have made more effort to finish the job. And I didn't see anyone. It was just an accident."

"I thought you don't believe in accidents."

Before he could argue, liquid fire tore across his scalp.

He yelped with pain. "What the devil was that?"

"Local gin. I told you, it cures all ills."

"Jesus. You might have given me warning at least."

She made a sound in her throat. "Oh, I'll give you a warning, Rhys St. Maur. Wind, fog, ghost, or man . . . it matters not. You shouldn't be sleeping out on the moor alone. It's not safe."

Rhys rested his chin on the back of the chair as the pain receded and the room came into sharper focus. He liked having her fuss over him, loved the concern in her voice. "I'd say you don't need to worry about me. But I rather enjoy it that you do."

"Of course I worry." She swabbed his neck and shoulders clean, then went to the washbasin and began to rinse her hands. "Just the same as I'd worry about Darryl or Cora or Father, or . . ."

"Really? Just the same as you'd worry about them?" He turned to face her and noticed that her hands were shaking as she washed. "Or do you worry about me differently?"

The soap slid from her grasp and landed in the basin with a splash. "Rhys . . ."

After a month of coming to understand Meredith Maddox, he knew better than to press the issue just now. He rose from his chair, slid a towel from its hook, and dried her hands himself. "You're trembling," he said. "Come sit close to the fire. Let me look after you for a bit."

"You're not fit to stand."

"I'm not fit for much of anything." He gave her his best stab at a cavalier grin. "Hasn't stopped me yet."

After seeing her seated by the fire, he took up the still-steaming kettle. "I see Cora's made tea." He poured her a cup.

She took the cup from his hand and lifted it to her lips. "I'd prefer the gin."

"I know you would. And I'd prefer you didn't drink quite so much of it."

Her eyes flashed at him over the teacup's rim.

"What?" he asked. "You're concerned for me. I'm not allowed to worry about you?"

She swallowed her mouthful of tea. "You should stay here tonight. With me."

God. He didn't think any part of his body could throb more forcefully than his wounded pate. But he was proven wrong.

With a rough sigh, he drew up a stool and sat across from her. "What are we to each other?"

She blinked at him. "You want to discuss the state of our relationship?"

He nodded.

"What sort of man enters this sort of conversation willingly?"

"A man who's tired of sleeping out on the moor alone." And not because he was worried about falling rocks or ghosts or Gideon Myles, but because he wanted her. He wanted her more than he'd wanted anything in his life, and he wasn't sure how much longer he could stay away.

"We're friends, Rhys. And I think I've made it clear that we could be . . . closer friends, whenever you wish."

"Closer friends," he repeated thoughtfully, reaching out to catch a loose strand of her hair. "How close?"

She set aside her tea, then inched forward on her chair. His heart began to pound, just from her nearness.

"Very close," she whispered, leaning in. Her lips brushed his. "Body to body." Another kiss. "Skin to skin."

He couldn't stop himself. He slid both hands to her waist and pulled her into his lap. She straddled his hips, locking her arms around his neck. Their mouths came together, open and willing and ready to meld into one.

And even though his eyes were closed, for a moment Rhys felt like his double vision had returned—because her hands were *everywhere*. There had to be more than two of them. He felt her grasping at his shoulders, cupping his face, clutching his neck. Not to be outdone, he cinched his arms around her and pulled her flush against his bare chest, anchoring her there with his forearms while his hands slid up to her hair.

Ah, her hair. So abundant, so soft. He thrust his hands in that thick, dark mane, sifting the strands through his fingers, and then grasping big handfuls close to her scalp and twisting, just a little, to repay her for that trick with the gin.

She moaned around his tongue. Bracing her hands on his shoulders, she rocked her hips.

And now it was his turn to moan.

She made a slow circle with her pelvis, grinding against his arousal. Much as he hated relinquishing his grip on her hair, he slid his hands to her hips and grabbed tight, dragging her over his hard length again. He needed this, he needed more of it . . . He just needed, so damn much. To feel good, for a change. To make her feel good, too.

He had a fresh head wound, and she'd been working hard from dawn to dusk and beyond—but all he could think of was getting under her skirt and working her all night long.

She writhed against him as they kissed, her motions increasingly frantic. He guided her hips with his hands, pressing her closer, increasing the friction, setting a firm, brisk rhythm.

Close friends, had she said? Well, Rhys was getting all kinds of close. And judging by the little mewling sounds she made in the back of her throat, so was she. Now it was just a race to the finish, and by God he wanted her to win. He wanted to give her pleasure even more desperately than he craved his own release. And he craved his own release more than he wanted air.

With a sudden gasp, she pulled back. "We can't, not here," she panted. "Let's go upstairs."

He sat stunned, open-mouthed, his lungs seizing and his loins painfully bereft of contact.

"Come along." She tugged at him.

After a moment, he released a curse and a sigh. Ten seconds ago, if she'd shoved aside her petticoats and hiked up her skirts, he would have buried himself in her warm, wet body without a moment's hesitation. But a few seconds of separation and the renewed pounding in his head, combined with the prospect of that long flight of stairs . . . There were just enough obstacles to his bounding lust that his tortoise-like intelligence managed to catch up. "It isn't enough."

"I know," she said. "I know. Too many clothes between us. Let's go upstairs." She kissed his neck.

His hands went to her shoulders. "No," he repeated, pushing her back. "It still won't be enough. Body to body, skin to skin. It's not enough. I don't want . . . friendship without clothing. I need a marriage."

She traced the line of his jaw. "Why must you always be thinking of the future? Just think of tonight."

Damn his eyes, how ironic. For so many years he'd never considered the future. Not once. In fact, he'd spent a great deal of effort and spilled a great deal of blood—his and others'—trying to ensure there wouldn't *be* a future, not for him. And now . . . now he had plans and desires, and a half-built cottage up on that slope. A future. He couldn't simply give that up, collapse it all to one fleeting night of pleasure with no promise of more.

"I *am* thinking of tonight." His voice was a low rasp. "I am thinking—in shameless detail—of taking you upstairs, stripping you bare, and doing unspeakable things to you all night long. Touching you everywhere. Tasting you everywhere. And I know, as sure as I know my own name, it still won't be enough. I will want you again tomorrow, and then the day after that, and again and again and again. That's why I need those vows. I need to hear you say you're mine forever before I have you at all. Because I know I will never, ever get enough."

She stared at him. A whole parade of emotions marched through those silvery eyes. Surprise, desire, vulnerability, disappointment . . . something he fancied might be genuine affection.

"How can you say such things to a woman and not take her directly to bed?" she asked. "It's cruel, I tell you. Cruel."

"It's a cruel, cruel world," he teased. In a serious tone, he added, "It's not only about bedding you, I hope you know. I want to take care of you. I can't bear to see you working so hard." He cast a glance around the humble kitchen. "Once we're married, I'll rescue you from all this."

"But I don't *want* to be rescued from all this. This is my life. I enjoy working here, just as you've enjoyed building that house." Her hand went to his wounded head. "If anyone needs rescuing, it's you. You're in danger here, the longer you stay."

"I keep telling you—"

"You keep telling me you're indestructible. And I'm telling *you*, I just scraped your unconscious body off the floor." Her hands laced behind his neck. "Don't go back to the moor alone. Stay with me tonight."

"I can't." He stood, setting her on her feet as he did. "I should be going."

He couldn't imagine staying under this roof without bedding her. And this night was *not* going to be their first night. Just as well. With his throbbing head, he wouldn't have been in top lovemaking form.

"It's all right out there," he assured her. "Just two more weeks, two more rises—and the walls will be done. The paring and timbers . . . another week, maybe. Then all it will need is some thatch and a few coats of limewash. Well, and window glass, doors, shutters. And furnishings. I'll be making some trips to Plymouth over the next few weeks, to place orders."

Calming, she made a slow circle of the room. "There are things I'll be needing for the new guest rooms, too." She smoothed her hair with her hands. "When you go, may I send a list with you?"

"I suppose."

She began ticking items off on her fingers. "Old Mr. Farrell will make me the furniture, but I'll be needing mattresses. And washbasins, chamber pots, fabric for bedding and curtains . . ."

"Wait, wait. I know nothing about fabrics."

"I know nothing about Plymouth. I've never been farther than Tavistock. And . . ." She bit her lip. "And I don't really know what a guest of quality expects, anyhow. I mean, I try to ask roundabout, when travelers come through. But you're a lord. You've traveled all over England and the Continent besides. You'll know far better than I how to select quality goods."

The idea struck him—so swift, so brilliant—his head ached with it. A smile pulled at his mouth as he massaged his pounding temple. "You'll have to come with me," he said.

"To Plymouth?"

"No, not to Plymouth. If you want guest rooms fit for

people of quality, you ought to go where they go, shop where they shop. You'll come with me to Bath."

Oh, it was so beautiful—that bright shimmer of excitement in her eyes, before her practical nature doused it.

"Are you mad? I can't go to Bath. It must be two days' journey in either direction."

"I'll hire a coach to drive us straight through. If we leave before dawn, we can manage it in one day."

"And what of the inn? Who'll take care of the inn?"

Rhys looked toward the bar. "Who's taking care of it right now? You said yourself Cora's doing well. Between her and Darryl and your father, they'll manage without you for a few days."

She crossed her arms. "We can't travel alone together. It's not proper."

"Who in this village is going to care? But if you're anxious about how it will look to strangers, we'll present ourselves as a married couple at the hotel. For appearances only."

"For appearances only?" She arched a brow.

"I'll be a perfect gentleman. You did want romance." Oh, yes. This was how he was going to get everything he wanted. Meredith's body and her troth. By giving her a taste of her future life as Lady Ashworth.

"A perfect gentleman? Truly?" She leaned one hip on the counter. "Do you really think you'll be able to spend all day with me in a private coach, then night after night in the same room, with one bed, and still resist temptation?"

He pretended to think on it. "No."

She shook her head and laughed.

"You'll come with me, then?" he asked.

"Yes. Yes, I'll come with you. Fool that I am. I'd like to see Bath once in my life."

"It's only the beginning," he told her. "There are so

many places we could travel together. We could see the country, Merry. The Continent too, if you like. There's a whole world out there to be discovered."

"Funny. There's a whole world out there. And the one place I'm interested in discovering with you is the underside of a bedsheet."

"I understand they have bedsheets in Bath."

She smiled. "One night, Rhys. Your perfect gentleman act won't last. You'll be sharing my bed before the night's out."

"I'm counting on it. Because I know your innkeeping aspirations won't survive a day beyond the borders of this village. Before the night's out, we'll be officially engaged."

There. The battle lines were drawn. They just stood there for a moment, gazing at each other and letting all that pent-up sensual excitement prickle over and around and between them, like electric fluid in a thundercloud.

"This is fun," he said.

"What is?"

"This." He gestured into the space between them. "Just this."

It *was* fun. It was near-unbearable, the tension between them, and possibly doing irreparable damage to his breeding organs. But it was also wonderful, and something he'd never experienced before. She wanted him, he wanted her, and the air around them just smoked with it. This was the force making him feel so alive, so driven, so directed toward a goal.

Because she *was* his future. And somewhere, deep down, despite all her protests, she knew it too.

With a dry smile and a mock salute, he turned to leave.

"Rhys?"

He stopped. An absurd hope bloomed in his chest,

that maybe she'd finally acknowledge it, give in. The trip to Bath could be their honeymoon.

"Take the hounds with you?" she asked. "I'll sleep better if I know you're not alone."

He nodded and whistled to the dogs. Not quite what he'd been hoping for, but he'd take it. For now.

Chapter Fourteen

"Oh, ma'am. It does look well on you. You'd hardly know it was a strumpet's gown."

"Are you sure?" Meredith fretted in the predawn darkness, twisting and turning before the mirror. This was the largest looking glass in the inn—the one adorning her finest guest room—and still she couldn't get a sufficiently reassuring view.

Proper-sized mirrors, she mentally added to her shopping list.

It had been two weeks since Rhys had issued the invitation to Bath. Why had she waited until the last possible moment to pack?

"The color's lovely," she said, running her hands over the ruby-red silk. Did genteel women truly wear such colors? "Are you absolutely certain I won't look like a whore? That wouldn't do at all." She threw Cora a guilty look. "That is . . . I beg your pardon, dear."

Cora smiled. "No need, Mrs. Maddox. I understand perfectly."

Did she? Well, in that case, Meredith wished the girl would enlighten *her*. For she scarcely understood herself at all. Here she was leaving tomorrow morning to travel alone with a gentleman for several days, with the express purpose of making love to him several times, and no intention to allow said activities to culminate in marriage. And she was concerned that a red dress might make her look the tart?

She tugged up on the neckline. "I need a fichu."

"I don't think so, ma'am. The cut is not so very low, and your . . ." The girl's voice died, and she cleared her throat.

"And I don't have so very much to put on display." Meredith smiled, patting her modest bosom. "Of course, you're right. And you've done a fine job with the fitting."

"There wasn't much to alter, save the hem. You and the owner had quite similar measurements."

"This wasn't your dress, then?"

"Oh, no. I never had anything half so fine."

"Then where did it come from?"

"When Mr. Bellamy had me staying at the Blue Turtle in Hounslow, there was a lord and his mistress stopping over. Well, the two of them had a noisy row right in the middle of the courtyard, in the wee hours of the morning. He'd cast her out into the cold, then flung her dresses out the window."

Cora shook her head. "That was the scene that made me realize I never wanted to be any man's whore again. The lady who owned these dresses, she had what all us girls wanted—a wealthy protector to buy her nice things and treat her well. And still, when he had no more use for her, he cast her out like rubbish. I didn't want that to ever be me."

A little smile curved Cora's lips. "Evidently, the fancy lady had too much pride to pick her garments out of the mud. She simply left them on the ground and ordered her carriage, and that was that. So I gathered them up, brushed out the dirt as best I could. I planned to make them over for myself someday, but they suit you better." She carefully folded a leaf-green muslin frock edged with ecru lace and laid it in Meredith's trunk. "There's this, too, for the daytime. And a traveling cloak."

Touched, Meredith caught the girl in a warm hug. "Thank you. You'll have the dresses back, I promise."

"Well, I did leave the excess inside the seams, just in case," Cora admitted, reaching to undo the row of tiny closures down the gown's back.

As Cora helped her change from the red silk gown into her plain, serviceable traveling habit, Meredith drilled the girl on all the details of minding the inn. Where to find the extra stores of Madeira if wealthy guests happened through, how to start watering down the drinks a good hour before closing, and where to find Skinner's mother if he had one of his bad nights.

"Don't be so anxious, ma'am," Cora said, packing away the silk gown. "With Mr. Lane and Darryl and Mrs. Ware all helping, we'll be fine."

Meredith wished she could tell her to call on Gideon Myles in an emergency, but she couldn't trust him anymore. They'd scarcely spoken two words in the weeks since Rhys's "accident" at the ruins. Much as Meredith hated to believe Gideon was responsible, it was the only explanation that fit.

As Rhys said, his attacker certainly could have finished the job, so clearly the incident had been meant as a warning. Not just a warning to Rhys, but a warning to *her*. Only a few weeks remained of the two months' grace Gideon had extended. The other night, she'd worried aloud to Rhys that Gideon might make good on his threat to kill him, if he didn't leave the village soon.

Rhys had only laughed, much to her dismay. He refused to see Gideon as a threat. While Meredith had no doubt that Rhys would come out the victor in a fair fight between the men, this wasn't an army skirmish or a boxing match. Gideon had time to bide, knowledge of the terrain, loyal men to assist him. The ambush at the ruins proved all too well that Rhys was not as indestructible as he claimed. As she knew from experience, she couldn't bear to stand helplessly by while he courted death.

There was a knock at the door just as Meredith finished tying the traveling cloak in front. Before she could even call, "Come in," her father entered.

"Father." She kissed his cheek. "You're up early."

" 'Course I am. Did you think I wouldn't see you off?" He patted her arm. "And I wanted to talk to you, just a minute, before you go."

She bit her lip, making a great effort not to openly cringe. She hoped he didn't mean to discuss the implications—moral or otherwise—of her traveling alone with Rhys. They'd never spoken of Maddox, not in any marital context at least, and though Meredith supposed her father must know she'd taken a few lovers since her husband's death, they'd mercifully never discussed that, either.

"I'll carry your valise down, Mrs. Maddox." With that, Cora left them alone.

"Let's sit," she said, guiding him to the bed.

He sat beside her on the edge of the mattress, using his arms to settle his weight. The worse of his crippled legs extended at an awkward angle. Since the fire, when his leg was crushed by the weight of a burning rafter, he'd never regained the ability to bend it properly at the knee. Her heart twisted in her chest. After so many years, she suspected he'd learned to ignore his injuries better than she had.

The old man's face was very grave. "Meredith . . ."

"I'll stay," she said, clasping his hand. "If you don't want me to go, only say the word, and I'll—"

"No, no." He gave a gravelly chuckle. "Go, child. Enjoy yourself. I wish I'd been able to do this for you, for your mother. You deserve a holiday far grander than this. What I wanted to say was just . . ." He squeezed her hand. "Rhys is a good man, Merry. He's had a hard time of it, but his heart is in the right place. Give him a chance."

"Oh, Father," she whispered. A bittersweet smile tugged the corners of her mouth. "Believe me, I'd like nothing better. It's Rhys who doesn't believe in chance." She squeezed his hand and whispered, "May I ask a favor?"

"Anything."

"If you happen to see Gideon while I'm gone, make this little speech to him."

"Are you ready to leave?" Rhys appeared in the doorway, dressed for travel.

Father stood and greeted him warmly. Meanwhile, Meredith took advantage of the diversion to discreetly swipe at her eyes. If Rhys did leave Buckleigh-in-the-Moor, her father would be so disappointed.

Between Rhys, Gideon, her father, the inn, the village—Meredith felt her loyalties stretched in too many directions of late. At night, she lay wrung out and restless in her bed, racking her mind for a solution. A way to keep everyone happy and secure. No answer had come to her yet.

Farewells were exchanged in the first gloom of dawn. Rhys handed her into the carriage, settling her on the front-facing seat. He spoke a few words to the coachman, heaved his weight onto the opposite bench, gave the carriage roof a smart rap . . . and then they were under way. The hounds yipped after them, chasing them all the way out of the village. Poor beasts, they'd probably miss Rhys far more than they'd miss her. They'd grown quite attached to him in recent weeks.

Meredith's stomach danced with every swaying motion of the coach, and excitement fizzed through her veins. She stretched her fingers inside her traveling gloves, and the seams chafed her work-roughened hands.

Here we go, she told herself, as the village's last thatched roof rolled past. *This is really happening.* She was truly departing Buckleigh-in-the-Moor, and not for a half-day's bartering in Tavistock, but for an indulgent stay in Bath. Best of all, she was going there with Rhys. She resolved to leave all her worries in the village, where they belonged, and simply enjoy these precious days. A giddy smile stretched her face, and she unglued her gaze from the small window in order to share it with him.

He was asleep. Arms folded, chin tucked to his chest. Boots propped possessively on her seat, but thoughtfully well clear of her skirts. The coach swung into a turn, and a low, soft snore rumbled from his chest.

She pressed her wrist to her mouth to keep from laughing.

Well, he was a soldier. She supposed he could nap anywhere. And since she knew his sleep to be all-too-often disturbed by unpleasant dreams, she didn't want to rob him of his well-earned rest. Not presently, anyhow. If she had anything to say about it, he'd be getting little sleep in Bath.

But for her part, Meredith could scarcely bring herself to blink. As dawn warmed the countryside, she kept her face pressed to the window glass, the better to greedily consume every detail. She'd never passed by this route before, and she might pass a lifetime without traveling it again.

After some time, the carriage lurched to a halt. Rhys woke with a start. His boots hit the carriage floor with a jarring thud.

"All's well," she assured him quickly. "I believe we're stopping to change horses."

He glanced out the window. "We're nearing Exeter. That's good. Shall we climb out and stretch?"

They walked a bit, away from the inn, strolling through the fringe of a wooded glen that bordered the lane. It amazed her, what a short distance they'd traveled and yet how many plants grew here that she did not know by name.

"We never talk about you," she said, taking his arm. And their opportunities to do so might be dwindling by the day.

"There's not much to discuss."

"But of course there is. You've traveled all over. What's the most beautiful place you've ever been?"

"Anywhere you are."

She blushed like a girl, despite herself. "This from the man who claims no talent for romance. No, be serious. I truly want to know. French mountain ranges? A Belgian cathedral? The open sea?"

"Tulips." He lifted his chin and stared hard into the thickening trees. The pause grew so lengthy, Meredith wondered whether he meant to say anything else. Perhaps he just had a particular fondness for tulips.

"A whole field of them," he finally said. "In Holland. Red tulips, in endless waves. And a clear blue sky overhead."

"Sounds lovely."

"It was." A dull note landed on the word *was*. Looking over his shoulder, he said, "I believe they have the new team harnessed."

And that was the end of that.

As the coach got under way a second time, he stacked his arms on his chest and propped his boots beside her, as though he would sleep again. But this time, she did not hesitate to interrupt.

"Tulips," she said. "So they're the most beautiful sight. What about the ugliest?"

He shook his head. "Even if I could decide between

the many contenders for that distinction . . . I'd never answer you that."

"Never? Why not?"

"Because you should never witness the hell of war. You shouldn't even hear about it secondhand. That's the whole reason we were fighting, to spare innocent people like you such ugliness. I'll be damned if I'll personally acquaint you with it now." He turned his head to the window. End of discussion.

She sighed, wishing he wouldn't close himself off to her. If he only knew how much of his pain she'd already witnessed.

"Thank you," she said.

"For what?"

"For your service. For fighting. I'd imagine you don't hear that enough." At least, he likely hadn't heard it from anyone in the village, including her. "Your regiment was England's most decorated, I understand."

"Who told you that?"

"I read it in the newspaper once." Or twice. Or several dozen times.

"I had the honor to serve with many good, valiant men."

"And you were one of those good, valiant men. You *led* them."

He shrugged. "I'm here. Far too many of them aren't."

She didn't dare admit it, but she knew every last ribbon and medal and citation he'd been awarded. They numbered almost as many as his scars. The thought that he'd incurred them all with the vague idea he'd be sparing her and others a bit of ugliness . . .

"I admire you," she said.

The poor man. He looked utterly panicked. As if she'd lobbed him a snarling weasel, rather than an honest compliment. Actually, he probably would have dealt with the weasel more handily.

"Truly, Rhys. I admire you. And I wish you'd allow yourself more credit for everything you've accomplished, instead of throwing it back on fate all the time." She gave him a sly smile. "And to that end, I think I'll honor you by hanging a plaque in the tavern, engraved with your name and rank. Our local war hero."

He just laughed and rubbed his eyes. "There are all kinds of courage in the world, and most of it takes place far from battlefields." His gaze caught hers, warm and honest. "That whole inn is a monument to your bravery, Meredith Lane Maddox. And I'm going to buy you every ribbon in Bath."

Oh. A lump formed in her throat. And her heart . . . her heart just melted. It meant so much, that he recognized the hard work and love she'd poured into that place.

"What is it?" He leaned forward until his knees knocked against hers. "What's troubling you?"

"I'm just a bit fatigued," she lied.

He crossed to sit beside her, putting an arm about her shoulder and drawing her head to his chest. She breathed deeply, enjoying his comforting male scent.

"There, now," he said. "Are you comfortable?"

She nodded.

"Then sleep. You've all day to rest."

They fell into an easy, companionable silence, which somehow spoke more eloquently than any of their conversations. Impulsively, she reached out to take his free hand in hers. Their fingers tangled. His thumb settled over her wrist, and her pulse pounded against it. She couldn't help but lean against him and snuggle into his warmth, under the guise of sleeping. But she was doing no such thing. She was wide awake, unwilling to miss a single moment. Scenery in entirely new shades of green was flitting by outside, and she might never have another chance to view it, but she couldn't be bothered to lift her cheek from his lapel. Instead, she closed her eyes, scrupulously memorizing each sensation he caused within her. Every yearning, every thrill, every ache.

This, too, was the experience of a lifetime.

Chapter Fifteen

❦

With dry roads in their favor, they reached Bath just as the late summer sun kissed the horizon. Rhys was well pleased with the fair weather, and with his fair companion.

Meredith remained pasted to the window as they drove through the city, eyes wide and lips parted. As though it were not enough to look her fill of the surrounding landscape—she must drink and breathe it, too.

He watched her as intently as she watched the scenery rolling past, smiling to himself all the while.

When they arrived at the hotel, he was forced to abandon the pleasant occupation of noting her every gasp of wonder and reluctant blink. After procuring the finest suite of rooms, as previously arranged, he directed the footmen to unload the valises. He reserved for himself the pleasure of handing Meredith down from the coach.

"Good heavens," she breathed, staring up at the hotel's Roman-styled façade, all Bath stone columns and carved balustrades.

"It gets even better inside."

She said not a word as a servant led them through the entrance hall, up a carpeted staircase, and down to the very end of the corridor. Rhys allowed her to pass through the door first, then followed her into the suite. The servants followed soon thereafter, and he exchanged a few words with them as they deposited the baggage.

Once they'd left, he turned to Meredith. There she stood in the center of the sitting room, a smudge of gray wool and dark hair against the cream-colored walls and carpet. She just remained there, perfectly still, hands clasped and eyes wide. Silent.

Rhys frowned. Her amazement had been entertaining to view earlier, but this continued silence was beginning to concern him. "Merry? Are you well?"

She shook her head. "I may cry."

He hesitated. "Is that good or bad?"

"It's terrible." She swallowed hard, then pressed both hands to her cheeks as she tilted her neck to view the elaborate carved ceiling.

He took a step toward her. "Is there something wrong with the rooms?"

"Oh, no," she said. "Nothing. That's the problem."

Now he was thoroughly confused.

She finally took pity on him and explained. "Rhys, this suite is . . . stunning. Elegant. Palatial. It's enough to throw me into abject despair. If these are the sort of accommodations to which people of rank are accustomed, how can I ever hope to appease them at the Three Hounds? Why, one of the inn's new bedchambers would likely fit in that closet!"

"That's not true."

"That's not the point." Sniffing, she turned to him. "Just look at this place. How can the inn ever hope to compete with establishments such as these?"

So. The superior quality of the place had her upset, not some deficiency. Smiling with relief, he crossed to her side and slid an arm around her shoulders. "Don't you worry. You're not competing with establishments like this one. This is one of the grandest hotels in all England. A resort for the country's wealthiest lords and ladies. The Three Hounds is a coaching inn. Even the nobility have modest expectations when it comes to coaching inns."

"Ah," she said. "I see. So I still have some hope of meeting those 'modest expectations'?"

Tsking softly, he squeezed her shoulder. "You're already exceeding them." When her shoulder muscles remained tense under his fingers, he added, "I've ordered a hot bath and a hot meal sent up. I know you find this suite devastating in its refinement, but try not to fling yourself off the balcony."

She laughed and brightened instantly. "I'm sorry. I know I'm being ridiculous." Turning in his embrace, she kissed his cheek. "Thank you. It's simply magnificent."

"Well, that's better." He released her, giving her an affectionate pat on the backside, and she immediately left his side to begin a closer inspection of a decorative alcove.

"Should I call for a servant to help you unpack?" he asked, crossing to their baggage where it sat by a large wardrobe. "Or do you trust me to play lady's maid?"

"As you like," she muttered distractedly, craning her neck to peer atop a high shelf and testing its cleanliness with her fingertip.

Rhys doubted she'd heard a word he'd said, but he took it upon himself to unpack the valises. The army had given him years of experience in packing and unpacking quickly. After shrugging out of his greatcoat, he set to work. He shook out and refolded their inner garments, then hung his coats next to her gowns. Of course, he had separate closets planned for the cottage, but he had to admit—he liked seeing their clothing mingled in the same wardrobe, her stockings nestled next to his cravats. It looked right, and—if a hulking brute of man like him could say such a thing—it looked sweet.

It also aroused him something fierce.

As he worked, Meredith made a slow circuit of the sitting room. She stopped to peer at each small object, inspected each stick of furniture and decorative detail. He could sense her making mental notes, storing up ideas and inspiration to bring home to the Three Hounds.

"I could never hang velvet drapes at the inn," she lamented, fingering the edge of one dark blue curtain. "The dust would be horrible." Her head tilted. "But I do like the way they've hung these draperies near the ceiling and let them fall almost to the ground. Makes the window appear larger than it is. I'll have to remember that."

Chewing her lip with concentration, she wandered off into the bedchamber.

Rhys sighed. When was she going to realize that a return to innkeeping wasn't in her future? With an impatient yank, he dragged a pale, gauzy shift free of her valise. He wished she would cease paying so much attention to the furnishings and spare a thought for him.

"Oh!"

Her exclamation of surprise tugged him across the room. From the arch separating sitting room and bedchamber, he spied her at the side of the bed.

The *enormous* bed. The carved mahogany posts were hung with rich draping, and the bed itself was a billowing cloud of snow-white pillows and counterpanes.

"Oh, my," she said. "What a bed. I've never seen its like." Placing both hands flat on the mattress, she leaned forward, testing its softness and give. As she bounced her arms up and down, her bosom and backside teetered cheekily, as if in invitation.

Rhys's hands fisted in the tissue-thin muslin, wrinkling it irrevocably. He cleared his throat. "Yes."

She turned and looked at him. Her dark eyebrows rose, as though she expected him to go on.

He didn't have a damn thing else to say. The only word in his brain was *yes*. *Yes, yes, yes*.

Well, and perhaps the word *now*.

She knew it, too. Those slender brows arched with amusement. "Yes," she said, hiking her heavy traveling skirt and lifting one hip onto the mattress. "It is indeed a remarkable bed."

Transferring her weight to that hip perched on the edge of the bed, she slowly reclined sideways, stretching out her arm as she did. It was a slow, sinuous motion, like that of a cat stretching into a patch of sun. Propping herself on an elbow, she made her body one long, dark ribbon of femininity unfurled atop the fringed white cushions.

At last. Now he had her complete, undivided attention.

His heart battered his ribs, threatening to splinter apart the old, imperfectly healed bones. Other parts of him stiffened to iron.

She gave him a coy, seductive smile. "Won't you join me?"

Rhys's mouth went dry. Despite all his intentions to wait, to tease, to ply her with ruthless, exquisite temptation, and finally seduce her into a formal engagement . . . they'd been here five minutes and he was the one with *yes* on his lips. *Yes, yes, yes*. He could not have said anything else.

"It's useless to resist," she said in a sultry voice, picking open the top button of her jacket. "We both know you'll give in." She hooked her finger under the second button and gave it a playful tug. "I'm a woman, Rhys.

When it comes to the bedroom, my will is stronger than yours."

He laughed a little. But the words gave him pause.

On instinct, he should have dismissed the idea out of hand. No one's will was stronger than his. That was why he'd survived so many fights. Hadn't he spent eleven years in the infantry, always charging into the first wave of blood, hoping to meet a stronger opponent? The man who would knock him to the ground and finally end it all, at last?

It had never happened.

Until now. And it wasn't a man threatening to vanquish him with sabre or musket, but a woman. A woman with curves of satin and a spine of pure steel. *Give in,* she said. *My will is stronger than yours.*

On this point, he suspected she was right. His resolve was quickly softening, even as his groin went rock-hard. Wasn't this precisely what he'd spent a lifetime chasing? Sweet, blessed defeat?

And to find it on such a lush, silky field of battle . . .

Destiny whispered in his ear. She was beautiful, and she was his for the taking. Whether it happened today or next year, this was fated to be.

He would have her. Today. Yes.

Yes, yes, yes. And *now.*

With a deep, resonant sigh, he stepped toward her.

Her expression changed quickly, from one of seduction to one of surprise. Despite her teasing, she hadn't expected him to give in.

He stopped. He hadn't expected her to be surprised.

Tenderness warmed her eyes. In a generous, fluid motion, she reached out a hand and beckoned. "Oh, Rhys," she whispered. The words were so soft they might have been a caress. "Come here."

A sharp rap at the door halted him mid-step.

God damn it. Fate was playing cruel games with him tonight.

"That'll be our dinner," he said. He muttered to himself, "Blast it."

"Our dinner. And our bath?" She rose to a sitting position.

Our bath. Well, there was a happier thought.

Rhys twisted the muslin in his hands, wondering which would be worse—answering the door with a wad of frilly muslin in front of his groin? Or greeting the servants with an obvious erection?

Smiling at his predicament, Meredith saved him by answering the door herself. Rhys took his turn studying the draperies as a parade of maids bearing steaming pitchers marched through the suite, each adding her cargo to the rapidly filling tub. He pretended to admire the view of the park as a manservant wheeled a small table into the sitting room, whisking away silver dome after silver dome to reveal a feast.

"Thank you, that will be all." Meredith's voice. And then the soft snick of the door.

Releasing his breath, Rhys turned to her. Grinning sheepishly, he held up the abused, twisted night rail for her inspection before tossing it aside. "You won't be needing it anyway."

Her breath caught. "I won't?"

"No."

"Good." She took a deep breath. "So, how do we proceed? Do we eat first? Bathe?" Sparkling eyes met his. "Neither?"

"Dinner first," he said, drawing two chairs up to the table. "Then bath. Once I have you in bed, I'm keeping you there."

"Oh, I like the sound of that." Her cheeks pinked as she settled into her chair and raised a glass of wine. "Shall we have a toast?"

He raised his own claret. "To the lovely Mrs. St. Maur, Lady Ashworth. And to a most enjoyable honeymoon."

She giggled. "Be serious, Rhys."

"I am perfectly serious." He waited for her defensive laughter to cease. "As far as society's concerned, you're here in this room as my wife. And as far as I'm concerned, this night is the beginning of forever."

She made a strange sound in her throat as she studied her wine. At length, she put it down. The glass met the table's surface with a clink.

"Meredith, what is the matter?"

She picked up her knife and fork and began to eat.

"I mean it," he insisted. "Tell me."

"I don't know, it's just . . . I'm *not* your wife."

"You will be." He jabbed at a hunk of beef, and his fork screeched across the plate. "Listen, Meredith. Life's made you cautious, I know. And I know I was gone for fourteen years and I've only been back for a matter of weeks. Some reluctance is understandable, and I've been prepared to wait it out. But surely by now you have to know I'm not just some randy traveler passing through the inn."

"I do know that." She chased a pea around her plate.

"Do you? I've had the banns read, twice, in front of the whole village. Threats, vandals, rocks to the head— I've endured all of these in recent weeks, and none of them have shaken my plans to rebuild Nethermoor, nor my belief that we're meant to marry. But you still don't trust me on this."

"On what? Marriage?" She raised her eyebrows and her voice. "You don't trust me on the subject either. If you did, you'd offer me a real choice in the matter. I don't recall ever being *asked* if I'd like to marry you, simply told that it's inevitable. Instead of a proposal, I get . . . autocratic commands and prophetic pronounce-ments. Where's the trust in that?"

Rhys shook his head. "Eat," he told her. "The bath-water's going cool."

"You're right. Let's not argue." She gave him a self-effacing smile. "We'll laugh about this in the morning."

He frowned. Was that what she thought? That every-thing would change by the morning? Maybe this was the source of her reluctance. She thought that his determina-tion to marry her would disappear once he'd purged the lust from his system.

Well. He'd simply have to prove to her that those fears were groundless. And the way to do so was to make love to her tonight, make it very, very good, and show her none of his intentions had changed the next morning.

Not exactly a chore, that.

He ate quickly, as always. When he looked up from his plate, he found her watching him, circling the rim of her wineglass with a fingertip.

"Are you finished?" he asked, wiping his mouth with a linen napkin.

"Oh, yes." She rose from her seat.

"Now, can we make the bath just as speedy as the meal?"

"If we bathe together, we can."

Rhys rather liked that suggestion. Parts of him liked it very well indeed.

He ushered her over to the bathing area, where she spent a good minute cooing over the glazed ceramic tiles and painted washbasin while she removed her hairpins at the vanity.

While her attention was diverted, Rhys took the op-portunity to quickly and discreetly undress. No matter how many times she assured him she wasn't repulsed by his scars, that she found his body—against all reason—

attractive, he still felt apprehensive about revealing *all* of himself. She'd seen him shirtless, but full nudity was another thing altogether. Between the lamps and the mirrors and the glittering white tile, there was simply too much light bouncing around, eager to illuminate his every flaw and imperfection.

And his body had a great many flaws and imperfections.

Once bared, he crossed the room silently and moved to stand behind her at the vanity. There was a mirror there, and she didn't startle. She must have watched him approach. Placing his hands on her shoulders, he pivoted her away from the mirror, not wanting to see his own damaged face staring back at him. She leaned back against him, settling her weight against his bare chest.

Rhys sucked in his breath. He reached his arms around her, and with stiff, clumsy fingers, he yanked at the closures of her traveling jacket.

Sighing, she leaned forward and lowered her arms so he could shake the jacket free. He cast it aside and started on the buttons of her crisp, high-necked chemisette. Her breathing came more quickly now. His fingers worked lower, and lower still, and her breasts rose and fell. As though they were as eager to be displayed as he was to view them.

When he'd eased the last tiny button free, he drew the halves of her chemisette to the sides, baring her creamy neck and chest, her small breasts covered by the frailest layer of muslin and supported by tightly laced stays. The dark valley between her breasts held secrets and suggestions.

"Lovely," he breathed, moving his hands to the small of her back so he could loosen the knot of her laces. He'd wanted to do this for so long. So many nights he'd lain awake dreaming of it—first on the rocky ground, then on the stony plinth, at last on the wood-planked floor. Every night, he'd tried to ignore the uncomfortable surface beneath his weary bones by filling his mind with thoughts of her. The gentle curves of her body, the exquisite softness of her skin.

And here she stood before him, half bared and fully willing, and he couldn't work the damn knot. It wasn't the tightness of the tapes or the limitations of his mangled hands. He was nervous as hell. Unable to make his fingers work, yet impatient to taste her, he bent his head and kissed the side of her throat.

She gasped, letting her head roll to the side.

Taking what she offered, he kissed his way up the elongated slope of her neck. Licking and nibbling at her delicate skin, suckling the tiny pearl of her unadorned earlobe.

"Oh, Rhys," she sighed, tilting her head back.

The way she moaned for him . . . it made his blood catch fire.

"Oh my God," she said, craning her neck a bit more. "Just look at the scrollwork on that ceiling."

He froze. That was it. She'd just found the cure for his nerves.

"To hell with the damned ceiling," he growled, tugging angrily at the ends of her laces.

She gave a sharp intake of breath as he momentarily cinched them tight. The knot gave way to him this time, and the stays fell away from her body.

"To the devil with tiles and drapes," he said, whirling her to face him. He pulled down the neckline of her chemise, ripping it just a little in his effort to expose her breasts.

She swallowed hard, then gasped. Her eyes went wide as she took in the sight of her ruined shift and exposed bosom. Then the sight of him, naked and aroused.

"Close your eyes," he told her, snaking his hand inside

her chemise to palm her breast. He squeezed. "Close your eyes. Stop examining everything. Just feel."

She obeyed.

He fumbled open the closures of her skirt and pulled it down over her hips. Then he divested her of her petticoats. Garters and stockings too—taking caution and pleasure in rolling the flannel sheaths down her slender, shapely legs.

Then she stood before him in only her chemise, her eyes still closed. He left her for a moment. Tracing a slow circle around the room, he extinguished all but a few candles.

There, much better.

"Rhys?" Her long, dark lashes trembled against her cheeks. "May I open my eyes now? I promise not to speak of tiles or ceilings."

"Not yet." With a swift yank, he widened the rent in her chemise until he could draw it over her shoulders and pull it downwards, all the way to the floor.

"That's two shifts you've ruined now," she joked, curling into herself to hide her nakedness.

"I'll buy you a dozen more tomorrow, but for tonight . . ." He gently pulled her arms away from her body. "It's my turn to admire the most beautiful, exquisitely crafted thing in this suite."

And he did. He brushed a fall of dark hair away from her breast, pushing it behind her shoulder so it wouldn't obscure his view. And then he stood back a pace and took a long, unhurried look at her body, from her elegantly turned toes to the arrow-straight part of her dark, shining hair. Tongues of candlelight licked over her pale skin. Her slender arms hung straight at her sides, bracketing the sensuous curves of her breasts and hips. As he watched, the rosy points of her nipples gathered to tight nubs. Between her thighs, a triangle of dark curls and shadow guarded her sex.

He'd never seen a woman so beautiful in his life. And that wasn't an exaggeration. Rhys simply hadn't seen all that many unclothed women, and most of those he had seen, he'd purposely tried *not* to examine too closely. Even so, he'd wager that women of Meredith's loveliness were rare indeed.

Hell, even if they numbered in the thousands—she was the only one for him.

As he stared, his already-stiff cock hardened further. Until it literally pained him to look at her. Fortunately, life had gifted him with a formidable tolerance for pain.

"Rhys, please," she said, twisting with impatience. "The water will have gone stone-cold."

He could only hope. A stone-cold bath was what he needed right now, if he was to keep from spilling his seed all over the floor.

"Very well." Gently, he took her by the hand. "Come, then."

"I'm opening my eyes."

"Of course."

He helped her into the deep copper tub, testing the water first with his hand. It had gone a bit cool, but the tepid temperature felt good, considering the warmth of the evening.

He stood behind her as she eased into the bathing tub.

"Aren't you joining me?" she asked, quickly sinking up to her neck in the lukewarm water.

"You first," he said, crouching beside the tub and handing her a sponge. "It's not big enough for two."

The corner of her mouth quirked. "It is, if we sit close together. I thought that was the idea. We were going to make this fast."

Rhys worried it would all be over before it started.

She put a hand to his cheek and pressed a sweet kiss to his lips. "Please. I want to bathe with you."

A little groan escaped him. How could he refuse? Rising to his feet, he swung one mighty leg over the curved copper lip of the bathtub and plunged it into the cooling water. A wave surged from the spot, splashing water onto the floor.

"Never mind it," she said.

So he managed to swing his other leg in, with the effect that he straddled her legs, and his rampant arousal bobbed right above her face. It didn't seem to trouble her any, but just to be safe, he lowered himself into the water without delay, sending another, larger wave of water splashing out.

"Rhys, do you forget I'm a widow? It's not like I've never seen a man unclothed before." She reached for the soap and sponge, rubbing them together to form a thick, sweet-scented lather. "Although I'd be lying if I didn't say you're by far the most pleasing man I've ever beheld."

She ran the sponge down the slope of his shin. He jerked with surprise.

"I'm sorry. Are you ticklish?"

"No," he replied curtly, as if she'd accused him of something dastardly and weak.

She soaped his leg again, and once again his knee jerked.

She laughed. "I think you *are* ticklish."

"Perhaps I am," he admitted.

"*Perhaps* you are?" Reclining against the neck rest, she raised the sponge to her own arm and lathered it from shoulder to wrist. "You don't know?"

"I suppose . . ." His voice trailed off as she tilted her head and soaped her neck. He stared, entranced, as a rivulet of foam trickled down between her breasts. Beneath the surface of the water, his erection throbbed. "I suppose I never had the occasion to find out."

Her hand froze, trapping the sponge against her chest.

"You never had the occasion to find out? I find that hard to believe."

He shrugged. "I've never bathed with a woman before."

"Yes, but surely you needn't bathe with a woman to—" She sat up abruptly, causing a little splash of her own. "You said it's been a long time for you."

"Yes." He drew out the word.

"Years, you said."

He nodded.

"How many?"

Rhys had to think about it. "Eleven? That sounds about right."

She stared at him. "Eleven years. You haven't made love to a woman in eleven years."

"I don't know that I've ever 'made love' to a woman, precisely. But I tupped a fair number when I was a youth. Whores, mostly."

"Mostly," she echoed, beginning to soap her other arm. She seemed too distracted now to make a true performance of it, but that didn't keep Rhys from enjoying the show.

"Aye, mostly." He hoped his honesty didn't offend her, but he didn't see any way around it. This was his wife-to-be. If she asked him a question, he would tell her the truth.

About most things.

He cleared his throat and continued, "My first was a local girl, at Eton. She was curious, and I was . . . sixteen. But the experience was so damned horrid for us both, I kept to whores after that. No more virgins."

"But how did 'no more virgins' become 'no more women'?"

Dipping his head, he scooped water in his cupped hands and sloshed it over his face and neck. When he surfaced, he shook himself and said, "I joined the army."

"Somehow I'd formed the impression that even soldiers can find time for women. You know, at least an hour or two here and there, over the course of a decade."

"Most do."

"But you didn't."

"No." He suddenly realized that he might be making himself sound rather pitiful. Or worse, less than virile. He hastened to add, "It's not that I stopped wanting women. Don't misunderstand. But I spent most of those years fighting or recovering from injuries, so my options were limited by circumstance. And more than that . . . I guess I just decided I'd rather not lie with women who didn't truly want me."

She stared at him. "What woman in her right mind wouldn't want you?"

He shook his head, uncertain how to explain it to her. To be sure, he'd had offers. Made by all the wrong women, for all the wrong reasons. Soldiers' widows looking for a warm tent and strong protector. Married ladies of the *ton* who wanted to be tupped by a big, strapping, scary-looking brute, but who were just snobbish enough to eschew the footmen. Whores who couldn't afford to be choosy.

He thought of Leo Chatwick, who could pick up a harlot in Covent Garden and have her half in love with him before the hour was out. Perhaps if Rhys possessed that sort of talent, he could have stomached paying for sexual pleasure. But the harlots seldom came to him willingly, and even when they did, they didn't care to linger.

"Once I'd gone that long without bedding any women, it seemed worth waiting to bed the right woman." Just in case it needed saying, he added, "That's you."

"Really?" Her face softened, set aglow with candle-light. "Rhys, that's terribly sweet."

Sweet? Well, he supposed he'd take sweet. It was better than pitiful.

She lifted one of her legs from the water and propped it atop his bent knee. Despite the cool temperature of the bath, he could have sworn drops of water sizzled between them.

When she leaned forward to soap her ankle, he took the sponge from her hand. "Let me."

"I thought you'd never ask."

Taking time to enjoy it, he dragged lather over every inch of her soft, supple calf and thigh. When he'd finished the first leg, she lowered it back beneath the water and lifted the other for his attention. As he stroked her, she hummed low in her throat.

Emboldened, he slid the sponge up her inner thigh. She caught his wrist and pulled his hand higher. Over the smooth slope of her belly, all the way up to her breasts.

"Wash them, too," she urged.

He obeyed, stricken mute with lust as he swirled white foam over each milky breast and pale pink tip. He teased her nipples to peaks with the rough sponge, then ran soap along the vulnerable, hidden curve beneath each breast.

Then, casting the sponge aside, he cupped her breasts in his bare hands. His fingers slicked over her soapy skin, and he clamped his thumbs tight over her puckered nipples to anchor them. She moaned her approval as he stroked and kneaded, but when he slid his fingers down toward her sex, she stayed his hand.

Hell. He'd done something wrong. Gotten too greedy. She didn't want him to—

"Your turn," she said, her lips curving in a seductive smile. She reached for the sponge and soap.

His turn? Was she serious? He was about to spill in the bathwater, just from washing *her*. He didn't think he could tolerate being on the receiving end of such ministrations.

But apparently she didn't mean to ask his permission.

Puffs of scented white foam bloomed as she squeezed the sponge. She began with his arms, washing each from wrist to shoulder. The jasmine fragrance calmed his nerves. Sensations rippled and slid over his skin. God, it felt so . . . so good. There was no other word for it. Just pure, simple, straightforward *good*. Damn good. She had him so relaxed, he thought he would dissolve into the bathwater.

Until, stretching forward, she swabbed him under the arm. He flinched and bolted upright.

"I knew it. You *are* ticklish."

"I suppose I am."

Looking pleased with herself, she kept right on working, lathering his chest, neck, shoulders, legs. And he loved every moment of it, even when she teased the bottom of his foot and he convulsed with shock and laughter, and they lost half the bathwater onto the floor.

"Come here." Grasping her waist with both hands, he pulled her to him. Her legs bent and doubled, forming a wall between his chest and hers. He wrapped his own big legs around her, planting his heels at the base of her spine. And then he kissed her, long and hard and deep. Tasting each of her lips in turn and exploring her mouth with his tongue. She tasted of wine and spice, and just faintly of soap. Both intoxicating and innocent. He went dizzy with the knowledge that tonight he needn't hold anything back.

Grasping his shoulders, she pulled up and repositioned herself until she knelt between his legs. He kissed her again, and oh, God. Now her firm, soapy breasts pressed to his chest, slipping and rubbing against his scarred flesh.

She wriggled one hand between them, and Rhys felt her slender fingers close over his erection. Pleasure jolted through him as she gently stroked. Up, then down.

"Stop," he said hoarsely, tearing his lips from hers. "Stop. It's been eleven years. If you keep that up, I won't last eleven seconds."

"I know," she said, pressing little kisses to his mouth and jaw. "I know. It's all right. Let me do this for you first, and then we can take our time." She sat back on her heels, still stroking him. "Let me touch you, Rhys. I've been wanting to touch you. You feel so good."

He groaned as her fingers explored his full length, tracing each vein and ridge, skimming over the swollen, sensitive crown. Rhys dug deep down inside himself, fairly down to the beds of his toenails, searching for the willpower to grab her hand and make her stop. It was a fruitless search.

"Merry . . ." Damn it, he thought he'd finished with these one-sided sexual encounters, where all the enjoyment was on his end. "I want to pleasure you."

"Oh, you will." Her eyes danced with ripples of silver. Her fist tightened around him, and she began to pump faster. "Believe me. This is for my pleasure as much as it is for yours."

He doubted that. As her hand sweetly massaged, he couldn't even put words to the sensations coursing through his body. No, no words. Just hoarse sighs and ragged moans. She worked him in a steady rhythm, and he reveled in the newness of it. All the ways it felt different from when he pleasured himself. Her hand was smaller and so much softer than his own. Her grip wasn't as tight, and her pace was slower than he would have set. Still, he fought the instinct to thrust his hips or urge her faster. Instead he closed his eyes and forced himself to be patient, to submit to her rhythm and the bliss mounting by steady, slow degrees.

Another small surrender, so torturous and yet so sweet.

"God." He gripped the sides of the tub, and every muscle in his body went rigid with the effort of restraint. "You have to stop," he said through gritted teeth. "You have to stop now, or I can't . . ."

"Shh. Just let it happen."

He didn't have a choice anymore. Free will had ceased to exist. The crisis building in his loins was as inescapable as destiny itself, and twice as powerful.

With one last snarling growl, he let the climax take him. His hips bucked off the tub's copper base, and he jerked into her tight fist, spurting jet after jet into the tepid water.

When the waves of pleasure subsided, he stared unfocused at the ceiling as he tried to catch his breath. All the while, she kept caressing and stroking him, smoothing those talented fingers over his spent body. He couldn't believe the small miracle of it: that she not only *wanted* to touch him, she would keep doing so willingly, after the deed was finished.

And he felt the same about her. He wasn't filled with self-loathing and a sudden, irresistible urge to yank on his clothes, toss a coin on the table, fling himself on a horse and ride away so hard, so fast, he just might finally outrun himself. No, he wanted to stay right here, and a team of draft horses couldn't have dragged him away. He would touch and caress and kiss and stroke and lick and pleasure her all night long. Just as soon as some strength returned to his limbs.

"You were right," he said moments later, still blinking up at the ceiling. "That is remarkably fine scrollwork."

She laughed and leaned forward to kiss his cheek.

He sat up with sudden purpose. "Let's get out of this bath."

Beside the tub were two pitchers of clean water for rinsing. He stood up and raised one over his head, quickly dousing himself clean, then shaking like a wet dog.

"Rhys!" she squeaked, holding her hands up as a shield.

"What? You're already wet." He stepped out of the tub and directed her to stand in the center. Hefting the second pitcher in one hand, he told her, "Now turn your back to me, hold up your hair, and be still."

She did as he asked, and he rinsed her slowly, allowing just a trickle of water to escape the pitcher as he moved it over her shoulders and neck. When the water cascaded down the elegant curve of her spine, she shivered and laughed. He poured water over the taut, pale globes of her backside, watching gooseflesh ripple over her skin.

"Turn around."

Smiling, she turned to face him. He dashed water over her collarbones. Then, with great concentration, he applied a small trickle to each of her breasts in turn. Carefully aiming the stream, he poured water directly over her nipple. Between the chill of the bath and this new stimulation, the round nub puckered tighter than ever. Which was, of course, exactly his hoped-for result.

Still holding the half-empty pitcher at his side, Rhys bent his head and sucked that lovely pink nipple into his mouth. She jolted with surprise, but he slid his free arm around her waist to steady her.

Damn, but he'd been waiting to do this forever. And thanks to her selfless efforts in the bath, now he could take all the time he pleased. Alternating between her breasts, he sucked and licked those delectable buds, pressing his face close to breathe in the fresh, clean scent of her skin.

Curling her fingers around his shoulders, she released a low, breathy moan. And though he'd just experienced a devastating climax not five minutes ago, Rhys felt his loins beginning to stir again.

Reluctantly, he pulled away from her breasts. Her nipples were darker and harder than ever. They looked like a pair of tightly furled rosebuds, glistening with dew. He moved the pitcher over her belly and poured a stream of water straight over her navel. The water quickly overflowed the small depression, channeling down to her pelvis and between her legs.

She gasped and stiffened. Her fingernails bit into his shoulders.

Evidently she'd liked that.

With measured caution, he pressed the pitcher's curved lip to the top of her mound, just above the triangle of dark curls that concealed her sex. Little by little, he tilted the pitcher forward, until a trickle of water came forth, coursing straight over her intimate flesh.

This time, she cried out.

He tilted the pitcher a bit more, increasing the flow of water. Her hips tilted and she spread her legs, until the tiny stream ran between the folds of her sex. Her throaty sounds of delight echoed off the tiles.

"Does it feel good?" he asked. He knew the answer, but he wanted to hear her say it. Over and over, not just once.

"It feels so . . ."—she gasped as he tilted the pitcher farther still—"I can't even describe it."

His chest swelled with a primitive, male sort of pride. "I'm out of water," he said, crouching to set the pitcher aside.

"Oh." Her whimper of disappointment was brief. "Perhaps that's best. I'm getting cold. I think there are towels in the—"

"Not yet."

He knelt before her, pressing his mouth to her core.

Chapter Sixteen

Meredith shrieked.

And very nearly fell on her arse. It was a fortunate thing she already had her fingernails hooked into his shoulders like talons. Still, he had to clutch her waist with both hands to keep her from losing her balance completely.

Once he had her steadied, he reapplied himself to his task, caressing her most intimate flesh with his tongue. Gently . . . so gently, his attentions felt just like the water had. Warm, subtle, unrelenting in their tenderness.

His hands left her waist, sliding down to her sex. Using his thumbs, he carefully parted and spread her feminine folds.

"Rhys." Her voice tweaked. "I've never . . ."

"Hush. Neither have I." The words sent huffs of delicious warmth rushing over her skin. "So neither of us will know if I'm doing it wrong."

He swirled his tongue over the swollen bud of nerves at the crest of her sex, and Meredith nearly lost her footing again.

"Oh," she said between gasps, "I'm quite certain you're doing it right."

No more joking now. He went silent with concentration, exploring her thoroughly with his lips and tongue.

Meredith moaned and sighed. She'd never felt pleasure this acute, so intense her bones threatened to melt with it. And it was so, so right that he would be the one to give her this feeling. He'd always been the one man to spark fiery sensations in her, even when she'd been barely more than a girl.

Patiently, with tender care, he worked her closer and closer to release. The muscles in her thighs began to tremble, and the copper tub seemed to undulate beneath her feet.

She cleared her throat. "I . . ." His tongue flickered over her, and for a moment she lost the power of speech. "Rhys, I don't know how much longer I can stand."

He didn't answer, simply hooked one arm under her thigh, until her leg rested on his shoulder. Then he framed her waist tightly between his arms, supporting her weight.

In this pose, with one leg planted in the inch of remaining bathwater and the other leg thrown over her lover's shoulder . . . Meredith felt a bit like a stork. She also felt very much on display. This posture revealed her most intimate places, spreading them wide to his examination and view. He pulled back for a moment, and she could feel him looking at her. Anticipation swirled in her blood, centering between her legs in a rapid, needy pulse.

After what must have been merely a moment but felt like an eternity, his open mouth covered her sex, and he circled his tongue, and everything exploded into pure, bright pleasure.

He held her tight as she came, never letting her weaken or fall, and all the while he kept up the slow, gentle swipes of his tongue, bringing her wave after wave of bliss.

Later, she scarcely remembered how they made it to the bed. He must have carried her, seeing as how her limbs had ceased to function. She recalled snuggling into a plush towel as she hit the mattress, and the way the heat of his body cocooned her shortly thereafter. They must have slept that way for a while. It was sheer joy just to lie next to him at last, nestled into his broad chest and pinned by the weight of one brawny forearm.

So much pleasure, and still they'd hardly begun.

It wasn't clear whether he woke her, or she woke him, but Meredith came to consciousness through a thick, cottony fog. Her limbs were so entwined with Rhys's, she had a tricky time of it, sorting out which strands of the knot belonged to her and which to him. She supposed it didn't really matter.

As her eyes fluttered open, his lips covered hers. Oh, how lovely, to be kissed awake. She closed her eyes again, wanting to prolong the drowsy haze. He began slowly, brushing light kisses over her mouth, cheeks, temple, and brow. The softness of his kiss was in delicious contrast to the hardness of his male organ, which pressed insistently against her thigh.

Wriggling in his embrace, Meredith reclaimed the use of her arms. She kissed him back—first lightly, then deep—and as they kissed, she ran her fingers over every inch of him she could reach. Through his short hair, over the nape of his neck, down the sculpted planes of his shoulders and back. A low moan rumbled through his chest when she flicked a thumbnail over his nipple. Encouraged, she did it again.

How could a man live to the age of one-and-thirty without knowing he was ticklish? To think that no nursemaid, no friend, no lover—for God's sake, no *parent*—had ever touched him in a playful manner. To know that he'd lived with constant physical violence and not the slightest scrap of physical affection . . . Her heart broke for him all over again, just as it had when she was a girl.

But she was a woman now, and determined to make up for lost time. Before they left this bed, she would touch him *everywhere*. Tenderly, desirously. With not only fingers, but lips and tongue, too. He was uncharted ground—practically virgin territory, she thought dryly to herself. But not after tonight. She meant to explore every inch of his body, noting every spot that elicited a laugh, a sigh, or a moan.

And somehow, by the grace of God, she would make him understand that he *deserved* this. He deserved to be kissed, stroked, pleasured, held.

He deserved to be loved.

Fully awake now, they lay side by side, facing one another. Meredith propped her head on one elbow and reached her other hand between them. It didn't take long to find what she was seeking. It was a big enough target, after all. Not exactly the proverbial needle in a haystack. She'd been delighted to learn that her memories of his body hadn't been some combination of time's distortion and her youthful inexperience. Over the years, she'd compared every man in her life to her memories of Rhys. Here was just one more way those other men had come up lacking.

She stroked him slowly, watching his eyes flutter with pleasure beneath closed lids.

"God, that feels good," he said.

"You sound so surprised," she teased. Gentling her tone, she asked, "Was it really so bad before?"

"The first time? Hell, yes." He opened his eyes. Brushing a strand of hair behind her ear, he said, "Worse for her than for me. Poor girl screamed like she was being murdered. We didn't even finish. Everything about it was just . . . wrong."

"Are you sure she wasn't enjoying herself?" Meredith smiled. "Maybe she was just the screaming sort. Some women are."

His brow creased. "Are *you* the screaming sort?"

"No," she said quickly, inwardly resolving not to make so much as a peep. "No."

"Then how would you know some women are?"

"I own an inn, Rhys. The walls aren't very thick."

She slid her hand further down, reaching to cradle his heavy sac in her hand and delighting in his low groan of pleasure. He clasped her hip and pulled her against him, grinding his thick shaft against her belly. She threw a leg over his narrow hips, opening herself to him. A clear invitation.

Still he hesitated.

"I'm ready," she assured him. "And I'm not a virgin or a screamer. Everything will be fine."

"It has to be better than fine." His hand ranged over her hip, and he reached down to stroke her cleft, probing with his fingers to test her readiness and groaning with satisfaction when he found her quite ready indeed. He slid his thumb to her pearl and gently massaged. "This has to be so damn unbelievably good that you want to do it again, and again, every day for the rest of our lives."

"Every day?" she teased. "Such stamina."

"We'll be making up for a lot of lost time." Pausing, he gave the appearance of serious consideration. "Every day for the next decade, at least. After that, it will depend on the state of my joints."

She threw back her head and laughed.

When he began to kiss the hollow of her neck, Meredith decided this was the time. She grasped his erection firmly and guided it to the damp, needy ache between her legs.

She stretched; he nudged.

And then he was inside her, just an inch. They drew a shaky breath together.

Now an inch more.

She bit her lip to keep from moaning. Truth be told, he *was* big, and she was very out of practice, had never given birth. She was probably as tight as a widow could be. It hurt, but deliciously so.

They stared into one another's eyes as he fed her another inch of his length, then two.

"Are you all right?" he asked.

She nodded, breathless. "Give me just a moment? Just like this."

"I'll try." He gritted his teeth through a few beats of her pulse. "God, I can't wait, I . . . I need more."

"I—"

A gasp took the rest of her willing reply, as he clutched her hip and thrust.

Meredith buried her face in his shoulder. *I will not scream. I will not scream.*

"Are you well?"

"Mm-hm."

"Are you certain?"

"Oh, yes," she squeaked through clenched teeth.

After a moment's rest, she dragged in a deep breath, then released it slowly. He rocked against her, in the gentlest of thrusts. Their natural moisture spread, easing the way. When he thrust again, she could tell he slid deeper than he'd intended. A groan rumbled from his chest, loosening her tense muscles.

And then, suddenly, it wasn't painful anymore. It was very, very good.

She worked against him, struggling to take him deeper, desperate for more. More heat, more friction. The firm slide of him against her taut, sensitive flesh.

She lifted her head and opened her eyes so she could watch his expression as they established a rhythm. Slow. Steady. Devastating. With each thrust, he sank a bit deeper, stretched her body a bit wider, prodded her one step closer to the brink of ecstasy.

His face was a mask of concentration—eyes intent, brow furrowed, lower lip folded under his teeth. He seemed to be gauging her reactions just as carefully as she was watching for his.

"Is it good?" she asked, breathless.

"Hell, yes. You feel so . . ." He grit his teeth as her intimate muscles squeezed in response. ". . . so much better than my hand."

"Your hands feel good to me."

Laying a hand over his, she dragged his touch from her hip to her breast. He cupped the small globe easily in his palm, kneading gently. Pleasure spread through her body as he chafed his thumb over her hardened nipple. A lusty sigh eased from her throat.

"You like that." He thumbed her nipple again.

"Oh, yes." She tightened her leg over his hips and flexed her thigh, drawing him deeper into her.

Relaxing her neck, she rested her head on her arm and simply stared into his beautiful eyes as together they worked their hips back and forth. In and out. "This is wonderful, Rhys. I'm so glad we're doing this."

"So am I. Believe me. Another week of holding back, and I think I would have imploded." One eyebrow arched. "Is it strange that we're talking so much?"

"Strange? Perhaps it's not usual, but it doesn't feel strange in the least, not to me. It feels . . ."

"Right." His breath hitched as he rocked his hips and sank deeper than ever. "It just feels right." Another thrust. "Doesn't it?"

Oh, Lord. It did. Of course it did.

His eyes drilled into hers, demanding and intense. Even with his arousal wedged against her womb, she felt more deeply penetrated by his gaze. There was desire there, and need . . . and just the faintest glimmer of fear. He gave another powerful buck of his hips. "Admit it. This is right, you and me. Meant to be."

A voice within her shouted for caution, urged her to put up a wall of defense. *Don't,* the voice said. *You'll reveal too much, risk heartbreak and worse.*

Go to the devil, she told it back.

Rhys was inside her, and next to her, and surrounding her with his embrace, and he needed so damn much. The man had suffered a lifetime deprived of affection, and he clung to all this destiny nonsense because—uncertain, wounded soul that he was—he couldn't bring himself to ask for hers. This was why he'd never offered her a choice. He was too afraid she'd say no.

She would not force him to ask. Not when she longed to give him everything. Affection, pleasure, a gentle lover's touch.

"Yes," she breathed, curling her arm around his shoulders. Stretching her neck, she brushed a kiss against his lips. "Yes, Rhys. It feels right." She kissed those strong, sensuous lips again, then again, running her fingers through his feathery hair as she did. "Utterly . . . perfectly . . . absolutely right. We belong like this."

He kissed her thoroughly, taking her mouth with feverish, driven passion. With a low groan, he rolled her onto her back and sank in deep.

Very deep. So deep, she gripped his shoulders in shock. In their side-by-side position, he obviously hadn't penetrated her fully. No, there was definitely more of Rhys to be had. And now he gave it all to her, thrusting hard, working deeper, until his hips met against hers and the breath left her lungs.

"Are you well?" he asked, bracing himself on his elbows.

She managed a nod.

"Good." *Thrust.* "Because I can't stop." *Thrust.* "God help me, I can't stop."

He thrust again, and his pelvis ground against hers. And she came, just like that. The feel of his strong body, the ragged need in his voice, all the emotion in her heart—she was overwhelmed, in every sense. The pleasure swept her in a hot, unrelenting rush, and she clung to him, riding it for all it was worth.

"God." The tight growl of his voice told her he was close, too. "*God.*" He fell on her, lowering his weight to hers. "Hold on," he whispered in her ear. "Hold me tight."

She did as he asked, as she wanted to do. Locked her arms around his neck and wrapped her legs over the tree trunks that were his thighs. She cinched her intimate muscles, holding him tight there, too.

And then, when she'd gripped him in every way imaginable—he let go. The force and tempo of his thrusts increased. His mouth fell on hers, and he probed wildly with his tongue as he took her faster, harder, deeper. As though there were something he desperately needed, something that resided at the very center of her being—and to get at it, he would break her apart.

Tearing his mouth from hers, he reared up a bit. Just enough that she could see his face. His eyes were unfocused, and his lips contorted with pleasure. And as the inevitable approached, an incoherent rush of words tore from his chest.

"That's so . . . Damn, it's . . . Merry . . . *Christ.*"

Joy swelled in her breast, and she nearly laughed with it. Because she knew the next thirty seconds were going to be the best of Rhys St. Maur's decade, and she was just so happy to be there, along for the ride.

He growled as he came, collapsing onto her and burying his face in her neck. She released her grip on his shoulders and soothed his back with caresses down his spine. Her fingers slipped over the sheen of perspiration as he shuddered in the aftermath of his release.

Eventually, she felt his breathing slow to a natural rhythm, washing gently over her ear. His arousal softened inside her. And yet the tremors in his muscles didn't abate.

"Oh, Rhys." As the realization dawned, she hugged him tight. "Oh, Rhys."

He was trembling. This big, strong, indestructible warrior was trembling in her arms. If there'd been any hope of protecting her heart, it slipped away that instant.

She was lost to him. Always had been.

"Thank you," he murmured, releasing a deep sigh of satisfaction.

She cradled his head, kissed his ear.

"Was it—?"

"Perfect," she assured him. "In every way." He rolled to the side, and she teased a fingertip along the whiskered edge of his jaw. Arching an eyebrow saucily, she asked, "So . . . every day? Truly?"

"Twice. For the first year, twice a day. At least."

She bit her lip and gave him a pensive look.

"What is it?" he asked, reaching out to playfully muss her hair.

"I'm just wondering whether that includes today. And if so . . ." She rose up on her elbow and peered at the clock. "How much time is left before midnight?"

The bed shook with his laughter. His arm shot out, flattening her to the mattress. With a flex of his biceps, he rolled her in close, nestling her snug against him. "Time enough, Merry. Don't you worry." His big hand stroked through her hair. "We have all the time in the world."

For the first time, she wished blind faith came so easily to her.

With a sudden burst of energy, she climbed atop him, stretching her body out over his. With her arms stacked on his chest, her toes hit him just about mid-shin. The hair on his legs tickled the arches of her feet. "I've just realized something."

"What's that?"

"I've spent a shockingly inadequate amount of time tasting the area between here"—she stroked a finger over his Adam's apple—"and here." She traced a line to the soft spot just below his ear. "Unless you have a complaint, I plan to remedy that immediately."

He grinned. "No complaint."

"Very good." She bent her head to his throat and touched her tongue to the underside of his jaw. The beginning of what would be, if she had her way, a sleepless night spent exploring every inch of his body.

They might not have all the time in the world, but they definitely had tonight. And she was going to make the most of every second.

Chapter Seventeen

Awareness filtered in some time well after dawn. When she woke to bright sunlight leaking through her eyelashes, Meredith kissed the forearm wrapped protectively about her chest. It was worth the lost time, just to wake up in his arms. She couldn't even remember the last time she'd slept through a sunrise. This was a luxury indeed. One to which she could too easily become accustomed.

Rhys stirred, nuzzling her hair. They lay on their sides, nestled like spoons in a drawer. At least one part of him was awake and ready to greet the day. The hard ridge of his arousal prodded her hip.

She wriggled her bottom just a little, teasing him. From the way his breath caught in his throat, she suspected he was awake. For all she knew, he might have been lying awake that way for hours, hard and patiently aching for her.

And in that case, he could wait a few minutes more. Keeping her eyes shut tight to feign sleep, she casually stretched and nestled deeper into the hard contours of his body. He dropped a kiss against the back of her neck, as if to test her wakefulness. Remaining immobile was a struggle, but she managed it. His hand came to life where it lay draped casually over her breast. He drew a lazy circle around her nipple, then tweaked it with a pinch. She couldn't help but moan.

He knew she was awake. She knew he was, too. But they kept up the little game they were playing. Somehow they'd tacitly agreed on the rules. Eyes closed. No words. Just touch and a steady, inexorable progress toward joining. It was a game they would both win.

She parted her legs a few degrees, and his erection slid between her thighs. The two of them lay that way for a moment, savoring that last bit of anticipation. She was wet for him, and he was impressively hard. A little tilt of her pelvis was all it took. He glided into her slippery cleft in one smooth thrust.

Though her breathing came fast, Meredith forced herself to be boneless. As passive as possible. She hoped the mounting tension of their game would drive him past the point of tenderness. All night long, they'd guided one another through an exploration of different positions, taken thorough tours of each other's anatomy. He'd loved her with a sweet, earnest purpose that touched her heart. But this morning, she wanted him to be the aggressor. She needed to feel all the strength and power in that big, hard body. She wanted to be overwhelmed.

When the wait became unbearable, she broke the rules and whispered, "Take me."

His teeth scraped her shoulder. With a low growl, he flipped her onto her stomach, wedging her legs apart with his thighs. He gave her just what she wanted, driving into her hard. So hard, she grabbed the pillow to muffle her cry. The bed creaked and rattled with each stroke.

Yes. *Yes.* This was exactly what she craved. To feel powerless beneath him, utterly at his mercy. She'd spent so much of her life being strong. Marshalling all her available fortitude to run the inn, take care of her father, look after the village. And she'd built up formidable shields to protect herself and those around her. It was a relief and a joy to be dominated, to relinquish all power and feel those barriers stripped away by someone she knew and trusted.

Someone she loved.

He rose up between her legs, grasping her hips in his massive hands and lifting her to her knees. His fingers curled around the cheeks of her backside, guiding her motions, spreading her open for his deepening thrusts. By the light smack of his thighs kissing hers and the roughened quality of his breath, she suspected he was watching their joined bodies. She wished she could watch, too.

He clutched her hips tighter still, kicked into a faster rhythm. "Come for me. Do it now."

Releasing the pillow, she slid one hand down her belly, between her legs. She pressed the heel of her hand against her mound and curled her fingers back, so they teased his shaft with every stroke. The pressure of her palm just where she needed it, the very proof of his own need, hard and hot against her fingertips—she hurtled headlong into a soul-shaking climax, crying out against the pillow.

He followed her seconds later, and together they collapsed to the mattress. He lay half atop her, half to the side. His breath was a rasp against her ear. She loved the heat and the weight of him, pinning her limp, wrung-out body to the bed. She could get used to this. She really could.

For the first time since Rhys had mentioned marriage over boiled eggs and coffee, Meredith let herself believe, just for a moment, that it might truly be safe to get used to this.

"You know," he said after a minute or two, rolling onto his back, "I think I've changed my mind."

"You have?" She propped her chin on one arm, tried to sound nonchalant. All the while, her heart was hammering the mattress.

"We'll have to find a bishop," he said. "Get a special license. There's no bloody way we're waiting another fortnight for that curate to come back."

She collapsed to the bed with relief.

"I'm serious," he said. "We'll take the coach and set off for London today."

"Rhys, we can't do that. Father's expecting me back on schedule. And we've all those things to buy for the inn."

"For our house."

"Well, yes. That, too."

His brow creased. "I don't understand. Why can't we—"

She kissed him, for no other reason than to cut short that question.

So strange. Ten minutes ago all she'd craved was for Rhys to take control, to leave her no choice, to overwhelm her senses completely. And never during their lovemaking had she felt anything other than cherished and safe. But an elopement . . . ?

"I was promised a tour of Bath," she said lightly. "There was talk of ribbons and romance."

"So there was." He gave her a smile, and she felt its warmth deep inside.

She loved him. After last night, there was no more denying it, not even to herself. And nothing would make her happier than to marry him. There were obstacles, yes. The inn's future, Gideon's threats . . . but from such a great distance, those obstacles seemed smaller now. Surmountable. Between them, surely she and Rhys had the strength and wits to sort it all out.

There was only one matter left to settle. Would marriage to her make Rhys happy? Not just satisfied in bed or at peace with his obligations, but truly *happy*? He deserved real contentment. With all this blind allegiance to the concept of destiny, she wasn't sure he even knew what he wanted anymore. Given the choice, would he truly prefer a cottage in rural Devonshire to the opulent life he could be leading elsewhere? Would he honestly prefer *her* to the elegant ladies he could have?

His words kept echoing in her mind: *It's not like I have something better to do.*

But he did. With his rank and wealth, he had so many options, and this holiday was likely to remind him of them. Before she could marry him, she needed time to observe, to gauge his thoughts and feelings in a setting outside their village.

"I just want to spend time with you," she said honestly. "What do the gentry do in Bath, anyhow?"

He pursed his lips. "Truthfully, I'm not so certain anymore. I only spent one summer here as a boy, when my mother came to take the waters. That's why people ostensibly come to Bath, you know. To take the mineral waters. If I recall correctly, the usual practice is to begin the day with a nice purgative, then travel by sedan chair to the Pump Room to sign the guest register and drink a glass or two of the rusty, foul-smelling stuff."

Good Lord. *That* was the reason wealthy people flocked to Bath? People of quality would spend their money on the queerest things. But she didn't want to offend Rhys by gainsaying the idea.

"Do *you* want to drink the waters?" she asked.

He chuckled. "What do you think? No, we'll confine ourselves to the shops by day. Perhaps a walk about the Circus and Royal Crescent. And then later tonight . . . should you like to go to the theater?"

"Yes, please." Inwardly she cheered. She would have a use for that red gown, after all. "That sounds like a perfectly lovely day. No purgatives or sedan chairs required."

Rhys had never been one for visiting the shops. But then, he'd never had a lady on his arm to spoil. This, he learned, made the whole experience more tolerable.

They didn't make it out of the suite until well after noon, but they dealt with the practical things first. He'd inquired at the hotel as to the source of the painted washbasin in their suite that had Meredith so enraptured, and they made that importer's warehouse their first stop of the afternoon. There they ordered complete sets of basins, pitchers, chamber pots, and mirrors.

"Four sets," Meredith told the shopkeeper.

"Five," Rhys corrected.

"But why?" She frowned up at him. "Oh, I see. So we have a spare, should anything break?"

"Make that six sets," he called to the shopkeeper. "Four for the guest rooms," he told her, "one for a spare, and one for our house."

"Oh." The little furrow in her brow only deepened. "But the set for the cottage doesn't have to be so fine."

"Yes, it does." And forbidding any further discussion with a look, he gave the shopkeeper the address of their hotel. That was, after adding to the order a full set of china and silver for the Three Hounds' new dining room.

"I'm going to repay you somehow," she murmured.

"Absolutely not. This was part of the arrangement. I agreed to pay all construction expenses in return for the labor."

"Yes, but most would not classify the washbasins and silver as construction expenses."

"Of course they are. How can a guest room be considered complete without a washstand? What use is a dining room without silver?"

"Very well," she consented as they left the importer's. "But I insist on paying for the fabrics from my own purse."

Rhys shook his head as he guided her out the door. Why did she argue over these small expenses? Once they married, all their money would be combined.

They strolled for a while, stopping in at Sally Lunn's for a bit of refreshment and a taste of the famous buns. Rhys declared them tasty enough, but vastly inferior to Meredith's own baking. That compliment earned him a toss of her dark head and a very pretty blush. All in all, he was modestly pleased with his progress in the romance arena.

Then it was on to the draper's. There Meredith took command. A mountain of fabrics amassed on the countertop as she asked for yard after yard of plain, but high quality linen for bedsheets, then printed dimity for curtains. And she insisted on paying for them from her own purse, to Rhys's frustration.

"What about for the cottage?" he asked.

"Oh, there's linen enough here."

"And the curtains?" He nodded toward a bolt of ivory lace. "Isn't that similar to the lace you liked so much at the hotel?"

She tsked. "It would be terribly impractical for curtains in the country. They'd become so soiled and would easily tear."

He tapped his finger on the counter. "How many yards would you need, to make a set? There are eight windows in all."

She shrugged and gave him a number. He tripled it in his mind and asked the shopkeeper to cut that amount and start a new bill.

"Enough for three sets," he told her. "When they become soiled, we'll change them for new. And when we run out of new, it's time for another trip to Bath." To escape the disapproving set of her mouth, he traveled down the counter to a glass case filled with a blinding array of plumes, ribbons, fans, and brilliants. Almost at random, he selected an assortment of silky and sparkly things, in as many colors as they came. The shopkeeper dutifully wrapped and tallied them as Meredith settled her fabric bill.

When at last she'd finished settling accounts and drifted down to stand at his elbow, Meredith's gaze wandered over the dazzling array. "Are you buying souvenirs for Cora?" she asked. "She'll be so happy. That lavender plume will look very well in her hair."

For *Cora*? With effort, Rhys swallowed a growl of frustration. Why wouldn't the woman allow him to give her a little taste of luxury? "They're not for . . ."

His voice trailed off as he noticed she'd gone quiet, too. She stared, lips slightly parted, at a silver dresser set in the case. The set included a boar-bristle hairbrush and matching engraved hand mirror, neatly arranged on a gilt-edged tray.

Wordlessly, he directed the girl behind the counter to remove the set from the case.

"It's lovely," Meredith sighed, picking up the hand mirror and turning it glass-side up.

Rhys moved to stand behind her shoulder. Catching her gaze in the reflection, he said, "It could be solid gold and encrusted with pearls, and it still wouldn't be as beautiful as the woman reflected in it. But thank God something has caught your eye." To the girl, he said, "We'll take the set."

"Rhys, no. It's too expensive."

He cocked an eyebrow. "Not for me."

"It's lovely, but it's not really the sort of thing I'd use. It would only gather dust."

"So we'll have a maid dust it."

"You can't—"

"Yes. I can." Despite all his efforts to remain emotionless, his blood began to heat. His cravat felt glued to his throat. Lowering his voice, he muttered, "It's a hairbrush and a tray and a bloody mirror. And I'm buying them for you, no matter how much you protest. So stop arguing."

She looked away, pressing her lips together into a thin line. "If you insist."

They stood in awkward silence as the shopkeeper finished wrapping their purchases and Rhys settled the account. After arranging for most of their packages to be delivered to the hotel, he turned to Meredith and handed her the parcel containing the dresser set. She thanked him demurely, then turned for the door.

And it was all ruined, damn it. Farewell to his fantasies of dragging that silver brush through her hair, arranging it around her bare shoulders and breasts. Now every time she looked in that hand mirror, she'd see an awkward moment when he'd lost his temper and snapped at her in the draper's. Just one more beautiful, shining thing he'd managed to tarnish.

He'd make it up to her somehow. In fact, he'd start right now, with an apology.

Catching up to her, he stopped her in the street. "Merry, I'm sorry. I shouldn't have pressed you to accept a gift you didn't want. We can return the dratted thing this instant, if you like."

Her hands tightened over the parcel. "Rhys, that's not it. You don't understand."

"I want to understand. Explain it to me." He gestured uselessly with his hands, hardly knowing how to form the question. "You have no problem buying fine things for your guests. Why can't I give you fine things, too?"

She sighed. "It's difficult to accept them."

"Difficult? You perform six difficult tasks before breakfast."

"Well, what about you? I don't see you buying any luxuries for yourself."

His chin jerked. "But that's different."

"No, I don't think it is. You deserve fine things, too, you know." Her eye settled on a shop window behind him, and he could see her gaze sharpening on something in particular. "I'm going to go in and buy you that, right now. And if you don't want to be called an insufferable hypocrite, you're going to wait right here while I do, and when I come out, you'll not say a word about it other than 'thank you.' "

He stood there, stunned, as she left him and entered the shop. Belatedly, he looked to the shop's window just in time to see a pair of hands removing a gentleman's shaving kit from the display. It was a quality set. The razor's handle and the knob of the shaving brush were both fashioned from horn, with gilt accents. He couldn't let her purchase that for him. She'd be spending straight down to the lining of her purse.

But if he tried to prevent her . . . she'd be furious. Poverty *was* an easier condition to remedy than a woman's displeasure.

A minute passed, and out she came, delivering the wrapped parcel into his hand. He stood blinking at it.

Lifting her chin, she regarded him with a challenge in her eyes. "And . . . ?"

He forced the words out. "Thank you."

"You see? It's not so easy to say as it would seem."

"I'm out of practice, I suppose."

"With gratitude?"

He cleared the emotion from his throat. "With gifts."

"Hm." She gave him a meaningful look. Taking his arm, she said, "If it helps at all, it was mostly for me. I discovered this morning how much I love watching you shave."

He gave a shout of laughter, remembering the way

she'd tackled him to the bed after he'd finished. God, her inner thigh had been like silk against his smooth-shaven cheek. His trousers pulled snug, just at the memory. That was it. Shopping be damned. He couldn't get inside her soon enough.

Without hesitation, he guided her into a hairpin turn and set a course back to the hotel. "We've had enough of the shops for today."

"Ahem."

Several pleasant hours later, Meredith cleared her throat as she emerged from the dressing room. One of the hotel's girls had helped her dress in the red silk gown and assisted her with a sleek upswept coiffure. Now she was anxious to see Rhys's reaction.

He stood before the wardrobe, peering into the small mirror hung inside the door as he tied his cravat. When he took no notice of her gentle clearings of the throat, she coughed. Loudly, this time.

In response, he swore. He tugged the half-knotted cravat loose and started all over again.

So much for a dramatic entrance from the doorway. The soles of her new slippers glided over the carpet as she covered the space between them. He flicked her a brief glance, then turned his attention back to his cravat.

"Well . . . ?" she prompted.

"Yes?" He frowned at the reflected knot of linen. "What is it?"

"How do I look?"

"Beautiful."

"Rhys! You scarcely looked at me."

"I don't have to," he said, his brow knitting in concentration as he unworked the knot for a third attempt. "You always look beautiful."

"But . . ." *But this will be my first evening out in fashionable society, and I'm terribly afraid that every person in the Theatre Royal will turn on cue, take one look at me, and instantly know I'm a country girl wearing a courtesan's discarded gown.*

With a growl of disgust, he picked apart the cravat again. "Goddamn fingers. Been broken one too many times."

"Calm down." She put a hand on his arm, turning him away from the mirror and toward her. "Let me? If a simple knot will serve, I can do it. I did Father's for years."

He closed his eyes and exhaled roughly as she wound and tied the cravat, tucking under the ends. "There."

"Thank you." His eyes fluttered open, and his sheepish gaze found hers. "You do look beautiful, by the way."

"As beautiful as tulips?" She smoothed her hands over his shoulders and lapels. Even if she had to feed him the compliments, she would take them. She was that desperate for reassurance.

"A thousand times more." He kissed her brow, then offered his arm. "Shall we?"

As they stepped out into the street, Meredith felt herself go pale. She'd wished she'd thought to fortify herself with some courage of the liquid variety.

"Ashworth?" The low voice came from behind them. "Ashworth, is that you?"

Chapter Eighteen

Meredith froze. Here it was, her first social test. That smooth, cultured voice could not possibly belong to a servant or shopkeeper. She would be introduced. She would have to *speak*. And before all that, she would have to somehow turn around in this voluminous red gown and manage not to tangle herself into something that resembled fresh sausage links.

Following Rhys's lead, she pivoted to face the newcomer. The tall, thin man bowed in greeting.

Rhys returned the bow, more fluidly than Meredith would have expected. "Corning," he said. "What an unexpected pleasure."

So curious, that she'd not seen Rhys bow before. All throughout their day in Bath, she'd noted an aristocratic grace to his movements that wasn't often on display in Buckleigh-in-the-Moor. Well, and to whom would he be bowing there? He was the lord. Everyone in Buckleigh-in-the-Moor ought to be bowing to *him*.

It was at that moment—several seconds too late for etiquette—that Meredith remembered to curtsy. Damn, damn, damn.

"Unexpected indeed," Corning said. "I wasn't aware you were in Bath."

"I wasn't," Rhys replied. "Until just last night."

They all stood there awkwardly for a moment, staring at one another. Meredith took in the understated luxury of the man's garments. They'd just come from the draper's that morning; she knew what such fine cloth cost. She knew that kind of quality tailoring came even more dear.

For his part, the newcomer's curious, mildly horrified gaze flicked over Meredith's red silk gown.

Oh, dear. She'd just *known* she must look like a whore.

Shifting his weight, Rhys brushed a protective touch over her lower back. "Mrs. Maddox of Devonshire, allow me to present Lord Henry Twill, Viscount Corning. I served with his younger brother in Portugal."

Good Lord. He must be a duke's son. The man inclined his head, and Meredith curtsyed again, more deeply this time. Panicked thoughts tumbled in her mind. Words stuck on her tongue. How did one properly address a duke's son, anyhow? As "Your Grace" or "my lord"?

In the end, she couldn't say anything. By way of compensation, she forced a wan smile.

"Mrs. Maddox, is it?"

She nodded mutely. She was a fool. It seemed anything she could utter would indict her as a fraud—but in the end, her silence made the confession on its own.

"Charmed." His tone communicated anything but.

Whatever mild degree of interest the man had shown in her cooled instantly. He pointedly turned his gaze, and it was as though she'd ceased to exist.

By mutual unspoken agreement, they parted ways with Lord Corning soon thereafter.

What a disaster. Meredith wondered if she could ever move amongst such people and not feel like an impostor. If she were to marry Rhys and become Lady Ashworth, she supposed she would have to learn to do just that. But she wasn't equal to the challenge tonight.

"Do you know," she ventured, "I'm not certain I really feel like going to the theater. Will you be terribly disappointed if we don't?"

He looked at her, as if to gauge her sincerity. "Not at all," he finally said. "Did you want to go back to the hotel?"

"Why don't we walk for a while? There's so much of Bath we haven't seen."

"Very well. Shall we head toward the river?"

Nodding her agreement, she put her arm in his, and together they strolled down the avenue. Slowly, in deference to Meredith's skirts.

"I'm sorry for earlier, with Lord Corning."

"Oh, don't be." She bit her lip, abashed by the fact that he'd noticed the gentleman's treatment of her, too. "It wasn't your fault."

He was silent for a moment, as if he were debating whether to take her comment as forgiveness or an invitation to further discussion. "It's hard, sometimes, for men like him to greet me. I understand it; it can't be helped. When Corning and I cross paths, naturally I remind him of the brother he lost. I can see it in his eyes, when he looks at me. He's asking himself why a man like me survived when his brother did not." Rhys sighed heavily. "It's a question I can't answer. There's no satisfactory answer at all."

"Wait a moment." Meredith slowed, tugging on his arm. Eventually they both pulled to a halt. "Are you saying you believe Lord Corning's awkwardness in that meeting was all about *you*?"

"But of course. What else would it be?"

"Me, you silly man." She laughed. "He thought he'd interrupted you with your lady of the evening."

He stared at her as though she'd gone mad. "No, he didn't."

"Rhys, I saw the way he looked at me. He dismissed me as he would a serving girl."

He simply shook his head and turned, pressing on.

After a few minutes, he said, "You saw him as disapproving of you. I thought him disapproving of me. Funny, isn't it?"

Not only funny, but a strange relief. Why hadn't she seen it? Rhys felt like an impostor here, too. She ought to have recognized it earlier, from the way he'd wrestled his cravat. He'd been nervous, just as she had been.

Tilting her head to the twilight sky, she mused, "Do you know what I think? I have a feeling that dour look on Lord Corning's face had nothing to do with either of us. Perhaps he'd just tasted something unpleasant. Or more likely, his purgative was taking effect at a most inopportune moment."

They chuckled together and continued strolling down the shop-lined street.

"Which way shall we go?" he asked. "Do you wish to see the Orange Grove?"

"Oh, let's. I adore oranges."

"There aren't any there. The park is named for William of Orange, not the fruit. No oranges to be had. Not much of a grove either, to be honest."

"Oh. Of course." She went silent, feeling inexpressibly stupid.

"But," he went on, "there are surely oranges to be had, somewhere. And if you adore them, you shall have them. Let's walk down to Sydney Gardens."

"And are there actual gardens there? Or will I reveal my ignorance again?"

"Actual gardens, yes." He bent his head and lowered his voice. "*Pleasure* gardens."

Her pulse responded quickly to that promise, and

only quickened as they made the walk across the Pulteney Bridge, crowded with vendors and shops.

As predicted, they soon came upon a girl hawking oranges. Rhys purchased three, tucking one in either of his pockets and tossing the third to her. Meredith held it between her hands as they walked, periodically lifting the exotic fruit to her nose and breathing deep.

She carried that orange in her gloved hands as they crossed the bridge and paused to gape at the grand homes in Laura Place. Just a short distance more, and they reached the Gardens themselves. Here there was yet more grandeur to be seen. The ancient ruins of a castle, which Rhys informed her was not truly ancient at all, but rather a modern construction. A bowling green and a labyrinth, and of course, all the fashionable people walking to and fro. Plumes bobbed in the perfumed breeze as a clutch of matrons approached. More than one turned a curious eye on Meredith and Rhys, and a titter of gossip rose as they walked past.

Here was that uncomfortable moment again, where they stood in silence. Meredith supposed both she and Rhys were suspecting the ladies' disapproval to be reserved individually for them.

"I hear music," she said. Because, although they hadn't been speaking, a change of subject seemed a welcome thing.

"There are concerts, most nights." He paused awhile before asking, "Did you wish to attend?"

"No," she answered quickly. "No, let's just stroll a bit."

They ambled aimlessly until they found a quiet, picturesque bridge overlooking a canal. Here they paused, listening to the faint strains of the orchestra waft through the trees. Alone with Rhys, she felt more safe.

He looked at the orange she still carried. "Don't you

want to eat it?" When she hesitated, he motioned to her. "Give it here. I'll peel it for you."

She surrendered the orange to him, and he bit the rind to make a flap. She watched as he carefully shelled the sectioned fruit within, removing every bit of peel and membrane, tossing the bits into the canal. Watching him reminded her of that first breakfast they'd shared, and the way he'd balanced an egg in his big, strong fingers.

Her mouth watered in anticipation. She removed her gloves. The aroma of orange grew stronger and stronger, and perhaps it was only her fancy, but the distant strains of the music seemed to grow more melodic, more sweet. The pleasure gardens began to live up to their name.

Dividing the fruit with his fingers, he offered her half. She accepted, separating one section and popping it into her mouth. The juicy tang of the orange flooded her tongue, and she gave an involuntary moan.

Side by side, elbows propped on the rail, they remained there. Two people who would never belong to the crowd, happily belonging to each other. Eating an orange in sticky, blissful silence, until it was completely gone.

Meredith licked her lips. They tasted of orange, sweet and tart with just a hint of bitter rind. She wondered if his lips would taste the same. But even dressed in a courtesan's gown, she wasn't bold enough to kiss him in a public park.

"Another?" he asked, withdrawing a second orange from his pocket.

She nodded and held out her hand. "Allow me, this time."

As she lifted it to her mouth, she reconsidered. It would look unladylike, perhaps, to bite the rind as he had done. Instead, she dug in with her thumbnail to separate the peel. She misjudged and pressed too deep. Juice erupted, splattering her hand. She bobbled the orange, and down it went. Down into the canal, meeting its poetic end with an extravagant splash.

"Oh!" Sticky hands frozen helpless in front of her, Meredith leaned her belly against the rail. "I'm so sorry. What a waste."

"Not at all." He took her juice-spattered hand and lifted it to his lips.

To the casual observer, it must have looked the most innocent thing imaginable—a gentleman chastely kissing his lady's hand.

The casual observer would have been deceived. Most wickedly so.

Pressing his parted lips to her knuckles, he licked each one. Then his tongue traced the sensitive seams between her fingers. Each furtive swipe sent a bolt of lightning shooting to her thighs, curling in the space between.

Once he'd finished her knuckles, he turned her hand palm up and bent his head.

"Rhys," she whispered. "There are people about."

He ignored her, lifting her hand to his face and curling her fingers over his cheek, so it would look to anyone passing by as though she were cupping his face. All the while, his tongue did wicked things, tracing the lines of her palm and loving the delicate pulse at her wrist. Her nipples went hard, and her sex went oh-so-soft.

And just when she thought she could not possibly become more aroused by a kiss on the hand, he proved her wrong.

He sucked her thumb into his mouth.

She almost cried out; it was a close thing. But his eyes held hers, forbidding her to make a sound as he swirled his tongue in insidious circles, then pulled with delicious, bone-melting suction. Her eyelashes fluttered and her breath came quick. A sudden weakness in her knees had her gripping the rail with her other hand and leaning her weight toward him.

At last, he gave her back her hand. He said simply, "There. Nothing gone to waste. Shall we walk back?" He offered his arm.

Still reeling from his kiss, she took it gratefully. "I'm not certain I remember how to walk just now." Licking her lips, she added, "There's still another orange, isn't there?"

"Oh, yes. I'm saving it." He leaned over to whisper in her ear. "I'll finish you later."

Well, and now she lost all sense of coordination.

Fortunately, he was tall and strong and steady, and he kept her tucked close.

"We *are* in Bath," he said as they crossed back over the River Avon. "It seems we ought to at least walk by the baths and Pump Room. They're on our way back to the hotel."

Meredith couldn't imagine why he would wish to prolong the walk back, but she said, "If you like."

They strolled a few blocks down the bank. The faint odor of sulfur reached her nostrils as they approached a grand stone building fronted with plate windows and a great many steps.

"The Pump Room," he announced. "You can't see them from the street, but the baths are just there, to the side."

"How very grand. But I imagine it's closed for the evening."

"It is." He gave her a conspiratorial look. "To most."

Chapter Nineteen

The night guard was an army man. Rhys had seen it straightaway in the way he patrolled, marching briskly back and forth, turning on a penny at the end of each pass. He introduced himself as Lieutenant Colonel St. Maur, newly Lord Ashworth, and all due deference was immediately forthcoming. After a few minutes of reminiscing and polite inquiries after the former soldier's family, Rhys only had to drop the hint.

"My lady here"—he tilted his head in Meredith's direction—"has been longing for a glimpse of the baths, but we're set to leave town early tomorrow. Don't suppose you could see your way clear to . . ."

A wink, a smile, and a rattle of keys—and he and Meredith were inside.

Alone.

"It's quite mysterious at night, isn't it?" Her voice echoed off the stone colonnade as they walked the edge of the rectangular pool. The colonnade was covered, but the water itself was open to the night sky. Above them, the moon and stars worked in concert to illuminate the space, unhampered by clouds and diffused by the steam of the hot spring.

Though it was impossible to see across the pool to the other side of the colonnade, Rhys could see Meredith quite clearly, and that was all he cared about. The steam curled the wisps of hair at her temples and loosened the creases from her gown. It also misted her pale complexion, and those strong curves of her face had the sheen of alabaster, carved and polished to a gleam.

She walked around the perimeter of the mineral bath, letting her ungloved fingertips graze each column as she passed. "So this is the center of Bath."

"Its *raison d'être*," he confirmed.

"People of means will travel from all over England to come here, spend untold sums on rented rooms and amusements, all to be near this smelly basin of water. Amazing."

"It's not just the waters."

"Of course not. It's the high fashion. The society. The promise of health and the allure of a pagan legend. I read the Romans had a temple to Minerva here."

"Care to have a bath?" he asked.

Her nose wrinkled. "Here?"

He nodded, running a fingertip along the slope of her shoulder. "There's no one to see." A moonlit, private bath in an ancient spring? If this wasn't romantic, Rhys didn't know what was.

"Thank you, no," she said stoutly. "We haven't any towels with us, and it smells horrid. I don't want to go back to Devonshire smelling of rotten eggs. Besides, don't invalids stew in there all day? It's . . . it's like a broth of disease."

Well, then. When she put it that way . . . Not so romantic after all.

He cleared his throat. "Shall we be off?"

As they left the baths, she said, "Please don't be offended. Thank you so much for showing me this place. I'm glad to have seen it. And I adore bathing with you, as you well know. I'd just prefer the tub at our hotel. Or the pool at home."

She gasped and stopped dead in the street. "But that's it. The pool. Of course, that's the answer."

Rhys had no idea what her little epiphany involved, but as she went quiet to sort it out, he seized the opportunity to admire her. The adorable way her brow wrinkled in concentration. The little flutter of her fingers as they made brisk calculations. The breathless excitement in her manner. He knew the signs. Whatever it was she was working out, it must have something to do with the inn.

A realization settled in his gut. It was always the inn. She lived for that place. It brought her trouble and hard work, yes. But it also brought her joy. All this time, he'd been assuming that once her initial wariness wore off, she'd gladly accept the advantages of marrying him. But now he wondered . . . if he offered her a true choice between the two, would he even stand a chance?

She bounced across the street to his side, and when she spoke again, her whole face lit from within. Like a small, round moon floating along in the dark.

"It's the pool, don't you see? We have a spring of our own in Buckleigh-in-the-Moor. One with water that flows crisp and sweet, not malodorous and revolting. And we have a natural place for bathing, far more picturesque than a Roman bath. Heavens, we have our own *actual* ruins. We don't need to go about constructing them, as they did for the Gardens."

She put her arm through his and pulled him along, keeping up her steady stream of plans. "Naturally, the village could never hope to have the fashionable or cultural pull of Bath, but we might be able to style it as some sort of spa. We only have to spread word of the waters, and their healthful benefits. And come up with some sort of pagan legend for Darryl to tell."

"Isn't there one already? I thought every nook and cranny of the moor had a story attached to it."

"True," she said, "but most of them are frightening. All witches and curses and . . ."

"Living phantoms?" He pinched her midsection playfully and whispered, "Boo."

She smiled. "No, I'm serious. The thing to do is start with a classic tale, but twist it to our purpose. You've had all that Eton education. What are some legends to do with pools and lakes? Romantic ones, not the ghoulish sort."

He thought on for a moment. "Do you want something Arthurian and medieval? There's always the Lady of the Lake."

"That won't do. Why would people want to take baths in a pool with some shriveled, soggy woman lurking at the bottom of it? She might grab their ankles."

"Echo and Narcissus?" he suggested.

"How does that one go?"

"I'm no storyteller like Darryl. I don't think I even remember it correctly."

She squeezed his arm. "Just do your best."

"Well, as I recall, Narcissus was a good-looking fellow. Beautiful, they said, and very vain. He spent all his time gazing at his own reflection in a pool. And Echo—she was a nymph—she was in love with him, I suppose. But she had a curse or something, and she had no words of her own. She was only able to repeat what others said to her. So he would sit by the pool, and she would just stand behind him quietly adoring. Until one day, Narcissus said to his own reflection, 'I love you,' and Echo was at long last able to say 'I love you' to him."

"And what happened?"

"The vain fool never took notice of her. She wasted away to just an echo of her voice. And he stared at his own reflection until he went mad with frustration and stabbed himself." Rhys chuckled.

Meredith didn't. She didn't say anything for a good long while.

They turned the street corner, and the way was more shadowed. The night had grown late, and they were alone. She clutched his arm in the dark.

"Merry? Are you well?"

"I used to watch you."

They stopped walking.

"I used to watch you," she repeated, turning to him by slow degrees. First her head pivoted, then her body. Finally, she lifted her chin and looked him in the face. "At the pool. When I was a girl. I used to follow you there in secret and hide behind the rocks."

"What?" Rhys felt as though he'd had the breath knocked out of him. He was stunned. "Why would you do that?"

"It was wrong, I know it." Her words were a rush. "I shouldn't have. But I was young and . . . and curious."

Curious? Anger swelled inside him. The same as it always did, when he picked himself up from a blow.

Grasping her by the elbow, he pulled her into a darkened alcove where a small flight of stairs met the street. "Just what did you see?"

"You." She swallowed hard. Her lip trembled. "All of you."

His heart stalled for a moment, until his vicious oath spurred it back to life.

That pool had been his refuge after a beating. His one safe place. There he would examine the damage to his body, soothe his wounds with the cool spring water, try to wash himself clean of the blood and shame. And to think, someone had been spying on him from the rocks, all that time? It churned his stomach. He'd been naked, in every way. Vulnerable. All those purpling bruises and raw, angry welts . . . she'd seen them. She'd seen them all.

It had taken him years to cover all the wounds his father had wrought. He'd healed from some and hidden the rest under other, newer scars. Or at least, he thought he'd hidden them. But he hadn't. Meredith had seen them. Every single one. Even the ones he couldn't have seen himself.

Adding to that mortification, he'd been an adolescent with natural male impulses, desperate for even a fleeting moment of pleasure . . .

Damn it to hell. So that's how she knew he favored his left hand.

He dragged in a breath and choked on the air. "I can't believe this."

"Rhys, please."

He turned away, disgusted. Disgusted with her, in some measure. But mostly disgusted by himself. Had he truly dreamed that Meredith would marry him? Willingly? Even women who hadn't been witness to such shame were repelled by his touch.

He tugged at his cravat, pulling it loose from his throat. The air felt too thick to breathe. She knew. She knew everything.

"Please." She grabbed his sleeve and laid her other hand to his cheek, tugging him to face her. He turned his head, but he still couldn't bear to meet her eyes.

"I'm so sorry," she said, her voice breaking. "It was terribly wrong of me, and I know that now. But I followed you everywhere. I couldn't help it. You were strong and wild and always in motion, and everything I wished I could be, and I . . . I was fascinated by you. Infatuated, to tell the truth."

A derisive laugh caught in his throat. "Infatuated."

"Yes," she replied, her voice strengthening. "Yes. I

adored you. I was mad for you. God help me, I still am now."

She slid both hands to his face and pulled his head down, brushing a kiss to his jaw, then the corner of his mouth. Then his cheek. Then each of his closed eyes in turn. His own hands stayed clenched in fists at his sides. Part of him was aching for the closeness, but he didn't trust himself to touch her.

"Please," she whispered, pressing her cheek to his. "Please, don't be ashamed. And don't be angry with me, I can't bear it. I'm so sorry. I was a foolish girl, with a girl's foolish dreams. I just wanted to be near you, in whatever way I could."

She kissed his lips. Desire ricocheted down his spine.

"Rhys," she whispered, sliding her arms around his neck. "I couldn't help it. It was just like the story. You were so very beautiful."

She rested her brow against his chin. He felt her breath drifting over his throat. Fast and hot, as if she were afraid, or aroused, or both. On his side, definitely both. His chest rose and fell with each ragged gasp.

He had no secrets left. No defenses. He had nothing, except that same vast, dark, empty, infinite ache that had resided in him for as long as he could remember. An endless flight of stairs, leading down and down into the cold, dark pit of his soul. Now, at long last, he'd reached the absolute rock bottom. And there she was, just standing there. She'd been there all along.

He cursed her. He blessed her. He needed her. Now.

"I want you." The words scraped from his throat. "Here."

"Yes."

The soft hiss of the word slid over his skin. He clenched his fists at his sides, grappling with his emotions. "I can't be gentle."

"I don't care." She lifted her face to his. "Just be quick."

And once they'd made the agreement to join, they immediately separated. They each took a step back and began wrestling with their own clothing. Because that was the fastest way.

Rhys tossed a glance over his shoulder as he wrenched open his trouser placket and flicked loose the closures of his smalls. There was no one in the street. Even if there had been a crowd of onlookers, he wasn't sure he could have stopped. The need to get inside her was as intense and primal as any he'd ever known.

By the time he turned back, she had her skirts and petticoats hiked above her knees—just high enough that he could glimpse the ribbon ties of her garters and the milk-white skin above. Her inner thigh quivered. Perversely, he wanted to bite her there.

But there was no time for that.

"Hurry," she whispered, leaning back against the wall and canting her hips in invitation.

He freed his erection and knew a moment of cool night air before finding her waiting heat. Lifting her by the hips, he thrust into her tight sheath. Again and again, plunging a little deeper each time, feeling her body give him more, and yet more, but still not quite enough. He worked harder, boring into her with insistent thrusts, determined to penetrate her just as deeply as he could. It still wouldn't compare to how she'd invaded him.

"More," he growled. "Take it all."

At his words, she came apart. Her teeth scraped the tendon of his neck as she stifled her cry of ecstasy. Her intimate muscles clamped down, making his way even more difficult, but ratcheting the pleasure to an unfathomable degree. And he kept thrusting, pushing through the exquisite resistance, until he sank all the way to the root.

Ah, God. So good. So good.

"Stop," she whispered frantically. "There's someone . . ."

He froze. Light footsteps clattered down the cobblestone street, ever louder. Ever closer.

He pressed her into the furthest corner of the alcove, guarding her body with his. With his dark clothes, they would melt into the shadows and remain unnoticed. He hoped. Their combined breath was a dull roar in his ears, and his heartbeat knocked loudly against hers. He could only be still and pray their passion wasn't audible from the street.

All the while, the last tremors of her release caressed his arousal, teasing him to an unbearable peak of tension. Not helping the cause of silence.

By the time the footsteps finally faded, Rhys's legs were shaking with need. He withdrew and thrust again.

Sweet mercy. This was rapture.

Their forced interruption had heightened every sensation. Not just heightened—multiplied. In that spirit, he doubled his pace, stroking into her with abandon. The base of his spine tingled in anticipation. So close. So close.

A hoarse shout tore from his chest as pleasure exploded inside him, blanking his vision and driving out everything else.

He slumped against her chest, pinning her to the wall. Pure joy simmered and hummed in unlikely parts of his body. His stiff finger. His damaged left knee. The scarred, wounded chest that covered his wildly thumping heart. For this one blessed moment, pleasure was all he knew.

"Merry, I . . ." Words failed him. He just stood there,

panting into her hair, just waiting for her to tell him what came next. Because damned if he knew anymore.

"Ask me," she whispered in his ear. He could hear a smile in her voice. "Know that I don't believe in fate, or destiny, or anything else except what lies between us, right here, right now. Now ask me to marry you."

Oh, God. As he pulled in a deep breath, her jasmine scent permeated his very being. He could taste her sweet nectar on his tongue. All this could be his, so easily.

And he was about to do the most damn fool thing of his life.

"I will." He cleared his throat and pulled away to look her in the eye. "But I must tell you something first."

Chapter Twenty

"You need to tell me something?" Meredith felt her smile spreading into a silly, cheek-stretching grin.

"Yes."

Please, she thought. Please let it be *I love you.* And then, like Echo, she could say the words back. Not just once, but a hundred times. *I love you, I love you. I have always loved you. I will love you so hard and hold you so tight, I will make everything better. Every instance of pain will be forgotten, and from this moment forward, you will only know bliss.*

But as the silence stretched, Meredith felt her smile fading. "Are there more than three words involved?"

He sighed. "Most definitely."

His eyes were so earnest, so troubled. He seemed to have missed her hopeful hint completely. Which, in that case, was probably for the best.

"Oh." She became suddenly conscious of the stone digging into her shoulder blade. "Then . . . may I lower my skirts?"

"Yes, of course. Sorry."

He withdrew from her body and tucked himself back in, refastening his trousers in haste. The cravat was a lost cause. He wadded it up and stuffed it in his pocket, where it shared the space with that last orange. Meredith felt, with a sad, sudden certainty, they would never eat it.

She shook out her skirts and smoothed them down.

"Let's walk," he said. "It's easier to converse that way." He took her by the hand and led her out of the shadows. The street being deserted, they promenaded down the absolute center at a stately pace. A parade of two. Her heart served as the pounding bass drum.

"After what you told me, earlier . . ." He rubbed his neck with his free hand. "I gather you know my father and I . . . Well, we didn't get on."

The understatement was so great, so absurd—she had to bite back an incredulous laugh. "Yes. I know he beat you. Regularly. Severely." For her part, she wasn't going to mince words. If he wanted to talk about it, they were going to *talk* about it. He'd been holding his silence for far too long. "Until that last summer," she added softly. "What made him stop?"

"I grew too big. I came home from Eton four inches taller and two stone heavier than when I'd left."

"I remember."

He looked askance at her, as though questioning why she should have noticed such a thing. She shrugged. How could she not?

"I came back to Nethermoor that summer," he said, "and for the first time I stood taller than my father. I was younger than him, and healthier, too. We both knew I could best him in a fair fight. So the next time he tried to order me into the cellar . . . I simply stood tall and said, 'No. Not anymore.' And that was the end of it."

She hugged his arm. "That was very brave of you."

"It was stupid, is what it was. He was enraged, and the fury had no outlet. One night, a few weeks later, I came back from a ride to find him in the stables. He was worked into a frenzy, whipping a mare for only the

Devil knows what reason. The grooms were powerless to stop him. Your father wasn't around."

Her whole body tensed.

He noticed. "I gather you know where this story is going."

She nodded. Queasiness puddled thickly in the pit of her stomach.

"I fought him," he said. "And in the scuffle, I knocked a lamp into the straw. That's how the fire began."

Oh, no. No, no, no. This was her every worst fear coming true.

She reeled to a halt and turned to him, eyes wide and burning with tearful fatigue. She wished she could shut them and just sleep. Pretend this conversation wasn't happening. "But . . ." The word fell off her trembling lips.

"Yes." He sighed heavily. "You know how it went from there. The horses . . . most of them died. Horrible, agonizing deaths. Your father was crippled trying to save them. The entire estate was lost, plunging the village into economic depression. And not a day has gone by in the fourteen years since that I haven't thought of that night. Dreamed of it. And wished that I'd died instead."

"Oh, no." Her hand went to her mouth. "You can't possibly blame yourself."

Fool thing to say. Obviously, he could. And had, for all the years since. The realization seized her heart and wrung it hard. She couldn't breathe.

He shook his head. "I shouldn't have fought him back. He wanted to beat that horse. I should have just let him beat me. I'd taken countless beatings from him over the years. If I'd just taken one more, none of it would have happened."

"How can you say such a thing? That fire, it . . . it was an accident. It wasn't your fault, Rhys."

"I don't believe in accidents. And it hardly matters whether or not I own the blame. The responsibility is mine, the duty to make it right. I'm Lord Ashworth now, much as I prayed I'd never live to inherit that title."

"I . . ." A wave of dizziness unsteadied her. "I think I need to sit down."

He pulled her over to a small row of steps leading up to a narrow stoop and urged her to sit on the topmost riser.

Then he sank to one knee before her.

"I couldn't bear to hide it from you," he said. "You deserve to know the truth. And I need you to know it. If you marry me . . ."

His voice trailed off. Meredith was struck by the significance of what he'd just said. *If.* For the first time, he'd used the word "if."

"If you marry me," he repeated slowly, "you'll be waking up every morning next to the man responsible for your father's injuries, the village's plight, your own years of work and sacrifice. I need to know you can live with that." He held up an open palm. "Don't answer me right now. Think on it, good and hard, before you decide. You were right. I owe you this much, to offer you a real choice."

His big hands engulfed hers where they lay folded in her lap. "I swear, if you give me the chance, I will fix everything." Sincerity rang in his voice. "I vow to you before God, I will take care of your father for the rest of his years. I will make certain the villagers never go hungry. And I will devote all the strength of my body and all the determination of my soul to the purpose of making you happy. All I ask of you is the chance."

She swallowed hard, shivering with emotion.

"I need this, Meredith. I need to make it right, or I don't know how I'll go on." His eyes squeezed shut. "Please. Marry me."

A tear streaked down her face. Lord, this was terrible. And not in the way he believed. Even if he had knocked over that lamp, she would never hold him blameworthy for that fire, nor any of its consequences. But could she truly consent to marry him, knowing that he viewed their marriage as a sort of penance for sins that weren't even his own?

Perhaps she could, and that was the worst part of all. Even now, the word "yes" hovered on her tongue. She wanted him so much. Maybe she truly had it in her to let him live under that perpetual burden of guilt and keep him for herself, always. Maybe she could even trick herself into believing that if only she loved him fiercely enough, it would all be for the best, in the end. Did she have the capacity for a lifetime of deceit? She was a little afraid to look within herself and find out.

"You'll think on it?" he asked.

She managed a nod. "Can we go home? Tomorrow?" She tightened her fingers around his. At home, everything would be clear. There, she would know what to do. "Rhys, will you just take me home?"

"If that's what you wish . . ." Wearing a grim expression, he rose to his feet. "Yes, of course."

She talked all the way home.

Rhys had never known Meredith could have so many words to speak and so very little to say. As the coach rolled on through Somersetshire and Devonshire, their cargo of porcelain and silver clinked in crates above them, whilst Meredith kept up a steady rattle of her own. He supposed she was afraid that if she stopped talking for any significant length of time, he would come forth with another shocking revelation. He didn't know how to reassure her that there were none left.

So he simply sat and listened—the sound of her voice was never hard on his ears. Every once and a while, she would go pensive for a bit, but soon she'd burst forth with an entirely new topic. All of them, however, had something to do with the inn.

"I've decided what to work on improving next, once the new wing is completed." Without waiting for his encouragement, she continued, "I need to help Mr. Handsford smarten up his house, and add a fresh coat of limewash to the church."

He silently pondered the meaning of those two gestures, knowing he wouldn't need to ask for an explanation.

Sure enough, one was soon forthcoming. "That's one thing I learned from the hotel in Bath," she said. "Remember we had that lovely view of the river? It's not only the outward appearance of the inn that's important, it's the prospect a guest will see from her room. The church and Mr. Handsford's cottage are directly across the road. They can be seen from each new room's windows, so we need to be certain they're looking their best. The entire village needs to look its best. Clean, bright, cheery. Perhaps we'll paint all the shutters and sashes red."

He didn't answer. Just gave a low grunt of agreement and turned his face to the window.

"Oh, but the visitors are the most important thing. If only we could be assured some guests of quality, to spread word of the spa."

"I don't suppose a duke and his duchess would serve?"

"A *duke*? Do you know one?"

"I know several. But the Duke of Morland owes me a favor. You'd like his wife a great deal, I think." Rhys had hoped to invite the couple to Devonshire sometime soon. But he'd envisioned Meredith welcoming them as Lady Ashworth, not as landlady of the Three Hounds.

"Oh!" She clapped her hands together. "That would

be ideal. I shall have to make up the new corner room to perfection. The ducal suite."

He sighed. Her answer must be no, then. That was the only explanation for her nervous energy and her persistent focus on the inn. She was already preparing for a life without him.

Damn it. He knew he shouldn't have told her the truth.

But she hadn't officially refused him yet. He still had some time to change her mind. Or perhaps the cottage could. She hadn't been out to see it in a while. With the windows and doors cut out and the roof freshly thatched, it looked cozy and welcoming, if rustic. And if it was scenery she'd grown to value, she should see the prospect from her dormer window. Perhaps she'd fall in love with the view.

Right.

Again they made good time on the journey, and a smoky dusk was just settling as they reached the border of the moor.

"Is it much farther?" she asked, peering out into the twilight.

"Ten or twelve miles, I should say. Another hour or two."

"I don't like the looks of this weather. A mist will be on us soon." She took a rug from the coach's underseat compartment and shrank into the corner of the bench, wrapping the woven blanket over her legs. To Rhys, seated on the opposite side, she looked very small. And very far away.

A mist did indeed bloom from the humid moorland air, enveloping the coach and making for much slower progress. The lamps illuminated a small section of the road ahead—enough that the carriage could safely continue, albeit at a slower pace. But the final hour of their journey stretched into three, and it was full night when they rolled into Buckleigh-in-the-Moor.

"They won't be expecting us tonight," she said.

He couldn't tell whether or not she looked forward to surprising them.

In the end, however, he and Meredith were the ones taken by surprise. The moment the coach rolled to a halt in the courtyard of the Three Hounds, a man rushed out from the stables to greet them. The mist was so thick, Rhys could barely make him out as George Lane until they'd alighted from the coach and he stood two feet in front of them.

"Merry, Rhys." He coughed, clearly out of breath. "Thank the Lord you're here."

"Father." Meredith gripped the old man's arm. "For heaven's sake, what is it? What's happened? Are you well?"

"I'm fine, it's—" He broke off coughing again. "It's Cora. She's missing. We only just realized it a half hour ago, but no one's seen the girl since the noon meal. Mrs. Ware says she might remember her expressing an intent to go up toward the cottage. The men were supposed to be working late up there today, finishing the floors. Perhaps she thought to take them some extra food? I don't know. But the men came back not an hour ago. None of them had seen her. And with this mist . . ."

"Oh, God," Meredith choked out.

She didn't have to explain the dangers to Rhys. Cora could be lost anywhere on the moor. She might have wandered into the bog or stumbled down a slope. And if she were caught out overnight with no protection from the elements . . .

He put an arm about Meredith's shoulders. "We'll find her. I'll find her." He tried to sound reassuring, but the truth was, if the girl had been missing for several hours in this weather, it didn't bode well. "Do you have the men searching?" he asked George Lane.

"Darryl's organizing them in the tavern."

Darryl Tewkes was organizing? Rhys groaned. God help them all.

His face grim with resolve, Rhys headed straight for the inn. Meredith followed a step behind, chilled to the bone with fear. Even if Cora were a complete stranger, she would have worried for her safety in this situation. But in just a few short weeks, she'd grown surprisingly fond of the girl. If they didn't find her . . .

This was her reward for leaving on holiday. This village could not function without her. She should have known something horrid would happen. She should have never left.

Rhys flung open the door to the public room, announcing his presence with a bang. Darryl, standing atop the bar, trailed off mid-sentence.

And then, a small miracle occurred. For the first time since Rhys's arrival in Buckleigh-in-the-Moor, the assembled men at the Three Hounds greeted him with a unanimously warm reception. Scattered words of thanksgiving rose up from the crowd, along with a hearty cheer. Relief softened every face in the room. Even the hounds came scrambling out from the kitchen, their claws clicking and sliding over the flagstones as they tumbled over one another in the race to nip at his boots.

And then all assembled went quiet, awaiting direction from their lord.

At some point over the past two months, Rhys had earned not only the respect of every soul in the village, but their trust, as well. In any other circumstance, Meredith's heart would have warmed to see it.

"Lamps," he said to Meredith. "We'll need lamps. As many as you can find. Torches, if you run out."

She nodded. After sending Darryl to collect the lamps from upstairs and the barn, she set about the task of filling and lighting them. From the storeroom, she could overhear all the goings-on in the tavern, where, with brusque, military authority, Rhys was rousing the men to action. He barked questions and waited for answers, divided the men into pairs and assigned each team an area to search. When the men came tromping through, single file, for their lamps, she and Darryl had them ready.

"Tewkes, you're with us. We're headed down the lane." Skinner jerked his head, and Darryl picked up a lamp and followed.

Rhys was last to come through. "I'm going up to the high moor. If she made it to the cottage, she probably had the good sense to stay there."

"You're going alone?" Meredith asked. The others had already departed in groups. Naturally, Rhys would have saved the most harrowing and perilous section of the area for himself.

He nodded. "Stay here, in case she comes back."

"Bollocks to that," Meredith said, lighting another lamp. "I'm going with you. I know the lay of the land better than you do. You're not going into that mist on your own." Before he could get the objection past his lips, she added, "Father's here, if she returns. Just let me retrieve my boots and cloak."

His jaw tightened with uncertainty. She held his piercing gaze, refusing to flinch.

Finally, he gave her a curt nod of assent. "Hurry."

She was up and down the back stairs in the space of a minute. Another few moments more, and she'd wrestled into her thickest boots and exchanged the courtesan's traveling cape for her own cloak of sturdy brown wool. "I'm ready."

They headed through the tavern door and forged out into the gloom.

It was an eerie sight—the men departing for the search. The cluster of lamps dispersing; the amber balls of light swallowed into the misty dark, one by one. The cries "Hullo!" and "Ho, there!" and "Cora, love!"— these too grew fainter and less frequent as the searchers scattered in every possible direction.

Meredith and Rhys began their slow ascent to the high moor. With visibility so poor, the ancient monks' path was the only safe route, though longer. The higher they climbed, the thicker the mist became, until Meredith felt as though she were swimming through milk. The lamps served only to illuminate the fog itself, giving it ghostly fingers and a deceptively comforting, cottony texture. They could see no more than a few paces in front of them.

"Cora! Cora, can you hear us?"

They took turns calling out into the darkness. Between the exertion of the climb and the strain of shouting and the oily smoke of the lamp burning her nostrils, Meredith's throat was raw by the time they crested Bell Tor. They had a choice here: Veer off toward the cottage or head straight for the ruins of Nethermoor Hall.

"Cottage first," Rhys said, answering her unspoken question.

They made their way over to the flat, picking up pace as they did. The even ground made for faster progress, as did the fact that in building the cottage, Rhys had cleared the area of stones.

Still, they almost stumbled right into the cottage as it rose up out of the mist. Meredith put one hand to the freshly pared earthen wall and followed it round, until her fingers met with a new texture—sanded wood.

"The door's been fitted and hung," she told him. She

hadn't seen the house for a few weeks now. She'd been so busy overseeing progress down at the inn.

"Good," he replied. "Glad to know the men weren't just loafing about while we were in Bath."

The door wasn't latched, however, and it swung inward noiselessly. The clarity of the darkness within the house was almost startling, as the fog had not penetrated the walls. Meredith lifted her lamp and flinched when a beam of light bounced back at her, reflecting off the new windowpanes.

"Cora!" They called out as one, lifting their voices to the rafters. "Cora, are you in here?"

No answer.

Meredith swore under her breath. Until this moment, she'd managed to hold panic at bay. Now she felt it rattling at the windowpanes.

"We'll check the whole house anyway," he said. "She could be asleep somewhere. You look down here. I'll go upstairs."

She nodded. Holding her lamp high, she began a slow circuit of the lower floor. The cottage had a simple arrangement, but a pleasing one. At one end was a large kitchen. It shared a double-sided hearth with the drawing room, which took up the center of the cottage. There were smaller rooms at the back—larder, closet. She didn't find Cora in any of them. Then, at the opposite end of the ground floor there was a bedroom suite with its own separate hearth, complete with a small dressing room. It was all very thoughtful in its simplicity.

The stairs hadn't yet been completed, but there was a ladder up to the second floor. Climbing with one hand and gripping her lamp with the other, she made her way up the rungs until her head and shoulders emerged into the loft. "Any luck up here?" she asked, pushing her lamp onto the newly laid floorboards so she could use both hands to pull herself up.

"None. Downstairs?"

Meredith couldn't answer him. And she wished she could say the reason for her silence was anxiety for poor Cora. But it wasn't. She'd just taken her first good look at the second floor of the cottage, and what she saw simply stole her breath.

"Rhys, this is . . ." She swallowed hard. "This is lovely."

"You weren't meant to see it yet." He came over and offered a hand as she managed the ladder's last few rungs.

The entire loft was open from end to end, making one large room. Only the chimney coming up from the kitchen divided the space. As below, it had dual hearths—one facing a nook tucked under the eaves, the other situated to throw heat toward the rest of the room. The sharply sloping roof soared high above them in the center, but tapered to meet the tops of the windows at each edge. The rafters and thatch were left exposed, giving it a homey feel. The scent of freshly planed wood shavings filled the air.

As she slowly toured the space, he said, "I hoped you'd approve of our rooms—or *room*, I should say— being upstairs. The place is meant to be your father's eventually . . . so with his legs, I thought it best to keep his bedchamber downstairs. Since it would be just us up here, and temporarily at that, I left it undivided and the ceiling unfinished. Gives us plenty of room for now, and once we move out the space can be used for storage or servants. I thought it cozy."

"Very cozy," she agreed.

"I thought I'd build a bed into this nook," he explained, walking over to the smaller space created by the hearth's division. "Nice and warm, you know, with the fire so close. And then"—energetic strides carried him to the opposite end—"shelves and cupboards at this end.

In the middle, a sitting area. A desk for all your papers and such, right under this window."

"What are these?" she asked, picking up a misshapen lump of wood from a pile near the window.

"Those are . . ." He darted over to take it from her hand, stepping between her and the rest of the heap. "Not finished."

She craned her neck, trying to look around him. "They almost look like—"

"They aren't."

She crossed her arms and cocked her head. "Very well. Don't tell me. We'll just stand here all night, denying the existence of little bits of wood."

He rolled his eyes and sighed. "Fine." He took the lump of wood from behind his back and lobbed it at her.

She caught it easily and held it up for examination, turning it over in her hands. "Why, it's carved. These look like leaves." Looking up, she raised an eyebrow at him. "Is it meant to be a pineapple?"

"No," he said impatiently, spearing a hand through his hair before snatching it from her grasp. "It is not a pineapple. It's meant to be a lily. I think." He kicked gently at the pile of wooden knobs, separating them. "There's a matching one here somewhere. As I said, they're not finished. The roses are coming out a little better. Have a look." He plucked another from the pile and held it out to her.

"Ah, I see." The object in her hand resembled a wooden cabbage more than anything, but she wouldn't have said so for the world. "What are they for?"

"Finials, for the curtain rods. There are four windows up here, you see. I've been working on a different set for each." He pointed to each window in turn. "Roses. Lilies. Daisies." His touch landed on the windowpane at their side. "Tulips."

He took the wooden rose from her hand and gave it a

rueful smile. "I know they're pitiful. But the work gave me something to pass the time if I woke in the night."

"Why flowers?"

He shrugged. "I promised you flowers, didn't I?"

She couldn't even answer, for the sharp pinch in her chest.

"My first attempts were far worse than these, if you can believe it. They came easier once I switched to my left hand. You gave me that idea."

Meredith turned to the window, unable to meet his gaze. "Tulips for this one, did you say? Then it must be the best."

"It is." He put his hands on her shoulders and nudged her close to the glass. "When it's a clear day, up this high, you can see for miles. And if you face the down-slope and look very sharp, you can just make out a thin slice of blue, a shade darker than the sky. That's the ocean, Merry. Right off the Devonshire coast." His thumbs stroked her shoulders. "Of course, you can't see it now."

No. No, she couldn't. All she could see was the blackness outside reflecting their own image, like a mirror. Even in this imperfect, dark reflection, she could see the excitement in his expression, the spark in his eyes. All the emotion he'd been holding back—he'd poured it all into this house. Not only emotion, but hard work and good faith.

They'd built something too, between them. Just as he'd said from the first. In the course of all those conversations and kisses and time spent in one another's company, they'd pieced together something wonderful— something with lace curtains and corner closets and an ocean view. Not just a house, but a loving home.

How would Rhys react when he learned it was all built on a foundation of misconceptions and needless guilt? Meredith didn't want to find out, but she needed to.

She had to tell him everything. Tonight.

His grip tightened on her shoulders. "You deserve so much more, but this is only the beginning. I'm going to rebuild the whole estate in time, and you're going to live in true luxury. The finest furnishings, a whole fleet of servants. I promise, you'll never lift a finger again."

"You needn't promise me anything."

"I want to. I owe it to you and your father both. You've suffered for years on my account, and now it's—"

"No." She turned to face him. "Please don't speak to me of fate or fires or obligation."

Frowning a little, he smoothed the hair from her brow. "Merry, I don't know what more I can say. I've tried my best with the romance, but—"

She gasped. *Romance.* "Oh, no. Oh, God."

"What is it?"

"Cora. We're here to find Cora."

Rhys swore viciously. How could he have forgotten their errand, for even one second? The guilt he felt was mirrored on Meredith's face.

Shrugging away from him, she went for her lamp. "We've spent enough time here. We've got to go search the ruins."

Together they scrambled up the bluff. Once they reached the ruins of Nethermoor Hall, they separated at what remained of the front entrance and circled in opposite directions. Rhys took the outer perimeter, and Meredith followed the inner wall. They each stumbled and shouted their way around the ruin, calling Cora's name until they were hoarse. Nothing.

He reunited with Meredith at the crumbling arch. The glow of her lamp bobbed in the mist. The wind was picking up.

"Any sign of her?" he asked.

"No."

Thunder rumbled in the distance. Perfect. Just what they needed, a storm. "I suppose we should be getting back to the village, then. Perhaps she's turned up elsewhere."

The bobbing glow stilled. "We haven't checked every part of the ruin yet."

"What do you mean?" he asked.

Though he knew damn well what she meant. Had he forgotten that place, truly? Or had he just wanted to forget it so fiercely that he'd managed to wipe it from his mind? But Meredith was right . . . if Cora had wandered up here, the cellar would have made a logical haven from the mist and cold. They would need to look.

"I'll go alone," she said.

"No," he said. "No, you can't go alone. It's not safe." That place wasn't safe, not for anyone. It never had been. But he'd be damned if he'd let her think that he—who'd faced down Napoleon's Imperial Guardsmen and hamfisted prizefighters alike—was afraid of a damned cellar, filled with nothing but cobwebs and shadow.

Her light swayed as she transferred it from one hand to the other, and for a moment, the features of her face were caressed by soft, smoky light. With her free hand, she reached through the mist to take his. "We'll go together. And we'll do it quickly."

He allowed her to lead the way to the cellar entrance. She seemed to know the way better than he did. It was well-hidden now, obscured by haphazard piles of masonry. Hand in hand, they picked their way over the strewn boulders and found the stairway. The rocks teetered and clacked a bit as they scrambled over them.

The cellar must have been built from a natural cave that his ancestors had widened and deepened with time. Or perhaps they'd quarried the stone for the house, then built right over the empty pit? At any rate, it made an ideal place for storing food and spirits—protected from the elements, cool and dark. Silent. It made an ideal place to keep secrets, too.

As they descended into the dark pit, the sounds of the wind outside were muted. Meanwhile, their every step and sigh echoed off the walls. This place caught every sound, trapped it to rattle about and amplify. Each footfall, each spoken word . . . each crack or blow . . . seemed to have the strength of dozens.

"Cora?" Meredith called out into the darkness. The name volleyed around the room, losing a bit of its consonant edge with each echo, until all that remained was a round, hollow ball of "Oh" bouncing about the dark.

She called again. "Cora, are you here?"

No answer.

Rhys would have added his voice to hers, but his throat had gone dry. His jaw seemed locked in place.

"She's not here," she finally said. "Let's go."

"Wait." The word creaked from his throat. He coughed and tried to master the emotions rising in his gorge. "We don't know that she's not here. We only know she hasn't answered the call. She could be hurt, or asleep. We have to check the whole cellar, every corner."

She was silent for a moment. Then finally said, "All right."

Sweeping his light around, Rhys noticed a great many crates and casks filling the room. Odd. He would have expected to find it stone-empty, especially after all this time. Looted by the locals long ago. Perhaps the rumors of ghosts had kept them away.

He knew they'd descended to the bottom of the staircase when his final footfall hit the ground with a thud that shivered his hipbone. He stumbled over something that felt like a wire.

"Cora?" Meredith called. Her voice was a bright, clear beacon in the blackness. "Cora, are you in here?"

No answer from the girl.

There was, however, an answer from God . . . in the form of a low, menacing groan at the top of the stairs.

"Oh, Lord."

Chapter Twenty-one

There was a crash of thunder.

A crash of stone.

And then a chorus of a hundred small collisions, each one bashing blindly into the next.

The difference was palpable, instantly. It had nothing to do with the lighting—pitch black was pitch black—but rather to do with the air. The cool, misty breeze was instantly sucked from the space, replaced with puffs of grit, and rank, ancient damp. The air was choked with earth and secrets, as if they'd been sealed in a tomb.

"Tell me," said Meredith, "that sound wasn't what I think it was."

"It was," he confirmed. "We're trapped."

Her fingers tightened around his.

"We'll be all right," he said.

At the same moment, she said, "We'll be fine, you know."

And after speaking over one another, they laughed a bit together. Fitting, that each of them should think of comforting the other. They were each of them so accustomed to being the stronger in any given pair.

Once the last bits of their echoed laughter had seeped into the cracks of the stones, Rhys took the lamp from her hand and held it aloft between them. Bravery aside, she was trembling a bit.

"Don't be concerned. You're with me. And I'm indestructible, remember?" It was this very place that had made him so. There was no way in hell he'd die here. Clearing his throat, he went on, "We need to look for something dry and wood. Something that will burn."

"Do you mean to start a fire? It's not that cold."

"No, but this lamp won't last all night. And once we have a bit more light, I'll go up and assess the damage." From the quality of the air, Rhys suspected the cave-in was complete, but he would check it himself to be certain.

Keeping her hand in his, he scouted the immediate area for wood. As his luck would have it, he stumbled into a crate almost instantly. He bent and began prying the boards apart with his bare hands. It was rough going. For a crate stored for more than a decade in a damp, underground room, the wood was surprisingly strong and dry.

Once he had the top of the crate pried off, Rhys waved the lamp over it to see what was inside. Brushing aside a thick layer of straw—again, remarkably fresh and dry—he uncovered several rows of bottles. Strange, that his father would have left this much of any spirit lying about, untouched.

Curling his fingers around a bottleneck, he lifted it to the torchlight. French brandy. And, judging by the rich amber color that swirled red in the flickering light, it was brandy of a fine quality.

Well, that sealed it. This hadn't belonged to his father. The old man had always valued quantity over quality.

"At least we won't die of thirst," Meredith said, taking the bottle from his hand. "I'd wager he has some foodstuffs stored in here, too. I thought he mentioned a crate of olives, some weeks ago. Or was it dates? And I know he was very proud of seizing some silver flatware recently. We could make a right fine meal down here."

"Myles," Rhys breathed. "This all belongs to Gideon Myles. He's been storing his smuggled goods *here*?"

She nodded. "Amongst his associates, he specializes in the hard-to-place items. When they can't find a buyer immediately, or none who'll pay what the goods are worth . . . he brings the goods up here and stores them until he can find a market for them in one of the cities. Some things stay just a week. Others, months."

"A tripwire. The bastard had this place rigged."

"What?"

"It wasn't lightning that caused that cave-in. I thought I'd stumbled over a cord, just before. It must have triggered a powder explosion somewhere."

"Yes, well. That makes sense. Gideon is very protective of his goods."

Rhys held the lamp aloft and blinked until the smoke stung his eyes, straining to make out more of the cavernous room. It was full to bursting with crates, casks . . . even furniture and rolled carpets.

"So," he said. "This is the real reason no one wants me to rebuild Nethermoor Hall. You're all living high off this trade."

"Not living high. Surviving, just barely. Gideon has had to take a great many risks. Harold, Laurence, Skinner . . . they all work for him as lookouts, and they help him transport and unload his cargo."

"And you hire out the ponies to him."

"Yes."

"And accept some of the goods in trade?"

She paused. "Yes, some. Stores for the inn."

He swore softly. What else could he say? The entire village of Buckleigh-in-the-Moor, including his intended bride, was complicit in a vast smuggling ring. He'd known Myles was dealing in unlevied goods, but he'd never dreamed of an operation of this magnitude. Truly, he wouldn't have believed the knave capable of it.

"It's not something I'm proud of, Rhys. I know it's unlawful, and I know it's dangerous. That's why I've been so determined to build up the inn and draw travelers to the district. If I'm ever going to convince Gideon to disentangle himself from this . . . this trade, the village needs another source of income to replace it."

Rhys's jaw tightened. "And the patronage of a new Lord Ashworth won't serve that purpose?"

"I don't know." She sighed noisily. "Not indefinitely. You've said yourself, you don't even intend to produce an heir. You know I'm barren. Unless you mean to marry another lady, but I don't know how you'd convince her to come live in this place." Her voice cracked. "I don't even know how *you* can stand to live in this place. I know what you went through here, Rhys. I grew up watching it. I saw every bruise, every welt—"

He shoved the lamp into her hand and bent to pry a board off the crate. "I need to make a fire."

He couldn't talk about this now. He'd rather not talk about it, ever.

"Rhys—"

Crack. He braced a board between his hand and the ground, then broke it in two with his boot. After throwing the splintered pieces into a pile, he wrenched another plank free and prepared to repeat the process. "Look at the smoke," he told her, determined to change the subject.

Her eyes went to the swirl of black soot coiling away from the lamp, rising into the air.

"It's drawing upward," he said. "That means there's ventilation someplace. A crack—either in the caved-in entrance, or above us somewhere. Once daylight comes, I'll be able to make us a way out of here. We just have to wait for dawn."

"And pray for poor Cora." She sniffed. "What can I do?"

"Gather some straw for tinder," he said. "And I don't suppose you've a screw for uncorking that brandy?"

"No, I haven't a screw. But I have my ways."

"I'm certain you do." If he was going to spend a night in this hole, at the least he was going to do so while warm to the marrow and drunk out of his skull.

They cleared a small depression in the ground to use as a firepit. Rhys arranged the broken planks, propping them against one another, and Meredith stuffed the gaps with straw. Then she cracked the top off a bottle of brandy with a stone and dashed a liberal amount of spirits over the kindling. One spark from the lamp, and . . .

Whoosh.

They had a fire.

For a moment, the flames blazed so high, so bright, that Rhys stood frozen, accosted by memories of the last time Nethermoor had seen roaring flames. His heart kicked into a gallop, and sweat broke out on his brow. But the brandy quickly flamed out, and the fire settled down to a small, respectable, unthreatening size. One might have called it cozy. Even romantic.

Adding to the effect, Meredith unrolled a fantastically expensive-looking Afghan carpet and arranged it alongside the fire. "Oh look," she said, prying open a newly revealed trunk. "Furs." A pile of sable and ermine soon graced the carpet's geometric design.

Good God. A small fortune was stored in this cellar.

While she dug about for cups, Rhys took the dying lamp and went to inspect the entrance. As he'd suspected, rocks had shifted and fallen, covering the opening completely. They might be movable, if he could wedge a board or bar in just the right place. But until he had some daylight shining through, he'd have little way of knowing whether his efforts were making matters better or worse.

When he scrambled back down to the cellar floor, he found Meredith brushing the packing straw from a silver tea service. Lifting her skirt, she reached beneath for a fold of clean petticoat to wipe the cups clean.

"There you are," she said, pouring brandy into a teacup and holding it out to him. "Is it hopeless?"

"No. But it's not worth trying to dig our way out tonight."

"Then come be comfortable, and save your strength for the morning."

They nestled into the furs side by side, but not embracing. A long, empty night together stretched out before them. It didn't seem possible to him that they'd get through it without having a certain conversation, so he decided to confront it head-on.

"So what is it, then? Your answer." In the ensuing silence, he took an anxious, overlarge swallow of his brandy. It burned all the way down.

She drank, too. Finally she whispered, "I'm still not sure."

Shaking his head, he quietly swore. This time, he tossed back an even larger draught of brandy. Because he knew it would burn, and he welcomed it.

"Are you angry?"

"Why should I be angry?"

"You have every reason in the world to be angry, Rhys. I don't know how you can even sit in this place and remain so calm."

He wasn't too sure himself. Brandy had something to do with it. He took another drink, then let his head roll back against the clammy surface of the wall.

"Do you want to talk about it?" she asked.

"Talk about what? Marriage, or lack thereof? I think we've talked that out."

"Not marriage. About . . . the past. About this place."

He kept quiet, hoping she would be clever enough to take his silence as a sign that no, he did not want to talk about it.

"I know he beat you here."

He tensed his jaw, to keep from growling at her to shut hers. She hadn't accepted him. She didn't have the right to keep poking at his wounds, tracing his scars . . .

"Everyone in service at Nethermoor knew."

"This pit is soundproof," he bit out. "No one knew what went on down here."

"Well, I suppose no one did know, not precisely. But it was impossible not to notice the evidence after the fact. And what do you think he did when you went off to school? Do you suppose he gave up violence for the winter term?"

A hot coal lodged in his chest. He could barely manage to form the words. "Did he hit you?"

"No. No, not me."

A drop of sweat rolled from his brow to his ear. Thank God. If he found out his father had hurt Meredith, Rhys truly would have lost control.

"My father was very careful," she said. "He never let me run about the Hall, never would have allowed me to work for the man. But there were others who didn't have a father looking out for them."

"And then there was me, whose father *was* the problem. No escape."

"Tell me what happened. Just have out with it, and you'll feel better."

He sincerely doubted that. But they were here all night, and he could tell she wasn't going to let the matter rest. Fine, then. He'd have out with it, and then he'd drink himself into oblivion. And when he woke in the morning and crawled out of this hole, he would leave this place behind. Forever.

He cleared his throat and prepared a dispassionate tone. "The month after my mother died, my father brought me down into this pit. He told me to stand in the empty center. He melted back into the shadows. And then a fist came out of the darkness. Sent me sprawling to the ground. I was stunned. It took me a minute to realize he'd hit me. I thought it had to have been an accident. He told me to get up, and so I got up. And then he hit me again, harder."

" 'Get up,' he'd say. 'Stand, you miserable wretch.' And so I would struggle to my feet. Only to be hit again. And again, until I couldn't stand at all. We played that amusing little father-son game a few times a week, for the remainder of my childhood. Me standing just about there"—he pointed toward the dark center of the room—"and him beating me until I could no longer stand. Took longer every time."

"For God's sake, why didn't you just stay down?"

"I don't know," he said. And he truly didn't. That would have been the clever thing, he supposed—to feign defeat. But he'd been nine years old, and the old man was his only parent left alive. It simply hadn't crossed his mind to disobey. His father said, "stand"—he stood. He stood and took another blow. It seemed to make the old man oddly happy. What else does a son long to do, but make his father happy?

And after so many years, it was as though that voice had become a part of him. In every brawl, in every battle. Whenever he took a blow or a musket ball and crumpled to the ground, he heard that harsh, brutal command echoing in his head. *Up. Up, you filth. On your feet. Stand and take another.*

So he always got up. No matter how desperately he'd wished to slip over into the next world and leave this one behind, that voice would never let him stay down.

"I don't know why he did it. And he's dead now, so I

never will. Maybe he'd been beating my mother and needed a substitute. Maybe he took some perverse thrill from it. Sometimes I think . . . he just wanted to make me strong. Stronger than he felt, in his own life. Indestructible."

"It's very hard for me not to touch you right now."

"Don't," he snapped in reflex. "I mean . . . I'd prefer you didn't."

"I understand." She paused. "You have every right to be angry. I've been angry with that bastard for nearly two decades now. When word reached us of his death, I wanted to take the next boat to Ireland just to spit on his grave."

"I'm not angry." But even as he said it, his speech grew clipped. "Just what is it you want from this conversation? Are you trying to convince me that my father was a sick bastard? Because I already know that, Merry. Or is this little talk supposed to make me feel better? Should it warm my heart to know that you and your father and every last footman and chambermaid were all perfectly aware that I was being beaten within an inch of my life, and yet stood by and did nothing?"

"No," she said, inching closer. "No, of course not. That's exactly why you should be angry. Not just angry at him, but at this whole place. We all failed you, Rhys. You don't owe this village anything." Her leg grazed his thigh, and he flinched. "You're holding so much emotion inside. I can feel it coming off you in waves. Just let it out."

What he let out was a long, steadying breath. "The man is dead," he said after a time. "If I get angry, I'll just end up taking it out elsewhere. Hurting someone or something that doesn't deserve it. And it won't change a damned thing." He cleared his throat. "In the end, I'm alive, despite his every attempt to kill me and my every attempt to die. Things happen the way they're meant to happen."

She growled. "I am so bloody sick of hearing you talk like that. You were not delivered to this place and time by the hand of destiny, Rhys. You survived, despite everything, by your own strength and wits and courage. I know it, because I'm a survivor too. And it's so frustrating, to hear you go on about fate and destiny and 'meant to be,' when I've been holding that village together with hard work and sacrifice for years. I stayed when others left. I kept working when others had given up. For God's sake, I married a man older than my own *father*. Don't tell me it was all for nothing, and that my life would have turned out just the same no matter what. You insult me when you speak that way. You insult yourself. You've stayed alive, and not because fate preserved you, but because you're a strong, courageous, quick-witted, resilient, good-hearted man. And it cuts me deep, every time I hear you deny it."

He didn't know what to say to that. He rose to stretch and add wood to the fire.

"More brandy?" she asked him, once he was seated again.

He accepted wordlessly.

"I think I've come up with the story. For Darryl to tell, about the pool. Do you want to hear it?"

He didn't, especially. But evidently she took his silence as a yes.

"It's a bit like the one you told me in Bath. Darryl will have his own way with it, but I think it should go something like this." She cleared her throat. "Once, back in the ancient times, when the moors were covered with forests and those forests were thick with magic, there was a small village where Buckleigh-in-the-Moor now stands. The village was plagued nightly by a blood-thirsty wolf. As they slept, the wolf would drag away their weak, their elderly, their children, and devour them. The people were helpless to defend themselves. Then one day a champion came. A strong man, and a good man, charged with protecting the villagers from harm. Every night, the champion would wage an epic battle with the wolf, incurring bites and gashes in his struggle to protect the town. In the morning, once the wolf had returned to its den, he would go to a sacred pool to cleanse his wounds and be healed.

"And there was a young girl. A very curious, often lonely girl. She would follow him in secret every morning, watching as he bathed in the pool, washing away the blood and allowing his wounded body to heal. To her, the champion was the most beautiful man she'd ever beheld, and the bravest. She fell in love with him, though he never noticed her. And the more her love grew, the more it pained her each morning to see the marks the wolf had wrought. Each day his wounds were deeper, more damaging, as the wolf grew more savage with hunger.

"One night, she stayed awake in secret and crept out of her cottage to watch the battle between man and beast. The champion fought with great skill and much heart, but this night the wolf's teeth were keen with desperation. As the girl looked on in horror, the wolf knocked the champion to the ground and stood over his senseless body, preparing to seize him by the throat in his savage, spittle-flecked jaws. The girl drew an arrow and fitted it to her bow. Just as the wolf reared to pounce, she shot a flaming arrow straight through the beast's heart, killing it instantly."

She stopped. "Hm. I suppose we'll need an explanation as to how this girl became such a skilled archer. And why she never killed the wolf on her own before, if so. More brandy?"

"No."

One last trickle into her own glass emptied the bottle, and she let it roll into the shadows. "At any rate, the girl pulled the wounded champion to the sacred pool, and doused him with cool water until all his wounds were healed. And just as he began to open his eyes, she slipped away to hide, afraid to shame him in his nakedness. The villagers, having found the dead wolf, all came running and rejoicing. 'All is well,' they cried. 'The wolf is vanquished, and the village is saved.' They cheered and feted the baffled champion, and he bid them farewell. His work there was done. He went on to fight other, even braver battles in defense of other innocents. The girl never saw him again. But she waited there by the pool, quietly hoping he'd one day return, ever faithful to her love."

Meredith drained her brandy. "She should turn into a rock or a flower or a tree, or something else we can point to now. That's the way these stories go, isn't it?"

"I don't know why you're asking me."

"Don't you? I thought I'd made it rather obvious."

Rhys rubbed his temples. He had a roaring headache from the brandy already, and he was tired of stories and games. "I suppose I'm not as clever as you give me credit for. Stop speaking in riddles, would you?"

"I followed you, Rhys. When I was a girl, I followed you everywhere, whenever I could slip away. And not only to the pool. Whenever you came to the stables, I would hide and watch you. If you took out your horse, I would follow on foot for as long as I could. When I couldn't keep up, I'd return to the stables and wait until you came home from your ride, just to catch one more glimpse of you as you handed the reins to a groom." She laughed a little. "God, the hours I spent in that hayloft, peering down. I perpetually had straw caught in my hair."

"And so . . . ?"

"And so I was there that night. The night of the fire. I was waiting for you to come home. I watched you fight him. You didn't overturn that lantern, Rhys. I threw it. Threw it at *him*, but I missed the bastard. He'd thrown down the whip and reached for the hayfork, and—" Her voice broke. "I will never forget the look on that man's face . . . It was pure evil. He would have killed you."

Rhys choked back a wave of bile. "You should have let him."

"How can you say that?"

"Better me than . . ." Damn it, he should have died that night. Somehow he knew in his soul he was *supposed* to have died that night. And because of her, he'd spent fourteen years stumbling through the world half-alive, looking in vain for an entrance to hell. All for nothing. Nothing.

Irrational rage welled within him. He clenched his hand into a fist. "For God's sake, Meredith. You are a stable master's daughter. You threw a burning lamp in a horse barn? You should have known better."

She buried her face in her hands. "I did know, I do know. But I wasn't even thinking. I just needed to stop him, and it was the closest object to hand."

"All those horses . . . Jesus. They died horrible deaths. Did you hear them screaming? Did you?"

"No." Her voice grew very small.

"Lucky for you. I still hear them." Even now. Even now, in this dark, dank hell, he could hear those screams echoing through his skull. He put his hands to his ears, but it didn't help, because the memories resided between them.

"I ran to raise the alarm," she said. "And then my father forced me to go home."

"Your father . . ."

"My father was maimed. I know it. I know it well. I'm

the one who has bandaged and bathed and dressed and tended him all the days since. And it may be horrible of me to say, but I would do it again. That man would have killed you. No matter what the consequences, I can't be sorry for having stopped him."

He bent his head to his knees, feeling ill.

"Don't you want to know why?" She put a hand to his shoulder.

He shrugged off her touch. "No. No, I don't want to hear any more. My head is killing me. Just leave me be."

He had an awful, sinking suspicion he knew what she would say next. And he didn't want to hear it. He didn't want that precious gift mixed up with all this anger and pain.

"Because I loved you."

Damn, there it was.

Her voice shook. "I have loved you for as long as I can remember, ever since I was a girl. I loved you all those years you were away. I read every page of every newspaper I could find, scouring the print for word of you. I dreamed of you at night. I went to bed with other men, wishing they were you. And I will likely love you until the day I die, because if I could have stopped loving you, I would have found a way to do so by now." She inhaled deeply, then released the breath in a rush. "There. I love you."

Chapter Twenty-two

Meredith waited in the flickering dark, afraid to say more. Afraid to move, or blink, or breathe. There it was, the truth she'd been hiding inside herself for decades now. Hiding so deeply, she'd even been able to deny it to herself. Not any longer.

The longer he went without reacting, the more anxious she became. Fear gnawed at her insides, working its way from the pit of her belly all the way to her limbs. Eroding her chin and fingers and knees from the inside, so that they trembled.

"I love you, Rhys," she said again. Because what was one more time, after all? She laid her trembling fingers against his wrist. "Rhys? Please. Say something."

And after a long, excruciating moment, he spoke exactly one word.

"Fuck."

She nodded. Not what she'd been hoping for, but somehow unarguably fitting.

"Fuck," he said again, louder this time. The curse echoed through the dark. "Why didn't you tell me?"

"I'm so sorry. Until yesterday, I had no idea you'd been blaming yourself all this time. I imagined you thought the fire was an accident. Because it was. It was a stupid, tragic accident."

He raised his head. "How could you keep that from me? Can you have any idea what difference it would have made, if I'd known that all this time?"

"That I threw the lantern? Or that I love you?"

"Both. Can you possibly imagine—" He made a strangled noise in his throat. "For God's sake, my whole damned wasted life . . ."

"I'm sorry. So sorry. I wish I could have told you sooner, but—"

"But what, Meredith? You *could* have told me sooner. You could have told me weeks ago. At least the latter bit."

Her heart squeezed. Scrambling to her knees, she turned to him and wrapped her arms about his shoulders. She simply had to hold him. "I'm telling you now, Rhys. I love you."

His muscles went rigid. "I said, don't touch me. Not in this place."

"All right. I understand." Reluctantly, she let her arms slide from his shoulders and settled back on the floor. "Don't you see? You don't owe this village anything. You don't owe *me* anything. But you owe it to yourself, after all this time and all this pain, to find your own happiness. If you could find true contentment here, I'd want nothing more than to share it with you. But if not . . ." Despite her quivering lips, she willed her voice to be strong. "Then you should go."

He sat in silence. His breath came so quick, she could feel the cellar's humidity increasing by the second. Brushing the dust from his trousers, he rose to his feet and tossed a plank on the fire before wiping clean another bottle of brandy.

"Don't you want to talk about this?"

Crash. The bottleneck broke against a stone. "Talk about what?" he asked tightly, sloshing brandy into his cup.

"You. Us. The past. The future." Could he forgive her, or couldn't he?

He didn't answer, only drank.

She forced herself to be patient. After all she'd told him tonight . . . about the fire, about her feelings . . . she'd altered everything he knew about himself, his past. And everything he knew about her. He must be overwhelmed, just struggling to make sense of it all. And to make it all worse, they were trapped in this place where he'd endured so much pain. Perhaps conversation was beyond him at the moment. For God's sake, she was surprised that standing wasn't beyond him at the moment.

It certainly didn't come easy to her. Using a nearby crate for support, she rose to her feet on wobbly legs.

"I know you must be upset," she said carefully.

"I'm not upset."

"Of course you're upset." How could he keep denying the obvious? "You're angry as hell. It's natural, Rhys. It's all right to show it."

"Why would I be angry?" He sliced the air with his hand, and brandy splashed from his cup. A few drops landed on Meredith's arm. Others spattered and sparked in the fire. His emotions, by contrast, remained at a quiet smolder. "The fire wasn't my fault. You say you love me, always have. The last fourteen years of torment were all just a big mistake. I should be happy, shouldn't I? Goddamned ecstatic. Stop telling me I'm angry."

"Very well. You're not angry."

A tense silence followed.

"Just what are you expecting?" he finally asked. His voice was flat. "Tell me what reaction you're waiting to see. Am I supposed to fly into a rage and smash crates against the wall? Lay my head in your lap and weep while you croon sweet words and stroke my hair?

Or . . . or I know. You're hoping I'll push up your skirts and pump you like an animal all night long. Because somehow a few hours of rutting will erase decades of living hell." He shook his head. "You're good, Merry. But not that good."

She tried not to let his words hurt her. "No. I'm not expecting any hysterics, nor any . . . rutting. But I've given you a great deal to absorb, and this place would make anyone feel a bit crazed." She reached out to lay a hand on his arm, striving for a soothing touch. "We'll make it through this. Come sit with me and wait out the night."

"I said, don't *touch* me." He whipped his arm from her grasp and took a lunging step back. He leveled a finger at her. "I mean it, Merry. Stay away from me right now. I don't trust myself."

"All right." Tears burned in her eyes as she slid back to the pile of furs. "All right. I won't bother you further."

She lay down on her side, hugging herself against the cold. He slunk to the opposite side of the fire and crouched there, leaning his back against a barrel and stacking his arms on his knees.

From this vantage, the flames and smoke appeared to dance around his face, distorting his features. His hands were clenched tight into fists. He was so tense, she could feel him vibrating with the force of his repressed fury.

He was fighting, she could sense it. Quietly doing battle over there in the corner. With himself, with his demons, with her. Maybe just with the rage itself . . . she couldn't be sure. All she knew was that he wouldn't let her help. He wouldn't even let her near.

She must have slept eventually, for the next thing she knew was the sound of rock grinding against rock.

She shivered. The fire had gone out, and the furs had

fallen away from her sleeping form. Her knees curled up to her chest, and she wrapped her arms about them, trying to warm herself.

After a moment spent blinking at the gooseflesh on her arms, a realization dawned. Or rather, *dawn* itself was her realization. The fire had gone out, but there was light enough to make out her surroundings. It had to be daylight. Weak, dusty daylight, but daylight just the same. The entire cavern was illuminated.

Rhys was nowhere to be seen.

"Rhys? Are you here?"

She struggled to rise from the carpet. Surely no matter how angry Rhys was, he wouldn't have left her here all alone. Would he?

"Rhys?"

Her call echoed through the cellar, unanswered. Meredith's heart began to race. Her skirts had tangled about her legs, and she tried to shake them out as she came to a sitting position.

Then, from the stairway, she heard a low, masculine grunt of effort.

Followed by a mighty crash.

"Rhys!"

Dust choked the air, but she clawed her way through it to reach the staircase. As the clouds of grit settled, she saw him silhouetted in the newly cleared entryway, hunched as he prepared to roll back one final stone. Wedging a length of iron beneath the boulder, he pried and heaved with all his strength. Certainly, they could have scrambled over the rock the way it was. The opening was already large enough. But she didn't interrupt. He was clever enough to have realized the same. For whatever reason, it was important to him to clear the entire way.

With one last straining effort, he managed to rock the

boulder onto its narrow end. A final shove with his boot, and the thing rolled clear.

"There," he said, wiping the perspiration from his brow. His knuckles were skinned and bloodied. "I'm done with this place."

His words had the edge of finality. She wondered what they meant. Was he done with this horrible cellar? Or with Nethermoor completely?

What about her? Was he done with her?

They descended back to the village, trudging along in silence. He seemed disinclined to converse, to put it mildly, so Meredith gratefully dropped a few steps behind. She ached all over. Her muscles complained about their night spent on cold, rocky ground, her head pounded, and her stomach demanded food. Worst of all was the wrenching pain in her chest.

The pain eased considerably when they entered the tavern of the Three Hounds to find the room filled to bursting with people.

"They're back!" Darryl called out over the room. "Mrs. Maddox and his lordship, they've returned!"

Stumbling his way through the cheering crowd, her father carved a path to her and all but fell into her arms. "Merry," he rasped, drawing her into a tight embrace and stroking her hair. "I was so concerned. I mean, I knew you were with Rhys and he'd look out for you, but still . . ."

"I'm well, Father." She hugged him in return. "I'm so sorry to have worried you. Is everyone else returned?" Craning her neck, she looked over his shoulder into the crowd. So many people—every resident of the village, it seemed—but no sign of the one person she sought.

Until she spied a basket of fresh yeast rolls, and her breath caught in her throat. She pulled out of her father's embrace.

"I'm here, Mrs. Maddox." Cora rushed out from the kitchen, clapping flour from her hands. "I'm here. I'm back to work. I'm ever so sorry, ma'am. And I don't know if you can ever forgive me, but I swear I'll never let—"

Meredith cut off the girl's speech by grabbing her into a tight hug. Cora immediately dissolved into tears. Meredith threw a glance of relief in Rhys's direction, but he'd moved into the crowd. She couldn't see him anymore.

She turned her attention back to the sobbing girl in her arms. "Poor dear girl. You had us all so worried." The layer of dirt and grit she wore mingled with Cora's dusting of flour. Regardless, Meredith stroked the girl's hair.

Cora twisted in her arms. "The rolls will burn."

"Never mind it." She quietly gestured to Darryl, directing him to rescue the bread. Then she directed Cora to the nearest table and helped her into a chair. "Where were you, dear?"

Cora bit her lip and turned her eyes to the flagstones. The room went very quiet.

"Don't be frightened," Meredith urged. "You can tell me."

"She was with me." A heavy, masculine hand landed on the girl's shoulder.

Meredith's gaze swept from hand to arm, from arm to shoulder, and straight up to the face she should have been expecting all along. Damn it, she ought to have known.

"She was with me," Gideon Myles repeated. "All night."

As she glared at him, red waves of anger swam before Meredith's eyes. She could only manage one word. "Where?"

"Someplace private. Someplace safe."

"We only went out for a walk," Cora said, sniffing earnestly. "But the mist came up, and Gi . . . and Mr. Myles said we ought to wait it out. That it wasn't safe to go home." Her grip tightened over Meredith's hand. "Ma'am, I swear to you. It weren't my intention. We only went out for a walk, and once the mist came up . . ."

"It wasn't safe to come home. I know." Meredith swallowed hard and turned to Gideon, confronting his unrepentant gaze. "It wasn't safe for *you,* who've called this moor home for more years than this girl's been alive, to walk home. But it was safe for everyone else in the village to go searching valley, tor, river, and bog for her? Someone could have been killed."

He shrugged and turned his gaze.

"Don't you look away from me." With a final squeeze, she released Cora's hands. Trembling with fury, she planted both hands on the tabletop and slowly rose to her feet. "Did you touch her?"

Cora bent her head to the table and wept.

Meredith firmed her chin and stared at Gideon until he met her gaze. "I asked you a question. Did you touch her?"

"It's not your business, Meredith."

"The hell it isn't." She kicked the chair out from between them and stepped closer. "Answer me."

"I didn't do anything she didn't want me to do."

She didn't even remember reaching back with her hand and letting it fly, she just heard the smart slap of her palm against Gideon's unshaven face. "You bastard. She's a girl."

"She's not a girl, she's a—"

"Don't you say it. Don't you call her that."

Before she could strike him again, he caught her wrist in a fierce grip. "Believe me, you have no idea what I was going to say." Releasing her, he raked her with a look of pure contempt. "What? It's all right for you, but not me? You're allowed to get tarted up and run away with Ashworth for a week's worth of high-class fornication, but I'm not allowed to—"

Gideon never saw it coming. One minute he was standing before Meredith, all but calling her a whore, and the next moment, Rhys had him smashed against the wall. And because it evidently wasn't enough to do it once, Rhys grabbed him by fistfuls of shirt, pulled him off the wall, and smashed him against it again.

All around the tavern, bodies launched from chairs and pasted themselves to the edges of the room.

Holding Gideon pinned to the wall with one arm, Rhys hauled back with the other and swung. At the last second, Gideon managed to twist in his grip, so that the punch glanced off his shoulder and hit the wall—rather than snapping his neck instantaneously. He put a forearm to Rhys's throat and wedged a boot in the larger man's gut, levering him away. With his other arm, he reached for the pistol at his side.

Rhys beat him to it. "No guns," he said, whipping the pistol from Gideon's waistband and flinging it aside. "Just fists."

The pistol skittered across the flagstones, coming to rest at Cora's feet.

Gideon gave Rhys a swift kick to the knee—the wounded left knee he always favored. The kick sent Rhys reeling back a pace, giving Gideon an instant to breathe, react.

Attack.

Lunging to the side, he grabbed a candlestick from the mantel.

"No!" Meredith cried.

Gideon's fingers closed around the heavy pipe of brass just as Rhys pulled back for another punch. They both swung at the same time. Rhys's fist connected with

Gideon's jaw first, altering the angle of the candlestick's descent, but not its velocity. The club came down on Rhys's back with a dull thud. Both men roared with pain, separating for a moment.

But not for long.

With an inarticulate battle cry, Gideon swung again.

Rhys dodged, and the candlestick hit a table instead, crunching straight through the tabletop. As Gideon struggled to withdraw the weapon from a bird's nest of splinters, Rhys picked up a stool and swung it hard. The stool smashed to kindling over Gideon's head.

"You bastard!" Relinquishing his grip on the candlestick, Gideon lowered his shoulder and charged Rhys with full force.

Though Rhys was the larger man, he was caught off-balance. He reeled backward when Gideon struck, and together they plowed the distance of the room, landing against the bar with a crash of glass and splintering wood.

Meredith's hands flew to her mouth. Good Lord. They would destroy the whole tavern.

If Rhys felt a single one of Gideon's punches to his chest and gut, he didn't show it. Instead he fisted his hands in Gideon's shirt and hauled him up and left, swinging him bodily onto the counter and dropping him flat on his back. Within seconds, Rhys had scrambled atop him, straddling Gideon's thighs to hold him down as he dealt blow after punishing blow.

"Stop this!" Meredith cried. "Rhys, Gideon. For the love of God, stop!"

Neither one of them heeded her pleas.

Gideon's hands shot up to grasp Rhys's throat. He locked his elbows, pushing up until Rhys's head smashed into the rows of hanging glassware. As they struggled, little bits of glass rained down on them both, followed by red trickles of blood. Whose blood, Meredith couldn't be sure.

Once the shower of glass cleared, the picture looked much the same. Gideon flat on his back on the bar; Rhys looming over him. Gideon's fingers cinched tight around Rhys's throat, cutting off his air. Meanwhile, Rhys took jab after powerful jab at Gideon's ribs. Meredith heard a sick crack.

Oh, God. This wouldn't stop until one of them was unconscious. Or dead.

Cora leapt toward the men, but Meredith grabbed the girl by the arm and held her back. There was no stopping these two. Anyone who tried to intervene would most certainly be injured, if not killed.

"*Die,*" Gideon growled, tightening his fingers about Rhys's throat.

In response, Rhys grated out two words. "*Make. Me.*"

Rhys's face had turned a frightening shade of red, but Meredith could tell Gideon's strength was waning. With an almost regretful expression, Rhys raised his fist and took one last swing at Gideon's jaw. Blood sprayed from the younger man's mouth, spattering Meredith and Cora both. Cora shrieked. Gideon's body went limp, his hands slumping back to the bar.

A tooth rolled to the floor and bounced off the flagstones.

And Rhys just kept dealing blows.

"Get up." *Thwack.* "Is that the best you can do?" *Thwack.* "Stand, you miserable piece of filth." He grabbed the senseless Gideon by the collar and shook him, slamming his head against the bar. "Wake up, you bastard, and try to kill me again."

He released Gideon's shirt, and the younger man's head rolled back to the bar. Rhys sat hulking over him, bleeding and panting and sweating. And maybe—

Meredith couldn't quite tell—weeping a little bit, too.

Just when she'd gathered the composure to go to him, Rhys firmed his jaw and raised his heavy fist again, as if to deal Gideon a death blow. The room sucked in its breath.

"No!" Cora cried.

Meredith said, "Rhys, don't!"

From behind them both, a man pushed through the crowd and rushed to grab Rhys's arm. Meredith recognized him as Rhys's friend and Cora's sponsor. Mr. Julian Bellamy. She never imagined she'd be so glad to see that man again.

"Save it," Bellamy said, breathing hard and using all his strength to rein in Rhys's fury. "Save that blow for one who deserves it. I've found him."

After a long, tense moment, Rhys lowered his arm, tugging it out of Bellamy's grip. He blinked down at Gideon's insensate form, like he didn't even recognize the man. His gaze wandered the debris-strewn bar, as if he'd no idea how he'd even come to be there.

"Rhys?" she ventured.

His eyes lifted to hers, soulless and cold. Swallowing hard, he wiped his brow with his sleeve. The linen came away streaked with dirt and sweat and blood. "You wanted me angry," he said, spitting a mouthful of blood to the side. "Are you happy now?"

She choked on a sob.

"So you're angry. Brilliant. The timing couldn't be better." Mr. Bellamy grabbed hold of Rhys's shirt and pulled, demanding his attention. "Save your wrath. I've found him. The man who killed Leo."

Chapter Twenty-three

The ensuing silence was profound. Everyone, Meredith included, was struck dumb by the tableau of carnage and destruction. This tavern had seen more than its share of brawls, but never anything like this. No one knew what came next.

Breaking the tension, Mr. Bellamy clapped Rhys on the shoulder. "Come along, Ashworth," he said gently. "Let's get you out of this place."

After a moment's pause, Rhys nodded. He slid down from the bar, landing with a resounding thud.

Bellamy surveyed Rhys's appearance, wrinkling his nose at the blood and dirt. "Have you a fresh suit somewhere?"

Rhys dabbed his bleeding lip. "Up at my house."

"Then up to the house we go." Bellamy inclined his head in Meredith's direction. "Mrs. Maddox, always a pleasure."

Meredith nearly hugged the man, she was so grateful. No one here in the village would have been able to stop that scene and talk Rhys back down to earth.

Bellamy turned an appraising gaze on Cora. "Are you well?"

The girl nodded.

"Mind you don't run off again. When we leave, you'll be coming with us."

Meredith tried to catch Rhys's eye, but he refused to meet her gaze. "Rhys," she said, grabbing his arm. "Look at me. Are you hurt?"

"Why do you care?"

"Of course I care."

"Don't. I don't want you to." He shrugged off her touch. "I can't be near you right now."

As the men left, the hounds trotted after them. Meredith stayed behind. She looked around at the wreckage and wondered to herself, which was in more pieces: her tavern, or her heart?

Cora rushed to Gideon's side. Within seconds, he was moaning curses and writhing atop the bar, proving that Rhys hadn't quite done him in.

For a long, fuming minute, Meredith contemplated finishing Gideon off herself. Then her practical nature prevailed. She didn't want that sort of mess in her tavern, or that sort of guilt on her soul. Gideon simply wasn't worth it. She did, however, want to keep him from bleeding all over the bar. She went for her kit of bandages and medicines, but when she carried the small box out from the kitchen, Cora took it from her hands.

"I'll take care of him," she said firmly. There was no girlish lilt in her voice now, only a woman's resolve. Harold and Laurence stood behind her, rolling up their sleeves. "We'll take him up to one of the guest rooms," she said.

Meredith nodded numbly. "I'll clean up down here."

After chasing everyone from the room, she latched the door. Alone, she swept up every sliver of broken glass and each piece of splintered wood. She mopped the blood from the countertop and scoured the flag-stones with sand. She righted the remaining furniture and returned the brass candlestick to its place on the mantel.

When noontime came, she went upstairs to wash and change her frock, and then she prepared a simple family meal. Bread, cheese, sausages. She called Father and Darryl in from the horse barn. Mr. Bellamy's team and carriage were still there, but there was no sign of the gentleman. Or Rhys.

After the men had taken their meal, Meredith prepared a tray and carried it upstairs.

"I've brought up some tea and broth," she said, pushing the door open with her foot. "And solid food for you, Cora."

Gideon was supine on the bed, still wearing his boots and trousers, but stripped to the waist. Cora sat in a chair beside him, holding a poultice to one side of his face.

"He's sleeping," she said. "I dosed him with laudanum for the pain."

Meredith set the tray on a nearby table. Then she crossed to stand over Cora's shoulder and reached to lift the poultice from his face. Lord. The man's jaw, cheek, and brow were all one giant, swollen bruise. He wouldn't be seeing daylight through that eye for a week.

"Well, Gideon," she said quietly, even though she knew he couldn't hear, "you deserved that."

"It wasn't how you're thinking," Cora said. She smoothed the hair from Gideon's brow. "The two of us, last night."

"Even so. He's had this coming to him." Ever since that night Rhys stumbled in from the moor with a gash in his scalp.

Meredith took her turn watching over the wounded man while Cora had a rest, then prepared an evening meal. And after all was swept and washed and put away, she sat down at her scratched and dented bar and poured herself a generous glass of wine. Then a second. A folded newspaper lay on the counter. She left it untouched. It couldn't tell her what she wanted to know today.

Near midnight, there came a knock at her bedchamber door. Meredith gathered a shawl about her shoulders, went to the door, and slid back the latch to open it a crack.

Rhys was there, dressed in a clean shirt and breeches. The small cuts on his brow had been tended and cleaned.

"I leave at dawn," he said.

She could only blink at him.

"It's the murderer. Bellamy thinks he's found the man who was with Leo the night he was attacked. Name of Faraday. Been hiding out in Cornwall. Bellamy's speaking with Cora now. She'll come along to confirm his identity."

"Why do you need to go?"

His eyebrow quirked. "Isn't it obvious? I'm the muscle. In case of reluctance, I'm to pound the truth out of him. Then mete out justice, if it's warranted."

"I see."

"Yes. You see. As did everyone else, this morning. It's what I do." Self-loathing flickered in his eyes. When he spoke, his voice was hoarse. "What about Myles? Will he—"

"He'll live. He's hurting, but he'll live."

His face stayed grim, but the corners of his mouth softened with relief.

She added, "He deserved it, for what he did to Cora."

At the mention of the girl, Rhys winced again. "She was under my protection. I should never have left her alone." He cleared his throat and gave himself a little shake. "I've unloaded the goods from Bath, packed up my things from the cottage. And I've brought back the hounds."

Her gaze fell. Two pairs of watery brown eyes looked up at her mournfully. A low whimper sounded from a canine throat.

"They'll miss you," she said.

"I'll miss them."

She opened the door wide, and the dogs rushed through, tumbling over one another in their race to the hearth. Even once the hounds settled, she kept the door open in invitation.

She allowed her shawl to slip from one shoulder. "It's hours yet before dawn." Shameless, she knew. But damn it, what use was pride? If he was leaving forever, she wanted one last night.

"Don't." His jaw tensed. "Don't invite me in. Because it's not in me to refuse, and I'd only be using you. The same way I used Myles this morning. I am angry as hell, and you'd be just another nameless person to pound. I'd work you hard and fast, until I forget who you are. Who I am." He swallowed hard. "I'd be using you."

Good Lord. If he was trying to discourage her, he was going about it all wrong. Meredith clenched her legs together as damp heat surged between her thighs. She'd never been so aroused, so quickly. What he described was exactly what she craved. One last hard, fast, unforgettable time.

Looking him bravely in the eye, she opened the door wider still. "We'd be using each other."

That was all it took.

Before she could even catch her breath, he'd moved through the doorway, caught her in his arms, and slammed the door shut, flattening her against it. She was pinned between the hard door of oak at her back and the harder wall of hot muscle before her, and she'd never felt more completely, deliciously trapped.

He slid his hands to her hips and lifted her, pressing her against the door. Letting her shawl slide to the floor, she pulled frantically at the hem of her nightdress, hiking it to her midsection so she could wrap her legs around his waist. Linking her ankles, she pulled his pelvis flush with hers. They both moaned as the hard ridge of his erection ground against her bared sex. She was already so wet for him, and he was unbelievably stiff for her. No need for preliminaries.

He held her up with one powerful arm as he jerked his breeches open with his free hand. With one hard, quick thrust he entered her, slamming her spine against the door. She gasped, and he thrust again, delivering everything he'd promised. A good, hard, nameless pounding into lustful oblivion.

He bit her shoulder, and she raked his neck with her fingernails. He responded with a growl of crude, unfettered profanity, the likes of which she'd never heard inside a bedchamber. She found it wildly arousing. As the pleasure mounted and coiled in her sex, her limbs went slack. His strength supported her entire body as he drilled her to the door again and again, and she made herself boneless, just trying to stay afloat atop the violent, churning sea of lust.

"Rhys." She slid her fingers through his cropped hair. "Yes."

And then he stopped.

He froze, deep inside her, panting against the curve of her neck.

Her hips writhed with need. God, she was so close. Did he mean to torture her?

"I can't do this," he said, gasping for breath.

"What do you mean?" She cinched her legs about his

waist. Her intimate muscles tightened around him, too, and he groaned with pleasure.

"I just can't. Not like this." He huffed against her neck. "The damned dogs are chewing my boots."

With a gasp, Meredith twisted and craned her neck to see. Sure enough, there the two hounds sat at his feet, nipping at the tassel of his Hessian where it tangled with the hem of her shift.

She couldn't help it. She laughed. And after a moment, he joined her, chuckling low against her neck.

He lifted his head to meet her gaze. They stayed like that for a moment, joined in body, both breathing hard, laughing with their eyes and speaking without words.

An unbearable sweetness bloomed in Meredith's heart, filling her chest and spreading out to her limbs. They'd begun this in a frenzy of anger and desperation, and all it took was one minute of his skin against hers for benign normalcy to prevail. It was just as he'd been saying from the very beginning. Being together just felt so right.

With trembling hands, she stroked his hair. His eyes shone with affection and vulnerability, and she had a sinking feeling that they looked that way because they were reflecting the unguarded emotion in hers.

He swallowed hard, and she cupped his face in her palms. "Oh, Rhys."

I love you, she thought. *I am hopelessly in love with you, and you're leaving me at dawn.*

"Don't say it," he said. "I know."

Still erect and deeply planted within her, he cupped her backside in his hands and lifted her away from the door. He turned, taking hobbled steps toward the bed, and gently laid her on the mattress without ever withdrawing from her body.

Easing her backward, he joined her on the bed, boots and all. The hounds, deprived of their amusement, returned to the hearthrug.

She was under him on the bed, completely surrounded by his strength and protected from the chill. And she'd never felt so afraid, so lonely and cold.

He tugged at the hem of her shift, pulling it up to her midriff. "Take this off. I want to see you. I need to see you—"

One last time.

The unspoken words gave her gooseflesh. But even though she shivered as she did it, she eased the chemise up and drew it over her head, casting it aside. She pulled at his shirt next, as he began to move within her again. Slowly, now. Gently.

By shifting his weight from one arm to the other, he helped her pull the shirt over his head. They were as bared as they could be without separating, and neither of them was willing to do that.

Balanced on one elbow, he traced the swell of her breast with his free hand.

"You're so damned lovely." His voice was a broken whisper, hoarse with yearning. "So beautiful." Flexing his thigh, he slid deep, nudging her womb. "I should have known better than to dream you belonged to me."

"But I do." She cupped his cheek. "I am *yours*. Body, heart, soul. I lo—"

"Don't." He kissed her quiet. "I can't bear it."

When he thrust deep again, she lost the breath to speak. She kissed him instead, pressing her lips to his mouth, jaw, throat, ear . . . any part of him she could reach.

He caught her arms and pinned her to the mattress, levering himself up as he stroked home, again and again. She didn't want this to ever end. *Please don't let this be the last time.* She struggled to hold herself back from climax. If he left her unsatisfied, her knowledge of the male mind argued, his pride simply wouldn't allow him to go.

But he was too much for her. Too big, too fierce, too tender, too wild. She couldn't resist him. Never could. He rode her to a bright, gasping peak, then released a savage growl as he took his own pleasure in her.

When he collapsed, spent and panting atop her, she wrapped her arms around him and held him tight.

"Stay," she whispered. Her tongue flickered over the salt of his skin. "Don't go."

"I have to go." He withdrew from her body, then sat at the edge of the bed, refastening his breeches placket. "I have to see to this business with Faraday. This is what I do."

"No." She rose to a sitting position, gathering the bed linens around her. "No, this is not what you do."

He reached for his shirt. "You saw me this morning. The whole village saw me this morning. That's how I've spent most of my life, Meredith. Fighting. Brawling. Tearing things apart. I thought I'd finally left all that behind me, but . . ." He leveled a hard, unflinching gaze at her. "I would have killed him."

"Perhaps. But Gideon tried to kill you first. That's not the case with this Faraday person."

"He's a murderer."

"You don't know that. From Cora's account, he could have been an innocent victim, just like your friend Leo."

"Determining his guilt or innocence isn't my job." He gathered white linen in his hands and jammed his head through the neck hole of the shirt. "I'm there to hit first, and Bellamy will ask questions later."

"You can't do that. You won't do that." She held his

cuff steady as he wrestled his arm into a sleeve. "All those battles and brawls over the course of your life— they all had one thing in common. They were all fair fights, evenly matched, with opponents who had it coming to them. You've never been a bully, Rhys. That's why I was so taken with you when I was a girl."

He scoffed. "When you were a girl, I paid you no notice whatsoever."

"Precisely." She smoothed the back of his shirt, draping the crisp linen over his rippling muscles. "Do you know how remarkable that is? Any other youth in your situation would have been *looking* for a target like me. I was little and awkward and irritating. I would have been so easy to torment. The stable boys, they always teased me when my father wasn't there. They were so used to being pushed about by their superiors, and they wanted someone to push about, too. It made them feel important, in control. But you"—she stroked his back— "of all young men, you had every reason to make my life miserable, and you never did. You respected my father. You were kind to the grooms. You cherished those horses. And you let me be." Haltingly, she raised her hand to his hair. "Call it foolish if you will, but . . . I loved you for it."

With a muttered oath, he braced his elbows on his knees and let his head fall to his hands.

"Don't you believe me? I still love you, Rhys. More than ever."

"I know. I know. And I don't know what's wrong with me." After scrubbing his face with one hand, he propped his chin on his palm. "You tell me you love me. I know in my mind that should make things better." He looked up at her. "Shouldn't it? I mean, it's the one thing I've waited my whole life to hear. And now that you've whispered those three little words, my anger should disappear, and the hurting should stop, and rainbows should burst through the clouds and a choir of angels should sing." His eyes glimmered with emotion as his fingertip traced the curve of her jaw. "Against all odds, this beautiful, clever, strong woman loves me. My life should be put to rights."

"But it isn't," she said.

Shaking his head, he withdrew his touch. "It isn't. You keep saying you love me. And it cuts deeper every blessed time. It hurts, Merry. I can't understand it, but it hurts like hell. Those words . . . they make me want to hit things, lash out in anger." He swore again, balling his hands into fists. "Something's wrong with me. Too many things are wrong with me."

"And I'm partly to blame. You can't forgive me."

"It's nothing to do with blame or forgiveness. It's about brokenness. I can't risk hurting you."

With a gruff sigh, he rose to his feet. "I should go."

From the bed, she reached out and caught his hand. "Stay awhile. It's not dawn yet. If it's hard for you, we don't need to talk."

"Yes, we do. Need to talk." He turned and crouched at the side of the mattress. His eyes were thoughtful as they roamed the knot of their joined hands. "I've done some good here, I think. The cottage is your father's to do with as he pleases. I'll see that his pension is restored. The men will finish the inn, and you'll have the posting horses, I promise. And I'll pay for the damage to the tavern."

"I'm not concerned about the inn, you fool man. I'm concerned about you." Her voice cracked. "*Rhys*. Stop acting like this is the end. You can't do this to me now. What happened to all that talk of destiny? I'm your fate, and you're mine?"

After pressing a firm kiss to her knuckles, he rested his brow to their joined hands. "I swear to you. If any woman could make it right, make me whole—it would be you. But I'm just too broken, Merry. It's too late for me. I wish to God that weren't the case, but—"

"Don't say it. Don't."

He wiped a tear from her cheek. "Some things just aren't meant to be."

❧

Chapter Twenty-four

"I thought your home county was forbidding," Bellamy said, squinting at the coach's small window. "This makes it seem right cheery in comparison. Is it just coincidence, Ashworth, or does a depressing fog *actually* follow you around?"

Rhys didn't answer. Forget the fog. He felt like a damned thundercloud rumbled within his chest. His heart seethed with thick, churning, violent emotion. Hurt, confusion, anger. And though he'd only left her a half day ago, he missed Meredith so much he could scarcely breathe. But he had to put distance between them. He couldn't let her get caught in the storm.

Absently, he worked his tongue against a cut inside his upper lip. The tang of blood helped him focus. The coppery taste coaxed a strange feeling in him, one vaguely akin to nostalgia. Just as that fisticuffs with Myles yesterday had given him a clarity of sorts. The dealing and taking of blows—this was what he did, what he knew so very well. He'd been raised to it, after all. It was the family trade.

"Tell me about Faraday. Is he big?" Rhys hoped so. He didn't like pounding on small ones.

Bellamy shrugged. "He's much like me, as Cora remarked."

Arching a brow, Rhys studied his companion with fresh interest. With an uneasy glance, Bellamy made a defensive shift down the seat.

"Then he'll do," Rhys said.

"Good." Bellamy tugged at his cuff. "It should have occurred to me months ago. At first, I thought Morland had arranged the murder. He wanted the Stud Club tokens, and he was there in the card room the night Leo and I made plans to attend the boxing match."

"But Morland had nothing to do with it." Rhys frowned. He thought they'd put this argument to rest in Gloucestershire.

"I know that now. And that's when I realized, for every token Morland collected, somewhere there was an angry former member of the Club. So I went through them all, making inquiries as to their whereabouts the night of the murder. I missed Faraday at first, because everyone seemed to think he'd left Town days earlier. Even his house staff confirmed it."

"But he hadn't."

"No. And he knew about the boxing match. It was Faraday's token Morland won that night. We were all watching them play. After Faraday lost, Leo—sporting fellow that he was—pumped Morland's hand, congratulated him on a game well-played. Faraday masked it well, but I could tell he was furious. When he announced his intent to head for the country immediately, we assumed he was out of funds. Never thought to question it. Finally, on my third round of inquiries, one of the footmen spilled the truth. Peter Faraday hadn't left Town until two days after Leo's death." He swore. "He has to be the one."

"Let's hope Cora can identify him with certainty."

The girl lay reclined on the front-facing seat, sleeping heavily. At least, Rhys thought it safe to assume she was asleep, because he didn't know any woman who would willingly display herself in front of two gentlemen with her mouth agape. This actual slumber came after she'd merely *pretended* to doze her way out of Devonshire and across Bodmin Moor. Her eyes hadn't met his since they'd left the Three Hounds. She was back to being afraid of him, and Rhys couldn't say he blamed her one bit.

The whole village would fear him again. He'd never forget looking up from Gideon Myles's bleeding face to find the bar destroyed and the assembled residents of Buckleigh-in-the-Moor staring at him in collective horror. And there, in the center of them all, his lovely Meredith . . . her face bleached to the shade of bone, and spattered with blood. Just the memory was enough to make his stomach turn and his head throb with pain. In all his wretched life, he'd never felt more monstrous.

"There's the sun," Bellamy said. "Thank God."

Leaning across him, Rhys peeked out the window. Cornwall was a lonesome place, but like Devonshire, it had a stark beauty. As they rounded a bend, the fog lifted. He glimpsed long, green fingers of earth grasping at a brilliant blue sea. The coves between them were dark, honeycombed cliffs. There was a sense of wobbling along the edge of the world as their coach and team navigated the coastal road, high above the breaking waves.

"What sort of place are we looking for?" he asked.

"According to my source, the house is perched above a rocky cove."

"Was your source any more specific? There seem to be a great many rocky coves hereabouts."

"We'll know it when we come to it," Bellamy said with confidence. "Last time we stopped, that crofter told me it's the only house of any size for miles."

The carriage tilted around another steep curve, and

Rhys grabbed the edge of the seat to keep from sliding into Bellamy's lap. That wouldn't go over well.

"Tell me something," he said after a minute. "You believe this Peter Faraday took Leo into an alleyway *knowing* they would be attacked? That he meant to lure Leo to his death?"

"Possibly."

"Why would he do that?"

Bellamy grit his teeth. "That's why we're on this little journey, isn't it? To find out."

"Well, if your theory is true . . ." Rhys peered out at the road. "How do you know we're not being lured into an ambush ourselves?"

"I don't." He tapped a finger against the window glass. "We'll be on our guard."

A house came into view, emerging from the mist as though it floated on its own low-hovering cloud. It was a small stone and brick affair, eccentrically designed. The window shutters' paint had peeled away from the wood. No lights emanated from within, and no smoke puffed from the chimney.

"Doesn't look especially welcoming, does it?"

"No," Rhys agreed. Neither did it look especially occupied. "Perhaps your sources were misinformed."

"No, just look at it. It's the perfect place to hide." He shook Cora awake. "You'll have to wake up now. Ashworth and I will go inside. You'll stay here. If we don't come out for you within a half hour, you're to tell the coachman to drive you straight back."

Blinking, Cora rose to a sitting position. After a lazy stretch, she peered out the window, just as they were drawing up to the house.

"La!" she said. "Isn't that just the picture of a fright. I'm not staying in the coach alone. I want to come in with you."

"We don't know what we'll meet with inside," Rhys said. "There may be danger."

"I thought I was here to identify the man. How can I do that from here? I tell you, I'm not staying in this coach."

As the carriage rolled to a halt, Bellamy leaned forward. "What will you do? Run off into the fog again?"

"I didn't run off into the fog. I do know better than that, it's just what everyone assumed." She sighed. "I suppose I'm used to being thought stupid."

"You'd rather be thought a whore?"

"I'm not a whore! Not any longer. I never took a penny from Mr. Myles. It wasn't at all like you're thinking." She cast a brief, fearful look at Rhys. "Or what you supposed, my lord. Gideon was very kind to me. We have a great deal in common, it seems. We talked all night. Mostly."

"Oh, *mostly*," Bellamy echoed. "And now I suppose you're in love with this criminal."

"What if I were?" Cora said. "I don't see that it's any of your affair."

"The way you were *so* in love with Leo after an hour in his company, then stripped his corpse of every last coin before dumping it on my doorstep?"

Cora's lip quivered. "I can't believe you'd say that. I might have left Leo there, you know. Let him die on the street, unclaimed and alone."

Rhys sighed heavily. "Leave off, Bellamy. God only knows what manner of lies the cur fed her, just to get under her skirts. She's not a bad girl, just too easily swayed."

Cora's bronze lashes trembled as she studied her hands. "Perhaps I am."

Bellamy said hotly, "I'm only—"

"You're only being an ass. I know. We're all getting weary of it. Let's hope it's a curable condition."

He suspected it was. Bellamy was clearly still mourning the loss of his friend. He was hungry for answers; Cora craved affection. Rhys sympathized with them both, but he wasn't good with comfort or diplomacy. He had precisely two methods at his disposal for remedying people's problems: his right fist and his left. Yesterday he'd dealt with Gideon Myles. Today he'd see about Faraday.

The coach door swung open. Bellamy curled his fingers over the rooftop edge to help himself out. "Come along, then. Both of you."

Rhys went first, then handed Cora out. They crossed an archipelago of stepping stones to reach the front entrance.

Bellamy extended his walking stick and rapped smartly on the door. "Hullo! We're here for Mr. Peter Faraday."

No answer. After a minute of waiting, Bellamy banged on the door again. "Hullo in there. Hullo!"

The latch scraped. Finally, the door creaked open a space of inches. An ancient manservant revealed a thin slice of himself through the crack. Not that he likely had much more to show them. He was rather a thin slice of a man to start, dusted with powder-white hair. He'd missed a button on his waistcoat, and as the result or perhaps the cause, his whole body was askew.

"Beg pardon," Bellamy told the aging servant. "We've traveled from London to speak with Mr. Peter Faraday on a matter of some urgency."

The old man grunted. "Urgency? There's nothing urgent in this neighborhood, save my need to make water in the night. Furthermore, it's not noon yet, so Mr. Faraday is not at home to callers."

"Good Lord, man. This isn't Mayfair. Damn your receiving hours. We're here now, and we demand to see him. If you won't step aside, we shall have to move you."

With a wheeze of indignation, the old man said, "You haven't even offered your card."

Sighing with impatience, Bellamy reached into his breast pocket and withdrew two coins. Rhys recognized one as a brass Stud Club token.

"This *is* our card. Show it to your master." In the old man's other palm, he dropped a guinea. "This one is for you."

The aging butler's hoary eyebrows rose. His fingers curled over the coins. "Wait here, gentlemen, if you'd be so kind."

Within the minute, he'd returned. He placed the brass token—only—back in Bellamy's hand. "Mr. Faraday will see you in the drawing room."

They followed the butler down a narrow corridor that seemed to have warped and twisted with age. The drawing room was empty, and the butler left them yet again, with no word as to when they might expect their host.

"You wait here." Bellamy dragged an armchair to the far corner of the room and settled Cora in it, partly behind a small screen. She wouldn't be immediately noticed there.

For his part, Rhys took a seat on a threadbare divan and propped one boot on the small, square table before him.

Bellamy did not approve. "You've been sitting in the carriage all day," he said. "Do you have to sit down now? You're supposed to hulk in the corner and look threatening. Menacing, not . . . cozy."

Ignoring him, Rhys stretched his arm across the back of the divan and surveyed the meager furnishings and cobwebbed corners. "I thought this was supposed to be a well-heeled dandy we're chasing. Perhaps all his fortune is sunk into gold embroidery. It's certainly not poured into the furnishings."

"He's in hiding. Why else would any man of means live all the way out here, in such humble accommodations?"

"Perhaps because he enjoys the bracing sea breeze?" An unfamiliar, cultured voice.

Rhys's gaze jerked to the doorway. There stood Peter Faraday, he presumed. And God, he could see what Cora meant. Faraday truly was the spitting image of Julian Bellamy. Or at least, a strikingly close resemblance. On examination, Faraday's hair was a dark brown, not jet black. He stood an inch or two shorter than Bellamy. His complexion was notably more pale. But in a darkened alley, the two would be virtually indistinguishable from one another.

"Gentlemen," Faraday said, leaning against the doorjamb, "to what do I owe this pleasure?" He wore a simple banyan over a shirt and loose-fitting trousers. His dark hair stuck up at odd angles. He looked as though he'd just rolled out of bed to greet them and had no intention of going anywhere, anytime soon.

From the looks of him, Rhys would wager he hadn't been out of bed in weeks.

"Believe me, there's no pleasure in it," Bellamy said. "And if you've seen the token, you know exactly why we're here."

Faraday's gaze sharpened. He remained absolutely still. "Do I?"

From his seat on the divan, Rhys shook his head. "If the two of you mean to be coy, we'll be here all day. Faraday, it's your house. Have a seat."

"Thank you, I'll stand."

Rhys leaned forward, eyeing the man. "Not for much longer, you won't." Faraday looked ready to swoon. So much for any plan of pummeling the truth out of him.

Rhys might be a violent brute, but it simply wasn't in him to beat invalids. Faraday had obviously already taken his share of blows.

He said casually, "Sit down. Does that old fellow rattling his chains around know how to make tea? We'll all gather round and talk this out."

Bellamy shot him a look. "In case you're wondering, that would be a complete and utter failure," he whispered, "at being menacing."

"Oh, come along," Rhys said. "Look at him. The longer he stands there, the more color drains from his face. The man won't even move, he's so stiff." He nodded at Faraday. "How many bones did you break, when you and Leo were attacked?"

The man paused. "My hipbone. Three ribs."

"That all?"

"My left wrist." Faraday raised the appendage before his eyes and peered at it. "I think there was a small fracture in one of the bones, but it seems to have knitted well on its own. Lost a few teeth. Other than that . . . just bruises, but they've long faded now." He cleared his throat self-consciously. "I was the lucky one."

Surveying the man's posture and pinched expression, Rhys could tell he wasn't lying. If anything, he was understating the extent of his wounds. In that moment, Rhys was convinced of the man's innocence. Of all people, he knew what a trial it was to recover from injuries so severe. There was no way a man would willingly incur them just to mask his own involvement in a crime.

He stood up and crossed the room. Without a word, he slid a hand under Faraday's arm and lifted, transferring the wounded man's weight from the doorjamb to his own shoulder. Then he slowly walked him the three paces to a chair and helped him sit.

"Thank you," Faraday said, giving Rhys an amused look. "That was rather forward of you."

"If I'd asked, you would have refused the help."

"True."

Rhys went back to his own chair. "The mending hurts worse than the breaking, I know. I've snapped a bone or ten myself."

"So I gather." Faraday tilted his head a fraction. His gaze trained on the scar on Rhys's temple, then slid to the fresh split in his lip. "You must be Ashworth, the great war hero. Still doing battle, it would seem. Any teeth left?"

"Most of them."

"Good. Giles makes excellent shortbread." He called over his shoulder. "Giles!" When the ancient manservant appeared in the doorway, Faraday instructed, "Tea, Giles. And shortbread, and a few sandwiches if you can muster them."

"I don't suppose you have chocolate?" Cora asked hopefully from the corner.

"Well, hullo there." Faraday gave the girl a rakish smile. "I thought Giles mentioned a pretty girl. Was beginning to think he'd gone dotty and mistaken Mr. Bellamy here."

"Wonderful," Bellamy muttered. "Tea and shortbread. It's a regular party."

Faraday settled in his chair. "I thought you loved nothing more than a party. That was always the word around Town."

"Your use of the past tense is appropriate. I don't get around to so many parties of late."

An ironic smile crooked the wounded man's lips. "That makes two of us."

"So what happened that night?" asked Rhys. "Start from the beginning."

Faraday took a deep breath. "I went out to the East End for the boxing match, just like everyone else. Afterward, I happened to cross paths with Leo in the street. He called me over, and—"

"That's not the way Miss Dunn tells it."

"Miss Dunn?" Faraday folded his hands with a careful air of indifference. "Who is Miss Dunn?"

Bellamy gestured toward Cora. "Miss Cora Dunn, the prostitute who found you after the attack. The one you directed to transport Leo to my address."

"Oh." Faraday blinked at the girl with new interest. "So sorry, dear. I didn't recognize you. It was dark that night."

"She says you were the one who called out to Leo."

"Really?" He worried the edge of his fingernail and shrugged one shoulder. "Perhaps I did. Honestly, I don't remember. I don't see how it's important."

"If you're lying to us," Bellamy said, his voice a low threat, "that is important."

"What did you and Leo discuss?" Rhys asked. "Cora says she heard arguing, shouting."

"Oh, yes. Leo was vexed with me. You recall, I'd lost my Stud Club token to the Duke of Morland a few days earlier. Leo was angry with me for wagering it. He knew Morland was out to collect all ten and disband the Club, and he'd warned me not to play with him."

"But you did."

"I did. As I told Leo, I'd grown weary of his silly Club. With the likes of you two for members, it wasn't fun anymore. And I don't even breed horses."

"What *do* you do with your time?" Bellamy asked contemptuously.

"Much the same as you, my friend. Spend money, when I have it. Perfect the art of leisure. Work at being very good at being good-for-nothing."

"So," said Rhys, "if that's your life's ambition, why have you come all the way out here to the edge of England?"

"I needed a place to convalesce. I'm my uncle's heir, but for now I have no property of my own. This place came to mind. I once brought a sweet little blond here for a very pleasant summer holiday." He swept Cora with a gaze that Rhys did not appreciate. "The rent's cheap, and the servants are discreet."

Giles entered the drawing room, carrying a tea service that rattled precariously on its tray. Cora accepted the duty of pouring and began to distribute cups of the steaming brew to each gentleman.

"Why the need for discretion?" Rhys asked him. "You were injured in a violent attack, and yet you fled the scene, leaving Leo in the care of a stranger. You left Town in secret, squirreled yourself away in this remote cottage, and never once attempted to have your attackers identified or brought to justice. Why?"

Bellamy snorted. "Because he's hiding something, obviously."

"Thank you, love." After taking his cup from Cora, Faraday cautiously sipped his tea. "What would I be hiding?"

"If I knew that, I wouldn't be here, now would I?" said Bellamy, growing agitated.

"Tell us about the attack," Rhys interrupted. "What exactly happened in that alley?"

"As I told you, Leo and I were having words about the tokens while Miss Dunn over there waited just round the bend. From the other end of the alley came two ruffians. We were taken unawares. Before we knew what was happening, they were upon us, slinging fists. We made our stab at defense, but the men were . . . large. And determined."

"What else can you tell us about them?" Rhys asked.

"Cora said one was bald," Bellamy said. "And the other . . ."

"Was Scottish, from the sounds of him," the girl put in. "I'm almost certain of it."

Rhys leaned to the edge of his chair. "Would you know them again, be able to identify them if they were caught?"

Faraday put his hands to his temples. "Honestly, once the beating started, I remember little. Bald or ginger, Irish or Scot, pug-nosed or six-fingered . . . I've no recollection. If I didn't even recognize Miss Dunn, how would I know those brutes again? There was no time to get a proper look. They didn't even go for our money before they started in on us."

"Well, if they weren't cut-purses, what were they after?"

A strange look crossed Faraday's face. "Don't you know?"

Rhys and Bellamy looked to one another, nonplussed.

"I'll be damned. You truly *don't* know." Faraday rubbed his eyes for a long moment. Then he gave a throaty chuckle as he reached for a piece of shortbread. "You, Mr. Bellamy. They were after you."

Chapter Twenty-five

Bellamy paled. "What the hell are you saying?"

"I meant just what I said," Faraday replied. "That attack was meant for you."

Bellamy leapt from his chair. A teacup crashed to the floor, and Cora flinched.

"Easy, there." Faraday quirked a brow at Rhys. "Your friend's hotheaded, isn't he?"

Raking both hands through his dark hair, Bellamy paced the room with agitation. Every few seconds, he punctuated his steps with a muttered oath.

Faraday watched him with a dispassionate gaze, leaning back in his chair. "You have to admit, it only makes sense. Everyone expected Leo to be with you that night, and the two of us share a strong resemblance. In the dark, we could easily be confused. The brutes weren't after money, just blood."

Rhys frowned. "Even from that, you can't be sure—"

"Leo was sure."

"What?" Bellamy stopped pacing.

"He said, 'Tell Julian,'" Faraday said. He blinked a few times, cleared his throat. "Those were his last words to me. He said them twice, as a matter of fact. Clear as day. 'Tell Julian.' Why do you think I gave Miss Dunn your address?"

"Oh, Jesus." Sinking his weight onto the windowsill, Bellamy put a hand to his eyes. "I knew it. I knew his death was my fault." His voice broke. "How will I ever look Lily in the face again?"

Faraday said, "If you value her safety, you'd best stay clear of her entirely. Evidently, you're a dangerous man to be around. Leo never did know how to choose his company. This is what happens when you start a club and open membership to just anyone."

Rhys gave their host a scrutinizing look. "If all this is true, why didn't you wait for Cora to return? Go with her to Bellamy's house? Instead you slunk off and left Leo alone."

Bellamy said, "He's right. That makes no sense."

Faraday gave a defensive shrug. "I don't know . . . I suppose I panicked."

"What did you have to fear?"

"Questions. Suspicions. Being found alone with a dead man."

"But if your story is truthful . . ." Rhys began.

"*If*," Bellamy emphasized.

"If your story is truthful, you would have nothing to fear from an inquiry," Rhys finished. "Not to mention"— he eyed the man's legs—"you walked back to your carriage with a broken hip?"

"No." Faraday winced as he said the word. "I crawled."

That answer didn't sit right with Rhys. The man had dragged a broken leg and his gold-threaded waistcoat through the gutters of Whitechapel, rather than wait for assistance?

Faraday absorbed Rhys's skeptical look. "As I said, I panicked. And . . ." He blew out a slow breath. "I knew he was going to die. And I didn't want to watch him go. Just couldn't."

"So you left him to die alone," Bellamy choked out. "In a dark, filthy alley, with a whore for company."

Faraday picked up his teacup and stared into it, hard. "Do you know, I believe I've had enough society for today. Miss Dunn, once again your pretty face has improved a very bleak occasion. It's been lovely, but I really must ask you all to leave."

"You're a lying bastard," Bellamy snarled. "I'm not going anywhere until you tell us the truth. I want answers."

Faraday's eyes snapped up. "I've given you answers. A good many of them. Here are some more. What are my parents' names? Jason and Emmeline Faraday. My childhood home? In Yorkshire. Where did I have my education? At Harrow and Cambridge. I'm just full of honest answers to those kinds of questions, Mr. Bellamy." He set his teacup down with a crack. "What about you?"

"My history has nothing to do with this."

"Oh, I suspect it does. And I think I deserve to hear it, considering that I've spent the past months recovering from blows meant for you."

A tense silence saturated the room. Bellamy tapped Rhys's shoulder and jerked his head toward the corner. Taking the hint, Rhys rose from his seat on the divan and followed him.

"What?" he said.

"Time for muscle," Bellamy whispered.

Rhys shook his head. "For God's sake, the man's already injured."

"You have to see he's lying."

"I suspect he's not being entirely truthful."

"Call it what you want, he's hiding something. If you hit him hard enough, you'll shake his secrets loose."

"Perhaps." Rhys gave him a cool look. "And if I hit you hard enough, I could shake loose all of yours." He let the threat sink in a few seconds before adding, "But I'm not going to do it. I'm not a bully, as someone reminded me recently." Someone he missed more acutely with each passing minute.

"Goddamn it, Ashworth. Leo—"

"Leo," Rhys interjected, "wouldn't want me to hit him. I'm certain of it."

"I'll do it then."

"No, you won't." Rhys put a hand on Bellamy's shoulder. Then he tightened his grip, by slow degrees, until he was sure the man comprehended his meaning.

"Mr. Bellamy," Faraday said, bracing his hands on the armrests and struggling to his feet, "I assure you, I've given you all the help I can. If you want to find Leo's murderers, there's really only one question that needs answering."

"Oh, really?" Bellamy said. "What's that?"

"Who wants you dead?"

"Who wants me dead?" Bellamy muttered to himself from where he'd sunk into the corner of the coach. "The better question would be, who *doesn't* want me dead?"

"I don't want you dead," Rhys said. Then he added honestly, "But then I'm rather ambivalent to your general existence."

His teeth rattled as they jounced over a rut in the lane. "Weren't you with a woman that night?" he asked. "A married lady, if I recall. Thought she was the reason you cried off the boxing match. What was her name again?"

"Carnelia. Lady Carnelia Hightower. But if her husband intended to murder her lovers, I'd be holding up the end of a very long queue." Bellamy sighed. "No, it wasn't him. But there are others."

"Other jealous husbands? Or other enemies?"

"Both. What do you care?"

Rhys shrugged. "I suppose I don't. Where are we headed, then?"

"I'm for Town. I'll have to go to ground, skulk around a bit and see what I can find."

"What about the girl?" Rhys asked. "I can't offer her protection anymore." He'd go to London, too. See his solicitor there, discuss arrangements for the estate and George Lane's pension. Then he'd think about what to do next. Perhaps the army again. He could buy back his commission. Or there was mercenary work, if he wanted a change of pace. England wasn't currently at war, but surely there was something that needed destroying somewhere. Preferably somewhere far away. Maybe if he put an ocean between himself and Meredith, this fierce ache in his chest would ease.

"Kindly don't discuss me as if I'm not here," Cora said, hugging her arms across her chest. "I should think I'd be free to do as I please, now that you've found Mr. Faraday. And I want to go back to the Three Hounds."

"Why would you want to return there?" asked Bellamy.

"I like working at the inn. I like the villagers, and they like me. I was happy there."

The coach took a sharp curve in the road, and they all leaned into the turn.

Bellamy said, "This is about that Gideon Myles, isn't it?"

"Not completely," the girl replied, blushing. "But yes, in part."

"Nothing good will come of it, you know. The man's a petty smuggler."

"Smuggler or no, he cares for me." She glanced at Rhys. "There's someone in Buckleigh-in-the-Moor who cares for you too, my lord. Don't you want to go back?"

Rhys sighed and turned his head to the window. The carriage had turned off the coastal lane, and he caught one last glimpse of the dramatic Cornish cliffs as they began the gentle climb back to the main road. Gravity tugged on him as they made their way up the grade, and he slipped toward the edge of the rear-facing seat. He propped one boot on the opposite bench, bracing himself. "It's not a matter of whether I *want* to go back. It's a matter of what's best for everyone."

"Exactly," Bellamy said. "Listen, Cora. It's nice that you want to settle down. But pick a better man to settle down with. A scoundrel like that will bring you nothing but trouble. Believe me, I speak from experience. I've lived a devil's life, and now someone's out to kill me. I wouldn't wish myself on any lady, much less the one I actually—" He broke off.

Rhys finished the thought for him. "I think what Bellamy here is trying to say is, if Gideon Myles truly cared for you, he'd leave you alone."

Cora sat up on her seat. "What nonsense," she said hotly. "What absolute cowardly rot."

"*Cowardly?*" Bellamy and Rhys spoke as one.

"Perhaps he has done some bad things in his life," she said. "But why can't a man change? I changed. I'm not a whore any longer. I want an honest life now, and maybe Gideon wants the same." She shook her head. " 'If he cared for you, he'd leave you alone,' " she muttered, mimicking Rhys's deep voice. Her bold gaze met his. "If he truly cares for me, he'll stay. And do better."

Rhys stared at her, surprised. Was this the same girl who'd trembled in his presence not a few weeks ago? He wasn't sure about Myles's prospects for an honest life, but he felt certain Cora wouldn't be any man's whore again. The girl knew her own value now. Good for her. Meredith's influence was to thank, most likely. She had a way of letting people know their worth.

Maybe Cora was right. Maybe he *was* being cowardly. Back in Devonshire, there was a woman who loved him. Loved him enough to risk her own life to save his in a split-second decision, then devote the next fourteen years to coping with the consequences. Caring for herself, her father, the village. And she would do it all again.

Of course it terrified him. How could it not? The whole tragedy still traced back to him—but it wasn't the result of Rhys being unwanted or worthless. It was the result of his being loved. Meredith thought saving his life was worth every sacrifice, and if he wanted to be with her, he would have to somehow find the courage within himself to *agree*. Christ. And he'd thought accepting her gift of a shaving kit was difficult?

He'd never run from a battle in his life, but Rhys was running like hell from this.

The ache in his chest intensified. He couldn't understand why being loved hurt so damn much. And it didn't help matters any when the carriage gave a violent lurch.

"What's that?" Cora asked, flinching at the loud crack of a whip.

Rhys tensed. "I don't know."

He heard the coachman shouting at the horses from the driver's box, urging them forward. The entire carriage gave a violent shudder. There was another jolt, this one more jarring than the first. Rhys nearly lost his perch on the seat as the carriage came to a dead stop.

Bellamy looked to Rhys. "Would it help if we offered to walk?"

"Perhaps."

They never had a chance to act on the idea. With a low, foreboding creak, the carriage began to roll.

Backward.

For the second time in a week, Meredith slept through noon. The inn had no guests, thankfully. She didn't suppose any locals would be expecting full breakfast today, and if they did—well, they would learn to live with the disappointment.

When she finally gathered the strength to wash, dress, and trudge down the back stairs, she was stunned to find the public room full of men. They'd all gathered round the slate fixed to the wall, arguing and debating.

Standing atop a chair, Darryl looked to be defending both the slate and his very life with naught but a nub of chalk. "Now, gentlemen . . ."

"That purse should be mine," Skinner said, thumping his chest. "I had five weeks. Didn't nobody have money on longer."

Harry Symmonds shook his head. "But it's been more than five weeks, hasn't it? That doesn't make your bet right, just makes it wrong like the rest. Tewkes, just cancel the wagers and call it square."

Meredith couldn't believe it. After all that had happened yesterday, they were here this morning to argue over a ridiculous bet? From the bar, she put finger and thumb in her mouth and whistled for attention. When the lot of them swiveled to face her, she finally found her voice. "What the devil are you doing?"

Skinner shrugged. "Well, since Lord Ashworth's left the village . . . There are wagers to be settled, Mrs. Maddox."

Her face burned with anger. With a trembling hand, she retrieved a damp sponge from underneath the bar and threw it at Darryl. It hit his shoulder with a wet squelch, and he yelped with surprise.

"Wipe that slate clean," she ordered.

Darryl obeyed while the men looked on in silence.

"Now get out," she said. "All of you. The Three Hounds is closed until further notice."

The men didn't move.

"Out!" she shouted, jabbing a finger at the door. "Now!"

As they shuffled toward the exit, jostling and grumbling amongst themselves, an anxious-looking Darryl called over the din. "It's only temporary, gents! Don't count out the Three Hounds. We'll have this place fixed up in no time, me and Mrs. Maddox, and we'll be serving pints again before you know it."

"Don't make promises, Darryl," Meredith said. "Go see to the horse barn. Surely there's a stall that needs mucking out, if you're in the mood to shovel excrement."

"Now, Mrs. Maddox." Darryl moved toward her, apparently choosing not to take offense. "I know the place looks bad, but we'll have it back to form in no time. And it will all work out for the best in the end. It's like you said. Men come and go, but this road is always here. And so's the inn. We always have the Three Hounds. It's our home."

"Thank you, Darryl." The youth's words were well-meant, she supposed, but they didn't offer her much consolation. This inn didn't feel like home, not anymore. "Now, if you don't mind . . . I really would like a moment to myself."

"Of course, Mrs. Maddox. We'll sort out the glassware this afternoon."

Meredith stared after him, wondering if she needed to talk with Darryl about minding his place. The young man was growing a touch presumptive.

Once he'd left and she was alone, Meredith sat in one of the few remaining sturdy chairs. She looked around at the building she'd worked so hard to improve, taken so much pride in running with efficiency and style. She'd always said her heart was in this inn. And perhaps it had been, once. But it wasn't anymore. Her heart was with Rhys, and he was gone. She stacked her arms on the table before her and bent her head.

Barely a minute had passed before strong hands

landed on her shoulders, massaging gently. "There, there, Merry. It'll be all right."

"Oh, Father." She wiped her eyes with her wrist as her father rounded the table and slid into the chair opposite. She hated to tell him this, but postponing the inevitable wouldn't help. "He's gone. Rhys left."

"I know."

"I'm so sorry. I know you must be disappointed."

"Me? Don't worry about me, child." He wrapped her hands in his own scarred, arthritic grip. "Rhys will be back. You'll see."

"You truly believe that?"

"I'm not the only one. They're already starting another betting pool in the courtyard. Skinner's taking wagers as to when Lord Ashworth will return."

"Band of fools," she muttered, shaking her head. "Bloody ingrates. After the way this village treated him, why would he ever want to come back?"

"For you, Merry. Everyone knows he'll come back for you." His eyes warmed and crinkled at the edges. "And my money's on tomorrow."

Chapter Twenty-six

"Oh, God," Cora said. "What's happened?"

Rhys braced himself as the carriage began to move. Slowly at first. Then it picked up speed, rattling unimpeded down the slope they'd just climbed. "We've come unhitched from the team. Must have been the jolt just now."

"Lord," she said. "We're all going to die."

"Eventually." Rhys stood, as much as he was able, and braced his hands on the hardtop carriage roof. Leveraging his strength, he kicked at the carriage door, blasting the latch to pieces. "But not today."

"What are you doing?" Cora asked.

Rhys offered her his hand and a one-word explanation. "Jump."

Her mouth dropped open as she looked toward the now-open door and the accelerating landscape rolling past. "Are you mad?"

Rhys took a brief glance out the carriage's rear window. Just as he'd feared, the coach was speeding straight for the coastline—and those dramatic cliffs.

"It's jump now or plummet later," he insisted. When she still didn't move, he motioned to Bellamy. "Get her out of here!"

"Right." Bellamy shook off his surprise and leapt into

action, grabbing Cora by the wrist and tugging her toward the open door. He stood behind the girl, wrapping one arm about her midsection and bracing the other on the rooftop.

Rhys would have jumped with Cora himself, but he could barely fit through the door on his own, much less with a girl in his arms. He hoped Bellamy didn't cock it up. "Put your legs into it," he said. "You have to clear the wheels."

Bellamy nodded grimly. "On three, Cora. One . . . Two . . ."

Cora cringed. "Can't we do it on five?"

The carriage jounced against some obstacle, and she screamed as the whole business teetered on two wheels.

The moment the coach crashed back to all four, Rhys made the decision. No more hesitating. Planting his boot on Bellamy's backside, Rhys flexed his thigh and shoved with all his strength. *"Three."*

Oddly satisfying. He'd been wanting to give Julian Bellamy a swift kick in the arse.

The two disappeared from the carriage, and when the entire conveyance didn't snap an axle or overturn, Rhys assumed that meant they'd cleared the wheels. Time for him to follow.

But just as he made his way to the open door, the speeding coach hit a rock. Or perhaps it jumped the side of the road. No way to tell, but the thing went airborne for a stomach-launching second. Then it landed with a splintering crunch of wood, careening to one side.

Rhys was thrown away from the door, against the far side of the carriage. His head hit the window with a violent crack. The world oscillated between light and dark for a moment as he danced on the brink of consciousness.

When his wits returned to him, all he knew was that the carriage wasn't rolling anymore. But neither had it come to a halt. The wrecked cab bounced and tumbled from one obstacle to the next, skipping down the rocky turf as it obeyed the pull of gravity. Progressing steadily toward that cliff.

Rhys could go with it. He could.

He lay stunned and breathless, a jumble of limbs on the floor. His head was pounding with pain. It would be so easy to just stay there. Allow the wreckage to carry him over the cliff and dash him on the rocks below. End it all, today.

He kept waiting for that voice to speak up, echo off the walls of his skull. *Get up. Stand, you miserable wretch. Rise and take more.*

It didn't come. Unlike every other time he'd courted death, this time the dark cellar of his mind was eerily quiet. He didn't hear his father goading and taunting him, forcing him back to life. The old bastard had finally been silenced.

Instead, he heard her. He heard Meredith. His beautiful, strong, sweet Meredith. Her words were the sounds echoing in his ears. *I love you, Rhys. Stay. Don't go.*

What a bloody miracle. He didn't want to leave this earth today. He wanted to stay, and do better.

Which meant he had to get out of this deathtrap. Now, if not sooner.

A wild jounce of the hobbled carriage conveniently tossed him toward the door. The next bump would have thrown him straight back, but Rhys grabbed the edge of the door opening and gripped it with all his strength.

Another jarring blow and loud crunch of wood— some wheel or axle giving way. The resulting tilt sent the coach into a wild, spiraling skid. It also sent the door slamming shut on his fingers. Rhys growled with pain.

But somehow, despite the imminent destruction of the coach, he got his legs under him, shouldered the door open, spared one brief glance at the ground to judge his distance . . .

And jumped.

A moment too late.

It was a beautiful day to die.

The sun shone overhead, warm and comforting. A fresh, salty breeze wafted over his skin. For a moment, all Rhys could hear was the music of distant seagulls and the gentle rhythm of waves.

Then came the deafening crash, as the carriage exploded on the jagged boulders below.

He winced, clinging desperately to the rocky overhang. Two handfuls of crumbling basalt were all that kept him from following the same vertical path to his own doom. Twisting his neck, he looked down and caught a glimpse of the carriage. Or rather, the driftwood and flotsam that had once been a carriage.

Rhys kicked his feet in exploration, scouting for some surface he could push off from. His booted toes scraped the cliff's sheer face, but he couldn't get enough leverage. If only his fingers hadn't been slammed in that door a few seconds earlier. Then he might have found more strength in his hands—enough to hang on, pull up, swing a leg over the edge. As it was, he could barely keep himself from tumbling into the sea.

His vision grayed at the edges, rippling in the center like the surface of a pool. Damn it all. Wasn't this just the way his life went? He'd finally stopped wanting to die. And on the very same day, a stupid carriage accident would manage to kill him.

God, he loved Meredith. He loved her so much. Now he'd never have a chance to say it. He could only hope that she somehow knew. It was entirely possible she did know, even though he'd never said the words. She was a clever woman.

He shut his eyes and turned his concentration inward, bargaining with his weakened, aching fingers. *Hold on now,* he told them, *and you can stroke her later.* To distract himself from the dizzying height, he let his mind wander over all the parts of her body he most wanted to touch. Which was every part of her, truly. From her abundant dark hair to her neatly turned toes. And his lust for her body was nothing compared to the admiration he had for her strength of spirit, her generous heart.

As the strength ebbed from his arms, he began to shake. He turned his concentration inward, focusing on that steady beat of his heart. The heart that loved her so very much. He wasn't dead yet. Not so long as that heart kept beating.

Thump. Thump. A worrying pause. *Thump.*

Something landed on his arm, and he jerked reflexively, losing another fingerhold.

"Jesus, Ashworth. I'm trying to help."

Bellamy. It was Bellamy, come to help. Oddly enough, Rhys didn't feel especially rescued.

"Take my hand," Bellamy said, waving the suggested appendage in Rhys's face.

"Like hell I will," Rhys managed to growl. "I'm heavier than you. Unless you have a solid foothold to brace yourself against, you won't lift me up. I'll just pull you over."

"A valid point." Bellamy lowered himself onto his belly and peered down past Rhys's dangling feet.

"Don't suppose there's a convenient outcropping a foot or two beneath me?" Rhys ventured.

"No. The only thing beneath you is certain death." Bellamy shot to his feet and began digging his boots into the soil. "Back to the first plan. There's a ridge here. I'll brace my boots. You take my hand."

"It won't work."

"It'll have to work. Do you have some better idea?"

Rhys had to admit he didn't. "All right, then. On three."

"After that trick in the carriage?" Bellamy shook his head. "I don't trust you with counting. Just give me your hand."

His right hand had the more secure grip, so Rhys shifted his weight as far as he could to that side. Then he gingerly stretched up his left.

The instant he did so, two things happened. Bellamy's grip locked around his left wrist. And Rhys's right hand began losing ground. Grit crumbled under his fingernails as his splayed fingers slid down and down. Both men swore in unison. If Rhys lost that grip, he'd be dangling by one hand, a dead weight at the end of Bellamy's arms. Bellamy wouldn't be able to hold him for long, much less pull him up.

Rhys clawed wildly for a new grip. Nothing. His fingers only slid closer and closer to the edge.

Stomp.

Rhys roared with pain as Bellamy stepped on his right hand, pinning it to the ground with his boot. Tears pricked at the corners of his eyes. "Holy Christ."

"Come on, then," Bellamy grated through his teeth, tugging on Rhys's left arm. "Up with you."

The hand currently grinding beneath Bellamy's boot hurt like hell. But at least it wasn't sliding anymore. By flexing the muscles in his arms and abdomen, Rhys was able to hoist himself up enough to swing a leg over the cliff's edge.

A few grunting, heaving seconds later, he lay on solid ground, rasping for breath and staring up at the bright blue sky. Alive.

"Bloody hell." Bellamy joined him, collapsing on the rock-strewn grass. "I'll say this, Ashworth. Things are never dull when you're around."

The little finger on his right hand stood out from the

rest at an awkward angle. Rhys blinked at it, dazed by the familiar pain. "I think you broke my finger."

"I think I saved your life. And that's after you kicked me in the arse, thank you very much."

"Where's Cora?"

Bellamy tilted his head toward the upslope. "Her ankle's turned, I think. Driver looks like hell, but he'll live."

Rhys pinched his mangled little finger between thumb and forefinger of the opposite hand. Gritting his teeth, he yanked the broken digit straight out, then drew a breath and forced it back in its proper alignment, wincing at the bright slice of pain.

It was just as he'd told Faraday. The mending always hurt worse than the breaking.

He looked up to see Cora and the coachman limping down the slope.

Cora approached the cliff warily, took a peek over the edge, then reeled backward, pale and panting. "La."

Rhys took in the driver's torn clothing and scraped arms. In the accident, he must have flown straight off the driver's box. "Are you well?" he asked the coachman, pushing to his feet. "The horses?"

The driver nodded. "All safe, my lord."

"What the hell happened?"

"The traces just snapped. First the right side, then the left. Once they were gone, the splinter bar couldn't hold. A clean break between coach and team."

"Sabotage," Bellamy breathed. "Faraday was right. Someone's out to kill me." He ran a hand through his hair. "Maybe Faraday himself. Maybe he had someone working on this while you were enjoying your tea and shortbread."

"Or *maybe*," Rhys said, "the traces just snapped and not everything is about you." He scoffed at the idea of

Faraday's decrepit servant crawling under the carriage with a file or rasp. "Bad luck, plain and simple."

His curiosity finally overcoming his dizziness, Rhys peered down over the cliff. The ground fell away steeply. Far below, the sea chewed on the twisted wreckage with jaws of rock and wave. The entire coach had splintered to pieces. No man could have survived that fall.

Feeling suddenly breathless, he gave his cravat a vicious tug. The magnitude of the past few minutes' events began to sink in. "Good God," he said wonderingly. "I almost died."

"We all did," Bellamy said.

"Yes, but . . . that never happens to me." He rubbed the back of his neck. "I mean, I've come close dozens of times, but never like that. I really, *truly* almost died. I could not have saved myself."

"I'll take that as my outpouring of gratitude," said Bellamy. "Are you always this churlish when someone saves your life?"

Rhys winced, thinking of Meredith. "Apparently."

Cora indicated her own temple. "You're bleeding, my lord."

He touched a hand to his brow. His fingers came away wet with blood. Still huffing for breath as he straightened, Rhys reached for the handkerchief in his breast pocket.

Instead, his fingers closed over two odd-shaped coins.

He pulled one of them out and squinted at it. A thin disc of brass, stamped with a horse's head on one side and its tail on the other. Leo Chatwick's Stud Club token.

"Bellamy," he said. "Heads or tails?"

"What are you on about?"

"It's an experiment. Just call heads or tails."

The man shrugged. "Tails."

Rhys tossed the coin and caught it, slapping it flat

against his wrist. When he removed his hand, the horse's arse shining up at him seemed like the funniest god-damned thing he'd ever seen. Laughter rumbled from his chest. Leo always did love a good joke.

"Here. This one was Leo's." He tossed the token at a befuddled Bellamy, who caught it handily. "Now it's yours. I lost."

Who would have guessed it? By all things holy and profane, he'd lost. It would seem his cursed good luck had finally run out. He'd have to learn some new tricks—like the practice of caution. No longer would he stumble through the world, flipping that coin with "Life" on one side and "Death" on the other. He'd make his own fate now.

And Rhys knew just where—and with whom—he wanted to make it.

Chapter Twenty-seven

It was nearing noon when they returned to Buckleigh-in-the-Moor the next day, riding single file on the four draft horses. They must have been quite a sight. Villagers swarmed out of their houses to watch as, one by one, Rhys, Bellamy, Cora, and their much-abused driver clopped down the road and into the courtyard of the Three Hounds.

Rhys had hated stopping the night yesterday. Everything in him had wanted to return to Meredith as soon as possible. Fall on his knees, pledge his love, beg her forgiveness for everything. What words he'd employ in that effort, he couldn't begin to imagine. Well, three particular words were a given. Beyond that, he just hoped for inspiration in the moment.

But Cora's ankle had needed a doctor's attention, and they'd each had small injuries to tend. There were other basic needs, too: rest, food, proper saddles. He'd forced himself to be patient, wait.

Now they were here, and he wasn't waiting a second longer. The moment he slowed his horse, he dismounted and hurried toward the inn's door.

He was intercepted by Gideon Myles. The man came tearing out from the entrance. His face was one big bruise, and his steps were hobbled, and his mien was determined. He was a man with a destination in mind.

And Rhys wasn't it.

He brushed straight past Rhys and Bellamy both, rushing to help Cora down from her horse.

"Cora." He tugged the girl into his arms, burying his face in her hair. "Cora, thank the Lord you're back. I woke up and you were gone, and I didn't have the strength to go after you . . ." He hugged her close. "I would have never let you leave. You're not getting out of my sight again."

Rhys harrumphed loudly.

Myles pulled back from the embrace, surveying the bruise on Cora's cheek and the tattered edge of her cloak. "What's happened to you?" He turned a burning gaze on Rhys and Bellamy. "If you've hurt her, I'll kill you."

Rhys said impatiently, "Oh, suddenly you care about the girl's welfare?"

"Of course I care. And there's nothing sudden about it." He rubbed his hands up and down the girl's arms. "I love her, more than my own life. Would have said as much the other day, if someone hadn't smashed his fist in my face."

"Truly?" Cora asked, blinking hard. "You . . . you love me?"

"Aye, truly." He pulled her aside from the crowd, just a step. "I love you. And I've a question to ask you, but I'm just vain enough that I hate to ask it looking like this."

"Probably for the best," she said shyly. "It's come to my attention that I may be too easily swayed by fine looks and charm."

"I'm low on both at the moment."

"Yes, you are." She smiled, feathering her fingers

through his hair. "And if it's worth asking, the question will keep."

"I see," Myles said, a slow grin spreading across his face. "You mean to make me work for it."

She nodded, lacing her arms about his neck.

"Good girl. You should." Bending his head to hers, the man kissed her soundly. And quite thoroughly, considering the swollen state of his jaw.

As the assembled crowd cheered the young couple, Bellamy came to stand at Rhys's side. "Spares me the trouble of finding her a new place."

Damn Gideon Myles and his scene-stealing. Rhys wanted his own happy reunion. "Where the devil is Meredith?"

"Would you hand me the scissors, please?" From her perch atop the crate, Meredith braced her weight on the window frame and leaned sideways, extending an arm. "They're just there, over by the lace."

"Here?" Riffling his sandy hair with one hand, Darryl scouted the heaps of fabric and thread until he located the missing sewing shears. Then he loped across the cottage loft and delivered them to her hand with a gallant flourish. "There you are."

"Thank you, Darryl."

The youth smiled. "Anything for you, Mrs. Maddox."

Meredith returned to her task. She stretched a length of twine from the top of the window to the sill, then cut it to the exact length. Looping that strand around her neck for safekeeping, she started another measurement crossways.

"What are these?" Darryl asked.

"What are what?"

"These."

Craning her neck, she glimpsed him holding a misshapen lump of wood in his hand, turning it this way and that for examination.

"They're flowers," she said.

"Are you certain? Look like vegetables to me. Aren't these cabbages over here? And this one has the look of celery."

"It's a tulip. They're flowers." She smiled to herself as she turned back to her measurements.

"If you say so."

She heard a dull thunk as Darryl tossed the tulip finial aside.

"You surely are anxious to make these curtains," he said. "What's the hurry, Mrs. Maddox? I thought you'd be more concerned about repairing the tavern."

"That tavern is perpetually in need of something." Frowning with concentration, she folded her lip under her teeth. "There," she said, cutting off the final window measurement. To Darryl, she continued, "I just want this place looking nice by the time Rhys comes back. Looking like a home."

Darryl chuckled. "Mrs. Maddox, Lord Ashworth's not coming back."

"He is," Meredith said. "I know he left, but he'll be back. Eventually." Hopefully before another fourteen years passed. But no matter how long it took, she'd be waiting. Call it destiny. Call it faith. Whatever it was, she seemed to have caught the brain-addling contagion from Rhys, and she didn't want to be cured.

"No, Mrs. Maddox." Darryl's voice was strangely confident. "He isn't coming back."

Meredith turned her neck slowly. "What do you mean?"

His left eye twitched as he gave her a placid smile. "He won't trouble this place anymore. I've made certain of it. Buckleigh-in-the-Moor is free of the Ashworth line. Forever."

Her heart began to beat a little faster, though she bade herself to stay calm. This was Darryl Tewkes talking. Surely this was just another of his wild, imagined tales. She stepped down from the crate, and her feet hit the floor with a hollow thud. "Darryl, what are you saying?"

"I fixed matters for you. For everyone." He picked up a length of lace and began folding it. "Aren't you pleased?"

"No. No, I'm not pleased."

"Now, now. I know you're an independent woman and you like to do things your way, but you mustn't be angry with me, Mrs. Maddox. He left me no choice. We tried to give him the suggestion to leave, but the man can't take a hint. First the torches didn't work, and neither did moving his rocks about. Tried pitching a stone *at* him, and that didn't work either."

"That was *you*?"

Meredith was aghast. When Gideon had awoken this afternoon, the two of them had shared a pot of tea and a lengthy conversation. Among other things, he'd sworn he wasn't responsible for Rhys's injury that night at the ruins. Since he had no reason to lie about it now, she'd concluded the whole thing must have been an accident.

Evidently she'd concluded wrong.

Through sheer force of will, she kept her voice even. "Darryl, what did you do to Lord Ashworth? Tell me this instant."

"I didn't do anything to him. Let's just say I gave Mr. Bellamy's carriage a bit of special attention."

Meredith gasped. "Mr. Bellamy's carriage? But . . . but Cora went with them!" Hadn't Darryl been half in love with the girl? Every male in the village was half in love with the girl.

"Oh, you mean the harlot?" He shook his head, tsking softly. "She seemed nice enough at the beginning, but she showed her true colors in the end. We're better off without her, Mrs. Maddox. The Three Hounds isn't that sort of inn."

She could only stare at him, transfixed with disbelief.

"Do you know what I wonder?" His little smile crawled over her skin. "I wonder if he'll *truly* haunt us when he's dead. I hope he does. The travelers would like that. I'll have to change my story a bit, but that's all right. What do you think, Mrs. Maddox?" he asked, moving toward her. "Which sounds better? 'The Phantom Lord'? Or 'The Ghostly Baron'?"

"Neither," she said, stepping back. A floorboard creaked. Her fingers tightened around the sewing scissors in her hand. "Don't come any closer. You're frightening me."

"They're just stories, Mrs. Maddox. And it's only me. You know me."

"No, I don't think I do."

"Don't be angry." He moved closer. "I did it for you. For us. We were doing well for ourselves until Lord Ashworth came back. Bringing his fancy London friend and that harlot around, making trouble for the whole village. He tore up the tavern, tried to take you away." Darryl gestured angrily. "I couldn't watch him destroy the Three Hounds, Mrs. Maddox. I've worked too hard for that place."

He'd worked too hard? "Darryl, you fool. No one's worked harder for that place than I have. And I'm telling you, Lord Ashworth's return was the best thing to ever happen to Buckleigh-in-the-Moor. The best thing to ever happen to me. How dare you, you . . ."

Despite all her resolve to be strong, Meredith began to tremble. Her eyes fluttered closed, and horrid possibilities flashed behind them. Rhys always claimed to be indestructible, but no man was immortal. What if Darryl had somehow managed to . . .

No.

She opened her eyes, and she knew. She just knew, with a profound, bone-deep certainty, that everything was going to be fine.

"You're wrong, Darryl. Lord Ashworth *is* coming back. Not as a ghost or a phantom, but alive and whole."

"Now, Mrs. Maddox, you're not listening . . ."

"No, I'm not. I'm telling you, he's coming back. I've never been so sure of anything in my life."

"Why is that?"

"Because he's standing behind you right now."

Darryl froze. He gulped loudly. His eyelashes danced a wild jig as he turned by slow degrees, then tilted his head up.

And up.

And up, all the way to Rhys's waiting glare.

"Boo." With a lightning-quick motion, Rhys grabbed Darryl by the throat. The younger man squirmed and sputtered, clawing in vain at Rhys's grip.

"You scheming little bastard," Rhys snarled. "I knew I didn't like you."

"Is Cora well?" Meredith asked, nearly beside herself with emotion.

"She's well." Rhys tightened his grip, and the shade of Darryl's face deepened from scarlet to plum. "But she could have died. We all could have died." He gave the youth a shake. "I've a mind to throw you in the bog, let the wild pigs sniff you out."

Tears were streaming down Darryl's face by this point, and his violet complexion was tending toward blue.

"Rhys," Meredith said, tilting her head toward the youth. "Please."

He instantly released his grip.

"Damn," Rhys muttered as Darryl fell to the floor,

dragging in air with raspy gulps. "Lucky for you, this is the week I give up killing men with my bare hands."

"*Gads.*" Darryl writhed on the floor, clutching his stomach and gasping like a fish plucked from a stream. "*Can't. Breathe.*"

Rhys glared at him. "Burns, doesn't it?"

Darryl's head jerked in response.

"Good. I'm glad." Rhys turned to Meredith. "I know that feeling, Merry." He spoke low and only to her. "I've dangled at the brink of death more times than I can count. And that steep climb back to life, it hurts like hell. The pain of an injury is over in seconds. Everything that comes after is the pain of getting well." He gave her a heartfelt look, full of apology. "I'd forgotten that, you see. Coming back to life . . . It hurts."

She nodded, understanding him perfectly. His was a battered soul, and her love . . . it must have hit him like gin dashed over an open wound. But he was back here, ready to take more of it, no matter how it pained him inside. Because he was the bravest man on God's earth.

And he was hers. All hers, at last. Her heart swelled with joy.

From the floor, Darryl moaned.

"Get out," Rhys growled at him. "Get out, and begone. Unless you want to spend eternity haunting those ruins yourself, you will not let me find you."

Still gasping for air, Darryl crawled toward the ladder on his belly. At a painfully slow rate, he disappeared from the loft. A dull thud suggested he'd taken the last few rungs the hard way. At last, they heard the door swing on its hinges.

When Meredith and Rhys were finally alone, he turned to her. His brow furrowed with concentration.

"I love you," he said bluntly. "I have to say that, before anything else. Because it's the most important thing. I love you."

Dear, dear man. He spoke the words as though they were some sort of damning verdict on her life. "I'm very happy to hear it."

He heaved a sigh of obvious relief. He ambled his way across the room to her, looking around the loft. "You're hanging curtains?"

She nodded, sliding her scissors onto the windowsill. "The lace you bought in Bath."

"Pretty."

He stopped next to the window and surveyed the view over her shoulder. So close to her, but not touching yet. Her breathing came quick, and her heart began to pound. Every inch of her tingled with anticipation.

He said casually, "I think this would be an ideal nook for a dressing table. Little chair, a mirror." His big hands outlined a square in the empty space. Oh, how she wanted those hands on her. "Your silver hairbrush set can go right here."

"Right next to your shaving kit."

His big hand reached for hers. She looked up into warm brown eyes brimming with emotion.

"*Merry.*"

Her heart swelled as he finally pulled her into his arms. Just where she wanted to be. He inclined his head until his whiskered chin grazed her temple. And they stood there together, just breathing. The moment was too intense for a kiss, too profound for words. The relief, the joy, the sheer rightness of it all.

She pressed her forehead to his frayed lapel and the wall of muscle beneath. "I knew you'd come back," she whispered. "I just knew it."

His hands framed her waist, and he pulled her back to look at him. "Thought you didn't believe in fate or destiny."

"I still don't. But I believe in you."

"Good." His throat worked as he stared deep into her

eyes. "Because fate be damned. God and the Devil and every one of their minions could convene right here and now to drag me off to my doom, and I'd fight my way through each and every one of them to stay with you. Not because it's my destiny or my punishment or for lack of alternatives, but because I love you too much to be anywhere else. And if you refuse to marry me, I'll remain here still. Come down to the inn every night for a meal and a pint, just to look at you and be near you. I . . ." He brushed the hair back from her face, cupping her cheek in his weathered hand. "Merry, I love you."

"Oh, Rhys. I—" She hesitated, searching his eyes. "Can you bear it if . . . ?"

He nodded. "Tell me."

"I love you, too. I've loved you for so long."

His eyes closed briefly, then opened again. "Still hurts a bit. But it's getting better." His thumb brushed her cheek. "As I recall, you still owe me an answer."

"Remind me of the question."

"Will you marry me?"

She pretended to think on it. "Yes."

They smiled at one another. After all that time and all that discussion . . . yes, it really was that simple. Because it just felt right.

In a sudden burst of strength, he grasped her by the waist and tossed her into the air as if she weighed nothing. He caught her just under the hips, holding her fast to his chest and making her the taller of the two. Which gave her the immense joy of staring down at his wide, rugged smile. And then the very great pleasure of bending her head by slow, teasing degrees . . . until she finally kissed it away.

How she loved this man. Theirs would never be a soft, gentle kind of affection. They were both made of granite, chipped off this moor, and their love would be fierce and stubborn and even painful when they clashed. But also solid and enduring. A love to last for all time.

Finally setting her on her feet, he pressed his brow to hers. "Have I thanked you for saving me?"

Eyes still closed, she shook her head no.

"Well, then. I'll be certain to do that. Every day, for the rest of our lives." He kissed her brow. "I'm a broken man, Merry. I can't lie to you. It may take some time before I'm truly whole, and even then, the pieces may never come together quite right. But I'm grateful to you. Grateful *for* you. And I love you, more than I have words or strength to express. I will never leave your side again."

She threw her arms around his neck and pulled him close. "Even if you tried, I wouldn't let you go."

Sweet promises, both. But they didn't last long.

Rhys *did* leave her side, the very next morning. And Meredith gladly let him go, for the errand was one of some urgency. Rhys rode to Lydford and made a swift return, curate in tow. It wasn't the first Sunday of the month, but it was *a* Sunday. Therefore, Rhys had decided it would be their wedding day. Meredith was not inclined to argue.

Their tiny village church hadn't seen an Evening Prayer service in years, but it saw one that night. By candlelight, no less. Flickering tapers warmed each amber and red stained-glass window. The reading of the banns was followed by a marriage rite, with the entire population of Buckleigh-in-the-Moor in attendance. The groom wore immaculate black and white; the bride, a veil of Bath lace. Bellamy and Cora stood up as witnesses. George Lane looked on with pride.

And everyone—at least, everyone Cora could nudge into agreement—declared the scene to be the picture of romance.

Afterward they adjourned for dancing and merriment in the tavern. There, surrounded by increasingly tipsy well-wishers, Meredith laced her fingers behind her husband's neck as they danced some approximation of a waltz.

"Lady Ashworth," he said in a tone of mock formality, "you look uncommonly lovely tonight." He pulled her close and nuzzled her ear. "God, it's good to finally call you that."

"It's good to finally hear." She smiled. She'd been waiting for those words a great deal longer than he had. Since her twelfth summer, truth be told. Now she was here in his arms. His wife.

"When can we leave?" His tongue grazed her earlobe. "I want to take you home."

The word sent a pleasant shiver down her spine. The cottage wasn't much of a home yet. No furniture or fixtures. The curtains still weren't done. But she'd seen to the essentials that afternoon—a mattress, blankets, a few bottles of wine, and a healthy stack of peat for the fire. That was all they'd need tonight.

"Soon," she said, pulling back. "But first . . . I want to talk about the inn."

He concealed any irritation and gave her a patient smile. "What about the inn?"

"I had a chat with Gideon while you were away."

His smile faded. "Oh, did you?"

"He wants an honest life now, a family. With Cora."

"So I gathered."

She looked to the bar, where the younger couple were working together to serve drinks. "They're sweet together, aren't they?"

"I suppose." Rhys shrugged, as though to say a big, strong man like him couldn't possibly know a thing about sweetness.

Meredith smiled. She knew very well he did, but she

wouldn't force him to admit it. "Take my word for it, then. They're sweet. And my money says they'll be married by Christmas. Gideon's going to clear out your cellar and use that as a down payment on the Three Hounds." At the slight wrinkling of Rhys's forehead, she sped up her speech. "He and Cora will manage the place, under my supervision at first. We'll pay them with increasing shares of the inn, until they own it outright. Please say you'll agree."

"I'll agree to whatever you like, but . . ." His frown deepened. "Do you really mean to give up the inn?"

"Of course not. I really mean to sell it, at a profit." Smiling, she brought her hand to his face, rubbing her thumb along his lower lip. "It's what's best for the village."

"What about you?"

"You're what's best for me. Truly, Rhys. I'm ready to build a future with you."

She pressed a light kiss to his lips, and when she moved to retreat, he caught her, making that light kiss something dark, passionate. Deeply arousing.

"I'm glad you're parting with the inn," he said at length. "Because I have a new project for you."

"You mean Nethermoor Hall?"

"Yes. And I'm willing to bet you're already full of clever ideas for it."

She bit back a grin. She did have a few.

"I knew it. You're the most resourceful woman in England." He lifted his gaze, and a chuckle rumbled from his chest. "I'll never forget that first night, when I stood in that door"—he tilted his head toward the entrance—"and watched you smash that bottle of claret over Harold Symmonds's head."

She laughed at the memory. "Fell like a stone, didn't he?"

"I fell harder. Knew right then you were the only one

for me." He pulled her hand from his face, kissed her palm, then pressed it flat against his chest. "I know I don't have to tell you, I've seen a lot of unpleasantness in my life. Suffered a good many wounds, and a great deal of pain. But through it all, this heart kept beating. Do you feel it now?"

"Yes." His heartbeat thumped against her palm. Steady and strong, as ever.

"Beatings, battles, fights. No matter how bleak the circumstance, no matter how my soul despaired . . . this heart never once gave up." His voice deepened, went thick with emotion. "I've a theory as to why. Do you want to hear it?"

She nodded.

"This heart is yours."

Words failed her. Tears would have to do. Just a few tears now, then kisses all night long. Followed by a lifetime of passion and tender love. This was just the happy beginning.

"It's yours," he said. "It always will be."

Read on for an excerpt from
Three Nights with a Scoundrel by Tessa Dare
Available from Rouge

London, October 1817

Lily awoke to a rough shake on her arm. A searing ball of light hovered before her face.

She winced, and the light quickly receded. With caution, she opened her eyes. Blinking furiously, Lily strained to make out the lamp-bearer's identity. It was Holling, the housekeeper.

Good Lord. She bolted upright in bed. Something dreadful had occurred. The servants would never shake her awake unless it was a matter of extreme urgency.

She pressed a hand to her throat. "What is it?"

Yellow lamplight illuminated an apologetic face. "Downstairs, my lady. You're needed downstairs at once. Begging your pardon."

With a nod of assent, Lily rose from bed. She shoved her toes into night-chilled slippers and accepted assistance in donning a violet silk wrap.

Her sense of dread only mounted as she descended the stairs. And the feeling was all too familiar.

Nearly five months had passed since the last time she'd been summoned downstairs in the dark. No one had needed to wake her then; she'd been unable to sleep for an insistent sense of foreboding. Her fears were confirmed when she opened the door to find gentlemen crowding her doorstep—three men with nothing in common save their membership in the Stud Club, an exclusive horse-breeding society her brother, Leo, had founded. They were the reclusive Duke of Morland, scarred war hero Rhys St. Maur, and Julian Bellamy— the London *ton*'s favorite hell-raiser and Leo's closest friend.

One look at their grave faces that night, and there'd been no need for words. Lily had known instantly what they'd come to tell her.

Leo was dead.

At the age of eight-and-twenty, her twin brother was dead. Leo Chatwick, the Marquess of Harcliffe. Young, handsome, wealthy, universally-admired—beaten to death in a Whitechapel alleyway, the victim of footpads.

The last time she'd been summoned down these stairs at night, her existence had been torn in half.

Lily's knees buckled as she reached the foot of the staircase. She clutched the banister for support, then drew a shaky breath as a footman waved her toward the door.

Holling thrust her lamp out over the threshold. Gathering all her available bravery, Lily moved toward the door and peeked out.

As there was no one on the doorstep, her view went straight to the square. The first gray insinuation of daylight hovered over the manicured hedges and paths. The streets were still largely empty, but here and there she saw servants on their way to market.

At the housekeeper's insistent gesturing, she looked down. There, on the pavement at the bottom of the steps, lodged a costermonger's wheelbarrow. The wooden cart was heaped with carrots, turnips, vegetable marrows . . . and the body of an unconscious man.

She clutched the doorjamb. *Oh, no.*

It was Julian Bellamy.

Lily recognized the red cuff of his coat before she even saw his face. She clapped a palm to her mouth, smothering a cry of alarm.

There'd been one consolation in mourning Leo: the knowledge that she could never endure such a devastating loss again. He was her twin, her best friend from birth and, since their parents' deaths, her only remaining close kin. She would never love anyone so dearly as she'd loved him. Once Leo had left this world . . . pain could not touch her now.

Or so she'd thought.

Staring down at Julian's senseless form, it was hard to believe she'd ever felt this frantic. She sensed her throat emitting sounds—ugly, croaking sounds, she feared. But she couldn't make herself stop. Even when Leo had died, Julian had been there to stand by her. Devilish rake he might be, he was her brother's steadfast friend, and hers as well. Over the years, they'd come to think of him as family. If Julian left her . . .

She would truly be alone.

For the second time that morning, Holling gave her arm a shake. Lily looked to the housekeeper.

"He's alive," the older woman said. "Still breathing."

Tears of relief rushed past Lily's defenses. "Bring him in."

The footmen scrambled to obey, lifting his sprawled body from the wheelbarrow and hefting it up the steps.

"To the kitchen."

They all filed down the narrow corridor, headed for the rear of the house. Holling first with her lamp; then the footmen bearing Julian. Lily brought up the rear as they descended the short flight of steps to the kitchen.

Even at this early hour, the kitchen staff was hard at work. A toasty fire warmed the room, and a yeasty aroma filled the air. A scullery maid lifted floury hands from the breadboard and stepped back in alarm, making room for the footmen to pass.

They placed Julian by the hearth, propping his head on a sack of meal.

"Send for the doctor," she said. When no one sprang into action, she repeated herself at the top of her lungs. "Doctor. *Now.*"

With a hasty bow, one of the footmen hurried from the room.

Lily knelt at Julian's side. Heavens, he was filthy. Dirt streaked his face, and the smell of the gutter clung to his clothes. She put a hand to his forehead, finding it clammy and cool to the touch. Perhaps he needed air. Her fingers flew to his cravat, and she tugged at it, unwinding the starched linen from his throat. A day's growth of whiskers scraped her fingertips. She turned her cheek to his face, rejoicing at the warm puff of breath against her skin.

He suddenly convulsed, as if coughing.

She ceased her tussle with his cravat and pulled back to stare at him, not wanting to miss any word he might speak.

His eyes went in and out of focus as his gaze meandered over her form. "Hullo, Lily."

Relief washed through her. "Julian. Are you well?"

He blinked several times, in rapid succession. Then again, slowly. Finally he said, "Violet always was your color."

He slumped back, eyes closed.

Was he drunk? She leaned forward, sniffing cautiously at his exposed throat. No liquor. No gutter smells here, either. Just hints of starch and soap, mingled with the metallic, pungent odor of . . .

Oh, God.

She grabbed his arm, shook it hard. "Julian. Julian, wake up."

When he failed to respond, she withdrew her trembling hand and looked down at it. Just as she'd feared. Her fingers came away wet with blood.

Julian Bellamy had died sometime during the night.

That could be the only explanation. He'd perished, and there'd been some sort of divine mistake. Because this morning, he woke up in heaven. The sheer purity of it blanked his senses.

All was light. Fragrant. Lush. Clean.

The qualities of Paradise, as his boyhood self would have imagined it. The antithesis of everything he'd known from birth to the age of nine years: squalor, dirt, darkness, hunger.

Come to mention it, he still felt a faint pang of hunger.

Odd.

His bare arms glided between layers of crisp linen and quilted silk as he stretched, idly wondering if the dead felt hunger. And if so, what mead-and-manna banquet awaited him here?

"At last. There you are." A feminine voice. Husky and warm, like honey. A *familiar* voice.

His pulse stuttered.

His pulse? Bloody hell. To the devil with hunger. Dead men definitely did not have pulses.

Julian shot up on one elbow and forced his bleary gaze to sharpen. "Lily? Surely that's not you."

The elegant oval of her face came into focus. Dark eyes, anchored by a straight, slim nose. The rosy curve of her mouth. "Of course it's me."

Holy God. He was not in heaven; he was damned. He was in a bed—presumably a bed somewhere in Harcliffe House. And Lady Lily Chatwick sat on the edge of the bed, entirely too close. Within arm's length. And he knew this couldn't be a dream, because he never dreamed of Lily. He'd *tried* to dream of her, on a few occasions when he was feeling especially maudlin. It had never worked. Even in sleep, he couldn't fool himself. Every part of him, conscious and unconscious, knew he didn't deserve this woman.

Damn. He scrambled to remember the events of the night previous. What the devil had he done? What had he caused *her* to do?

"Lily." His tongue felt thick, felted. He swallowed with difficulty. "Tell me this isn't your room."

Her lips quirked in a half-smile. "This isn't my room."

He released the breath he'd been holding. Now that he flashed a quick glance about him, he could see that the bedchamber was decorated in masculine shades. Rich greens, dark blues.

A worse thought struck him. He sat up further. "Lily. Tell me this isn't *his* room."

Her smile faded, and sadness melted the laugh lines at the corners of her eyes. "No. This isn't Leo's room."

With a muttered curse of thanksgiving, he fell back against the pillows. It was one thing to disgrace his dead friend's memory. Another thing entirely to do it in his dead friend's own bed.

"It's just a spare bedchamber. How is your arm?" she asked.

In answer, the limb gave a fierce throb. The wave of pain pushed memories to the fore. The dusty storehouse. The panicked crowd. The escaped bull, smashing him against the rail.

With his right hand, he touched the bandage tightly wound about his biceps.

"The doctor's come and gone," she said. "He seemed to think you'll survive."

"Blast." He threw his wrist over his eyes. "How on earth did I get here?"

She clucked her tongue. "So dramatic. I should think this is a common occurrence for you, waking up naked in a strange bed."

Naked? Had she truly just said . . . ?

Julian lifted the sheet and glanced downwards. Thank God. Though he was undressed to the waist, the seven buttons of his smallclothes winked up at him. And they were lying flat and obedient in a tame row. At the moment. If she kept hovering over him, they wouldn't stay that way for long.

"Minx." When she only laughed harder at her own joke, he lowered the sheet and chided her, "You are an unforgivable tease."

"And you are an unmitigated ass."

When he shifted onto his side, she laid a hand to his bare shoulder. Her touch was a brand against his skin.

"Lily . . ."

"No, I mean it. You know I don't normally use such words."

She never used such words at all. Oh, she often *thought* them, he knew. But she never said them. And the scoundrel in Julian was perversely delighted that he'd provoked her into speaking her mind. Lily had a lot of thoughts worth sharing, and all too often she kept them to herself.

She handed him a glass of barley water, and he accepted it gratefully.

"You are making an ass of yourself, Julian, and I don't mean just this morning." Her eyes narrowed to angry slits. "But while we're on the subject, let's start with this morning."

"Must we?" Tucking the sheets close to his chest—to guard her modesty, not his—Julian sat up in bed. He drank as she continued, downing the barley water in greedy gulps.

"Yes. Do you have any idea what a fright you gave

me? A costermonger found you in the street before dawn. Lying in the gutter, bleeding."

Ah, yes. The blood. That was what had done him in. Jagged shards of memory began to piece themselves together.

"Fortunately, Cook recognized you when the costermonger brought you by in his barrow, tumbled in amongst the turnips and celery root." Her voice rose. "Really, Julian. Can you imagine?"

Yes, he could. He had a vague recollection of celery root. The night came back to him now, in a hot, sweaty rush. Setting aside the glass, he massaged away a sharp pain in his temple. "I can explain."

"Please do."

"There was a boxing match in Southwark."

She shook her head. "Not another boxing match. That's all you care about these past few months."

"I don't attend for love of the sport."

Julian had never shared the popular fascination with pugilism. He'd tasted too much of real danger in his life to take amusement from contrived imitations. But he wished to God he did enjoy bloodsport. If so, a good man would still be alive. Months ago, Julian had agreed to attend a boxing match at Leo's suggestion. At the last minute, he'd begged off, preferring to pass the evening in a woman's embrace instead.

Worst decision he'd ever made. And not just because Carnelia was uninspired in bed.

Leo had attended the fight without him. And afterward, he'd been attacked and beaten in a Whitechapel alleyway—murdered in the street by a pair of footpads. A random act of thievery, it was concluded by most.

Julian knew better. That attack had been meant for him. In recent months, he'd attended every boxing match, cockfight, dogfight, and bear-baiting within a day's travel of London. If the scent of blood hung in the air, he followed it—no matter how the spectacle turned his stomach. He could not rest until he reckoned with Leo's murderers, lest they become his killers, too.

"Do you really think attending these matches will lead you to them?" she asked. "You have scarcely any description of the men. They could be standing next to you on the street, and you would never know."

"You don't understand." He knew well how ineffectual the search was. It didn't matter. Giving up was unthinkable.

"No, I don't understand. I don't understand a great many things you do lately. For example, just how do you get from a boxing match in Southwark to a costermonger's wheelbarrow in Mayfair?"

"After the bout, there was a bull-baiting. The beast snapped its tether, and the crowd panicked." Julian closed his eyes and pinched the bridge of his nose, his thoughts crowded out by memories of noise. The men shouting, the dogs' frenzied barks, the thunder of footfalls as everyone rushed for the exits at once.

He raised both hands between them—one balled in a fist, the other extended as an open palm. "The bull charged." In illustration, he drove the fist into his palm. "I was in the way."

"I don't suppose you were doing something noble, like diving in front of the beast to save a hobbled grandfather." She put a hand under his chin and tipped his face to the light, examining his cheek. Her finger traced a slanting line toward his mouth—he must have a scratch there, he supposed. He licked his cracked lips.

Her touch skipped to the bandage encircling his arm. She ran her fingers over the binding, tucked a raw edge under the fold.

The casual intimacy of her touch was affecting. Too affecting.

Shaking his head, he pulled her hand away. "Nothing

noble. I was just the one stupid enough to be wearing red."

"Julian." Her dark eyes glimmered with emotion as she squeezed his fingers. "You must stop making yourself a target."

"I was only squashed. No real injury, save the pain in my arm. I decided to walk home to shake it off."

"*Walk* home? From Southwark?"

He shrugged his good shoulder, easing his hand from her grip. "It's not so far." Not for him. Lately he spent most nights wandering all quadrants of the city.

Last night, he'd made his way back so far as the square where Harcliffe House was situated. This house was always the last stop on his nightly rounds. He would pause on the corner down the street. If he stood half on the pavement, half on the green . . . then craned his neck . . . he could *just* glimpse the fourth rightmost window on the second floor. The one he knew belonged to Lily's bedchamber. If the window was dark, she was sleeping and at peace. He, too, could relax. On the nights he found a lamp burning, he ached for her sorrow. And he simply stood there, quietly sharing her grief, until that light went dark or the sun came up—whichever occurred first.

In the weeks after Leo's death, he'd found that lamp burning more often than not. As the months passed, however, her bad nights had grown less frequent. Last night, he'd been comforted to see the window dark. And just as Julian had turned to seek his own home, that faint pain in his arm shifted to a deep, persistent throb.

Available this month from *Rouge Romance*:

Tessa Dare's 'Stud Club' Trilogy:

ONE DANCE WITH A DUKE
Spencer Dumarque, the fourth Duke of Morland, has a reputation as the dashing "Duke of Midnight." Each evening he selects one lady for a scandalous midnight waltz. But none of the ladies of the ton catch his interest for long, until Lady Amelia d'Orsay tries her luck.

TWICE TEMPTED BY A ROUGE
Brooding war hero, Rhys St. Maur, returns to his ancestral home on the Devonshire moors following the murder of his friend in the elite gentlemen's society known as the Stud Club. There, he is offered a chance at redemption in the arms of beautiful innkeeper, Meredith Maddox, who dares him to face the demons of his past.

THREE NIGHTS WITH A SCOUNDREL
The bastard son of a nobleman, Julian Bellamy plotted to have the last laugh on a society that once spurned him. But meeting Leo Chatwick, founder of the exclusive Stud Club, and Lily, his enchanting sister, made Julian reconsider his wild ways. When Leo is murdered Julian vows to see the woman he secretly loves married to a man of her own class. Lily, however, has a very different husband in mind.

THE HUSBAND TRAP by Tracy Anne Warren
Violet Brantford has always longed for Adrian Winter, the wealthy Duke of Raeburn, who is set to marry Violet's vivacious twin sister, Jeannette. But when Jeannette refuses to go through with the ceremony, Violet finds herself walking down the aisle in her sister's place in order to avoid a scandal. But keeping up the pretence with a man as divine as the Duke will take all of Violet's skills...

THE WARRIOR by Nicole Jordan
Ariane of Claredon is betrothed to King Henry's most trusted vassal, the feared Norman knight Ranulf de Vernay. But cruel circumstance has branded Ariane's father a traitor to the crown and Ranulf is returning to Claredon, not as bridegroom...but as conqueror. But though he has come to claim her lands and body as his prize, it is the mighty warrior who must surrender to Ariane's passion and her remarkable healing love.

ROUGE
SUSPENSE

WILD HEAT by Bella Andre

Maya Jackson doesn't sleep with strangers. Until the night grief sent her to the nearest bar and into the arms of the most explosive lover she's ever had. Six months later, the dedicated arson investigator is coming face to face with him again. Gorgeous, sexy Logan Cain. Her biggest mistake and now her number-one suspect in a string of deadly wildfires.

CRASH INTO ME by Jill Sorenson

Ben Fortune is the world's most famous surfer, known as much for his good looks as for his skill. He's also a suspect in a series of brutal murders that may have begun with his late wife. FBI Special Agent Sonora "Sonny" Vasquez has been sent undercover to make friends with Fortune, but soon they have collided in an affair that is both intense and irresistible.

ROUGE
PARANORMAL

BLOOD MAGIC by Jennifer Lyon

Darcy MacAlister is about to discover that she is a witch and the key to breaking a curse that has plagued witches and the men who hunt them. For if a Wing Slayer Hunter kills an innocent witch by mistake, the price is a piece of his soul. When gorgeous leader of the Wing Slayer Hunters Axel Locke's sister is cursed by a demon witch, he discovers that Darcy MacAlister may hold the cure...

www.rougeromance.co.uk

ROUGE

Red-hot romance...